6.00
M
pa

BRIGHT'S KILL

BRIGHT'S KILL

A Campbell Young Mystery

J.D. Carpenter

A Castle Street Mystery

THE DUNDURN GROUP
TORONTO

Editor: Barry Jowett
Copy-editor: Andrea Pruss
Design: Jennifer Scott
Printer: Webcom

National Library of Canada Cataloguing in Publication

Carpenter, J. D.
   Bright's kill / J.D. Carpenter.

(Castle Street mysteries)
ISBN-10: 1-55002-564-3
ISBN-13: 978-1-55002-564-4

   I. Title. II. Series: Castle Street mystery

PS8555.A7616B74 2005   C813'.54   C2005-900169-0

1   2   3   4   5   -   09   08   07   06   05

We acknowledge the support of the **Canada Council for the Arts** and the **Ontario Arts Council** for our publishing program. We also acknowledge the financial support of the **Government of Canada** through the **Book Publishing Industry Development Program** and **The Association for the Export of Canadian Books**, and the **Government of Ontario** through the **Ontario Book Publishers Tax Credit** program and the **Ontario Media Development Corporation.**

Care has been taken to trace the ownership of copyright material used in this book. The author and the publisher welcome any information enabling them to rectify any references or credits in subsequent editions.

J. Kirk Howard, President

Printed and bound in Canada
Printed on recycled paper ♻
www.dundurn.com

Dundurn Press
8 Market Street, Suite 200
Toronto, Ontario, Canada
M5E 1M6

Gazelle Book Services Limited
White Cross Mills
Hightown, Lancaster, England
LA1 4XS

Dundurn Press
2250 Military Road
Tonawanda, NY
U.S.A. 14150

For Jon Dawson and Rod Jamer

A Horse misus'd upon the Road
Calls to Heaven for Human blood.

William Blake, *Auguries of Innocence*

Thursday, June 1, 1995

Debi ran across the parking lot towards the barns. Once again, she was late for work. As she passed the mountain of manure steaming in the pre-dawn light, she pushed back the sleeve of her lumberjack shirt and glanced at the luminous dial of her wristwatch: 6:12. Shorty would be furious. There were just the two of them, and Shorty expected her to be in the barn by 5:45 to lead the horses out to the walking machine before she started mucking out their stalls.

Debi rehearsed her excuse as she rushed along: *I'm real sorry, Shorty. I got Jamal to the sitter's in plenty of time, but the traffic across the 401 was impossible.* No. *The traffic across the 401 was insane.* That sounded better.

As she hurried from the outside darkness into the brightly lit entrance of Barn 7, a familiar mixture of aromas greeted her: sweetness of hay, reek of manure, pungency of liniment. The morning sounds were there, too:

rattling of buckets, pawing of hooves, the grooms' animated chatter as they went about their chores.

When she reached Shorty's shedrow, she stopped short. Each trainer or groom was expected to turn on the lights for his or her section of the barn, but the lights for Shorty's section weren't on yet. Not only was *she* late, but so, it seemed, was Shorty. She flipped on the lights and listened. While everyone else's horses were snorting and whinnying in their stalls, her horses — Shorty's and hers — were moving about restlessly.

She looked in the first stall. The roan filly, Software, was banging her forehead against her empty water bucket. In the next stall the new horse, Prince, was walking in tight circles, and he cast a resentful glance Debi's way as she looked in. Next to Prince, crazy Gig was weaving, swinging his head left and right as he faced Debi. Gig was a cribber — he would clamp his teeth to the bars of his stall door and suck air — and the leather cribbing strap Shorty used to keep the colt from doing so was still in place. One of the first things Shorty did each morning was remove Gig's cribbing strap. Where was he? He was never late. *And traffic can't be the excuse*, she thought, *because he sleeps right here in the barn*. "What's going on, Gig?" she said. "What have you done with Shorty?"

She jogged towards the bunkroom at the end of the shedrow where Shorty lived during the long summer meet at Caledonia Downs. *If he's slept in*, she thought, *I'll really give him the gears. And* — she smiled at the thought — *he'll never know I was late*.

"Heads up!" a voice called, and Debi looked up in time to avoid smacking into the rearing Doll House, Tom Wright's huge chestnut mare, Tom himself desperately hanging onto the shank. "Whoa, missy, what's the hurry?"

"Sorry, Tom, I can't —"

"You know better than to run in the barn."

"I can't find Shorty, have you seen him? The horses haven't been tended to, and I can't find him."

"No, I ain't seen him." Tom settled the mare and stroked her nose. "You made her all jittery."

"I said I was sorry. It's not like Shorty to —"

"I told you I ain't seen him, and you know better than to run in the barn."

Debi ran off down the shedrow to the end of the barn and knocked at the door of Shorty's bunkroom. She knocked again and tried the knob. The door swung inward. Debi leaned into the darkness of the room. "You in here?"

There was no answer.

She reached around the door jamb and flipped on the light. The room was empty. The blankets on the single bed were rumpled, but that didn't mean anything: Shorty never made his bed. The card table was littered with fast food wrappers, copies of the *Daily Racing Form*, and a nearly full mickey of Lamb's Navy Rum, but this, too, was nothing new. Although Debi had never known Shorty to be a neat man in the five years she'd worked for him, recently he'd been getting worse. His gambling. His drinking. In a few short years, he had fallen from being one of the best public trainers at Caledonia — with a foreman, six grooms, eight owners, and two dozen horses — to being an also-ran, a has-been with one groom, three owners, and five horses. Debi corrected herself: four horses. She kept forgetting — or maybe it was some kind of mental block — that Download, an expensive three-year-old colt, had died in his stall two months ago, only days after his owner, an Internet millionaire, had hired Shorty to be his trainer. Debi shook her head. As soon as a small piece of good

luck rolled Shorty's way, a big piece of bad luck followed. She turned out the light, closed the door, and
started back towards the stalls. *Where the hell's he got
to?* she wondered.

As she walked back along the shedrow, it occurred
to her that there was one stall she hadn't checked: Bing
Crosby's. She stopped at the door to Bing's stall and
peered through the bars. The horse was standing in the
shadows at the back of the stall, his head in one corner.
When she clucked to him, he didn't move. *That's odd*,
Debi thought. *Old Bing always comes when I call him.*
"Come here, baby," she said, but the horse didn't move.
Debi looked at him more closely, squinting into the
gloom, and that was when she saw his shoulder twitch-
ing, his hindquarters shaking. She ran her eyes down his
trembling forelegs. And there, on his face, half-buried in
the straw, lay Shorty Rogers.

Campbell Young reached for the phone on the floor
beside his bed. His fingertips were orange and greasy
from the bag of cheesies he'd eaten the night before, and
the receiver slipped out of his grip and clattered on the
floor. "Fuck," he said, and picked it up. "What?"

"Daddy!"

"Debi?" he said, instantly alert and struggling with
his sheets. "What is it? Are you all right? Is it Jamal?"

"Daddy," the voice sobbed, "it's Shorty."

"Shorty? What about him?"

The clock radio on the bedside table said 6:25. Young
had been dreaming. His dream had changed from a chase
down a back lane — not a police chase; instead of guns
there was a girl with long blonde hair wearing green knee
socks and a short plaid skirt who kept disappearing down
alleyways and around the corners of garages, her laugh-

ter leading him on — to a dream about the racetrack. He was in line at the betting window, and the old man ahead of him was taking forever to place his bet, and Young was becoming impatient because it was already post time and he had a sure thing. Finally Young peered over the old man's shoulder to see what the holdup was, and instead of money or tickets lying on the counter between the old man and the cashier there was a bloody handkerchief with three teeth on it, and the old man, turning his face towards Young — like the little girl in *The Exorcist* — was weeping. Young had become aware of a ringing in his head, and at first he'd mistaken the ringing for the bell at the racetrack when the starting gate opens and the horses charge out, but then it dawned on him that the ringing he was hearing was a telephone, and that was when he had awakened.

"He's dead. He's been murdered."

"Murdered? Go slow, Debi. What happened?"

"I found him in a stall. Ten minutes ago. I phoned 911, then I phoned you."

"I'll be right there, sweetie. Forty minutes. You still in the same barn?"

"Yes," his daughter said, the tremolo still in her voice. "Barn 7."

Caledonia Downs was not in Young's precinct — he was downtown, and the track was out in the monster home suburbs — but there was no doubt where he was going. Firstly, his daughter was in distress; secondly, he knew a thing or two about horse racing, so if he needed a rationale for treading on someone else's turf, that was it; and thirdly, he was close enough to retirement that he no longer paid any attention to protocol or procedure. He just did what needed to be done.

But the whole thing gave him pause. Accustomed as he was to death and its adjuncts, it still shook him when the dead person was someone he knew, especially, as in this case, when it was an old friend. Years ago, Campbell Young and Shorty Rogers had been as close as two men married to the same bottle could be. They had been drinking buddies, but because of certain half-remembered things they'd done in each other's company, they had not been close for almost a decade. Five years ago, however, when Debi had been on the ropes and had come to her father for help, one of the things Young had done to get her back on her feet was to phone Shorty and ask him if he could do him a favour, for old time's sake, and give Debi a job. Shorty had said yes, she could pick up stalls and walk hots. Debi had been with him ever since. In fact, she was the only one who had stuck by Shorty during his gradual slide from the top of the heap. She had been with him when times were good — she was Shorty's old route horse Too Many Men's groom when he won the Horizon Stakes in 1993 — and she was with him now, two years later, when he was lucky to win a bottom claimer for non-winners lifetime. It was hard to say what had gone wrong, exactly. Shorty just stopped winning races. He lost his touch. And last October he had been in trouble with the stewards because one of his horses had tested positive for phenylbutazone, a sore-horse drug, and he'd had to serve a thirty-day suspension. His drinking increased. He got in fights. And then, one by one, just about everybody abandoned him: the owners who for years had trusted their horses to him, his fellow trainers, his grooms, his friends; even Bunny, his wife of fifteen years, walked out on him. Shorty seemed to have lost everything and everyone — except Debi.

* * *

Young usually started his day with a shower, a shave, a one-a-day vitamin with a large glass of extra-pulp orange juice, a lozenge of flaxseed oil, a zinc tablet, a bowl of Grape-Nuts, and half an hour of breakfast television. This morning, however, all he did was feed Reg, his ancient British bulldog, let her outside to stretch and relieve herself, and phone Homicide to speak to Staff Inspector Bateman.

"Do you want Wheeler with you?" Bateman asked after Young had explained the situation. Detective Lynn Wheeler was Young's partner.

"No, I'm going straight there."

"She'll be here any minute, Camp. She could drive herself up, or I could send Barkas or Urmson."

"No, the place'll be crawling with their own people. I don't want to get their backs up. Let me handle it."

The last thing Young did before leaving his apartment was knock back about three ounces of Pepto-Bismol. He hated the taste and even the texture of the thick pink fluid, but he'd had a stomach ache for the past three days, and all he could think of to ease it was Pepto-Bismol. That and Tums. *Maybe I'm getting an ulcer*, he thought, as he locked his front door.

Young walked down the driveway beside his low-rise to the small parking lot where he kept his mini-van. A year earlier, he had been forced to dispose of his previous car, a 1978 robin's egg blue Plymouth Volare so badly in need of a valve job that an OPP cruiser had pulled him over on the Don Valley Parkway; its driver, a young patrolman with a boiled face, had described to Young how he'd followed a black cloud of smoke all the way up from the lakeshore, curious to discover its source, which had turned out to be Young's Volare. He'd told Young he could either repair the car or junk it. So Young had gone out and bought a used Dodge minivan, faded maroon, missing its middle seat.

As he fought his way through gridlock towards the track, Young thought about his daughter. A few images of Debi as a little girl flashed through his mind, but they were overtaken by the more disturbing images that always seemed to appear in his mind's eye of Debi as a teenager, pink-eyed with dope, tattooed and pierced and overweight and filthy. Whenever Debi had come to spend the weekend at her father's apartment after his separation from her mother, his passing attempts at cleaning up were quickly overwhelmed by his and his daughter's combined sloth. They never sat down to have a meal together: she would eat her frozen dinners and junk food in front of the television in her bedroom, and he would eat his in front of the television in the living room.

Young stopped for a traffic light. He fished a cigarette out of the pack on the passenger's seat beside him. He had tried to quit smoking when Jamal was born, but he was too attached to it. He tried to keep himself to a pack a day, but if he was drinking he might smoke two packs. He loved everything about smoking. When he opened a fresh pack, he would push his nose against the silver foil for the raisin smell. Yes, he loved it. *Hell*, he thought, *aside from shortness of breath and heart palpitations and the threat of lung cancer, what's not to love?*

The light turned green, and Young drove on. He remembered the night he'd left his wife. She had grown tired of his drinking, his carousing with workmates, and had given him an ultimatum: "If you don't quit the force our marriage is over!" He had snorted at the very idea of not being a cop, thrown a couple of changes of underwear into his overnight bag, grabbed his Bob Seger CDs and several unironed shirts Tanya had washed and hung on hangers on the back of the bedroom door, and driven away from his wife and child, a hole in his heart the size of a bus, but absolutely convinced he was doing the right thing. A week later, more or less settled into a malodorous flat above a souvlaki joint on the Danforth, he had wandered — drink in one hand, cigarette in the other — into the bathroom and had stood in front of the shirts he had brought from home. They were hanging from the curtain rod in the shower and still hadn't been ironed; Young knew that he would never iron them himself — he'd never used an iron in his life — and he knew that without Tanya to look after him, it was going to be downhill for a while.

But that was six years ago, and although Jamal's father had flown the coop long before his son's birth — or perhaps because of it — Debi had straightened herself out, and Young had straightened out, too. He was still a slob, but he was a much happier slob than he had been back then — for one thing, he had discovered a dry cleaner's right around the corner, and for another, his daughter and grandson were a daily presence in his life.

By the time Young reached the racetrack, the police had established themselves, and the ambulance crew was standing by. The stall door had been rolled back, and yellow police tape was stretched across the opening. Bing Crosby had been moved to another stall.

A uniformed officer was standing by himself.

"Are you First Officer?" Young asked him.

"Yes, sir."

"Young, Metro Homicide. What's your name, and what've we got here?"

The man swallowed. "Peebles, sir. To tell you the truth, sir, I think this is an accident scene, not a crime scene. I think the horse just kicked him."

"Any other detectives here yet?"

"No, sir."

Young nodded and turned his attention to the stall. The police photographer had set up a light stand that was shining on the straw bedding and on the figure of a man in a dark suit kneeling over the corpse of Shorty Rogers.

Young crouched and lifted the yellow tape above his head and then stood up in the entrance to the stall. "What've you got?" he said.

The kneeling man looked up, and the first thing Young noticed were the black-rimmed half-glasses that were the trademark of Elliot Cronish, Pathologist. Cronish slowly rose to his feet and brushed the straw from his knees. "Hardly your neck of the woods, Young."

"Yours neither," Young said.

"Regular man's on vacation."

"What have you got? Kid over there thinks the horse kicked him."

"That's what it looks like, but the young woman who phoned it in — he was her boss," he nodded down at Shorty, "— she claims it's murder."

"Coroner already been here?"

"Come and gone."

"Mind if I take a look?"

"Be my guest." Cronish made a sweeping motion with his arm, like a chauffeur would for someone stepping into a limousine.

Carefully, Young manoeuvred himself into the stall. He swallowed as he looked down at the body of his friend. He wanted to kneel down and stroke him or pat him and say something, but he didn't. He couldn't. Cops didn't do that sort of thing, especially cops with as many years under their belts as Young had. Especially in front of people like Cronish, who would watch such a display of emotion with amusement and file it away.

Shorty was on his stomach. He was wearing blue jeans and a white Toronto Maple Leafs hockey sweater with the number 93 in blue. There was blood spatter on the left shoulder. Young bent his knees and lowered himself into a half-squat. On the left side of Shorty's head, near the temple, the gray hair was darkly matted with blood.

"What do you know so far?" Young asked.

Cronish looked back down at the body. "Blow to the head. Could have been a kick, like the First Officer said."

"How long?"

Cronish stretched his left arm and looked at his watch. "It's 7:45 a.m. My best guess at this point is he's been dead since midnight."

Young pondered. "What would he have been doing in a horse's stall at midnight?"

Cronish smiled and shook his head. "Are you just thinking out loud, Young, or do you really expect an answer? What I know about racehorses you know about, oh, let's see — opera?"

Young wasn't listening. "He bunked nearby, I know that. Maybe he heard something. Horse in trouble, maybe. Where's Debi?"

"Who?"

"Debi. The groom. My daughter."

"Oh, that's your daughter?" Cronish smiled his Cheshire smile. "The plot thickens."

"Where is she?"

Cronish shrugged his shoulders. "Somebody took her for a coffee."

Young stepped back out of the stall, lifted the yellow tape over his head, nodded to the uniformed officer, and trudged back through the barn and outside through the early sunshine towards a low square building painted Parks Department green that served as the track kitchen and cafeteria. Young was a big man — so big, in fact, that as he passed a pair of exercise boys in their flak jackets and helmets, they looked up in alarm, like two kids in a canoe who've suddenly found themselves in the path of a freighter.

Inside the kitchen, as he walked past the counter with its enormous coffee urns and its trays of pancakes and scrambled eggs and sausage and bacon and home fries, he smiled. He smiled because he spotted her — a big young woman in coveralls with a fire-engine red crewcut sitting opposite a smallish-by-comparison young man in a blue uniform — his baby girl, who, thanks to him, had the shoulders and strength and vocabulary of a linebacker.

"Daddy!" she shouted when she saw him. She stood, knocking her chair onto its back, and ran into her father's arms. "Why would anybody want to kill him?"

Young pulled back so that he could see her face. "Sweetie, sweetie, what makes you think he was murdered?" He kissed away a tear. "The horse —"

"The horse!" she interrupted, her eyes blazing. "You think Bing did it? You think Bing kicked him? Bing loved him. Bing loves everybody. Daddy, you know horses. This is an eight-year-old gelding. He's like a trail horse at a goddamn riding stable. He's a pussycat. He wouldn't hurt a mouse, let alone a man, let alone Shorty, who he loved. No, no, somebody murdered him. Somebody murdered him and made it look like an accident."

"The pathologist says he died around midnight."

Debi took a step back from her father. "I bedded Bing down myself at eight o'clock last night. Shorty was with me. He did Prince and Softy, and I did the other two. Then I left to pick up Jamal at Mrs. Ferri's. Shorty wouldn't have had any reason to go back into Bing's stall at midnight. Besides, he would have been in bed by ten. *Law & Order* at nine, a couple of rum and Cokes, then bed. Like clockwork. I'm telling you, Daddy, somebody killed him."

But Shorty did go into Bing Crosby's stall around midnight. Maybe he was in his bunkroom and heard something and went to investigate and someone attacked him. Or maybe he was taken there by force. Dragged maybe. Or maybe the First Officer was right, despite what Debi said, and Shorty got kicked in the head. These were among Young's thoughts as he headed back to Barn 7. Debi had told him about her encounter with Tom Wright while she was searching for Shorty, and Young wanted to talk to him. He found Tom grooming Doll House in her stall. "Terrible business," Tom said. "Me and Shorty was friends."

"It's a shock, all right. You were here early this morning, weren't you, Tom? Did you see anything suspicious?"

Tom shook his head. "No, I didn't see nothin'."

"What about last night?"

Tom paused, currycomb suspended in air. "I tucked this old thing in about seven, seven-fifteen, then I went home. I don't remember nothin' out of the ordinary."

Young nodded towards the stall. "She ran last weekend, didn't she?"

"Yes, sir, she run second in a starter allowance." Tom didn't take his eyes off the mare. "Nice spot for her. She's entered a week from tomorrow."

"Any chance?"

"Well, she's sound as a bell."

"I'll take that as a tip."

Tom shook his head. "Don't bet the farm. She's gettin' a little long in the tooth, ain't you, Dolly? You ain't gonna win no stakes races."

"How old is she?"

"Seven, which is old for a mare to still be runnin', but like I say, sir, she's sound and she still enjoys her work."

"You've been around the races all your life, right, Tom?"

Tom was rummaging in his tack box. "Yes, sir, since I was knee high."

"I remember when you won the jockey championship two years in a row."

Tom held up a hoof pick. He bent over and lifted Doll House's off fore. "Seventy-five, seventy-six."

"That's right, and I remember the year you finished second in the International on ... what was the colt's name?"

"Signifier. That was seventy-eight."

"That's right, Signifier. My money was on you that day."

"We didn't quite get up. Another couple of jumps. Then I went with him to a big race at Arlington. We finished fifth, but you could of throwed a blanket over the bunch of us."

Young knew Arlington Park in Chicago. One of the great racetracks of North America; Citation and Round Table had set track records there. At Arlington, people didn't toss their losing tickets on the floor, the way they did everywhere else, they dropped them in trash barrels. Cleanest track he'd ever seen, and the most beautiful, and he'd been to most of the famous ones — Churchill Downs and Saratoga and Santa Anita.

He'd still been with Tanya when he'd gone to Chicago. It seemed a long time ago now, although it was only six years. He remembered seeing an old blues singer named A.C. Reed in one of the bars on North Clark Street, which he thoroughly enjoyed, and an exhibit of sculptures at an art gallery Tanya made him go to, which he didn't enjoy at all. The sculptures were all made of pipes and fittings and all looked like plumbing to him; despite Tanya's oohing and ahhing, he couldn't understand how any of it qualified as art. It wasn't that Young had anything against art — art in general, or sculpture in particular. In front of that same racetrack in Chicago, for example, there was a life-sized bronze sculpture of the great grass horse John Henry, fully extended, Willie Shoemaker aboard with his whip raised, nosing out The Bart in the 1981 Arlington Million. In Young's opinion, that was art, that was sculpture, but hey, as he liked to tell anyone who would listen, although he wasn't a complete ignoramus, what he knew about culture you could fit in a thimble.

"You were a fine rider, Tom."

Tom stood up and stretched his back. "Kind of you to say so."

"I guess you know my daughter, do you?"

"Your daughter, sir?"

"Debi Young. Shorty's groom."

"Oh," Tom said. "Yes, I bumped into her this mornin'." He looked up at Young like a pony at a plough horse. "She has to learn not to run in the barn." He dropped the hoof pick back into the tack box. "How can I help you, sir? Me and Shorty went back a long ways."

Young said, "We were friends, too, at one point, and he was good to my daughter, and I want to find out whether his death was an accident or whether there's some other explanation."

Tom said, "What can I do?"

"You can tell me who else to talk to. Who else Shorty had daily contact with. Jockeys, agents, owners. Whatever."

Tom took off his grimy fedora and scratched above one ear. "Well, gosh, let me see..."

"Who did he spend the most time with?"

"Oh, well, if you put it like that" — Tom smiled — "that's easy. That would be Percy Ball."

"Name rings a bell. Wasn't he a rider?"

Tom said, "That's right. Rode a few years at the Fort, and a little bit at Greenwood. B-tracks mostly. Didn't last long. Couldn't keep the weight off. Now he's an exercise rider. Works all of Shorty's horses."

"Him and Shorty spent a lot of time together?"

"Oh yes," Tom said and nodded.

"They drank together is what you're saying."

"You could say that, yes, sir."

"You think Percy might be able to help."

Tom smiled and shook his head. "He's an aggravatin' little so-and-so, and I wouldn't trust him as far as I could throw him, but maybe he knows somethin'."

"Where'd they drink?"

"JJ Muggs, mostly. It's in the Caledonia Mall. If he's not there, then he's probably at McKenzie's. You know where McKenzie's is at?"

Young nodded. "What time's he usually get there?"

Tom raised his left wrist and squinted at his watch, then shook his head. "Wife gave me this for my birthday, but whenever I wanna know the time, it takes two minutes to figure it out. Blasted thing's got no numbers to it." Tom squinted at the watch again. "Let me see, let me see. Well, it's only nine. He'll ride his last horse around ten-thirty, so you're likely to find him over there around eleven, or whenever they start servin'."

"How will I know him?"

Tom thought. "He's got a sort of a Beatles haircut, dyed blond. He likes to flip it around for the girls."

* * *

Young spent the next two hours examining the crime scene and talking to grooms and trainers whose horses were stabled in the same barn. The only useful piece of information came from Morrison, the evidence man, who determined that no one had been dragged into the stall. But Young realized that that didn't prove much, because Shorty was small enough for a strong man to carry. A detective from King County Homicide finally arrived shortly after eleven, delayed, he claimed, by a wee-hours drug-related shooting in the Finch Hills projects, in his southeast quadrant. When he asked Young, somewhat suspiciously, why a detective from downtown was on a case that was, geographically speaking, none of his business, Young smoothed the man's feathers by explaining his personal interest in the situation and by giving him a rundown on everything he knew. Mollified, the man, whose name was Keogh, invited him to lunch, but Young begged off. "Got a lead to run down," he said, and Keogh said, "Another time, maybe."

At eleven-thirty Young parked his minivan outside JJ Muggs. Inside, he had to wait until his eyes adjusted to the darkness. And there was Percy Ball, just as Tom Wright had predicted, sitting at the bar, his back turned, but the unmistakable blond mop fully in evidence.

Young walked towards him. Percy was wearing cowboy boots, black jeans, and a black vinyl jacket that was supposed to look like leather. When Young was two feet behind him, he said, "Percy Ball?"

Percy hopped off his stool like a man in trouble. He stood there with his chest stuck out, and his head wouldn't stay still, poking this way and that like a pigeon's.

"Are you Percy Ball?" Young said.

"Who wants to know?"

Young had his badge in his hand. "Police. Used to ride, didn't you?"

Percy stuck his chest out even further. "Yeah, some. Here and there. Greenwood, the Fort. Out west mostly."

"Did you ride for Shorty Rogers?"

Percy hesitated. "Some."

"What's that mean, some? Did you ride for him or not?"

"I worked horses for him."

"Ah, you were his exercise boy."

"That's right, but he put me on all the best ones. He wouldn't let nobody else get on the good ones."

"What good ones? Shorty was fresh out of good ones."

"He let me ride Too Many Men."

"Sure, that was his money horse for awhile, but you know what, Percy, that's old news."

"Yeah, well, I was the only one Shorty'd let on him."

"In the mornings."

"Yeah, in the mornings. That horse was a mean motherfucker. Liked to snap his head back."

Young looked closely at Percy's face, the eyes too close together, the broken nose. "The reason I'm here, Percy, is I need to know where Shorty was last night."

"What're you askin' me for?"

"Because Shorty's dead, that's why." He waited, but Percy didn't react. "You knew he was dead, didn't you?"

Percy lifted his chin as if his collar were too tight. "Yeah, I knew."

"You seem real broke up about it."

Percy shrugged.

"And," Young went on, "the reason I'm asking you is because you were with him."

Percy's bird eyes looked left and right.

"You didn't just work for him, you were his drinking buddy, right?"

Percy scratched his dirty hair. "We was here."

"What time?"

"I got here about one or so. I don't know what time he got here. An hour later, maybe. We was here all afternoon, had a few beers, something to eat. He musta left around seven-thirty. Had to go back to the barn and bed down his horses. I never seen him after that."

Young waved to the bartender. "Couple of beers here," he said. Then, to Percy, "Do you think his death was an accident?"

Percy picked at a scab on his knuckle. He didn't look up. "Shorty knew his way around horses, and besides, that old Bing Crosby wouldn't hurt a flea. It wasn't no accident."

"Who should I talk to?"

"Whoever he owed money to, I guess."

"Who might that be?"

"Hey, what do I know? Maybe he was in trouble with a bookie." The bartender placed two bottles on the bar. Percy took one and drank deeply from it. He wiped his mouth with the back of his hand. "Maybe one of his owners got fed up with him not winnin' any races."

"Who were his owners?"

"Old lady he'd been trainin' for for years. She owns Bing Crosby." He paused, as if unsure whether to continue. "And some guy who owns a computer store or something. Calls himself the Internet King. He owns the other horses. Shorty only had the two owners."

"Who owned the colt that died?"

Percy looked up at Young, then away.

Young's eyes narrowed. "Someone told me about a colt that died. What was its name? Down something. Downtown?"

Still looking away, Percy said, "Download. The Internet guy owned him. Paid a ton of money for him, but he didn't do much. Won a special weight maiden race at the Fort last fall, which, as I'm sure you're aware of, don't mean fuck all, and after that he couldn't cut it with winners. Anyways, he died."

"In his stall?" Young asked.

Percy nodded at his beer bottle.

"What killed him?"

"Vet said colic."

"How old was the colt?"

"Three."

"Young horse. Otherwise healthy?"

Percy nodded again. "Seemed so." He finished the first bottle of beer and eyed the second. "Aren't you gonna drink yours?"

"You can have it."

Young studied Percy a moment, dropped some money on the bar, and walked outside into the sunshine.

He was unlocking the door to his minivan when a voice behind him shouted, "Hey!" Young looked up. With one hand Percy was shielding his eyes from the sun, and with the other he was holding open the side door of the bar. "He had three!"

"Three what? Who had three?"

"Shorty. He had three owners. Picked up a new one. Guy won the lottery or something. Dresses like *Saturday Night Fever*. Shorty claimed a colt for him. Won his first race for them, and won it very impressive, too. He was supposed to run him back Sunday in the stake. I don't know what'll happen now. All's I know is Shorty didn't like the man." Then he disappeared back inside the bar, and the door closed.

* * *

Detective Lynn Wheeler came into Young's cubicle at Homicide at 2:00 p.m., shortly after he had returned from his visit with Percy, to tell him that the pathologist, Elliot Cronish, had called. Wheeler knew there was no love lost between the two men. Young complained that Cronish never took anything seriously. He was more interested in the murderer's modus operandi than he was in the pain and suffering of the victim.

"What did he want?" Young asked. He was sitting at his desk. She was standing beside him. Because he was so tall and she was so much shorter, their eyes were at the same level. Wheeler had a physical peculiarity: one of her eyes was brown and the other was blue. When she was being especially businesslike or when she was angry, she somehow drew Young into her brown eye. When she was happy or light-hearted, he found himself staring into the blue one. Right now he was looking into the serious eye, the brown one.

"It was about your friend," she said, tucking her blonde pageboy behind her ears. "After they took the body back to the lab and cleaned it up, they found a mark."

"What kind of mark?"

"Dr. Cronish described it as horseshoe-shaped. Above the left temple."

Young frowned. "Shit. I was so sure."

"About what?"

"That he'd been murdered."

"They found horsehairs, too. Stuck in the wound."

"Horsehairs? Well, that ices it, I guess. Shorty got kicked to death by a horse that everyone swears up and down wouldn't hurt a flea."

* * *

That night Percy Ball partied in an empty tack room in an empty barn at the far reaches of the backstretch of Caledonia Downs Racetrack. With him was a young man named Marvis and a woman whose name Percy never learned. As an exercise rider Percy considered himself superior to the other two, who were both grooms.

Marvis had a cube of hashish wrapped in foil. He said Percy and the woman could have some if they paid him ten dollars each. Neither of them was carrying any money, but they promised to pay him the next day, so he agreed. He slid the end of a safety pin into a small chunk of hash, and the three of them, squatting like peasants in the smelly room, inhaled the smoke through a plastic drinking straw.

Later, the woman, who was skinny and tattooed and had dyed her short, spiky hair lemon yellow, sat beside Marvis and traced her fingers through his cornrows.

They were drinking Black Ice, and after a while Marvis lay down and went to sleep.

Because the barn was not in use, its power had been shut off, and now, as dusk fell, Percy picked up the flashlight Marvis had brought with him and, accidentally-on-purpose, flipped back his blond hair in its beam. When the woman didn't react, Percy said, "Both of us, we dye our hair, eh. Same colour, almost."

The woman took the flashlight from Percy's hand and showed him a tattoo of a scorpion on the back of her neck. Then she pulled up the left sleeve of her T-shirt and showed him a tattoo of a teddy bear on the point of her shoulder. Percy asked if she had any other tattoos, and could he see them. She said no, but he didn't know if she meant that she didn't have any others or that he couldn't see them.

There was a silence, and soon the woman seemed to forget about Percy and resumed playing with Marvis's cornrows.

Percy set his chin. He reached for the flashlight and turned it off. In the darkness, he said, "You like black guys, do you? You like doin' it with black guys?"

The woman scrambled to her feet and bumped and stumbled her way out of the tack room. Percy thought about going after her — he had a jackknife in his pants pocket — but even though the beer was all gone, he was content to stay where he was. He wished he had some snacks, though — Bar-B-Q Fritos, maybe, and a couple of cans of Dr. Pepper.

Friday, June 2

This time, instead of chasing a private school girl, Campbell Young was himself being chased — by Shorty Rogers, his white Maple Leafs jersey splattered with the bright blood that sprayed from his blond Beatles mop at every twist and turn of the same series of alleyways that had appeared in the first dream. *But it's Percy Ball, not Shorty, who has the Beatles haircut*, Young told himself in the dream. And when he looked again, it was Percy chasing him. Young gasped and opened his eyes and stared at the ceiling, his chest heaving. He sat up, swung his feet onto the floor, careful not to wake the still-snoring Reg, curled at the foot of the bed, and made his way to the bathroom. There was an open *Racing Form* on the vanity beside the toilet, and as he stood there urinating he looked down at it, his head at an angle, and became so engrossed in the past performances of a filly named Small Wonder that he was still standing there, penis in hand, thirty seconds after the last drop.

A few minutes later he was at his kitchen counter pouring milk over a half-bowl of Grape-Nuts when he heard the clicking of Reg's nails as she made her way down the hall.

Young opened the door onto his little balcony and discovered that it was a fine, sunny morning. As he held the door, Reg waddled out and slowly and painfully made her way down the wooden steps to the backyard. Young watched from the balcony as she snuffled around before settling down on her haunches. When she was finished, she returned to the bottom of the staircase, studied the first step long and hard, made several false starts, and then finally, with one protracted effort, mounted the stairs to the balcony and walked past Young, who was still holding the door for her, back into the kitchen, where her breakfast of Iam's Senior Diet, topped by a torn-up piece of caraway rye, was waiting in her bowl.

"Don't expect me to start carrying you up those stairs," Young said to her as he sat down in his dining nook with his Grape-Nuts. "No free rides around here."

With age, Reg had become not only arthritic but constipated as well. She had developed a rectal itch and was now in the habit of dragging herself in a sitting position across the living room carpet, her forelegs doing the pulling, the paws of her rear legs up by her ears, her anus making hard contact with the abrasive material of the broadloom. This caused her to grunt with pleasure. Young's cleaning lady complained that the dog was staining the carpet. "It's dark red," Young said, "with black designs all over it. You can't see anything. Anyway, just vacuum it. That'll pick up any little dagmarbles that break loose."

When he had finished his cereal, Young considered the bottle of Pepto-Bismol that stood beside his juice glass. His stomach ache had pretty much faded, but he wasn't convinced it was completely gone. Young didn't have vast experience with stomach aches, but this one impressed him. For three days it had felt as if his guts were in the grip of a cold vise. He hadn't felt nauseous or feverish, just a little dizzy, and the pain in his stomach came in waves, sometimes so intensely that sweat popped out on his forehead. He removed the cap, upended the bottle, and chugged about three ounces of the glutinous liquid.

He ran hot water over the dishes he had used and placed them in the rack, then checked the three horseshoe-shaped farmer's sausages hanging from the knobs of his kitchen cupboard doors. He had bought them fresh at the St. Lawrence Market a week earlier and was drying and hardening them. Over a period of several days, a drop of grease would collect and hang like a golden pearl from the bottom of each sausage. He'd placed a square of paper towel beneath the sausages to catch the drops.

Half an hour later, after showering and shaving and dressing, Young was behind the wheel of his minivan on his way to work. He wondered what his old partner, Arthur Trick, would have to say about Shorty's death. He was usually pretty good at smelling out leads. But Trick wasn't on the case. In fact, he wasn't even on the Force anymore — all the result of a bullet in the neck he'd taken three years earlier during a stakeout, leaving him in a wheelchair. The stakeout had been part of an investigation into a series of hostage-takings. Young's daughter, Debi, had been one of the hostages.

I'll see both of them at the track on Sunday, he thought. When he had talked to Debi on the phone Thursday night, she'd told him that both the old lady Percy had mentioned and the secretary for Mahmoud Khan, the Internet King, had contacted her and asked her to continue looking after their horses. Not as groom, however. As trainer. At least for the time being, until things settled down. She hadn't heard from the lottery winner yet, she said, which struck her as odd, because his colt, Someday Prince — as Percy Ball had told Young — was scheduled to run in Sunday's minor stake for three-year-olds. *Shorty was awful high on the horse,* Young remembered as he turned into the parking lot behind Headquarters and pulled up beside Wheeler's Sidekick, *at least according to Percy. Maybe I should speak to Debi about the horse's chances. A small wager may be in order.*

As he shut off the engine, Young thought, *Debi's my favourite person in the world. Well, Jamal's up there, too, of course. And Trick. And don't forget Wheeler.* In the three years that they had been partners, Wheeler had proven herself time and again to Young. Courage, smarts, dedication. And, Young smiled to himself, he liked to think that after a rocky beginning to their partnership he'd proven himself to her. He shook his head remembering the crush he'd had on her. How stupid could he have been? First of all, he was almost twenty-five years older than she was. A quarter of a century. Twice her age, for fucksake. Secondly, since his marriage to Tanya had gone belly up — his first and only marriage — he had pretty much avoided anything resembling attachment or domestic responsibility or falling in love. And then there was the fact that he was big and ugly and had kinky red hair, and whatever minute amount of charm he had once possessed where the ladies were concerned was long gone. And lastly, how stupid could he have been not to twig to the fact that Wheeler liked girls? It had been a shock to his system when she came right out and told him. He'd left her little choice, really, hitting on her as he had. *Nevertheless,* he thought, as he walked towards the rear entrance of HQ, *I have four favourite people in the world. My daughter, my grandson, my best friend, and my partner. I'm a lucky man.*

* * *

Shortly before eleven in the morning, Elliot Cronish showed up, unannounced, at Young's cubicle.

"Clumsy, clumsy," he said cryptically once he had Young's eye, but Young wasn't biting. Despite his happiness in the parking lot, he had turned surly. Some part of him still refused to believe Shorty's death was an accident, but he had nothing to go on. He waited Cronish out. After fifteen seconds, Cronish sighed and continued. "I refer not to you, you great lummox, but to the murderer or murderers of your daughter's employer."

Young blinked. "I thought you said it was an accident."

Cronish shrugged. "We were, if only momentarily, duped. Upon closer examination it was discovered that there were several horsehairs stuck to the wound on the side of the deceased's head."

Young said, "I already know that. You already told Wheeler that, and she already told me. Tell me something I don't know."

Cronish held up a hand like a stop sign and inclined his head. "Bear with me, please. After removing the horsehairs from the wound, what caught my eye — well, my technician's eye, to be truthful — was that the horsehairs appeared to have been cut. I got Morrison to look at them under the microscope, and he agreed that they'd been cut with a sharp instrument, probably scissors. So then I phoned an associate of mine at the Guelph School of Veterinary Medicine. She works in the large animal department there. I sent the hairs to her."

"When was this?"

"Yesterday afternoon, by FedEx. The results came in an hour ago."

"And?"

"I should tell you as well that I also sent along several other horsehairs. For comparison."

It was as if Cronish had turned on a light bulb above Young's head. "They didn't come from the horse that was in the stall where Shorty died," Young said. "Bing Crosby. You suspected the cut hairs weren't his, so you cut some of his hairs and sent them along for comparison."

Cronish patted his hands together in mock applause. "Very good. And guess what?"

"You were right, the hairs came from different horses."

"Wasn't that clever of me?"

"What made you think the horsehairs were planted?"

"Because we also compared the imprint of the horseshoe on the side of Shorty Rogers' head with Bing Crosby's horseshoes, that's why. They didn't match. The one on the side of his head had left an unusual impression. It left an extra mark. We made a diagram of it and sent it to my associate in Guelph, along with the hair samples, and she identified the impression as having come from what is known as an outside sticker, which is a special type of horseshoe — "

"Trainers put them on their horses when the track comes up muddy."

"That's right, that's what my associate said, but when we checked Bing Crosby we discovered he was wearing normal shoes."

Young nodded. "Debi was right. She said there was no way Bing Crosby killed Shorty." He paused. "But tell me something, how would horsehairs have gotten into the wound anyway? The hoof would have hit him, not any part of the horse's hide."

"Believe it or not, compadre, the same question troubled me. So I asked my associate and she said that while it was unlikely, it was possible. The hide on the back of a horse's leg runs right down into its hoof."

Young nodded. "Plus it made the whole kicked-by-a-horse scenario more believable."

"There you go."

"Anything else?"

"Well, far be it from me to tell you how to do your job, but maybe you need to find the outside sticker. If it's an uncommon type of horseshoe — "

"It's not, though. Every trainer has a stock of them in case of an off-track. Might as well look for a needle in a haystack."

"All I'm saying is the one you're looking for might have hair or blood on it."

Young nodded again. "I hear you. Anything else?"

"No, that's it. But I thought you would want to know about the horsehairs. Now you know what you're looking for."

"That's right, I'm looking for a killer."

The first task Young gave Wheeler was to find out whatever she could about Shorty Rogers' family. "There's an ex-wife," he told her. "Bunny. Actually, they may still have been married, but they weren't together. What I heard was she ran off with a veterinarian. I don't think her and Shorty had any kids, but you better check. Find out if Shorty had any brothers or sisters. And find out who might have wanted him dead."

Wheeler strode out of Young's cubicle full of purpose and determination, and while she was checking out Shorty's family Young set to work on some of the people they did know were involved in Shorty's life: Percy Ball, the exercise rider; Shorty's regular jockey, Trinidad Grant; and even Grant's agent, a shadowy character named Ronald Outhouse. All afternoon Young made phone calls and talked to people he thought might have useful information, but nothing he learned led anywhere. Percy Ball appeared to be nothing more than a not-too-bright drunk. The jockey was clean. His agent had a record — he had served two years for extortion after bilking several old ladies out of their pension cheques by impersonating a bank officer — but there was no immediate reason to suspect him of Shorty's murder.

At 5:00 p.m., Young decided enough was enough. On his way out of the building, he stopped by Wheeler's desk to see what she had accomplished. He hung his head over the wall of her cubicle.

She favoured him with her blue eye. "You look like a big old moon up there."

"Any luck?"

She nodded and looked down at the chaos of papers on her desk. "I'd say the ex is clean. She and the veterinarian moved to Arizona a year ago. They opened a dog restaurant in Tucson."

"A dog restaurant? People eat dog?"

"No, no, a restaurant for dogs. The dogs eat there. And you were right, she and Shorty didn't have any children. Shorty had one brother, Harold, but he had Downs Syndrome. He lived in an institution in Barrie. Died six months ago, aged fifty-two."

Young was shaking his head. "I like dogs, you know that. I love them. But a restaurant, when people are starving in the streets, all the homeless people."

"In fact, his only other living relative that I can find is an uncle, Morley Rogers, who lives up in the Caledon Hills."

"It's a crazy fucking world, Wheeler, that's all I know. Come on, it's Friday and it's past five. Let me buy you a beer. Harold and Morley can wait till Monday."

"Thanks anyway, Sarge," she said, turning to her computer screen, "but I'm going to stay a bit longer. I don't want the trail to go cold."

"You working this weekend?"

"No, I'm off."

"Well good, that's good." Young nodded his head thoughtfully. "But let me tell you something, Wheeler: Shorty was a friend of mine, and I *will* find out who killed him, but he ain't going to be any colder Monday than he is today."

Wheeler just looked up at him — brown-eyed — until he nodded his head again and walked away.

Saturday, June 3

Like Wheeler, Young was supposed to have the weekend off, but Saturday morning he went to work anyway. He began to research the people Shorty trained horses for: the old lady, the Internet king, the lottery winner.

The old lady was revealed to be Helen McDonagh, a wealthy spinster who had maintained a small stable of racehorses for over thirty years. In her youth she had been a champion tennis player. She was a member of the Granite Club and lived with a companion in an old house in the affluent Willowdale area of the city.

Young was about to shift his focus to the Internet king, but something that Percy Ball had said as he stood in the doorway of JJ Muggs tweaked Young's interest in the third owner, the lottery winner: "All's I know is Shorty didn't like the man." The man, a former junior high schoolteacher named Douglas Buckley, turned out to have a CV not nearly so straightforward as the old lady's. In his former life, before he won $8 million by selecting numbers that corresponded to the birthdays of his three children, Buckley had taught physical education and had been a Cub Scout leader, a sports card collector, and a scratch golfer. In those days, he'd driven a station wagon. In his new life, he drove a sports utility vehicle. Young learned some of this information in a phone call to Debi late that morning, but most of it he reconstructed during an afternoon visit he paid to Kathy Buckley, Doug's wife, in her pleasant, post-war, suburban brick bungalow in the Don Mills area of Toronto. There were beds of white hydrangea out front, the grass had recently been cut, one of the children — a boy — passed through the neatly appointed living room looking like he hated the world, and Kathy herself appeared ready to unravel.

The day after he won the lottery, according to Kathy, Doug took a leave of absence from Berrywood Middle School — he wanted to resign outright, but she put her foot down — and began spending his afternoons at Caledonia Downs. Although his friends and neighbours were unaware of it, Doug had a gambling problem. And although his children — Jason, fifteen, Jennifer, thirteen, and Jessica, seven — knew nothing of their father's compulsion, Kathy knew. She had seen him in action during their annual getaways to Las Vegas. "A light came into his eyes," she said, serving Young a glass of lemonade, "as soon as he stepped into a casino. Myself, I hate casinos — the crazy carpets, the noise. There isn't a clock anywhere. I'd spend my time shopping or going to shows, but I always knew where to find Doug. He loved the slots, but what he *really* loved was the horse race room at Bally's, where he could bet tracks all over North America and watch the races on huge telescreens while young women with hardly any clothes on brought him drinks." After he won the lottery, again according to Kathy, Doug's enthusiasm for Scout jamborees waned, and within months of his windfall he had dyed his mouse-brown Brillo-Pad hair jet black, had taken to wearing orange aviator glasses and a diamond ear stud, and had purchased, without Kathy's knowledge, a three-year-old thoroughbred racing colt named Someday Prince. When Kathy found out about the horse — Doug carelessly left a vet's bill in a shirt pocket — she demanded an explanation. Doug admitted that several months earlier he had talked to a horse racing writer named Priam Harvey. Harvey, Doug told her, had put him onto a trainer named Shorty Rogers. When Kathy ordered Doug to sell the horse and terminate his relationship with Rogers, Doug simply smiled at her, turned and walked out the front door, climbed into his fully loaded, cow-catchered, pewter-coloured Ford Expedition, drove to the Airport Hilton a mile from the racetrack, and moved in.

Young asked if Kathy had any photographs of Doug that she could show him. "Jessica has one in her room," she said. "I'll get it." When she returned, she polished the glass of the frame with the elbow of her sweater before showing it to him. The photograph revealed Doug to be muscular, baby-faced, and — Young thought — full of himself.

As Young was standing up to leave, Kathy asked if he would be speaking to her husband in the near future.

"I haven't actually met him yet," Young said.

"Well, when you do meet him," Kathy said evenly, "tell him to drop by sometime and pick up his belongings. They're in the garage."

Young found a phone booth outside a Sunoco station a short distance from Kathy Buckley's house. He phoned the offices of *Sport of Kings* magazine and asked to

speak to Priam Harvey. He was informed by a receptionist that Mr. Harvey no longer worked there.

Young phoned McCully's Tavern. Dexter, the bartender, answered. "Dexter," Young said, "is Mr.
Harvey there?"

"Right here, Sarge. You want to talk to him, I'll
have to wake him up."

"Wake him up."

Thirty seconds passed, and a groggy voice said,
"Priam Harvey, at your service."

"Were you really sleeping?"

"To whom am I speaking?"

"Young. Dexter said you were sleeping."

"I may have been having a little rest, but I certainly
wasn't asleep. Dexter was exaggerating." Harvey
paused to cough. "What can I do for you?"

"I need some information on a man named
Douglas Buckley."

"Never heard of him."

"A few months ago he asked you to recommend a
trainer, and you gave him Shorty Rogers."

"Oh, poor Shorty. I just heard this morning."

"Yes, well, it looks like foul play, Mr. Harvey, so I'm
doing a little research on his owners, and Doug Buckley
was one of them."

There was a pause as Harvey lit a cigarette. "Won
the lottery, if I'm not mistaken."

"That's right."

"I never met him, but I remember he sounded very
bubbly over the phone. I guess I'd sound bubbly, too, if
I won the lottery. Said he was interested in getting into
the racing game, but didn't know anyone in the business, so he called me. Claimed he devoured every issue
of *Sport of Kings*, and my column in particular. He
wanted the name of a good trainer. I asked him how big

a stable he wanted and how much money he wanted to spend, and he said just one horse to start, twenty to thirty thousand dollars. I told him I had just the man for him and gave him Shorty's number."

"What happened then?"

"Well, about a week later, I bumped into Shorty at JJ Muggs and he thanked me for sending a new client his way. By that time, he already had his eye on a horse."

"Someday Prince."

"That's right. I know that Shorty himself had coveted the colt since watching him as a two-year-old the previous fall. He'd finished third twice, and Shorty felt he could be a late-kick sprinter. Trouble was he didn't have anywhere near the money it would take to buy him. The arrival on the scene of Doug Buckley and his fat purse was timely indeed." Harvey inhaled deeply on his cigarette.

"Then what?"

"In late May, Someday Prince made his first start as a three-year-old, running for a tag — thirty-two thousand — and Shorty claimed him. The jockey took him immediately to the lead and, as Shorty predicted, he faded in the stretch. Finished eighth. Buckley, who was sitting with Shorty in the clubhouse, was disturbed by the horse's poor showing. Shorty told me later he had been quite firm with Buckley. Told him the colt would prove out, but to show how strongly he felt, he would buy a twenty-five percent interest in him. So Doug kicked in twenty-four thousand, and Shorty, by begging and borrowing and maybe a little stealing, scraped together eight, and three weeks later, in his first race for his new owners, Someday Prince came from off the pace in a special weight maiden race and won handily."

Young said, "He's entered Sunday."

"Well, if he wins, he'll have more than recouped the original investment."

"Too bad Shorty won't be around to enjoy it."

Next, Young phoned the Airport Hilton, had his call transferred to Doug Buckley's room, found him in, and, after a few minutes of introduction and explanation, succeeded in persuading Doug to meet him in the dining room a half-hour later, at five-thirty.

Young wove in and out of traffic all the way up the Don Valley Parkway and across Highway 401 to the hotel, flipped his keys to a valet, and found Doug — as advertised, muscular and baby-faced — standing at the entrance to the dining room, shooting the cuffs of his powder blue leisure suit and smoothing his coiffure.

Young said, "I thought those outfits went out of style about 1979."

"It's retro," Doug said, colouring slightly.

The maitre d' seated them at a corner table and gave them menus. When the waiter arrived, Doug ordered a half-litre of gewurtztraminer and the fettucine alfredo. Young ordered two bottles of Labatt's Blue. "No glass," he told the waiter, "and no food."

Young began the conversation by asking Doug about his new life. "It must have been hard to leave the wife and kids."

Doug nodded. "It's not something you do every day, but I'd just made a fortune, and it turned out to be a very liberating experience. It taught me that I was not a prisoner of my marriage or my job or my role as a father. I was a free agent. I could do all the things I'd always wanted to do."

"Like what, for instance?"

Doug looked around. "Like pay cash for a top-of-the-line car. Like buy a new wardrobe." He fingered the lapels of his leisure suit. "Like buy a racehorse, or move out of suburbia and into a nice hotel where you can get a massage at three in the morning, if that's what turns you on."

"Speaking of racehorses," Young said, "Shorty Rogers was your trainer, right?"

Doug lifted his napkin from his lap to his lips and patted them. "I'm sure you already know that."

"Him and you get along okay? I mean, you were his boss, right? No problems between you two?"

Young's first impression was that Doug was not the sort of man who would look you in the eye at the best of times, and he seemed particularly evasive right now. "I hardly knew him," he said. "He'd only been training for me for a few weeks. I've been told that he drank too much, but I really wouldn't know."

"You got his name through Priam Harvey at *Sport of Kings*, right?"

Doug shifted in his chair. "That's right."

Young examined his fingernails. "That's kind of interesting about Priam Harvey. He happens to be a friend of mine. As a matter of fact, when my daughter was looking for a job a few years ago, Mr. Harvey told me I should talk to Shorty."

"Your daughter worked for Shorty?"

Young looked back at Doug. "She's taken over his horses for the time being. Debi Young? You should know her, she's looking after your horse."

Doug's brow furrowed and he peered into his wineglass. "I think I met her when Shorty claimed Someday Prince, and I went to the backstretch to see him up close." He looked back up at Young. "So that's your daughter? His groom?"

"That's my daughter. She's heard from the other owners, but not from you. They want her to stay on as trainer."

Doug couldn't contain a smile. "Big girl?"

Young smiled, too. "Well, look who her father is." He stood up to his full height, leaned across the table towards Doug, and extended his hand. "You going to be around for a while?"

Hesitantly, Doug lifted his hand. "When, tonight?"

Young took Doug's hand and squeezed. "I mean are you likely to stay in this hotel for a while? No second thoughts about going back home to the wife and kids?"

Doug shook his head. "No, I'm not going back."

"No plans to move over to the Holiday Inn next door?"

"Hey," Doug laughed nervously, beginning to blanch in Young's grip, "massages at 3:00 a.m. Why would I leave?"

At 9:00 p.m., Young was at home and happily ensconced in his La-Z-Boy, which was so impregnated with back sweat and whose crannies were so littered with loose change and pens and pencils and balled-up Kleenexes and dusty kernels of popcorn and worms of cheesies that it resembled a stork's nest more than it did a chair.

Jamal was on Young's lap. Jamal's favourite place in the world was his grandfather's lap; at age two he would sit facing his grandfather, pulling his lips, tugging his ears, whacking his forehead with a tiny fist while Young was trying to watch TV. Now, almost six, Jamal faced the same direction his grandfather did, and together they watched TV sports. Tonight, they were watching baseball. When a batter rapped a grounder to short with a runner on first and nobody out, Young shouted, "Two, two!" and Jamal yelled, "Two, two!" in a serious little-boy voice, and when the throw to first beat the batter by two steps, Young shouted, "Got him!" and Jamal yelled, "Got him!"

As she did every time voices were raised, Reg struggled to her feet from her ragged mat in the middle of the living room carpet. Raised voices in Young's apartment were always sports-related. Sometimes Reg would bark if there was too much commotion, and Young would take her outside and put her in the front seat of the minivan, which was Reg's favourite place in the world, reasoning, Young figured, that if she was in the minivan she couldn't be left behind. How many times, after all, had he seen her silhouetted in the living room window as he drove away? But on this occasion she simply limped over to the La-Z-Boy and nosed under Young's wrist. He patted her head, saying, "That's okay, you old smelly thing, you stinky girl." Then he said, "She wants you to pet her, too, honey," and Jamal leaned over and patted her, saying, "That's okay, you old fatty," his small mocha hand on top of his grandfather's great freckled white slab of a hand, and after a minute or so Reg returned to her mat, sniffed a bit, and with a soft grunt lay back down.

Young often babysat Jamal, especially Wednesday and Saturday nights when Debi and her live-in boyfriend, Eldridge, went bowling. Eldridge was a jockey, but even though he wasn't Jamal's father — he and Debi had only been together a year and a half — and even though Debi was eight inches taller and eighty pounds heavier, they seemed to get along. They bowled in a league of racetrack employees — trainers and grooms and jockeys and jockeys' agents and valets and kitchen staff. They bowled year-round, and on Saturday evenings in the winter Young and Jamal would watch their favourite hockey team, the Toronto Maple Leafs. When a Leaf winger would cut from the boards across the slot, Young would shout "Shoot!" and Jamal would echo him, and if the puck found its mark they would shout "Yaaaaayyy!" and Jamal would swivel and high-five his grandfather.

One of the stories Young was most fond of telling, in his cups at McCully's Tavern, to anyone who would listen — especially complete strangers since his friends would howl in protest when they recognized what he was launching into, having already heard it themselves innumerable times — concerned the evening when Jamal, only three years of age, was sitting on Young's lap watching the Leafs play New Jersey, and Toronto tough guy Wendel Clark fought Devils left winger Mike Peluso. After the bout was over and the sticks and gloves had been picked up off the ice, Young listened intently as the penalties were announced. Clark was given a five-minute fighting major and a game misconduct. The TV commentator said, "That's all for Wendel Clark," and Jamal looked up at his grandfather and solemnly repeated, "That's all for Wendel Clark." Young would shake his head and laugh and then set off in search of someone else to tell the story to. People who knew him would see him coming and look for a place to hide. They knew that if he buttonholed them and started in on one of his stories, there was no escape. They would have to listen to the story all the way through. Even if they interrupted him partway into the story and said, "Stop right there, Camp, I've heard this one before, it's the one where Jamal makes some cute comment about Wendel Clark, right? It's a great story but I've heard it six or seven thousand times!" it wouldn't do any good. Young would simply stand there, stone-faced and single-minded, and wait until they were done protesting and then pick up the story at the point at which he'd been interrupted and tell it right through to the end.

An hour later Young realized that Jamal, still in his lap, had not uttered a sound for at least an inning.

Gently, he hefted the boy and could tell by the limpness of the small body that he was sound asleep.

Young adjusted his chair to its upright position, extricated himself as quietly as possible, and carried his grandson into the bedroom. Young laid him down on the king-sized bed, and as he constructed a rectangle of pillows around him, Jamal opened his eyes and said, "Tell me a story, Poppy?" Young lowered his weight onto the creaking bed and smoothed the curls off the boy's forehead. "The Adventures of Bert and Ernie," Young said. "Chapter One Hundred and Twenty-Four. Bert and Ernie Take Riding Lessons." Young could still do Bert and Ernie's voices convincingly, just as he could when Debi was little and he told her similar stories. He made them up as he told them, lying there in the dark beside the child, and no two were ever the same.

Partway into the story, Jamal said, "I'm just going to close my eyes for a minute, but I won't be asleep." Young continued with the story until the boy's breathing changed, then he carefully raised himself off the bed and tiptoed out of the bedroom.

In the living room the telephone was ringing. Young picked up the TV remote, hit "mute," and picked up the phone. "What?" he said.

"Young?" a voice said.

"Who's this?"

"Percy Ball. I wanted — "

"How'd you get my number?"

"I uh … I asked your daughter for it. Debi. I seen her at the bowling alley. She gave it to me."

"Well, she shouldn't be doing that. What do you want?"

"I have some information I think you might want to know about."

"I'm listening."

"Well, um, before I tell you what I know, I think there oughta be somethin' in it for me."

"Oh," said Young, "a shakedown."

"Man's gotta eat."

"I have to tell you, I'm a little disappointed. Making money off the death of your drinking buddy. Shame on you."

"I need the money. Shorty was the only one who'd let me work their horses, and now that he's gone — "

"I'll give you fifty dollars."

Percy stopped. "Make it a hundred and — "

"It's fifty, Percy, or you can stick your priceless information up your hole."

"Okay, okay, when can I get it?"

"I'll give it to Debi, and you can pick it up from her on Tuesday. Barn 7. Now spill."

Young heard the flare of a match and Percy pulling on a cigarette. "When me and Shorty were sittin' in JJ Muggs that last time, he told me that new owner I told you about —"

"The *Saturday Night Fever* guy?"

"That's right, the guy that won the lottery."

"His name's Buckley."

"Fine, okay. The point is Shorty told me this Buckley guy was offered a hundred thou' for Someday Prince."

Young's eyebrows lifted. "On the basis of that one win?"

"That's right, but you have to remember he won very impressive, and it seems some Jap interests caught wind of it. But Shorty didn't want no part of it. Just tellin' me about it in the bar there, he got seriously agitated. He said he told Buckley the colt was gonna be a champion, he was gonna run him in the fall classics, maybe even the Breeder's Cup. Buckley told him he was a fool to hire him in the first place, he was a drunk and a loser, and if he wasn't part owner of the horse he'd fire him, and he'd fire him in any case if he didn't watch out."

"What did Shorty say to that?"

"He said, 'That's right, I own part of the horse, one quarter to be exact, and you can't do nothin' without my say-so. Even if you fire me,' he told him, 'I still own one quarter of the horse.'"

"Shorty told you all this?"

"That's right," said Percy. "At JJ Muggs. Last time I seen him alive. Then the next day he shows up dead."

"So when I talked to you the other day, you already knew all this."

"Yeah, that's right."

"I bought you a couple of beers, and you still held out on me?"

Percy dragged on his cigarette, then in a grave tone said, "Never show your cards before you have to, what I say."

Young phoned the Airport Hilton and asked for Doug Buckley's room. The concierge at the front desk told him that Mr. Buckley was no longer a guest at the hotel.

"When did he check out?" Young asked.

The concierge paused, checking the register. "Mr. Buckley checked out about an hour ago."

"Did he leave a forwarding address?"

"No sir. He paid his bill and left."

"Listen," Young said, "maybe you can help me. My name's Michael Hunt, I'm Mr. Buckley's brother-in-law, he's married to my sister, see, and he's run out on her, and if there's anything else you could tell me, I'd be awful grateful. He's a deadbeat dad is what he is, and we're trying to catch up with him. He hasn't paid Lisa a cent in alimony, and the little ones … well, I guess you can see where I'm coming from."

The concierge paused, and when he spoke again his voice was low and conspiratorial. "Well, Mr. Hunt, I do sympathize because my sister has found herself in very much the same situation."

"No shit."

"No, I'm serious, and her husband's an orthodontist, for God's sake."

"It takes all kinds."

"Exactly my point, Mr. Hunt. Now, while it's entirely against policy here at the Hilton to divulge information of a personal nature about our guests, I can tell you that I was the one who checked Mr. Buckley out, and, like I said, he paid his bill, I had a valet bring his car around, and all I can really add is that his departure was, well, I guess you could say abrupt. I asked him if he wanted to leave a forwarding address, and he said no. He said he was lighting out. That was the expression he used. Lighting out. It's a cowboy expression, isn't it?"

"How the fuck should I know?"

"Oh, well, I believe it is, but anyway, I asked him where he was lighting out *to*. I just kind of enjoyed using the expression myself. And he said he was lighting out for greener pastures."

Young phoned Wheeler. He was several sheets to the wind, as he always was when he made these late-night calls, which he did once or twice a month. "Wheeler," he said when she picked up, "I got one for you."

"Sarge, it's eleven-thirty."

"Come on, Wheeler, it's a good one."

She sighed. "Fine, all right. Wait till I get my drink."

He was encouraged. "What are you drinking?"

"Warm milk."

"Get the fuck out of here. Warm milk! It's June, for fucksake."

But she had put the phone down. When she came back, she said, "All right, so let's hear it."

"Okay, in the final scene of *All Quiet on the Western Front*, what's the German kid reaching for when he gets shot?"

"A butterfly. I thought you said it was going to be a good one."

"I thought it was a good one."

"Anybody who knows anything about movies knows it was a butterfly. What was the kid's name?"

"What, the German kid?"

"Yes, the German kid."

"Lew Ayres."

"No, Sarge, that's the actor's name. What's the character's name?"

"How the fuck should I know?"

"Paul."

"Okay, that's one for you." There was a brief silence, then Young said, "Did you know they've started showing commercials when you go to the movies? I went to see a John Goodman movie last week, and the bastards made me sit through ten minutes of commercials. And what's worse is, I'd seen most of them on TV, except these ones were longer. Jeez, Wheeler, I thought the reason we pay to go to the movies is so we *don't* have to watch commercials."

"You should have stood up and booed."

"I did."

She laughed. "You did not."

"I did! I stood right up and booed. Fucking right I did. But it didn't do me any good."

"Nobody paid any attention?"

"Oh yeah, everybody yelled at me to shut up and sit down."

There was another silence. Then Wheeler said, "Okay, so what's on your mind, Sarge? You're not going to ask me to marry you again, are you?"

"No, I'm not going to ask you to marry me again" — Young belched softly — "and do you know why?"

"Why?"

"Because it hurts too much when you say no, but I would do it, you know, I would marry you."

"As soon as I come to my senses and realize I'm not really a lesbian."

"That's right. It's only a matter of time."

"So why did you phone?"

"Just wanted to hear your voice."

"Goodnight, Sarge."

"Goodnight? It's Saturday night, it's early, don't go yet."

"I'm tired."

"You gotta get up early?"

"Maybe I do."

"What for, church? They got a church for dykes?"

She was silent.

"Sorry."

She said nothing.

"I just wanted to talk some more."

"About what?"

"About … I don't know. John Goodman in *Barton Fink*."

"What about it?"

"I didn't get it. It was too intellectual. I thought maybe you could explain it to me."

"Goodnight, Sarge."

Sunday, June 4

———————————————

"I don't know what the world's coming to," Young announced.

"Oh boy," Debi said, "now we're in for it." She turned to Trick. "Remember, Uncle Artie, last week it was how they're making TV shows with shaky cameras. 'I have to close my eyes, I can't watch, it gives me a headache behind my eyes,'" she said, imitating her father.

Last week they had been sitting at the same table as they were now, in the clubhouse dining room at Caledonia Downs. Every Sunday Young picked Trick up at his high-rise at 11:30 in the morning. They would drive the fifteen miles out to the racetrack and meet Debi by 12:15. By 12:30 they would have returned from the roast beef buffet with their first plates of food in front of them.

"And the week before that," Trick said, "he was going on and on about the price of gas, and how the Arabs, or somebody — your father thinks everybody from the Middle East is an Arab — were holding back the oil shipments to jack up the price internationally. Which is true, but it ain't the Arabs."

Young ignored him. "I'm serious, I don't know what the world's coming to. I went to the barbershop yesterday to get a shave, and they wouldn't give me one. I've been getting my hair cut for twenty years at the same place, and whether it's Albert or Connie, whoever's chair I'm in, all I've ever asked them for was a haircut. I've always shaved myself. But yesterday I thought, *What the hell, I'll treat myself to a shave*." Young shook the saltcellar over his meat. "But Albert said they couldn't give me one."

"Why not?" asked Debi.

"At first I just laughed at him. I thought he was joking. 'You're joking, right?' I said. He said — he talks like this — he said, 'I'ma so sorry, Meesta Young, no canna geeva shave.' Then he pointed to the list of prices on the wall. 'See. Eesa not even onna de board.' 'Why not?' I asked." Young looked first at Debi, then at Trick. "What do you think his reason was?"

Debi shrugged her shoulders.

Trick said, "AIDS. He's afraid of getting AIDS. If he nicks you with the razor and if he's got an open cut on his finger, it's game over."

Young glared at him. "That's right. That's what he told me. He said I couldn't get a shave anywhere in Toronto. No barber in the city will shave anybody because they're afraid of catching AIDS. But the thing is — and this is what frosts me — I don't have AIDS."

"You're frosted because you don't have AIDS?"

"You know what I mean."

"Albert doesn't know you don't have AIDS. Maybe he thinks you're queer."

Young placed his hands palms down on the table. "Do I look queer to you?"

Trick shrugged. "Okay, so maybe he thinks you're a drug addict."

Young appealed to his daughter. "You'll listen to reason, I know you will. Your Uncle Artie won't, because he thinks his purpose in life is to argue with me, but I know you will. Getting a shave at a barbershop — even though it's not something I regularly do, it's not something I actually ever do — is as basic a right as … I don't know … as climbing up on a stool at McCully's and ordering a beer. And now, because of this AIDS crap, I can't get a shave. I said to Albert, 'You've known me for twenty years, and you won't give me a shave?' And he said no."

Trick said, "It's been a while now since barbers have been giving shaves. It's hardly news."

"It's news to me," Young said, picking up his fork, "and I don't like it. It's just one more thing gone. One more simple pleasure. You can't walk downtown anymore for fear of getting mugged, you can't read a newspaper or watch TV without somebody telling you the world is getting more fucked up by the minute. And I can't get a shave. Well, it makes me mad, goddamn it. Next thing you know, they'll be making sitcoms about queers."

Debi said, "Uncle Artie, who do you like in the first? We've gotta get a move on here or we'll miss the Double."

Trick craned his neck over his *Form*. "I like the seven."

"What about the second?"

"Five."

"What about you, Daddy?"

Young leaned over his *Form*. "Yeah, I like the seven in the first, but Trick's full of shit about the second. The five will die by the middle of the lane. You want the four in there."

"Fine," Debi said. "We'll bet both of them. Give me some money and I'll go make the bets — seven-five, seven-four — while you two argue about something else."

"I want some more of that roast beef," Trick said, and using the keypad on the left arm of his wheelchair, he backed away from the table, swivelled, and aimed himself at the buffet.

"Trick," Young said.

Trick stopped and turned his head slightly.

"Bring me back another one of them Yorkshire puddings."

Trick had been sitting in his cruiser on Queen Street in October 1992 when he took a bullet in the neck. There was damage to his spine, and he lost the use of his lower body. The extent of his injuries wasn't known at first because he remained semi-comatose for six weeks after the shooting, and it appeared to Young, and indeed to the doctors who were monitoring his condition, that his biggest challenge was to regain consciousness. Because he was not fully comatose, restraints had to be applied: basically, he had to be belted to his bed. He would twist and turn and lash out with his left arm; his right was rigidly cocked at the elbow, like a man making a muscle — a condition, Young learned, called flexor tension.

At first, Trick had a number of visitors. His cousin Eartha came up from New York State and stayed for three days. His girlfriend of two weeks, a Japanese-Canadian named Yukio, was so upset by the cards Fortune had dealt her that she disappeared after her first visit to the hospital. Trick's parents were both dead, he had no brothers or sisters, so it fell to his colleagues to do most of the visiting. Wheeler came often, as did Staff Inspector Bateman and several of the others. But Trick's most regular visitor was Young, who came daily, rain or shine, often accompanied by Debi. He would talk to Trick, hoping for a reaction, a sign he was in there, that he wasn't damaged beyond repair. Young talked to him about horse racing, hockey, women, movies, dogs. But mostly he talked to him about baseball.

And when the Toronto Blue Jays won the 1992 World Series, Young was with Trick in his hospital room. He felt sure that after four or five weeks without improvement, without emerging from his semi-conscious state, this amazing victory with all its noise and celebration — doctors and nurses and patients and orderlies and interns dancing arm in arm through the corridors of the hospital — would snap Trick out of it, would bring him back.

But it didn't. He continued to lie on his back in bed, his eyes at half-mast, snot in his moustache. And then even Young gave up. The visits were depressing him to the point that he didn't want to go anymore. It was like talking to a corpse. *Time to move on*, he told himself. So he, too, bowed out. He, too, stopped visiting. He took a week off work and flew to Las Vegas. In three or four bourbon-blurred days he lost $3,600 on the slots, then flew home. When he called Debi, she told him there had been some improvement and, cautiously optimistic, Young hurried down to the hospital. There was a new patient in Trick's room. At the nurses' station Young asked what was going on. The nurse pointed to the lounge area, and there was Trick sitting in a wheelchair watching a rerun of *Hill Street Blues*. "Trick!" Young bellowed and rushed over to him, and when Trick turned to face him, one eye was focused, the other lay off to the side. He raised his left hand. His right, Young couldn't help notice, lay curled in his lap like a fetus. "Hey, man," Trick said weakly, "where the hell you been?"

It was only after his return to consciousness that it became apparent that Trick had lost the use of his legs. The way he had thrashed around on his bed made it appear that his legs were active; in fact, they were nothing more than doll's legs, dragged around by the furious actions of his upper body. Everyone had been fooled.

Months passed. Hopes of further physical recovery dimmed. There was an operation to correct his vision, which was successful, and several months of physiotherapy, which accomplished little. Then he was sent home.

Staff Inspector Bateman offered Trick a desk job, but he wouldn't even consider it, and when the police department presented him with a disability package, he accepted it. He resigned from the Force. He sat in his apartment with the shades drawn. He watched TV. He asked Young to do something about his car, a mint-condition 1968 Cadillac Seville, burgundy with white leather upholstery. "What do you want me to do with it?" Young asked. Trick shook his head. The car had been his pride and joy. Young arranged to have it stored in a remote, unused corner of the police garage. He had one of the mechanics drain the oil, put it up on blocks, and cover it with a tarpaulin.

Now, almost three years since the shooting, Trick was still bitter. Sometimes, if Young picked him up, Trick would have a beer at McCully's, but more often than not he refused. "I will not be an object of pity," he told Young. "Whatever my new role in life may be, it's not so those fools at the bar can feel superior, it's not so they can feel lucky they're not me." The only public place Trick felt really comfortable was the racetrack. Nobody knew him there. Nobody except Young and Debi. And the other horse-players were too focused on their gambling to pay attention to a cripple.

"Shorty was always good to me," Debi said. "That's all I can say."

The third race had just gone, and the money the threesome had won on Harbour Master and Conniving in the Daily Double they had given back on a semi–long shot named Pine Cone.

"I know some people didn't like him," she continued. "They thought he was — I don't know — untrustworthy. But he was never anything but good to me."

Young said, "Maybe he was afraid of you. You could have flattened him with one punch."

"He was little, but he was fearless," Debi said. "Remember that time he broke Brian Reese's nose."

Young laughed. He turned to Trick. "Reese was the jockey on some horse in the same race Shorty had one in. Shorty's horse was winning with about fifty yards to go when Reese's horse caught up to him, they hung like that for a few seconds, then Shorty's horse bobbled, and Reese's horse won by a neck, and when Shorty's rider dismounted he told Shorty that Reese had hit his horse across the eyes with his whip. He said they would have won otherwise. So Shorty marches over to the winner's circle where Reese is sitting proudly on his horse, and the owner and his family and the trainer and the groom are all posing, and the photographer is just about to take the picture, and Shorty hauls Reese off the horse and jumps on top of him and clocks him right in the nose."

"Short fight," Debi said, nodding. "Blood everywhere."

"That's right," Young said. "Shorty wasn't afraid of anything. And proud? He had that small man's pride."

Debi said, "Like how all the jockeys and exercise riders have to have these really big girlfriends, just to show all the normal-sized men that they can get any girl they want. Just 'cause they're small doesn't mean ... well, you know."

"Doesn't mean they got small dicks."

"Daddy!"

"Well, it's true. Right, Trick? Every man worries about the size of his dick."

Trick said, "Not me. Not anymore. My dick could be a yard long and it wouldn't matter to me."

Young grimaced. "Sorry."

Trick shrugged.

Debi forged on. "So what happened was, for the New Year's Ball that the Horseman's Association puts on, Shorty brought this unbelievable woman. Not his wife, I might add. This was during one of his bad spells when he was drinking like it was going out of style. Anyway, this woman must have been six-two, two hundred pounds — bigger than me, even — and she had this gigantic goddamn chest."

Young nodded his head. "That's right. I had the pleasure of being Debi here's escort that night, and that woman had the biggest kazoobies in the world, and there's Shorty strutting alongside her like a rooster, big stupid grin on his face, hanging onto her arm like a little boy and his momma."

"Well," Debi said, "he had his flaws, I guess, but I still can't figure out why anybody would want to kill him. He wanted people to respect him, sure, and he wanted to be successful, but who doesn't? I mean it's not like he was a goddamn serial killer or something."

Trick looked at Young. "Any leads yet?"

Young shook his head. "All I know is he was down on his luck. He had that horse die on him a couple of months ago." He turned to Debi.

"Download," she said. "Shorty'd just had the owner a few days when it happened. The vet said it was colic."

Trick said, "What's colic?"

"Any kind of intestinal problem, but usually it's a twisted bowel."

"What causes it?"

"Any number of things. Coughing can cause it. The horse might cough so violently it flips its stomach. Or if a horse lies down and then gets up suddenly, that can cause it. There's about seventy-five feet of intestine in a horse's stomach. Or if food gets impacted, that can cause it, too. We have to check our horses' droppings every day to make sure they're not too hard."

Young said, "Something fishy about that horse's death. Soon as I get a chance, I'm going to ask around a bit."

"Did all this hurt Shorty's business?" Trick asked.

"His business was already hurting. By then pretty much everybody — everybody but Debi, that is — had jumped ship on him. My guess is he owed somebody some money, but I don't have any evidence yet. I've checked into two of his owners. One of them — an old lady — she's clean, but the other one, Doug Buckley, he's a crafty son of a bitch. Tomorrow I'll check into the Internet guy."

"Mr. Khan," Debi said. "Mahmoud Khan."

"The man whose horse died?" Trick said.

Debi nodded.

"Rich?"

"Oh, yeah, he's rich. You pretty much have to be rich to own thoroughbreds. Mr. Buckley's rich, too."

"How'd he make his money?" Trick asked.

"Won the lottery. Eight million. He owns Someday Prince, which I'm saddling in the stake today."

"Which reminds me," Young said to his daughter, "please don't go around giving out my phone number to scumbags like Percy Ball."

Debi made a face. "He said it was important, Daddy. I thought he might help you with the investigation."

"Well," Young said grudgingly, "he did. He told me somebody offered Buckley a hundred large for Someday Prince."

"When? I never heard about this."

"Couple of weeks ago."

Debi thought for a moment. "But Shorty was part owner. He wouldn't have agreed to it. He was gaga over that colt."

"That's right, he vetoed it."

Debi shook her head. "He thought that colt was his come-back horse, the next Secretariat. He thought he'd be back on top again."

"So I've got a question," Trick said. "How does a trainer so down on his luck that everybody abandons him suddenly acquire not one, but two millionaire owners?"

They laid off the fourth and lost the fifth. Then Debi had to excuse herself to prepare Someday Prince for the eighth. She was more than a little excited, not only because it was her first time listed as trainer but because the first horse she was saddling was entered in the feature race of the day, the $75,000 Bold Ruckus Stakes for three-year-old Ontario-bred colts and geldings.

As she stood up to leave, her father said, "Good luck, sweetie."

"Do I look all right?" she asked. She was wearing a three-quarter-length lime green dress with a black ivy pattern up one side. She had cleaned and polished her old white eight-hole Doc Martens. She had tinted her hair for the occasion; no longer was it fire-engine red, now it was blood red. She was so nervous she was perspiring, and her nose stud twinkled.

"You look great," her father said. "Sort of Christmassy."

"I don't feel Christmassy."

"Why, what's wrong?"

"It's so soon after what happened to Shorty. I should be wearing black, but we're supposed to look nice in the saddling enclosure. The owners expect it."

"Besides," said Trick, "you may have to get your picture taken."

She smiled. "If that happens, Uncle Artie, I want both of you in the winner's circle with me."

Young said, "What about Buckley? He might have something to say about a big fat cop and a guy in a wheelchair taking up space in his photograph."

"I don't think we'll see him. He phoned yesterday to say he wouldn't be able to make it."

"Interesting," Young said. "He moved out of the Airport Hilton shortly after I paid him a visit. Did he say where he was?"

"No, he just said something about some meeting or some previous commitment. I can't remember for sure."

"Have you met him yet?"

"I saw him once or twice early on, when he first hired Shorty, but not since what happened. I've just spoken to him on the phone, that's all. Listen, I gotta go."

She hurried off.

The waitress came by, and Young said, "It's like a desert around here."

"Four?" she asked.

Young looked at Trick, and Trick nodded.

When she'd gone Trick said, "I've got a bone to pick with you."

"Oh yeah, what's that?"

"I'd appreciate it if you wouldn't discuss certain things in front of me."

Young had a forkful of Yorkshire pudding halfway to his mouth but drew up short. "What are you talking about?"

"Like dick size, or anything to do with dicks. Or anything to do with sex."

Young shook his head. "I'm sorry, buddy, sometimes I forget —"

"It's all right, I know you didn't mean anything, but I'm sensitive about that sort of thing."

Young stopped shaking his head. "But weren't we talking about Shorty? We weren't talking about you."

Trick gave him a look. "You were talking about dick size."

The forkful of Yorkshire pudding finished its journey, and Young chewed. "Okay, so let me see if I got this right: from now on I can only discuss things in front of you that don't involve dick size."

"Or sex in general."

"Are you nuts? How am I supposed to know where some topic of conversation's going to go? How did I know talking about Shorty would lead to a conversation about dick size?"

"Shorty's lucky," Trick said darkly. "His troubles are over. Mine have barely started. I'm looking at the rest of my life like this." He waved his left hand over his wheelchair, his useless right arm, his useless legs. "I could live another forty years."

"Your troubles have barely started, is that what you said? You've been in that wheelchair three fucking years, I would've thought by now —"

"By now what? I'd be used to it? How'd you like to piss in a bag all the time and not even know you're pissing? It's humiliating. And sometimes I smell like piss."

"You do not."

"Don't tell me I don't. I know I do. I can smell it. At first I think it's somebody else, and I say, 'What the fuck?' and then I realize it's me. That's a good feeling.

I'm sure you'd enjoy that feeling. Believe me, brother, it's not something you get used to."

The waitress returned and placed four bottles of Labatt's Blue on their table.

After she left, Young put his fork back down on his plate and said, "So, basically what's happening is you're feeling sorry for yourself?"

"Damn right I am."

"Never thought I'd see the day."

"Well, get used to it. And while you're getting used to me feeling sorry for myself, I'll get used to smelling like piss."

Young took a deep breath, then said, "You need another interest."

"Another interest?" Trick said. "Oh really. Like what, for instance?"

"Like, I don't know, like" — Young waved his arms around — "like computers."

"Computers?"

"Well, I don't know. There must be something."

"Computers?" Trick shook his head. He was so angry his black face glowed. "You don't get it, do you? Everything I was I'm not anymore. I was a good cop and I was good with the ladies. Now I'm neither."

"You can still do both. You just won't be able to do as much."

Trick's mouth fell open. "I can still do both? How? How can I still do both? I can hold their hand? Camp, when I see a naked woman in a movie, I still get sexual thoughts, just like any other guy, but down below there's nothing happening. It kills me. And how can I still be a cop? Arrest guys from my wheelchair? 'Excuse me, sir, would you mind stepping over here so I can cuff you?'"

"Bateman offered you a desk job. You could still be involved."

"Yeah, on a computer. I'd rather shoot myself than sit at a computer."

"What've you got against computers?"

"I don't know. It's like ... it's like playing old-timers hockey after you've played contact all your life. I can't sit at a computer and call myself a cop, no thank you. It's all or nothing for this mother's son."

"So what you're saying is it's nothing. Since 'all' is no longer available, you're choosing 'nothing.'"

Trick looked away.

"All I'm saying is," Young said, in a quieter voice, "the offer was there. It's probably still there."

"Right, and they also offered me permanent disability insurance, which as you know was a whole whack of money which I wouldn't have got if I went back to work, which is why I took it."

"Right, so now you're a rich man who mopes around all day watching TV and telling his friends what a shitty hand you got dealt and being pissed off for the next, what, forty years?"

"You should talk. A few years ago, you were ready to pack it in. You could hardly wait to retire. They offered you a package, too."

"Yeah, well, that was then. After you got hurt, and after I almost lost Debi and Jamal, things changed. I regained my ... I don't know, I started to care again ... about my work. So, when the time came, I turned the package down."

"That's the difference between you and me. I never stopped caring about my work, and I'm the one that can't work anymore. I'm the one that got fucked."

"Yeah, but what I'm telling you is maybe you can work again. You'd just be doing something different is all I'm saying."

Trick was silent. Then he said, "I was never a com-
plainer before this happened. I never complained."

"I know that."

"But it's hard, brother. I think about police work all
the time. It was my life. And I think about sex, too."

"Sex isn't such a big deal."

"Maybe for you it isn't. You probably haven't got
laid in a year."

"A year? I haven't got laid in three years!"

Trick laughed. "You're not serious."

"Hell, I am! I haven't got laid since the old Polish
woman that cleans for me fell asleep in the La-Z-Boy."

Someday Prince made a late kick, but the pace was slow
and the horses in front of him didn't back up. He finished
fourth. A small slice of the purse for Doug Buckley, wherever he was, but no photograph for Debi, and the large
amount of money Trick and Young wagered wound up in
the coffers of the Ontario Jockey Club.

Monday, June 5

Young had just sat down in his cubicle and was peeling the lid off his coffee cup when Wheeler arrived.

"Morning," he said.

"Morning."

He followed her down the hall. "How was your weekend?"

"Not bad, how was yours?" She opened the door to the half-fridge that stood beside the coffee maker and placed her lunchbox on the top shelf. "Is this your banana in here?" she asked. "It's all black."

"No, it's not mine. Me and Trick — "

"How about this bagel? The one with the mould."

"Nope, not guilty. Me and Trick lost about two bills each at the track." He wasn't looking at her. He blew into his coffee. "Listen, sorry about Saturday night. That phone call. Did I say anything stupid?"

She took off her HOYAS ballcap and shook out her short blonde hair. "I wish people would be a bit more responsible. It's like living with animals."

"Wheeler —"

"Yes, you said plenty."

"Like what?"

"That's for me to know and you to find out."

"Oh, come on, that's not fair." But he knew he wasn't going to make any headway. "How about you? What did you do this weekend?"

"I visited my mother Saturday. We went to a craft show." She looked tired, and she was using her brown eye on Young.

"Yeah, and what about yesterday?"

"I worked."

"You worked? You had both days off."

"Staff Inspector Bateman okayed me to do some overtime, so I worked four hours in the afternoon." She sat down at her desk.

"You should let me know when you decide to do something like that. I could have —"

"I wanted you to enjoy yourself. Staff Inspector Bateman told me you worked Saturday."

"Yeah, so?"

"So you worked Saturday, I worked Sunday. You saw Trick, right?"

"Yeah, I told you, we lost two bills each."

"And Debi?"

"Yeah, she was there. What the fuck —"

"That's good. Do you want to know what I've got on the Shorty Rogers case?"

Young arched his eyebrows. "Yeah, of course." He sat down in the chair opposite Wheeler's desk.

"It's getting pretty interesting."

"What do you mean?"

"Among other things, you wanted me to find out what I could about Shorty Rogers' uncle, right?"

"Right."

"Well, once I found out that Morley Rogers was Shorty's only living relative, I drove up there —"

"Up where?"

"Up to his farm. In the Caledon Hills. It's not really a farm anymore, he's sold most of the land. It's really just a farmhouse, and a falling-down one at that."

"So what happened?"

"I interviewed the housekeeper."

Young shifted in his chair. "Did you talk to the old man?"

"I tried. I told the housekeeper I was part of the murder investigation and that I needed to talk to Shorty's uncle, but she wouldn't let me. She said that even though Mr. Rogers had little use for his nephew, he was too upset about what had happened to see anyone. She said he was in seclusion, praying."

"So you talked to her instead."

Wheeler nodded. "She told me all sorts of stuff. But the really interesting thing she told me was what happened a month ago. It seems Mr. Rogers held a special sort of top secret meeting at his farmhouse to discuss the possible sale of his property, and the list of people who attended — by invitation only, I should point out — is pretty interesting."

"Interesting how?"

"Well, the lottery winner, Doug Buckley, was there, and Mahmoud Khan, the Internet King, he was there, too." Wheeler took her notebook from her jacket pocket and flipped several pages into it. "And a man named Richard Ludlow, who's like a huge land developer and president of the King County Golf and Country Club. And Summer Caldwell, who's some sort of important socialite. I wrote down here that she's a horticulturalist."

"That's flowers, right?"

"Right. Also, a man named Stirling Smith-Gower was there. He sounds like a bit of a nut. He fights for animal rights, that kind of thing. By profession, he's an ornithologist."

"Birds," Young said.

"And the housekeeper herself was there. Her name's Myrtle Sweet. And Mr. Rogers' bodyguards."

"Bodyguards?"

"Yeah, apparently he's got two bodyguards."

Young nodded. "Okay. Anybody else there?"

"Yeah, Shorty himself was there."

"No shit. When was this meeting?"

Wheeler referred to her notes again. "May 17. Two weeks before he was murdered."

"So tell me about the meeting."

"I can do better than that." Wheeler lifted her briefcase onto her desk and opened it. She held up a VHS cassette. "When I was about to leave, Miss Sweet asked me to wait. I stood by the door while she went upstairs. When she came back, she was carrying this. She said Mr. Rogers wants us to have a look at it. It's a videotape of the meeting."

After the blue screen was replaced first by snow and then by diagonal black bars that rose and fell for several seconds, the face, in close-up, of an old man appeared. "Are we ready, Kevin?" the old man asked in a reedy voice. Another voice, off-camera, said, "Ready, sir." The old man was wearing a charcoal gray suit coat, a white shirt frayed at the collar tips and yellow at the neck, and a thin black tie dusty at the knot. He was hunched at the shoulders and had difficulty keeping his head up. The camera backed off shakily to reveal that he was leaning heavily on the handlebars of a walker. "All right then, I think we'll begin," he said. "Ladies and gentlemen, welcome to Bright's Kill. Glad all of you could make it. I hope you're comfortable. Some of those card table chairs you're sitting on are a bit wonky, but I'm afraid we're a bit challenged — as the bureaucrats like to say these days — in the furniture department. And I apologize for the humidity, but I thought the solarium would provide a picturesque setting for this little shindig of mine. As you can see, we're surrounded by a paradise of lilies and orchids and various ferns and other tropical plants. This room is my pride and joy, ladies and gentlemen, my only extravagance, and the rock garden to your left with its statue of a little boy tinkling, and the tiled pool below him, and the Chinese carp which are resident there, are but a sampling of the added touches I have allowed myself."

A scraping of chairs was audible as members of the audience moved in their seats to better see the solarium's features. The camera, however, remained on the old man as he said, "My name is Morley Rogers, which should come as no surprise to any of you, being as you're all here for one reason and one reason only: to separate me from my property. Some of you, I dare say, think I'm nothing more than a feeble old hermit taking his own sweet time to die, that I'm nothing more than a Bible-beating Baptist and an old miser, that something perverse in my nature makes me hang on to these twelve acres you crave so desperately." He raised a hand to his mouth and suppressed a cough. "But I forget my manners. While some of you may know me, I doubt that any among you has made the acquaintance of this delightful creature." He fluttered a trembling liver-spotted hand in the direction of a woman standing a few feet behind him. The camera swivelled and zoomed in slightly on a handsome black-haired woman dressed in a navy jacket, white blouse, and red necktie. "My assistant, ladies and gentlemen, Miss Myrtle Sweet." The old man coughed into his fist. "Miss Sweet is more than just my assistant. She is my nurse, my secretary, my cook, my housekeeper, my helpmeet, my friend, my companion. If I weren't a God-fearing man, I'd add rod and staff, because in her gentle ministrations she comforts me. But now to the business at hand." More scraping of chairs could be heard.

"My farm, or what's left of it, is named after a Dutchman, Jacob Bright, who settled here in the 1830s. It's been in my family a hundred twenty years. According to the deeds, all of which I have in my possession, Bright used to be spelled B-r-i-e-t or B-r-e-e-t, and may have been pronounced *Breet*. Nobody knows for sure because the signature on the deed of 1834 is smudged, and the township records for that period carry both spellings. *Kill*, in case you are unaware, is Dutch for creek or stream, and the creek or stream that bears Jacob Bright's name, and that I once swam in and watered the Clydesdales in and caught perch and sunfish out of, is now part of that accursed golf course next door. All I have left is the house and twelve acres and the grove of black walnut trees you drove past on your way in. My grandfather Anson Red Rogers planted those trees. They're ninety-seven years old, almost as old as I am!" As his audience laughed politely, he stopped, turned his head to the side, and coughed again. "But getting down to business," he said, "I've been hearing that a number of different parties are covetous of my property. Well, I say beware the tenth commandment: 'Thou shalt not covet thy neighbour's house, thou shalt not covet thy neighbour's wife, nor his manservant, nor his maidservant, nor his ox, nor his ass, nor any thing that is thy neighbour's.' Being as how I don't have a wife or an ox or an ass, and being as how my employees are more like family than servants, it's the part about the house that troubles me — the house and the field-land that goes with it. And lest you take me too lightly, ladies and gentlemen, be advised that I am on my guard against schemers and blasphemers, fornicators and flim-flammers." He stopped again, wracked by a fit of coughing. Myrtle Sweet stepped forward with a glass of water, but even as he sipped at it, his eyes surveyed his audience.

When he had recovered sufficiently to continue, he said, "Eric, would you fetch me a tissue, please." He cleared his throat. "You might be curious, ladies and gentlemen, about the presence in your midst of two dusky strangers. Their names are Kevin and Eric Favors, though which is which is a puzzle to anyone unfamiliar with them. They are identical in appearance, but in every other way they are as different as night and day. Kevin, who is manning the camera, is a devout Christian, like myself, who reads his Bible every night and who believes in turning the other cheek. He is a diplomat and a negotiator. He is a gentleman, God bless, but he is loyal to me and would, if necessary, use his considerable strength to protect me. Eric, on the other hand, couldn't give two hoots about the Bible. He would just as soon smite you as smile at you. He has the instincts of a beast of the fields, but he knows who feeds him and shelters him, and so he is loyal to me just as his brother is. The distinction between them is plain: where Kevin would take no pleasure in hurting you, Eric would. I do not speak of Eric this way because he's off finding me something to wipe my nose with; even if he were here, he wouldn't object. He's devoted to me, as is Kevin. Together, they are my muscle. They may exhibit a calm and quiet demeanor, but don't be fooled: they're as deadly as vipers. If murderous thoughts lurk at the back of your mind, if any among you would steal my purse, be forewarned: I am prepared; I am protected. Ah, here we are."

A black hand proffered a yellow Kleenex box. "Thank you, Eric." The old man blew his nose vigorously.

"But beg pardon, I've been yammering away like an old woman up here. If no one objects, I'll hear each of you out as you present your arguments. I am curious as to the various purposes to which my small empire might be put. I know that among you we have a real estate developer, an ornithologist, a horticulturalist, and a businessman who works with the Internet. I know what the first three do, but I'm not so sure about the Internet; is it some new-fangled kind of fishing tackle?"

More laughter could be heard.

"Mr. Richard Ludlow," the old man said, "if you're with us this evening, please approach the podium." As his eyes followed a progress in front of him, he said, "I hope you will not be discomfited by the presence of the camera, ladies and gentlemen, but for my own peace of mind I am recording the events of the evening. Consider it a form of insurance. If I appear not to trust you, it is because, quite frankly, I don't. You would rob me in my sleep if you could. Should anything untoward befall me in the future, this film will at least provide the police with something to go on."

The camera zoomed out to accommodate the arrival of a middle-aged man — tall, ruddy-cheeked, silver-haired, immaculately dressed.

"According to my information, sir," Morley Rogers said, "you are a real estate developer and a man of vast commercial experience. I hope you don't think me presumptuous if I ask you to go first, to set an example, so to speak, with respect to briefs and how they are presented. Please sir, say your piece."

Ludlow's face was tanned and handsome, his manner assured. "Mr. Rogers, ladies and gentlemen," he began, "my proposal is simple: I want to convert these

twelve acres into a condominium complex adjacent to
the fourteenth tee of the golf course. At present, the land
is unused, indeed unusable. It is marshy and buggy; it
contains nothing but bulrushes and blackbirds. If my
plan is accepted, hundreds of truckloads of clean fill will
convert this area into a thriving micro-community of
upwards of two hundred people. Think, Mr. Rogers, of
the economic boost such a project would provide. Not
to mention the humanitarian angle. There are a great
many people living in congested, polluted areas of
Toronto who would give their eye teeth to live out here
in the fresh air and the countryside —"

"Point of clarification!" a voice from the audience
shouted. The camera rotated to reveal a row of people
seated in front of a jungle scene. A pale, balding man was
standing up in front of his chair. He was dressed in paint-
stained jeans and an old cardigan and clutched a fuming
pipe in one hand. "Mr. Rogers, your twelve acres are neither unused nor unusable," he said in an unmistakably
British accent. "They are the natural habitat of a variety
of endangered birds. It is our duty to protect our avian
population, a threatened population —"

"Oh please," Ludlow could be heard to say, "spare
us the sermon."

"— that includes the King Rail, the Least Bittern,
the Loggerhead Shrike, Kirtland's Warbler, the Hooded
Warbler, and the Prothonotary Warbler. Corporate
greed has already eliminated most of the wetlands in our
vicinity, and —"

A banging sound was heard, and the focus of the
camera returned to the front of the solarium where
Morley Rogers was banging a garden trowel against one
of the handlebars of his walker. "Sit down, both of
you!" he shouted hoarsely. "You're both out of order.
Mr. Ludlow, you use the word *sermon* as if it were an

obscenity, and you — Mr. Smith-Gower, I presume — you call yourself a naturalist, an environmentalist, an ornithologist, yet you smoke that filthy pipe in a room full of orchids! Sit down, both of you!"

Ludlow opened his mouth to speak, then shook his head, smiled ruefully at the camera, and disappeared from view.

"Next!" Morley Rogers demanded.

A chair could be heard scraping, then the clip-clopping of high-heeled shoes.

The carefully coiffed woman who appeared on screen placed a pair of decorator bifocals on her nose, cleared her throat, and said, "My reason for being here is just as simple as Mr. Ludlow's and just as environmental as Mr. Smith-Gower's: Mr. Rogers, I think your land should be converted into a park. But not just any park: a flower park!" The woman's voice quivered with conviction. "The public could come and stroll along the crushed granite footpaths and observe the flower competitions." She spread her arms: bracelets jingled and rings sparkled. "Can't you just see it? Banks and banks of tulips and geraniums, and that's not all: duck ponds and gazebos and a little mill with a waterwheel and footbridges and —"

"Idle rich!" Smith-Gower's voice declared.

Morley Rogers beat the trowel against his walker. "Mrs. Caldwell," he said in his thin voice, the camera once again on him, his small head wobbling back and forth, "some of these people may not know that you are the perennial runner-up in Caledon Township's Beautiful Garden Competition, and the fact is you're just plumb jealous of the perennial winner, which happens to be me, God bless! Ladies and gentlemen, Mrs. Caldwell figures if she can dispossess me of my land and plunk me down to rot in some old folks home, then *she* might win! You know what I say to that? I say horse apples! Next!"

Summer Caldwell huffed her way out of view and was replaced moments later by a tall, thin East Indian man, who stood quietly until the clip-clopping stopped. Dressed in a light gray suit and royal blue tie, the man cast his piercing black eyes across his listeners and said in a richly accented voice, "Thank you, Mr. Rogers. My name is Mahmoud Khan, and like everyone else here, I have my own agenda. I have my own reasons for wanting your land. As you may know, I am the owner of Dot Com Acres, the farm next door, formerly known as Cedar Creek Stud Farm. That's right, I am the businessman of the Internet. The Internet, Mr. Rogers," and he inclined his head to his host, "in case you are truly unaware and were not just making a joke with us, is a form of global communication and information access. People use it on their computers. My success as a businessman did not come without struggle; nevertheless, it is, as you like to say in this fine country, a dream come true. However, my friend, I have another dream as well. I am embarking on an ambitious program that involves the breeding of thoroughbred racehorses. Foolishly, perhaps, I sold much of Cedar Creek soon after purchasing it, and now find myself in need of additional land to accommodate the broodmare band I am putting together. Your twelve acres would give me room for a larger barn and several pasture fields. It may interest you to know as well, sir, that two of my horses are currently in training with your nephew."

"Nephew?" Morley could be heard to bluster. "What nephew? I have no nephew!"

Khan was taken aback. "I beg your pardon, sir. I must be mistaken. You have the same last name, and I was led to understand that you were related. In any case, I want you to know that I am prepared to match and exceed any offer you receive from these other worthy candidates. I thank you for your time."

After Mahmoud Khan bowed and returned to his chair and Morley Rogers was once again on camera, he said, "This accursed housing project going up across the road here, it used to be part of Cedar Creek, am I right?"

Khan's voice could be heard to say, "Yes, sir, but at the time of the sale I had no idea what was to be done with the land."

Morley Rogers shifted his gaze. His eyes were like two arrows. "You the developer, Mr. Ludlow?"

Ludlow cleared his throat. "Well, in a manner of speaking —"

"I thought so. Next!"

After a few moments of shuffling, Doug Buckley appeared before the camera. He was wearing a salmon leisure suit over a lemon-coloured shirt whose collar wings extended four inches.

"Happy to introduce myself, Mr. Rogers," Doug said, nodding to his host. "Buckley's the name. I'm new to these parts, as John Wayne might say, but I hope to stay put. I'd be pleased and honoured to buy your land, just to put down roots in this fine community" — he gave a chuckle — "but I'll be darned if I know what to do with it. But I'll tell you one thing — I can afford it! Money is the least of my problems." He laughed again. "Happen to own a racehorse myself, Mr. Rogers. Shorty trains it — I know you're just pulling our leg about not having a nephew, he's sitting right over there! Well, pleased to make your acquaintance." He laughed again and disappeared.

The camera moved to Morley Rogers, who was glowering. "'For ye suffer fools gladly, seeing ye yourselves are wise.' Second Corinthians, eleven, nineteen. Next!"

More shuffling until the top of a feed cap appeared on screen. The camera lowered to reveal a sweating red face, in profile. "Uncle Morley," the man, who was wearing a Toronto Maple Leafs hockey sweater, began, "I know we ain't seen each other in a long time —"

Morley Rogers, off-camera, said, "I don't know you."

"It's Delbert, Uncle Morley. Your nephew. Shorty, as some call me. I was hoping you might … well, maybe this ain't the right place for me to be asking you this …"

"Ask me what?"

Shorty Rogers removed his feed cap to reveal a bald and glistening dome. "I'm a little down on my luck, Uncle Morley, and I was hoping you might —"

"Might what, you ingrate?" Morley Rogers' face appeared, also in profile, inches from his nephew's. "Might advance you a boatload of money? Might finance your next failure? You've got some nerve. I haven't seen you in years, not since your sainted father passed away, God bless, and here you are, you show up out of the blue looking for handouts. Well, forget it. Take a seat. Or better yet, crawl back to whatever liquor house you crawled out of."

Squeezing his feed cap, Shorty said, "But all I need is a few thousand —"

"Out of my sight, damn you! Back to your saloons and back alleys, your brothels, your Jezebels!"

"But Uncle —"

"May God have mercy!" Morley Rogers shouted, raising the trowel in a shaking fist. Shorty disappeared from view.

"Next!" Morley Rogers demanded, and when, after ten seconds of leaden silence passed, no takers appeared, he said, "Very well, that's it then. I'll take your proposals under consideration. Remember, ladies and gentlemen, that while I may look old and feeble, I am also rich and well-protected. When I sold off the rest of the farm I made a small fortune, certainly enough to live on for whatever God-given time I have left. In other words, don't hold your breath, don't sit by the phone. I have no need of your money, no purpose for it, and I am happy living where I do. But, as I say, I will consider your proposals. I bid you farewell. Don't knock anything over on your way out, don't trip on the creepers, and don't steal anything."

The images disappeared, and the screen went blue.

Wheeler pushed "stop" on the remote.

Young leaned back in his chair and put his hands behind his head. "So what was the outcome of the meeting? After Uncle Morley got everybody's balls in an uproar, did he sell the land?"

"No," said Wheeler, "he kept it. Miss Sweet told me that once Mr. Rogers saw how much everybody wanted his land, he decided — out of spite, she said — to hang onto it. I guess he's kind of eccentric. Considering how wealthy he is, he lives like a hillbilly."

"What about Miss Sweet? What else do you know about her?"

"Well, she's young — thirty-five or so — and she's beautiful, as you saw in the video, and although she claims to be nothing more than his nurse and cook, I'd like to be a fly on the wall."

"How long's she been working for the old guy?"

"A little more than a year."

"Myrtle," he said. "I used to think that was an old woman's name. Old-fashioned. Now it sounds kind of sexy. I wouldn't mind meeting the woman."

Wheeler smiled. "Drive up, why don't you. She's there twenty-four seven."

"Maybe *she's* after his land."

Wheeler's smile vanished. "That's a thought."

"Or maybe she's in his will." Young nodded to himself. "I wouldn't mind having a look at it, just to know for sure." He placed his hands on the arms of his chair. "All the rest of this information you got from Myrtle herself?"

"That's right. She seemed to know everything about everybody."

"She sure wasn't shy about talking to you."

Wheeler shrugged. "No. She sang like a bird. Which on the one hand makes me a little suspicious, like maybe she's trying to deflect our attention, but on the other hand makes me think she doesn't have anything to hide."

"She wouldn't let you talk to the old man."

"True, but maybe he really wasn't well enough to talk. She did pass along the video at his request."

"Maybe it was her idea to show us the video."

Wheeler sighed. "I don't know what to think, but it wouldn't surprise me one bit if she turns out to be exactly what she claims to be."

"His housekeeper."

"Right."

"Right, and I'm Tom Cruise." Young stood up. "Tomorrow morning, I'm going for a little drive in the country."

Tuesday, June 6

Young knocked on the rickety screen door of Morley Rogers' farmhouse.

He waited briefly, then knocked again. A shadowy figure slowly and haltingly approached, entering the daylight in the front hall.

"Mr. Rogers?" Young said through the screen.

"Who is it? Who's there?"

But before Young answered, a woman he recognized from the videotape as Myrtle Sweet hurried up behind the old man and said, "Sir, you know you're not supposed to be up and about." She turned and propelled him back the way he had come.

Young opened the screen door and stepped inside. A moment later Miss Sweet returned to the front hall. "You can't come in here!" she said. "Who are you?"

She was a knockout. Maybe thirty-five, as Wheeler had suggested, maybe even forty, but gorgeous. Olive skin. Black hair. Big black eyes. She looked Greek or

Italian — Sophia Loren-ish. She was wearing a house-keeper's outfit, black with a white apron. Not short, like a French maid's outfit, but sexy, Young thought, sexy as hell.

"Detective Sergeant Young," he said, flashing his badge. "Metro Toronto Homicide. Are you Myrtle Sweet?"

"Yes, I am. What do you want?"

"My partner, Detective Lynn Wheeler, was out here Sunday, and you answered some questions for her."

"I was happy to be of assistance. Delbert's death has been a terrible blow to all of us, but especially to Mr. Rogers."

"I was hoping I might be able to speak to Mr. Rogers."

"I'm sorry, he's in very delicate health, as I explained to Detective Wheeler, and I simply can't allow it."

Young nodded. "You sent along a videotape of the meeting —"

"Mr. Rogers instructed me to do so, yes, sir."

"— that was very interesting to watch, but I'm not sure what —"

A banging sound started up, a sound familiar to Young — trowel on metal. Myrtle seemed unaware of it and continued to look at Young.

Young said, "I think your boss wants you."

The polite smile on Myrtle's face froze into a hard line. "Wait here," she said.

Young studied the hallway while he waited. Several pairs of men's sneakers on the shoe tray. He stuck his head into the living room. Gloomy portraits of old people. Knick-knacks on the mantelpiece.

Myrtle returned. Her face was a mask of courtesy. "Mr. Rogers would like to speak to you. Follow me."

Morley Rogers was sitting at the kitchen table, a cup of tea and a digestive biscuit on a saucer in front of him. "Look at the size of you," he said, as Young entered the room. "You're big as a house."

"Sorry to bother you, Mr. Rogers."

"Nonsense," the old man said. "Creates a diversion in an otherwise uneventful life." He coughed into his hand. "There's not a whole lot I'm still capable of doing" — he glanced at Myrtle, who was standing in the doorway — "but I can still talk. Now what can I do you for?"

Myrtle said, "Sir, I really wish you wouldn't —"

"Go away, my beauty," Morley Rogers said, waving a limp hand in her direction. "I'm fine, and anyway what difference does it make if I die here or in my bed, today or a year from today? What difference, God bless? Now go away and leave the men to talk."

When they were alone, Morley said, "She says your name's Young. That right?"

"That's right."

"You get that movie I sent you?"

"I did, yes. I watched it yesterday with my partner."

"What did you think?"

Young shrugged. "There seems to be a lot of interest in your property. And seeing Shorty like that only two weeks before he died —"

"Before he was murdered, you mean."

Young nodded. "I knew Shorty. We weren't close, but I considered him a friend. My daughter worked for him for five years."

"Delbert was a not bad sort at one time, a sweet boy, really, but mischievous. Then, as young man, he got himself in with the wrong crowd." The old man shook his head. "I blame him for the heart attack that killed my brother."

"Why did you want us to watch the videotape?"

Morley Rogers looked up at Young. "Isn't it obvious? Whoever killed Delbert's coming after me next."

Young frowned. "To be honest with you, Mr. Rogers, the only person on the tape who seemed hostile towards Shorty was you."

The old man grunted. "I can imagine how it must have appeared, but what you need to understand is that Delbert was my only living relative. With him dead there's no one to inherit my property when I die. Or so the general public believes. Eventually it would be sold at auction to the highest bidder. My decision not to sell the land might have prompted one of the people at the meeting to kill my nephew. I think Delbert's killer is on the film, and I think I'm next to go."

Young considered, then said, "I was told this meeting of yours was top secret and by invitation only. If that's the case, why was Shorty there? From what I could tell watching the video, you had no use for him, and all he wanted to do was squeeze you for money. So how did he get invited?"

Morley Rogers said, "He wasn't invited, he just showed up. I was as shocked to see him as anyone. He must have heard about the meeting from one of those other vultures, Khan or that Buckley fool."

"Do you have a will, Mr. Rogers?"

The old man narrowed his eyes. "How does that concern you?"

"Would it be possible for me to see it?"

Myrtle Sweet bustled into the kitchen, saying, "I think that's enough talk for now, don't you, sir?"

Morley Rogers began to cough. Myrtle helped him to his feet, clucking at him. "I asked you not to overdo it, sir."

Young stood up, too. "I just have a couple more questions."

"Another time, perhaps," said Myrtle.

As she and the old man shuffled off down the hall, Young said, "Thank you for talking to me, sir."

The old man waved feebly. "Mustn't keep a lady waiting."

Young listened to their slow ascension of the stairs. He scanned the kitchen. He opened the fridge door and looked in. Milk, juice, eggs. A brick of cheese. A package of bologna. Ketchup. Mustard. A jar of pickles.

A six-pack of Red Stripe.

Young was standing in the front hall when Myrtle came back down the stairs. He had a flashback to the Raquel Welch cavewoman poster he'd had on the wall of his college dorm. "I'm sorry to cut short your conversation, Detective," Myrtle said, "but you saw for yourself he's in delicate health."

"You weren't listening in, were you?"

"I beg your pardon?"

"Your timing was interesting, that's all."

"I don't know what you mean."

"I'm going to have to talk to him again, you know."

"If you'll leave your number, I'll call you when he's stronger."

"This is a murder investigation. It's important we move quickly."

"I said I'll let you know."

Young opened the screen door and stepped onto the verandah. Myrtle began to close the inside door behind him.

Young turned to her. "Our business is just starting," he said quietly.

Her eyes widened. "What did you say?"

"You're in his will, aren't you?"

She closed the door. Young started down the steps towards his minivan. He heard the door open again. He turned and looked at her. She had pushed open the screen door as well, and was framed by the doorway. "Be careful what you say to me," she said.

Young smiled. "It's okay," he said. "I know what kind of woman you are."

She pointed a shaking finger at him. "I'm warning you. Nobody talks to me like that."

At 4:00 p.m., Young sat down on a bar stool at McCully's Tavern. Above the bar, four television sets were mounted. Each had an adhesive number stuck to it: TV #1 featured closed-circuit coverage of the horse races from Caledonia Downs, where a field of horses was just entering the starting gate; TV #2 was tuned to a sports talk show; TV #3 showed a tanned woman in a tiny orange bikini doing exercises on a beach; on TV #4, a man was fishing from a boat and speaking silently towards the camera.

On the stool next to Young was a ravaged, colourless man in his fifties whose white plantation suit was creased and stained, as if he'd slept in it and then eaten spaghetti in it. Yellow streaks in his gray hair added to the look of dissipation.

"Dexter," Young said, "two Blue, please."

The ravaged man had his head down, but at the sound of the voice beside him he looked up and around. "Detective Sergeant Campbell Young," he said.

"Mr. Harvey," Young said. "How are you making out today?"

Priam Harvey pursed his lips. In front of him on the bar lay a *Racing Form* open to the eighth race at Caledonia Downs, an empty pint glass, and an empty package of Player's Light. "My best recollection," he said, combing his thin hair with long, nicotine-stained fingernails, "is that I contributed generously to the retirement fund of a certain party who shall remain nameless."

"Oh, the bookies were in today?"

With his right hand Harvey made a zipper motion across his lips.

"Relax," Young said, as Dexter placed two bottles of beer in front of him. "Next time I want to bust a few bookies, I'll let you know. I'm here to talk about Shorty."

"To me?"

"Yes, to you."

Harvey shook his head. "I tried to interest my editor in a story about the life and times of Shorty Rogers, but there seems to be some suspicion that his death was not simply an accident, and of course if there's anything unsavoury about a story, *Sport of Kings* will avoid it like the plague. As you know, Detective, we only write what reflects well on our industry, an industry — I needn't point out to you — that depends for its success on the willingness of the poor, the halt, the lame, the stupid and benighted to gamble away their welfare and unemployment cheques, money that might otherwise be spent on milk for their babies or heat for their houses. No, *Sport of Kings* wouldn't touch a story like the death of Shorty Rogers — good man that he was, good horseman that he was — with a ten-foot pole."

"I heard you didn't work there anymore."

There was a pause before Harvey answered. "Who told you I didn't work there? Of *course* I work there. They wouldn't know what to do without me. I'm the only literate member of the staff, for God's sake."

"Well, I was hoping you could help me out in a different way."

"Shorty was a valued citizen among the racetrack community, and he was a friend of mine. Furthermore, he was named after Shorty Rogers, the jazz trumpeter. Therefore, I would be honoured to assist in any way I can."

Young scratched behind an ear. "I thought he was called Shorty because he was short. He was a jockey when he was younger."

Harvey gave Young a withering look. "I know he was a jockey when he was younger. I've done stories on the man. By the way, you might be interested to know that his real name was Milton Rajonsky."

"Shorty's?"

"Yes, Shorty Rogers."

"I thought his name was Delbert."

"No, I just told you. His name was Milton Rajonsky."

"The jazz guy or the racetrack guy?"

"The jazz guy, as you so quaintly put it. The trumpeter." Harvey was fishing for something in the pockets of his suitcoat. "Our Shorty's real name was … well, isn't that interesting. I'm not sure I know what Shorty's real name was."

"That's what I'm telling you, his real name was Delbert. That's why I was confused when you mentioned this Milton guy. And to tell you the truth, I'd be surprised if whoever gave Shorty his nickname had ever heard of the jazz guy."

Harvey's impatience turned to appraisal. Then he nodded his head. "You may be right. Anyway, proceed. How may I help?"

"Shorty Rogers was murdered. And it's more than likely that someone involved in horse racing is the killer, or at least hired the killer. I know a bit about betting the ponies, but I know dick-all about the ins and outs of the racing business. That's why I need you. You understand how it operates, who the big players are. You understand the politics. I need someone with that kind of inside information to help me with the investigation, to let me know what's being said on the backstretch."

Harvey lifted a fresh pack of cigarettes from a pocket and was trying to locate the tiny cellophane tab to unwrap it. "What's in it for me?"

"Fifty bucks a day. You'll be my consultant."

"Why me? There's lots of people who are knowledgeable about the track."

Young shrugged. "I owe you one. You told me to talk to Shorty about a job for Debi."

"I did? When?"

"Five years ago, give or take."

Harvey laid down his pack of cigarettes. "I don't remember anything about it. I have no recollection ..." He looked at Young, then away again. "You aren't just feeling sorry for me, are you?"

"Of course not. You're the best man for —"

"Isn't that Percy?" Harvey interrupted. "It is. That's Percy fucking Ball!"

During their conversation, Young had been watching the tanned woman in the bikini on TV #3. Young looked around to see Harvey pointing up at TV #1, the closed-circuit Caledonia Downs channel, where a short, skeletal man with bouncy blond hair was leading an exhausted thoroughbred away from the unsaddling area.

"No question about it," Harvey said. "That's Percy Ball. I thought he was dead. Skinny bastard owes me seventy dollars. I think it was seventy. I haven't seen him in months, and there he is, large as life. When old Dawson — you know him, sits here a lot — when he told me Percy was dead, I said, 'Oh well, I can kiss that seventy bucks goodbye,' and old Dawson, bless his heart, he says, 'That's okay, Mr. Harvey, all debts are paid in heaven.'"

Young, lighting a cigarette, said, "Oh, Percy Ball is very much alive."

"Little prick probably started the rumour himself," Harvey said, "just so I wouldn't come after him."

"As it happens," Young said, exhaling, "Percy Ball was working for Shorty at the time of the murder." He lifted his chin towards TV #1. "But it seems he's found a new barn."

"They all find new barns," Harvey said. "They're like rats that way." Then he sat up straight and waved his hand. "Dexter? A pint of Creemore, please, and a shot of Bushmills. Detective, allow me to buy you a drink."

"No, thank you, Mr. Harvey, I still have a full one here."

Harvey was leaning forward and looking around. "Where the hell's he got to?"

A tall red-headed woman approached them behind the bar. She said, "Dexter's downstairs getting a keg. What do you want?"

"Ah, the radiant Jessy," Harvey said. "I require a pint of Creemore and a chaser."

"Haven't you had enough?" Her voice had an Irish lilt to it. She looked at Young. "Hello there, sailor."

"Jessy," he said.

She continued to look at him for several seconds. Then she turned back to Priam Harvey. "I think you've had enough, Mr. Harvey. I think it's time you went home and lay down for awhile."

Harvey was about to protest, but Jessy wagged a finger in front of his nose. "No arguments. Get going. I'll add the bill to your tab."

As Harvey climbed unsteadily down from his stool, he said to Young, "Detective Sergeant, allow me to repeat myself: I would be honoured to assist in any way I can with your investigation. I'll just toddle off home, have a little rest, and I'll be in touch."

After Harvey was gone, Vinny, the owner of McCully's, a squat, sweaty man in a soiled apron, came out of the kitchen. "Hey, Vinny!" Young called from the bar, and when Vinny nodded to him, Young said, "I hear there was some business going on in here today."

"No idea what you're talkin' about," Vinny said.

"Rumour has it the bookies were in today."

Vinny turned and headed back towards the kitchen.

"Be careful, Vinny," Young said. "I don't want to have to call Vice on you."

Vinny disappeared behind the swinging doors.

Young decided to have one more beer. "Jessy," he called.

She came over, leaned her elbows on the bar, her chin in her hands, and gazed up into his eyes. "Mmmm?" she said.

"One more Blue."

"You make me blue, big guy," she said, "when you don't come around."

It had been a long time — at least six months — since Jessy had said anything of an encouraging nature to Young, and he wasn't sure how to handle it. Last December, he and Jessy had been seeing each other more or less steadily for two years, and he had been lulled into a false sense of security. It was in hindsight that he knew this, just as it was hindsight that helped him remember the warning she had given him when they first discovered their attraction to each other. Because she treasured her independence so much, she told him she had a policy where men were concerned: she would date each man only once. As it turned out, she was willing to bend her rule for Young and see him on a more or less regular basis because, as she put it, there was no danger of the two of them ever considering marriage or co-habitation or any other threat to her freedom. Although he sometimes wondered whether or not she actually liked him or had any genuine affection for him, the arrangement suited him fine: he was done with marriage. And, to his delight, she wasn't just willing to date him, she was also willing to sleep with him on a more or less regular basis.

Until last Christmas.

Young, sitting in his usual spot at McCully's one evening, had been surprised when Jessy told him she was going home for two weeks.

"You mean Ireland?"

"Of course I mean Ireland, you great ox. Dublin. See me mammy and pappy."

"I was hoping we might get away for a few days. Do something different. Maybe go down to New York City. Catch a couple of musicals."

She put her hands on her hips. She tossed back her red hair, flashed her green eyes at him. "Am I correct in thinking this is the first I've heard about any trip to New York? And when did you develop this sudden interest in musicals? You make it sound like you're president of the Gilbert and Sullivan Fan Club, like you hop down there every weekend for a bit of the culture. Have you, in fact, ever been to New York?"

The truth was he didn't want to be alone at Christmas. Debi and Eldridge and Jamal were flying down to Jamaica to visit Eldridge's brothers and sisters, and the prospect of being alone filled Young with dread. He knew suicides soared at Christmas. Not that he'd ever do anything like that, but it just showed how depressed people could get. And when Young was depressed he drank too much, and when that happened he usually ended up in a seedy bar in some completely unfamiliar part of the city with no recollection of how he got there.

"Forget it," he told her. "When are you leaving?"

She laid a freckled hand over his. "You know I don't like to be managed."

He nodded. "When are you leaving?"

"Tomorrow."

"Tomorrow!"

"It was kind of a last-minute decision, and that was the only flight they could give me."

He scratched his chin. "I got something for you. Just got it today, as a matter of fact. I was going to give it to you on Christmas, but since you're going away, I better give it to you now." He took a beautifully wrapped little package out of his coat pocket and placed it on the bar in front of her. "Merry Christmas."

Her hands flew to her cheeks. "Oh, Camp, you darling." She opened it, and when she saw the necklace she gave out a little squeal. She studied it for a moment, then looked up at him and said, "I'll go get your present. It's in the back."

Because Jessy was a favourite among the drinkers at McCully's, she received many Christmas gifts. Sometimes in her haste to open them she lost the name tags, and later she couldn't remember who gave her what. Mostly, she was given candy. Trick had shown Young a plum-coloured box of Belgian chocolates he had bought for Jessy. The name, Simryn, was spelled in raised gold on the lid. Trick said they cost him thirty dollars. That's why Young had spent over a hundred dollars on the necklace and had it properly wrapped in the jewellery store. He didn't want his gift to pale by comparison with Trick's. After all, he was the one she was sleeping with — if only occasionally. Not that Trick was any kind of threat in that department. Not anymore, at least. But nonetheless, it was only right that he buy her something special.

So when Jessy returned from the back room with a gift bag and presented it to Young, and he reached in and pulled out a box of Simryn chocolates with a little tear in the paper where the name tag had been removed, his stomach sank. *Is this how you do your Christmas shopping?* he wanted to ask her. *Recycle gifts you don't want, or have too many of? Somebody gives you a box of chocolates, you give it to somebody else?*

But Young said nothing. He just nodded his head.

"I hope you like them," Jessy said.

He couldn't look at her. *Not only are you giving me Trick's gift,* he said to himself, *but you know I hate chocolate. You* should *know I hate chocolate. At one point or other during the past two years I must have told you I hate chocolate. Can't abide the stuff. But that's what you give me. Because you know me so well, you give me Trick's thirty-dollar chocolates.*

The next day she left for Ireland. He drove her to the airport. He insisted she give him her parents' address. He made sure he had all the details about her return flight.

While she was away he wrote three letters to her and sent them priority post. He didn't hear from her at all and wondered if she'd received them. She didn't even phone at New Year's, and he didn't dare phone her.

On January 6, he picked her up at the airport. On the way back into the city he asked if his letters had reached her. "Oh, yes," she said. "Thank you. I'm sorry I didn't write you back, but, well, it was only two weeks, and besides, I'm not really the letter-writing type."

He wanted to ask if she'd kept his letters, but again he didn't dare. He was afraid of the answer. "Oh no," she might say, "I never keep letters." Or she might say, "I think they're in my luggage somewhere, but I've been so busy I haven't had time to read them."

So it was that after six months of cold war Young was surprised to hear Jessy say, "I'm off at ten tonight. Give a girl a ride home?" Her elbows were still propped on the bar, her chin still in her hands.

At 11:00 p.m., Young emerged from Jessy's shower and stood in the doorway of her bedroom, a purple beach towel wrapped around his waist. Candles were burning in various corners of the room. Jessy was lying on her back on the bed, naked. Her ankles were crossed, and she had her hands behind her head. Normally, Jessy's skin was so white it was almost translucent, almost blue, but in the candlelight it wore a rosy glow. She looked warm and content.

"Wow," he said.

"Hungry?" she asked, looking up at him with her flickering green eyes.

"Starving," he said.

Wednesday, June 7

It was after midnight at Bright's Kill, and Morley Rogers was lying in bed banging his garden trowel against the headboard. In another room down the hall, Myrtle Sweet ignored the noise for as long as she could. Finally she said, "Stop!"

"What?" a voice above her in the darkness said. "What wrong?"

She pushed Eric off and sat up.

"Where you going?"

"Can't you hear it?" she said. "I'll go see what he wants."

"He old, Miss, he forget in a minute. Stay here. I make you happy, I make you say my name."

The banging continued.

"I can't stand it." She stood up and felt her way along the wall for the light switch.

"Ow, my eyes!"

"Be quiet!" she hissed.

Tying the sash of her dressing gown as she hurried barefoot down the hall, she almost collided with Kevin coming around the newel post. "Oh!" she said. She laughed nervously. "You scared me."

"Sorry, Miss. I hear him from down in my room, so I figure I better have a look. I expect you's asleep and don't hear him."

She glanced back along the hall at the light cast through the open door of her bedroom. "That's okay," she said. "It's me he wants. I'll take care of it."

"You sure, Miss? I don't mind."

She looked again down the hall. She grasped the young man by the shoulders and turned him bodily towards the head of the stairs. "You just march yourself back to bed, mister. I'll handle it."

She waited until she heard his door close downstairs, then returned to her room. Eric was snoring face-first into a pillow. She turned off the light and eased the door shut behind her as she stepped back into the hall.

Morley Rogers was still half-heartedly banging the trowel against the headboard when she walked into his room. The lamp on his bedside table cast a yellow pall. "What is it?" she said.

"I've lost my Bible," he said weakly. "I had it with me when I went to bed, but now it's gone."

She padded across the carpet to his bedside. She lifted the bedclothes with her left hand and swept around with her right. "Here it is," she said, and handed it to him. "It was in bed with you all along."

"All's well," he said.

"Good night then." She started out of the room.

"Miss Sweet," he said.

"Yes?"

"There's something else."

"What?"

He patted the mattress beside him. "I'll show you."

Young and Tanya walked side by side down the steps
and joined the lineup of people waiting to view the
corpse of Shorty Rogers. Young was surprised that it
was an open casket, given the head wound Shorty had
suffered, but he was even more surprised that the cere-
mony was taking place outside in a public place, a picnic ground. He looked around at dogs chasing Frisbees
and aproned men in flip-flops flipping burgers. When he
turned back to Tanya she had transmogrified into
Shorty in his blood-spattered Leafs jersey. "Camp,"
Shorty said, "who do you like in the sixth?"

Young woke up. The stomach ache was back. It was
as if someone were tightening a vise on his guts. He
curled into a fetal position. He must have groaned,
because from her side of the bed, Jessy asked him what
was wrong. "Nothing," he said. "Just a gut ache."

When Young got to work that morning, Staff Inspector
Bateman told him that his counterpart at King County
Homicide had given him the okay to make Young lead
investigator on the Shorty Rogers case. Things were slow
enough at Homicide that Bateman could spare him and
his crew for the time being, and things were hectic enough
up at King County that they were grateful for the help.
Young gathered his detectives in the conference room and
assigned complete criminal, professional, and personality
profiles on all the people who had attended Morley
Rogers' meeting. He instructed Detective Gerald "Big"
Urmson to find out what he could about Stirling Smith-
Gower, the environmentalist, and he told Detective

Anthony Barkas to research the socialite, Summer Caldwell. When he added Richard Ludlow to Wheeler's worksheet, she was excited, but her smile disappeared when she looked up at Young's face. "My God," she said, "what's wrong with you? You're pale as a ghost."

"Nothing," he said. "Just a gut ache."

"How long have you had it?"

He shrugged. "I had one last week, then it went away. Now it's back."

"Have you seen a doctor?"

Young shook his head. "It's just a gut ache, Wheeler. Or heartburn, or whatever. It'll pass."

"Maybe it's an ulcer."

Young lifted his head to include Big Urmson and Barkas. "Okay, listen. Three o'clock tomorrow we'll meet here again and sit down and see what we know."

This time, instead of phoning the offices of *Sport of Kings* magazine, Young phoned McCully's first off, and, sure enough, Dexter said, yes, Mr. Harvey was at the bar. When Harvey took the phone, Young asked him if he would dig up whatever he could about Percy Ball and if he could attend the 3:00 p.m. meeting on Thursday. "On both counts, happy to oblige," Harvey said. "Perhaps I'll recoup my seventy dollars."

Satisfied that they had enough information on the lottery winner, Doug Buckley, for the time being, at least, Young turned his own attention to Mahmoud Khan, the Internet King, owner of Dot Com Acres.

Thursday, June 8

The stomach ache was still there when Young woke up, and he had to bring new supplies of Pepto-Bismol and Tums to work with him. At 3:00 p.m., when he assembled the members of his team in the conference room, the pain had changed from sharp, irregular jabs to a deep and constant ache.

When everyone had poured themselves coffees and the donuts had been passed around, Young asked everyone to sit down. He began by introducing Priam Harvey. Harvey was already known to the others as a local character, someone Young often referred to with great respect as a horse-player, writer, drinker, and all-around intellect, but this was the first time they'd had anything to do with him. "Mr. Harvey has offered to help us out with his specialized knowledge as regards the racetrack," Young explained, "so make him feel welcome."

Next, Young reviewed the information that everyone was so far privy to: Delbert Chester "Shorty"

Rogers, fifty-two, had been found dead in a stall at Caledonia Downs Racetrack early on the morning of Thursday, June 1. It was subsequently determined that Rogers had been fatally struck by a weapon — perhaps a baseball bat — with a horseshoe attached to it. Horsehairs had been placed on the wound to make it appear that Rogers had been kicked to death by a horse. But tests showed that the hairs were not from the thoroughbred Bing Crosby, whose stall Rogers was found in.

"Okay, you first," Young said to Tony Barkas. He checked the list in front of him. "Summer Caldwell."

Barkas, who was stocky, intense, and olive-complected, said, "Okay. Summer Caldwell's been married three times — her first husband died in a plane crash, the second of cancer — she does a lot of charity work, she's a member of the King City in-crowd and attends all the parties of the rich and famous, and she's a fanatic about flowers and gardens. I think it's pretty much unlikely that Mrs. Caldwell was involved in the murder of Shorty Rogers: she has no criminal record; she and her present husband, who's a land speculator, own a million-dollar property on the third hole of the golf course, and they've got homes in Nassau and Costa del Sol; and her pretty much regular placing behind Morley Rogers in the King County Beautiful Garden Competition does not, in my opinion, make her a priority suspect in the murder of her main competition's down-on-his-luck nephew. I'll conclude by saying that Summer Caldwell is a regular churchgoer and doer of good deeds, including volunteer work with handicapped and underprivileged children."

Young said, "Okay, good." He turned to Big Urmson. "Your turn. What've you got on the birdwatcher?"

Pink-cheeked and overweight, Big Urmson roused himself to a more erect posture in his chair, wiped the icing sugar off his fingers with a paper napkin, and began to read from his notes. "Stirling Smith-Gower is fifty-six years old. He's married and has a grown-up daughter. He writes a column on birdwatching for the *King City Chronicle*. He used to be president of the Save the Birds campaign and is worried about the vanishing wetlands and what's happening to certain kinds of birds, such as the King Rail, the Least ... Bittern, I think it is, some kind of ... shrike, I think it is, and a whole bunch of different kinds of warblers. Mr. Smith-Gower is six feet tall, skinny, is messy in his personal appearance, smokes a pipe almost all the time, has a habit of latching onto complete strangers and trying to get them to sign up for his Save the Birds campaign, and smells bad."

Young cocked his head. "He smells bad?"

"That's right. Body odour. I didn't get to talk to him personally because his secretary told me he just left yesterday for South America, but I did talk to a few of the Save the Birds people, and they all mentioned it. Apparently he stinks big time."

"What's he doing in South America?"

"Apparently he's looking for some rare kind of bird."

Young said, "Okay, good work."

"Sarge," Big Urmson said, "don't forget we got a game tonight." Big Urmson played second base for the precinct softball team.

Young, who was the catcher and team captain, said, "I won't forget. Just don't you forget that when the batter hits the ball in your direction, the idea is you're supposed to catch it, not let it roll between your fat legs into right field." He turned to Wheeler. "What've you got on Richard Ludlow?"

Wheeler cleared her throat. "Married for thirty years to the same woman, but by all reports a bit of a

Casanova. Two sons working in the same business —
real estate. He was the underbidder on the purchase
of Cedar Creek Stud Farm by your man, Sarge,
Mahmoud Khan. Still resentful about it, from what I
can gather, even though he made a pile of money bro-
kering the housing development that's going in.
Because he's a high mucky-muck at the golf and country club, he wanted to push through a proposal that
Mr. Rogers' land be turned into a housing development beside the fourteenth tee. Grew up with money.
Attended Ridley College and the University of
Western Ontario. No criminal record. Squeaky clean
except for the womanizing."

"How do you know about the womanizing?"

"Miss Sweet mentioned it when I interviewed her."

"Miss Sweet?"

Wheeler nodded. "She admits it's just hearsay, but
there's an authoritative tone to anything she says."

"What about Miss Sweet herself? Anything new
on her?"

"Not at the moment. I've left messages indicating
that we still want to talk to Mr. Rogers, but either she's
been out a lot or she's ignoring me. She's number one on
my list as soon as we're done here."

"Good." Young turned to Priam Harvey. "What
have you got on Percy Ball?"

Harvey lowered his eyes. "Nothing, actually. I've
been so busy with my magazine assignments that I
haven't been able to get to it yet. I didn't realize you were
all such keeners here."

There was a pause while Young narrowed his eyes
at Harvey.

Barkas said, "Chief, maybe this is a good time for
me to ask a question. Is this a good time?"

Young slowly shifted his gaze. "Go ahead."

"Well, these horsehairs that aren't Bing Crosby's, who do they belong to? By that, I mean which horse did they come off of?"

Wheeler said, "To figure that out, we'd have to take hairs from other horses and compare them."

"Which horses?" asked Big Urmson.

"Mahmoud Khan's," Young said.

"Why his?" asked Barkas.

"I've been sniffing around a bit with regards to Mr. Khan. Everything about him looks copacetic, except I've got this nagging suspicion that the horse that died a couple of months ago is a tie-in. What was its name?"

Wheeler said, "Download."

"Download. Mahmoud Khan owned Download. My guess is that Download's death might not have been natural. One minute he's young and healthy, but he's a complete failure as a racehorse. Next minute he's dead in his stall. There's something not right."

Barkas said, "You think somebody killed the horse on purpose?"

"What kind of an animal would kill a horse?" Big Urmson said.

"There was a guy in the States not too long ago," Young said. "The Sandman. Real name Tommy Burns. Fat cats in the hunter-jumper set would hire him to murder horses that were no longer wanted or, for whatever reason, had outlived their usefulness."

"But why?" said Wheeler.

"For the insurance." Young turned to Harvey. "You know more about it than I do, Mr. Harvey."

Harvey leaned forward in his chair. "The horses the nouveaux riches buy for their princess daughters often cost over a hundred thousand dollars. Some of these people, they'll import these magnificent Dutch Warmbloods that Olympic riders would kill to have and give them to their daughters who, more often than not, aren't skilled enough to ride them, let alone jump them, let alone show them, then they lose interest in them, preferring fast cars and fast boys, and the horses end up languishing in their stalls."

"But why not just sell the horses and get their money back?" Barkas asked.

Harvey shrugged. "I'm sure a lot of them do, but in certain cases — not very many — the princess will lapse into a crying jag if Daddy tries to sell her precious pet, or maybe the horse is chronically lame or has suffered an injury that ruins its value, so Daddy has it killed."

"And that's where The Sandman comes in?" Wheeler asked.

"Right. He'd sneak into the horse's stall in the middle of the night and kill it."

"How?"

"All sorts of methods have been used to kill horses and make it look natural, from an injection of insulin to ping pong balls jammed up the nostrils, but from what I understand The Sandman used an extension cord and alligator clips. Basically, he electrocuted the horse, and it looked like a heart attack or colic killed it. The insurance company had no choice but to pay up."

Wheeler said, "But those were jumpers. Download was a racehorse."

"A very expensive racehorse," Young said. "Khan paid a quarter-million for him, and it turned out he couldn't run a lick. But you can bet he was insured."

"If you're right," Wheeler continued, "who killed him? Not Mr. Khan."

"No, somebody he hired. Somebody on the inside. Somebody who's used to being around horses, who isn't afraid to get in a stall with a twelve-hundred-pound thoroughbred."

Barkas said, "Maybe someone was about to kill Bing Crosby, and Shorty stumbled upon the situation, tried to be a hero and save the horse, and got killed for his efforts."

"Maybe it was Shorty himself," Big Urmson said. "Wasn't it strange for him to be in that horse's stall at midnight? Maybe he was going to kill the horse for the insurance, but someone killed him instead."

Young shook his head. "No, Bing Crosby's just an old claimer. He's not worth anything. Besides, he doesn't belong to Khan. The old lady owns him. He'll wind up a pensioner on somebody's hobby farm. He's probably not even insured."

"So who else might have done it?" asked Wheeler.

"Well," said Young, "it could have been just about anybody in the backstretch who wasn't above making a quick buck."

"What about The Sandman himself?"

Harvey shook his head. "Last I heard, Tommy Burns was a guest of the state of Illinois."

"So what's next?" said Barkas.

Young said, "I'm going to pay a visit to Dot Com Acres. Have a look at Mr. Khan's horses. See if he's got any the same colour as Bing Crosby."

"What colour's Bing Crosby?" Barkas asked.

Big Urmson said, "White, right?"

"He's a bay, which means his body's brown, and he's got a black mane and tail. Unfortunately, most thoroughbreds are bay."

"About seventy percent," said Harvey.

"Oh," said Big Urmson, "that Bing Crosby."

"What are you going to do," Barkas asked, "pull a hair out of each horse's tail?"

"I'm not sure how to handle it yet," Young admitted. "But the hairs found on Shorty's wound weren't from the tail or mane. They were from the hide on the lower leg, and they were white."

"But I thought you said he was brown," said Barkas.

Young nodded. "He is, but he's got stockings on both back legs."

"Stockings?" Big Urmson laughed. "What the hell?"

Harvey said, "It's a natural marking. Some horses have stars or blazes on their faces. Some have stockings on their legs. The lower part of one or more of their legs is white."

"That's right," said Young. "And whoever killed Shorty lured him into Bing Crosby's stall, and Bing Crosby has rear stockings. The killer knew that before he murdered Shorty."

"And brought some white hairs with him," said Harvey.

"But wait a minute," Wheeler said. "Debi says Bing Crosby is a real teddy bear, he wouldn't hurt a flea. Why wouldn't the killer commit the murder in the stall of a more dangerous horse to make it more believable?"

Young considered. "Maybe the killer was afraid of what the horse would do while a murder was going on in its stall. Or, if Mahmoud Khan was involved, maybe he didn't want the murder to take place in one of his stalls."

"Or maybe," said Wheeler, "the killer didn't know that Bing Crosby was harmless."

"But he knew enough to bring the white hairs with him."

"Maybe he was instructed to bring them," Harvey said.

Wheeler said, "Do we even know that the murder took place in the stall? Maybe Shorty's body was moved to the stall after he was killed."

"That would make sense," Young said, "except there's no evidence of that, no drag marks or anything."

"And why wouldn't the killer use Bing Crosby's own hair? If he was such a calm horse, it would have been easy to clip hairs off of him."

Young scratched his chin. "That's assuming the killer was somebody local. But maybe you're right, maybe he came from outside and didn't know one horse from another. Anyway, the point is that if Mahmoud Khan was behind Download's death, he may be behind Shorty's, too. That's why I'm going out to Dot Com Acres and see what I can see." Young lifted himself from his chair, placed his hands on the table, and leaned forward. "Good work, everybody, but we're far from done. Wheeler, I want you to find out what you can about Morley Rogers' bodyguards. What are their names again?"

"Eric and Kevin Favors."

"Right. If you need to talk to them up close and personal, I want Barkas to go with you. And I want more on Myrtle Sweet. She's a little too involved with the old man for my liking. She's got her finger in the pie somewhere. Urmson, I don't need you for anything right now, so see if Staff Inspector Bateman has anything. As for you, Mr. Harvey, if you wouldn't mind hanging back a minute."

When it was just the two of them, Young stretched his neck up out of his collar and looked down at Harvey. "How come you came up empty on Percy Ball. What's the problem?"

Harvey laughed lightly. "No particular reason." His face was sallow. "I'll have something for you tomorrow."

"I'm counting on you to help me out on this," Young said, standing up. "I'll meet you at McCully's at noon tomorrow. You can show me what you've got then."

* * *

In that evening's slo-pitch game against Narcotics, Homicide took an early 12-5 lead, due in large part to a pair of three-run homers by Big Urmson. However, with the bases loaded, none out in the bottom of the fourth, and Homicide's infield playing in, Big Urmson stopped a line drive with his forehead. The ball fell at his feet, but Big Urmson was unable to play it because he was lying on his back staring first at the crazy flight of cartoon stars above him and then, a few seconds later, at a circle of concerned faces.

When Big Urmson was able to stand up, two things became clear: one, the stitch marks of the softball were imprinted on his forehead in the shape of the) (symbol used on road maps to indicate bridges, and two, not only had all three of the Narcotics base runners scored on the play — merrily rounding the bases while Young and Barkas and Wheeler and Staff Inspector Bateman and Desk Sergeant Gallagher and fingerprinting expert Wicary and the rest of the team except team manager Trick, whose wheelchair had stalled in the sand at third base, hurried to the assistance of the downed man — but the batter, too, had sprinted around the bases. While Young and his teammates slowly returned to their positions — all of them glaring into the opposition dugout — the batter, who wore number 99, was high-fiving his bench and acting as if he'd hit a moonshot so far out of the yard that street kids in Chicago were scrambling after it.

The fourth inning ended with the score 12-9.

The sixth ended with Homicide still in front 15-14. Young led off the top of the seventh, the final inning, with a double. As he lumbered into second, he saw number 99 on the back of the shortstop, who was awaiting the throw from the left field corner. Using a blocking technique he'd learned as an offensive lineman in college, Young lifted the shortstop from behind and propelled him ten feet into left field, where he landed on his face. Leaning on his knees to recover his breath, Young could hear his bench cheering. The shortstop got to his feet, dusted himself off, turned and stared at Young, pointed an imaginary gun at him, and pulled the trigger.

Two minutes later Young scored on a triple by Barkas. Barkas then scored on a Lynn Wheeler single. Much high-fiving ensued.

Narcotics managed one run in their last ups. Final score: Homicide 17, Narcotics 15.

After the game, both teams retired to McCully's. Dexter and Jessy were working, as usual, as well as a new girl — an attractive blonde. For a while members of both teams shouted epithets at each other. The new girl helped Jessy serve, and after many pitchers of beer and half a dozen baskets of chicken wings, the mood of hostility was replaced by camaraderie. Later in the evening, a disk jockey named DJ Dan set up his equipment on the little karaoke stage. It was the night of the monthly Twist Contest at McCully's, and DJ Dan asked Jessy and Young if they would help him decide the winners. Big Urmson — the stitch marks on his forehead now accentuated by pink dabs from a fluorescent bingo dotter belonging to a blowsy woman who had attached herself to the group but whose name no one knew — and Mona Higgins-Hubbard, right fielder for Narcotics, were declared Twist King and Twist Queen. Big Urmson was a horrible dancer: he flung his limbs every which way; he looked like a man being struck by lightning. Ms. Higgins-Hubbard wasn't much better. Nevertheless, Jessy adjudged them the winners on the basis of their enthusiasm, and Young did likewise on the basis of Big Urmson's heroic performance during the slo-pitch game. Trick and Wheeler finished second — Trick twisting drunkenly, rhythmically, in his wheelchair. Desk

Sergeant Gallagher and the blowsy woman with the bingo dotter finished third.

An hour later, after most of the ballplayers had left, Trick and Young were themselves preparing to leave.

Trick called to Jessy at the bar and asked for the bill, and the new waitress brought it to their table. On the back she had written, "Thank you! Freedom!"

"Is that your name," Trick asked, looking up at her, "or your philosophy?"

She smiled. "Both."

"Well, it's a beautiful name *and* a beautiful philosophy."

"Thank you," she beamed. Despite a lazy left eye, she was the picture of health, tan and fair.

Young said, "To give you a name like that, your parents, were they like hippies or something?"

She turned to him and her brows furrowed. "No, my parents named me Cheryl."

"So how come you're Freedom now?"

"If you really want to know, I've been travelling for the past four years, and towards the end of my travels I spent some time meditating on Mount Shasta. In California? And that's where my transformation took place."

Young was puzzled. "That's where you got your new name?"

She frowned. "No, you don't understand. I didn't *get* it. The mountain gave it to me."

As she walked away from their table, Young started chuckling, and Trick said, "Nice going, partner. I finally engage a woman in conversation, and you drive her away."

Young stood up. "The mountain gave it to her." He shook his head.

Trick said, "Fine, forget it. You ready to go?"

"In a minute. I got to take a leak so bad I can taste it. Be right back." Young headed off to the men's room. As he walked up to the urinals, a man came out of one of the cubicles. It was number 99, the Narcotics short-stop. He could barely walk. Young nodded to him and said, "You all right? Where's all your buddies, they run off and leave you?"

"Fuck off," the shortstop said. He staggered towards the exit, then turned abruptly and vomited into one of the wash basins.

"Nice," Young said. He regarded the man. "When I saw you come out of that cubicle I said to myself, 'Well, if it ain't our old friend the super star, the Wayne Gretzky of slo-pitch, the man who likes to take his home run trot while the other team's guy is rolling around in pain.' Then I saw how you were walking, and I said to myself, 'Poor boy, is he having trouble walking because he's drunk or because of that hit I laid on him out at second base?'"

"Fuck you," the man said, spitting into the basin.

Young laughed. "You shouldn't talk like that while you're puking. You look like a fool."

He waited to see if the man had more to say, but he didn't, so Young, zipping up, said "Next time on the diamond, fuckhead," and left the men's room.

When he returned to their table, he wanted to tell Trick about the shortstop, but Trick was slumped in his wheelchair, his chin down against his throat.

"What's the matter with you?" Young asked as he sat down.

Trick wouldn't answer.

"Trick," Young said, "what's the matter?"

Trick said nothing.

"Trick, for fucksake —"

"That new waitress."

"What about her?"

"She won't dance with me."

"She won't dance with you?"

"No. I thought she liked me." Trick looked at Young. "While you were in the john I asked her to dance. Hell, I won the Twist Contest, didn't I?"

"No, I believe you finished second to Big Urmson and that big-assed girl from Narcotics. Anyway, it's probably because she's working she won't dance with you." Young consulted the Blue Light clock above the bar. "It's almost one. We'll stay for last call. Maybe she'll dance with you when her shift's over."

"No, she won't."

"How do you know? What did she say when you asked her?"

Trick was silent for a moment, nodding. Then he said, "I asked the bitch to dance, and she smiled so sweet and said, 'No, thank you, I don't dance with niggers.'"

Young sat forward in his chair. "Get the fuck out of here, she didn't say that."

"She might as well have. Bitch named Freedom. Ironic, ain't it?"

"Her not dancing with you has nothing to do with you being black."

"That's where you're wrong, brother."

"No, *you're* wrong. I told you, it's because she's on duty. She's serving."

"No, it's because I'm a nigger."

"Fine, fuck it, I'm not going to listen to this." Young stood up to leave.

"Nigger in a wheelchair."

Friday, June 9

Dot Com Acres was smaller than Young had expected. He had envisioned a two-hundred-acre spread with rolling fields, ponds, and oak trees lining both sides of the lane that led to the century farmhouse and its attendant barns. Then he remembered that shortly after Khan had purchased Cedar Creek Stud Farm, he had sold off most of the land, so that what Young found instead was an urban ranch with a kitschy Ponderosa-style archway at its entrance proclaiming "Khan's Dot Com Acres" in burnt cursive. Next to it was a green and white barn-shaped mailbox with "The Khans" painted on one side. Young drove under the archway, followed a short red brick driveway, and stopped in front of a colossal pink monster home. To his right, beyond a late model Dodge Ram pickup truck and a black Porsche Carrera, was a chain-link fence that enclosed a cedar deck and a teardrop-shaped swimming pool. To his left, Young could see a stable and two or three other buildings — a barn, an implement shed, and a squat structure the size of a school portable. The stable wasn't all that large; it might have accommodated eight or ten horses. After Young parked his minivan and began to walk towards the stable, he could see that Khan's land was bordered to the west by a vast, treeless, lawnless, still-in-progress housing development, to the east and south by the sprawling King County Golf and Country Club, and across the road to the north by a small strip mall. Right next door, just across a split rail fence, and for maybe three hundred yards — interrupting the smooth confluence of Khan's land and the golf course — lay Morley Rogers' Bright's Kill. From this perspective, unlike the up-close-and-personal view he'd had on Tuesday, Young could see just how dilapidated Morley's farmhouse was; he could also see the glassy new solarium at the back in which the meeting of May 17 had taken place. Morley owned twelve acres altogether. Young did a slow three-sixty. Mahmoud Khan's farm was only fifteen, maybe twenty acres, tops. Two small squares on the giant quilt of Caledon horse country.

It was 9:00 a.m., and Young was expected. Immediately after yesterday's meeting had concluded he had called to make an appointment. When he phoned the number he had for Mahmoud Khan, it turned out to be the downtown offices of MK Internet Services. A receptionist had told him that Mr. Khan was not in at the moment, but that she would page him and he would call Young from his cell phone. Five minutes later the call came through. Young told Khan that he was a homicide detective investigating the murder of Khan's former trainer, Shorty Rogers. Khan said, "Ah, I wondered when I might hear from you people. The circumstances of Mr. Rogers' death were, well, unsettling." Young remembered the rich tones of Khan's voice from the video. When Young said that he had a few questions for Khan and asked if it would be possible to meet in person, Khan consented, saying, "It's the only way to do business. When would you like to meet?"

"Tomorrow morning," Young had said, "if it's not inconvenient."

"Not inconvenient at all," Khan had said, "as long as you don't mind driving up to my farm at King City." Young couldn't help smiling to himself. Sometimes it was too damn easy.

The front door of the huge home opened and a tall, dark-skinned man in blue jeans, loafers, and a pink golf shirt emerged. "Detective Sergeant Young, I presume?" he called cheerfully, and Young nodded. Khan trotted down the front steps and across the driveway to where Young was standing. His handshake was firm and dry. "My golly," he said, "I thought I was tall." Khan was an inch or two over six feet, but Young towered over him and outweighed him by a hundred pounds. Because of his size and his curly red hair, Young would sometimes remain behind the scenes if he was concerned that his appearance might queer a situation. At other times, to make a show of strength he would reveal himself early. He enjoyed watching the eyes of tough guys when they looked at him for the first time. Khan was still smiling, but his dark brown eyes looked like cold coffee. "Come on," he said, "I'll show you around."

As they walked, Young talked about horse racing, how much he loved it, how much he had admired Shorty, how his daughter had worked for him and was now, in fact, Khan's trainer, information that clearly surprised Khan. "Ah, Miss Young," he said. "Of course. I knew that Shorty was the nephew of the old gentleman next door" — and here he waved his hand in the general direction of Morley's property — "but I would never have made the connection between Miss Young and yourself. It's a small world, my friend. What is it they say about six degrees of separation?"

Khan showed Young the rose garden, the pool, a drive shed behind the house with a brand new John Deere tractor in it as well as a baling machine and a hay wagon.

"How many horses do you own, Mr. Khan?" Young asked.

Khan said, "Well, there are the two in training with your daughter, and here at the farm I've got two brood-mares, both with spring foals at their sides, and a young stallion."

"A stallion? Do you breed him commercially?"

Khan frowned. "I've been trying to attract outside mares, but so far I've not been very successful. When I bought him, I was assured he would be attractive to breeders."

"What's his pedigree?"

"He's by Mr. Prospector out of a stakes-winning, stakes-producing Northern Dancer mare."

Young raised his eyebrows. "In the purple. What was he like on the track?"

"He never raced. He bowed a tendon before his first start and never recovered his action. But he's half-brother to two graded stakes winners."

"What's his stud fee?"

"Five thousand."

Young nodded. *Pretty steep for an unraced, unproven sire*, he thought. *No wonder nobody's knocking at the door.*

"I paid a hundred thousand for him at a breeding stock sale in Kentucky last September. He's a beauty. Would you like to see him?"

"Very much. How old is he?"

"I bought him when he was five. He's six now."

Khan led Young into the stable. Out of the sunshine, it took a few seconds for Young's eyes to adjust. He could smell fresh hay and manure. "This is Angel Band," Khan said, nodding his head towards a stall, "and her colt by Promethean." Young looked through the bars and saw a dark bay mare looking straight at him. Her legs were black right down to the hoof. Her foal was hiding behind her, but he could see the foal's legs were black, too.

"And this," Khan said, moving along to the next stall, "is Top of the Morning and her filly, also by Promethean."

A beautiful chestnut mare with a bay foal. Not a stocking between them.

Young looked into the next stall, which contained a small black Shetland pony. "Who's this guy?"

"Ah, that's Max," said Khan, smiling. "He came with the farm when I bought it. My daughters love him. They're too big to ride him, but they treat him like a pet. And he actually performs a useful function. He acts as teaser for the stallion."

"Teaser?"

"We use him to determine whether or not the mare is in season before we bring in the stallion."

"In season means, like … "

"Um, receptive, I guess you might say. Willing." Khan indicated an empty stall. "The stallion's not here. I guess Pat's already turned him out."

"Who's Pat?"

"Pat's the stud groom."

As they walked through the open doors at the other end of the stable, Young asked, "What's his name?"

"The stallion? Sam McGee."

As if on cue, the morning quiet and the birdsong were shattered by a piercing whinny, and Young looked up to see the stallion standing at the corner of his pasture, thirty feet away. Young walked towards him, and the horse sniffed the air. He was a rich blood bay, almost red. He held his head in regal hauteur, then snorted. When Young was only a few feet from him, Sam McGee turned and bolted away towards the far end of the pasture, neck bowed, head tucked under towards his chest, thick black mane and tail streaming behind him, the blinding white of his knee-high off-rear stocking punctuating his flight.

"Bingo," said Young.

"I beg your pardon," said Khan.

"He's fantastic."

"Yes," Khan agreed, "but he's also a money pit."

Young fingered the nail scissors in his pants pocket.

"Come on," said Khan, "I'll show you the breeding shed." He headed off in the direction of the building shaped like a school portable. "Both mares are bred to him for next year. It's too early yet to tell if they've caught, but he certainly seems spunky enough. In fact, we're breeding Angel Band back to him this morning."

"Mind if I hang around? I've never seen how it's done."

Khan stopped. "Well, it's different. Not like humans." He laughed, embarrassed. "The stallion is all business, savage almost."

"Really?"

"Oh yes. No foreplay, for one thing. And it's over very quickly."

"Makes sense to me," said Young.

Young drove straight from Dot Com Acres to a phone booth in the little strip mall across the road. The phone booth was in front of an adult video store. While he waited for Desk Sergeant Gallagher to connect him with Wheeler, he read the blurb on a poster advertising a film called *Pussies Aplenty*: "Little did L'il Abner know when he planted those mysterious seeds he'd found in his uncle's tool shed what a bumper crop he was in store for —"

"Wheeler here."

"I got the hairs."

"What?"

"I got about a dozen hairs off the only stockinged horse at Dot Com Acres. And it wasn't just any horse, it was a stallion. And he'd just bred a mare. It was quite a show."

"Slow down, Sarge."

"I watched them breed him. It was something to see."

"I'll bet. All that nature."

"One of Mahmoud Khan's daughters, a very beautiful young woman named Cheyenne, brought the mare in one door of the breeding shed, and another daughter, not so beautiful, named Tiffany, brought a Shetland pony named Max in the other door. There's this wall about four feet high in the middle of the shed. The mare and the pony looked each other over for a while, and when the mare showed she was interested, the pony was led out of the shed, and then the stud groom, an old Irishman named Pat, brought the stallion in."

"How did the mare show she was interested?"

"It's called 'winking.'"

"She winked at the pony?"

"Not with her eyes."

"I don't understand."

"Never mind."

"Oh, I think maybe I do understand."

"Good, because I'm not going to explain it to you."

"So the pony got the mare all excited, then they took the pony away?"

"Right."

"Poor pony."

"He's what they call gelded, Wheeler. He's got no

nuts. He couldn't bang her even if he wanted to. Besides, he's not tall enough. He could barely see over the wall in the breeding shed. He's just there to help them figure out if the mare's keen on the idea. He's called a 'teaser.'"

"Why can't the stallion figure out for himself if she's keen?"

"Well, he could, of course, but if she's not keen, she'll try to kick him, and he's too valuable to risk getting injured. Hence the teaser."

"Who's clearly not valuable."

"What can I say, it's a business."

"It's no life being a teaser. You've learned a lot today, Sarge."

"So then Pat, who's got these dentures he clicks all the time, brings the stallion into the shed, and up he goes — the stallion, that is — and Pat makes sure the plug hits the socket, if you know what I mean —"

"He does what?"

"I'm not kidding. He gets right in there and makes sure everything's the way it's supposed to be. Like I say, it's a business."

"If you say so."

"So then when the stallion's finished his business and dismounts, old Pat throws a bucket of cold water on his privates, and he shrinks up like a little boy."

"Serves him right. Is that when you got the hairs?"

"Damn straight. Old Pat led him back to his stall, so I tagged along, and when Pat went off to get some oats, I slipped into the stall and did a little clipping."

"Weren't you scared? My God, clipping hairs off a stallion!"

"Nah, nothing to it. Gentle as a lamb. That's the way us guys are after we get some."

"Right. So what happens now?"

"So now I give the hairs to Cronish, he ships them

off to his friend in Guelph, and the friend in Guelph tells us whether the horsehairs that came off Shorty Rogers' wound came from Khan's stallion. If they did, then we're getting warm."

"And if they didn't?"

"Then we keep looking."

"Where?"

"The other horses in Barn 7, I guess."

"Aren't there like a hundred horses in each barn?"

"Hundred twenty."

"Yikes."

"Yeah, well, they won't all have stockings."

Inside McCully's, the wide-screen TV beside the karaoke stage was showing a strong man competition. A giant blond man was hauling on a rope, one step at a time. Behind him, the other end of the rope was attached to the front bumper of a school bus filled with screaming children.

Young and Priam Harvey settled themselves on stools at the bar. Harvey always sat on the stool at the end of the bar, on the corner. There were two stools and an Infinity video card game machine between him and the wall to his left; straight ahead of him, the rest of the bar extended towards the kitchen like homestretch would if you were horse and rider coming out of the far turn and heading into the lane. All the regulars knew that the corner stool belonged to Priam Harvey, and if one of them was sitting on it when he walked into the bar, whoever it was would quickly relinquish it. If a stranger was sitting on the corner stool when Harvey walked in, he would tap the stranger on the shoulder and tell him it was his stool he was sitting on and to get the hell off it. If the stranger protested, Harvey would summon Dexter. Dexter would approach the stranger and say, "Get the fuck off Mr. Harvey's stool," which, given Dexter's menacing demeanor and imposing physique, always did the job.

After Dexter had brought a pint of Creemore for Harvey and two bottles of Labatt's Blue for Young, their eyes were drawn upwards to the bank of television sets mounted above the bar. TV #1, as usual, was tuned to the afternoon card of thoroughbred racing at Caledonia Downs — post time for the first race was in twenty minutes; TV #2 showed a man demonstrating a golf swing; TV #3 showed a nubile young woman in workout gear doing stride jumps; TV #4, like the wide-screen TV, was tuned to the strong man competition: the same blond muscleman who had been pulling the school bus only minutes earlier was now carrying in his bare arms a boulder the size of a doghouse. The volume on all four bar TVs and the wide-screen TV was turned down. The music on the jukebox, which was located beside the exit to the lobby of the small chain hotel that housed McCully's Tavern, was ambient and unobtrusive. The only time the volume on the jukebox was turned down was when a horse race was being broadcast. Right now on the jukebox the Eagles were urging a desperado to come down from his fences.

Harvey raised his pint glass to his mouth, and fifteen seconds later it was empty.

Young said, "Remember that conversation we had about why Shorty Rogers is called Shorty, and you thought he was named after some jazz guy, and I figured it was just because he was short?"

Harvey let go a long, *sotto voce* belch. "Yes, of course I remember. You were right and I was wrong. Why must you bring it up again, unless it's to humiliate me further?"

"No, it's not that. I just wondered where you got your name?"

Harvey looked up at him.

"Hey, if it's something pretty personal, forget it. I was just curious."

Harvey eyed his empty beer glass. "No, it's all right. It's only natural you'd be curious. People have been asking me that question all my life. My mother's to blame."

"Who said anything about blame? I think it's a great name."

"My mother was a professor of mythologies at a small liberal arts college in upstate New York."

"You're an American?"

Harvey smiled. "I was an American. I grew up in Corning, New York. When I was twenty, I dodged the draft. I came up here. Now I'm a Canadian. I'm one of you!" He patted Young on the shoulder. "Anyway, my mother named me after the king of Troy." He motioned to Dexter down the bar, and Dexter nodded. "There are certain ironies you may be unaware of. King Priam was beloved by his people. He was kind, judicious, respectful of the gods. He sired fifty sons — Paris and Hector among them — and fifty daughters. I, on the other hand, am beloved by no one, man or woman, I am far from kind or judicious, I laugh uproariously at the notion of even one god, let alone many, and I have no issue. Oh, and I am also not a king. My mother loved stories about kings and heroes. She loved stories about brave knights who risked their lives to save damsels in distress. The rope of hair out the tower window. The sword in the stone. The sword laid on the grass between knight and maid when they're forced to sleep in the forest. I guess she was hoping I'd be like King Priam, but, as it turned out, I couldn't be less like him. Just another of life's little ironies." Harvey shook a cigarette loose from his pack and lit it. "King Priam was respected, even idolized; Priam Harvey — if you'll excuse my crass use of the third person — is merely mortal."

"Well," Young said, "at least she didn't name you Dwayne or something."

Dexter set a fresh pint of Creemore on the bar. "There you go, Mr. Harvey."

"Thank you, Dexter. Dexter, do you believe in God?"

Dexter frowned. "I guess I do most of the time, but when something awful happens, like an earthquake kills a whole pile of people, or some little kid gets murdered, then I'm not so sure." He stopped. "Ready for a couple more, Sarge?"

"No, I'm good," Young said, and after Dexter moved back down the bar, he said, "See, you're wrong, Mr. Harvey. You are respected. Dexter calls you Mr. Harvey. Jessy does, too. Even I call you Mr. Harvey. Everybody calls you Mr. Harvey."

"Big deal," Harvey said. "I'm respected by barflies and members of the service industry."

"And you've got your own barstool, for fucksake. How do you explain that?"

"It's not charisma, I can tell you that. It's not even my somewhat seedy, down-at-the-heels, philosopher-prince persona. It's quite simply that I win more than I lose on the ponies and I'm better than anyone else at the trivia game. I'm smarter than them, that's all."

Young nodded and smiled, then glanced at the Blue Light clock above the bar. "So," he said, "excuse me if I cut to the chase, but what have you got on Percy Ball?"

Harvey almost choked on his beer. "There's a non sequitur if I ever met one."

"I don't know what that means, but I do know that yesterday you told me, and I quote, 'I'll have something for you tomorrow.'"

Harvey shrugged. "I'll need another couple of days on that one. It's turning out to be more difficult than I anticipated."

Young said, "Look at me, Mr. Harvey," and when
Harvey wouldn't look at him, Young said, "You're a
pretty interesting guy, and I know you're smart and all,
but how difficult can it be to get the goods on a small-
time crook who drinks all the time in the same place and
who talks too much? You haven't done anything, have
you? You haven't even begun. That offer I made you —
fifty dollars a day — that only applies to those days
when you actually do something. I hope you understand
that. So far you haven't earned a cent."

Harvey was looking into his glass. "Why don't you
talk to him?"

Young shook his head. "I've already talked to him.
Twice. He's leery of me. That's why I want you to do it.
He won't have his guard up with you."

"Fine," Harvey said. "I'll have a full report for
you tomorrow."

"I find that a little hard to believe," Young said,
standing up from his stool, "seeing as how you're settling in so nicely here. When exactly, between now and
tomorrow, do you plan to talk to him?"

Harvey's hand shook as he reached for his pint.

Young put his hand on Harvey's wrist. "You said
you'd help, but you haven't done fuck all. If you
won't help me — or can't help me — I'll find someone who can."

Harvey nodded.

"Tomorrow," Young said. "I'll give you till seven in
the evening. I'll meet you here. Me and Trick are stopping by for a drink." He rattled his car keys in his
trousers pocket, then turned and headed for the door.

Harvey waited until Young was gone, then lifted his
head. "Dexter, my good man," he said, "a shot of
Bushmills, please."

Saturday, June 10

Young was out at Caledonia Downs by 6:00 a.m. Officially, he had the day off, but he figured he could kill four or five birds with one stone: he could watch the morning workouts, interview Shorty Rogers' regular jockey, Trinidad Grant, and Trinidad's agent, Ronald Outhouse, visit with his daughter, and stay for the afternoon's card of racing. He'd be back on Sunday with Trick, of course, but this was a special treat. He was excited about watching the morning workouts — the rumble of hooves as the horses galloped out of the mist at the head of the stretch — and propping himself against the rail with the trainers and grooms and hot-walkers and clockers.

But just as he stopped his minivan at the backstretch gate and showed his badge, the gathering clouds let loose, and even though plenty of horses would still do their workouts, Young decided the rain was too heavy to stand out in and jogged from the parking lot to Barn 7, where he found Debi mucking out a stall.

"Daddy!" she said, dropping her pitchfork. She stepped out of the stall and hugged him. "What are you doing here?"

"Business. I'm looking for Trinidad Grant and his agent, a guy called Ronald Outhouse."

"Well, you'll probably find Outhouse in the track kitchen, hustling mounts. Trinny's most likely still out at the training track. You don't think they had anything to do with —"

"No, sweetie, I just want to ask them some questions. I'll catch up with you later."

The rain had let up, and Young walked out to the training track. He wanted to catch the last of the workouts. He stood at the rail for a few minutes, one railbird among many, before he recognized the small man standing near him with a pair of binoculars raised to his eyes.

"Morning, Mr. Wright," he said.

Tom Wright lowered his glasses. "Oh, it's you, Detective."

"You working Doll House?"

"No, she ran yesterday. She's all tuckered out. I expect she's snoozin' in her stall."

"How'd she do?"

"Never got untracked."

"I forgot she was running. Guess I saved some money."

"She's back on July 2. Mile and a sixteenth. It's a Sunday, I think."

"I'll be here."

"Looks like a good fit for her, but as I always say, Detective, don't bet the farm." Tom raised his glasses to his eyes again. "So how you doin' with the Shorty Rogers case?"

"Still chasing down leads. Actually, that's why I'm here. I'm looking for Trinidad Grant."

Tom lowered his glasses again. "Well, you're in luck," he said, and pointed at a black horse cantering past them. "That's him right there."

Five minutes later, Young and Trinidad Grant were walking towards the track kitchen. Grant was small and handsome and looked like Harry Belafonte.

Young said, "You know my daughter, Debi Young?"

"Sure, I know Debi." Grant looked carefully up at Young. "She's with Eldridge Carver, right?"

"That's right."

"He's good people. He's my homey."

Once inside the kitchen, Grant led Young to a table in the corner occupied by a cadaverous man smoking a cigarette. Pale and unshaven, he was wearing an Expos cap and had a *Racing Form* and a Hilroy scribbler open in front of him. "Ron," Grant said, "this is Detective Young. He wants to talk about Shorty."

The man nodded at Young. He crushed his cigarette in the ashtray and lit a fresh one. "I got you a mount in the eighth."

"Excellent," Grant said, as he and Young sat down. "Any chance?"

Outhouse shrugged. "Not much."

"How many I got altogether?"

Outhouse checked the Hilroy. "You got the favourite in the first, you got a two-year-old in the third, first-time starter, and this one in the eighth." He turned his attention to Young. "So, what can we do for you?"

"Answer a couple of questions is all."

"Fire away."

"Mr. Grant, am I right in thinking that you rode most or all of Shorty's horses, and that you, Mr. Outhouse, arranged those mounts with Shorty?"

Grant nodded, and Outhouse said, "Right on both counts."

"You were on good terms with Shorty?"

"You asking me or him?"

"Both of you."

They looked at each other. "Yeah, we was on good terms with Shorty," Outhouse said. "He wasn't the same man he was a couple years ago, before he lost all his owners, but he was square with us."

"He drink too much?"

Outhouse smiled, and Young saw his crooked yellow teeth. "Way too much."

"Did he owe anybody money?"

Grant said, "He always paid me on time. I never had any complaints."

"As far as you know, did he get along with his owners?"

Outhouse said, "I didn't like his new owners much. That Khan guy, he spent way too much money way too fast, with no clue what he was doing."

Grant nodded. "He spent a quarter-mill on a colt with a crooked leg. Turned out to be an expensive mistake. He's one of these guys who makes a pile of money in some kind of business — in his case it was computers, right? — and then he thinks, 'Well, I know everything about computers, I guess that means I know everything about racehorses.' He didn't ask for advice, and nobody offered him any."

"The horse with the crooked leg," Young said. "That the one that died?"

Grant nodded. "Yeah, Download."

"The vet said it was colic. Seems unlikely for a three-year-old."

Again the two men looked at each other, then Outhouse said, "Far as I know, colic can happen at any age."

"What about Percy Ball?" Young said. "He was Shorty's drinking buddy, right?"

"One of them," Outhouse said.

"Well, how did Percy figure in all of this? He told me one of the other owners, a guy called Doug Buckley, was offered a hundred grand for Someday Prince, and he wanted to sell, but Shorty wouldn't go along."

Grant said, "Shorty owned part of that colt, he had every right —"

"That Buckley," Outhouse interrupted, "was another bad owner Shorty picked up. Get-rich-quick guys."

"Did Buckley have any reason to go after Shorty?"

Outhouse shook his head. "Buckley's a jerk-off. I seen him in his green suit and his white shoes and white belt and those stupid fucking sunglasses. Even if he did have a beef, he don't have the balls to do anything about it."

"Well, what about Percy then?" Young said. "Why would he offer up all this information on Shorty and Buckley unless there was something in it for him?"

Grant started to speak, but Outhouse raised a hand to stop him. "Shorty's dead," he said, showing his crocodile grin, "and there's no harm saying certain things were this way or that way, but Percy's still alive, at least for the time being — he's not too bright, that lad, and he gets himself in enough trouble without no help from the rest of us — and here in Shedrow one thing we don't do is we don't rat each other out."

His stomach ache once again in evidence, Young was standing at the bar waiting for Dexter to pluck a pickled egg out of the jar for him when he heard laughter behind him. He turned and saw Jessy walking away from the table where Priam Harvey and Trick were sitting, and the two of them were killing themselves over something. The music on the jukebox was drowning out whatever they were saying, but Trick was laughing so hard there were tears in his eyes. He seemed to have recovered from his Thursday night funk. The new waitress, Freedom, was nowhere to be seen. Young wanted to go back to the table and ask them what was so funny, but he was waiting on Dexter, who was still trying to lift an egg out of the jar with a spoon.

"Where's your tongs?" Young asked. "Usually you always use your tongs."

"Fucked if I know," Dexter said. "Ask Jessy. She's always moving stuff."

Young looked back over at the table. Trick was mopping his face with a paper napkin, and Harvey was going on about something. Young felt an urge, a physical need, to go back to the table. He was missing out on something, he didn't know what, but it was something good, something funny. Seeing Trick laugh like that was a rare enough occurrence, and he hated to miss out on it. He turned back to Dexter, who was still bent over the jar, pink tongue visible at the corner of his mouth. "Fucker keeps sliding off," Dexter said.

"Forget it," Young said. He took a step away from the bar, his eyes fixed on his laughing friends, then stopped as Dexter said, "Got it! I got it!"

By the time Young had paid for his egg and walked back to the table, Trick and Harvey were back to their normal unsmiling selves. "What was so funny back then?" he said.

"Back when?" Trick said.

"Two minutes ago, the two of you were laughing your heads off, and two minutes later you can't remember?"

"Oh that," Trick smiled. "Mr. Harvey asked Jessy to bring us some wings, so she said, 'How many?' and Mr. Harvey said, 'Forty,' and she said, 'How do you want them?' and he said, 'What are the choices?' and she got pissed off because he knows what the choices are, but she's always polite to him, right — Mr. Harvey this, Mr. Harvey that — so she says, 'Mild, medium, hot, suicide, or honey garlic,' and he says, 'Bring us forty medium,' and she says, 'Okay,' but then he says, 'But Jessy, make sure you only bring us left ones.' 'What ones?' she says. 'Left ones,' he says. 'We only want left wings.' 'Are you serious?' she says. 'Why do you only want left ones?' And Mr. Harvey says, 'Well, most chickens are right-winged, and consequently their right wings are tough. We only want left wings, because they're more tender.'" Trick started to crack up again.

Young's eyes narrowed, then he turned to Harvey. "So what did she say?"

Harvey shrugged. "She didn't seem to find it amusing. She said, 'I'll give you a left,' then she stomped off. Is that a pickled egg you've got there?"

"What the fuck's it look like?"

"May I have a bite?"

"Here, take the whole damn thing!"

Harvey's eyebrows raised. "What's wrong with you?"

Young shook his massive head. "I hear you guys laughing and I think how great it is, how I don't even have to be a part of it or anything, or know what it's about, it's enough just to see the two of you laughing like that, and when I get back over here and ask what it's all about, what was cracking you up like that, I find out you were making fun of Jessy."

"I wasn't making fun of her," Harvey laughed. "I was just —"

"You were just seeing how far you could take it."

Trick said, "He didn't mean anything, Camp."

Young kept his sights on Harvey. "How are you coming with Percy Ball? Anything to report? No, don't answer, let me guess. You've been too busy, right? Too many magazine articles? This is the third time you said you'd do it and you haven't. What the fuck's wrong with you?"

Harvey watched Young until he was done. "Are you doing her?"

"What?"

"Are you doing Jessy? You seem awfully protective of the wench. Doesn't he seem that way to you, Arthur?"

Trick said, "I'd leave it alone if I were you, Mr. Harvey."

"No, I'm serious." He sat up straighter in his chair. "Are you doing the barmaid?"

Young came around the table, grabbed Harvey by the lapels of his rumpled white plantation suit, and lifted him into the air like a father would an insolent child. "You sorry drunk," he said, "if you were half a man I'd break your neck." Then he did a half-turn, dropped Harvey on the floor, and steamed for the exit.

Outside, the streets were quiet. The stars were out. Young's gut was bothering him, so he tried to walk it off. He headed south on Donlands to Cosburn, then turned west and walked across to Pape, then north to O'Connor and back east towards McCully's. While he was walking he thought about disappointment, how everything turned to shit: Trick was a good man who deserved to be happy, but after the shooting his life turned to shit; Young's relationship with Jessy was okay at first, but they were basically fuck-buddies, that was all, and that, in Young's opinion, was pretty much shit; even his notions of friendship were shit, as was evident tonight — he had tried to repay a favour Priam Harvey had done for him by giving Harvey a chance to earn a few bucks, but now that, too, had turned to shit. Nothing was what it was supposed to be. Everything was disappointing; everything turned to shit. There weren't many things you could count on in this life, that was for sure. Dogs, maybe. But that was about it. But even dogs had their shortcomings: horrible breath, that was number one, plus they liked to roll in dead things.

When Young returned to McCully's twenty minutes later, Trick was still there, his wheelchair parked at the same table as before. There was no sign of Priam Harvey.

Young sat down. "I realized you had no way of getting home."

"If I'd wanted to go home," Trick said, "I would have done just that."

"How?"

"Boum-Boum." Boum-Boum was a cab driver who drove a wheelchair-accessible Econoline van.

"What if Boum-Boum wasn't available? Maybe it's his night off, or he phoned in sick. Don't be stupid. Any other cabbie'd probably just dump you on the sidewalk. How would you get up the stairs?"

"I'd pay him extra if I had to. Don't worry about me. And don't call me stupid. Dropping Mr. Harvey on the floor, that was stupid. Don't you need him for the investigation?"

"Yeah, well, he's got a big mouth. Anyway, you could do just as good a job. Better."

"I already told you no. No means no."

"Mr. Harvey was supposed to dig up the dirt on Percy Ball, who my guess is the key to the whole business, but he just keeps on finding excuses. What do you want, your own office down at Homicide?"

Trick shook his head. "I'll admit I'm interested in the case, but the way things are today, unless I knew how to operate a computer and the Internet and websites, all that sort of thing, I'd be no use to you." He lifted his left hand, palm up. "Look at me, Camp. I'm a prisoner of my limitations."

"So that's what you want? You want somebody to give you lessons on how to operate a computer?"

Trick didn't answer.

Young said, "At home or at Homicide?"

Trick said, "At home."

"Why not at Homicide? I'd get a car to pick you up every morning, bring you to work. Drop you off at home, too, unless we're coming here, which in that case I could drop you off myself if I'm not too drunk."

"When are you not too drunk?"

"Hey, be nice, I'm offering you your old job back."

"I'm not sure you have the authority."

"You watch. I'll talk to Bateman, and you'll be back at work on Monday."

"No, brother, I'm tempted, and I'll take a computer course if you think you can set it up, but I'd rather work at home."

Young spread his arms. "Why?"

"I don't want people looking at me."

"They look at you here."

"No, they don't. They just stare in their beer."

Sunday, June 11

Four races in, Young and Debi and Trick were up almost a thousand dollars. They had boxed three horses in the third race triactor, and the horses had finished in the optimum order: the 12-1 long shot had won, a 5-1 overlay finished second, and the 9-5 favourite was third. Furthermore, Young was happy because Trick was officially on board with the Shorty Rogers case. Young had phoned Staff Inspector Bateman early that morning and caught him just as he and his wife were going out the door to church. He spoke to him of Trick's willingness to help out with the investigation, as well as Trick's need to feel useful and productive. Bateman said that although Trick's acceptance of the long-term disability package prevented him from being rehired by the Force, he could work in an advisory capacity, and he okayed Young's request for a consultancy contract and computer training for Trick.

When Young mentioned all of this as the three of them were sitting down to eat their lunch in the club-house, Trick just nodded. Debi clapped her hands, came around the table, hugged her father, and kissed Trick's cheek. "That's wonderful news!"

"Yup," said Young, "your uncle's back in the world again."

After the fourth race, Debi left. Bing Crosby was running in the seventh, and she had to meet Mrs. McDonagh at the backstretch gate. Before each of Bing Crosby's races, Mrs. McDonagh visited him in his stall and gave him a brandy-soaked sugar cube. It was one of those extra little indulgences good trainers allow their more eccentric owners.

Shortly after Debi left, Young stood up to use the men's room. Just inside the entrance, a man in a wheel-chair was urinating into a plastic bottle, which made Young think of the Maxwell House jar wrapped in sil-ver duct tape that Trick kept in the backpack he carried on his wheelchair. Another man was standing bare-assed at the urinals, his pants down around his ankles. Young took a spot three down from the bare-assed man and unzipped. He heard the man in the wheelchair fussing with his paraphernalia and then heard him propel him-self out of the men's room. The bare-assed man looked over at Young and said, "Fix was in on that last one, eh. Fuckin' jock on the seven rode right into traffic." Young stared at the white ceramic tiles in front of his face and said, "Maybe you just picked the wrong horse." He waited for the bare-assed man to say something back, but he didn't. A few seconds later the bare-assed man pulled up his pants and wandered off. Young heard the door swing to behind him, and he started thinking about the whole hand-washing thing, how neither the man in the wheelchair nor the bare-assed man had washed his hands, but really why should they if they didn't get piss on them — after all, their dicks were probably as clean as any other part of their bodies; well, maybe not the bare-assed man's dick, he definitely needed a bath, nor, for that matter, the other man's dick, because sometimes personal hygiene can be a challenge for the handicapped — when he sensed that someone was standing behind him.

"Don't turn around."

Young felt something hard press into his back, just behind his heart. Startled, he suddenly had urine on his pants and on his hand.

"I got some advice for you, mister, and it be free so you better listen."

The pressure was removed from his back, and Young relaxed slightly. He could hear the man's breathing, shallow and rapid, behind him. The man's breathing sped up, then stopped. Young stepped quickly to his left, spun, and assumed a defensive posture, his knees bent, arms spread, hands fisted. In front of him stood a black man with one arm frozen in mid-air like a pitcher halfway through his delivery. The hand at the end of the arm held a crowbar. The man's eyes locked on Young's, then panned slowly downward. When they reached Young's still exposed penis, they widened, then panned back up to Young's face.

The man lowered the crowbar and slapped it against his palm. He smiled and shook his head in apparent good humour. "You wet yourself, man. And look how small it be. How come it so small?"

The door to the men's room swung open and in wheeled Trick. As soon as he saw the man with the crowbar and Young in a linebacker's stance, he steered his wheelchair around behind the man.

The man's head swivelled from Young to Trick.

Young eased himself away from the man, his back to the bank of urinals.

Trick stopped and aimed his wheelchair at the back of the man's legs. He said, "What up, motherfucker?"

"It okay, mister, I got it covered."

Trick said to Young, "What's going on?"

The man looked from Trick back to Young.

"Gentleman's got some advice for me," Young said, still in his crouch, still moving, "but I don't believe him. I think he just wants to suck my cock."

"That right, motherfucker?" Trick said. "You want to suck his cock?"

The man looked back at Trick. "Stay away from me."

Young took two steps and lunged. The man spun and slashed at him with the crowbar. Young felt a glancing blow to the side of his head and a flash of pain. His face smacked the white tiles of the floor. He rolled, and there was a *dwoing* and a spray of white shards beside his head. The crowbar leapt from the man's hand and cartwheeled through the open door of a cubicle. Trick rammed his wheelchair into the backs of the man's legs. The man yelled and fell to his knees. Still on his stomach, Young reached for him, grabbed the collar of his shirt, and pulled him flat. Prone, the man swung around on one hip and brought his knee up between Young's legs. Young gasped and let go his grip, and the man jumped to his feet and ran out of the men's room.

The seventh race of the Sunday afternoon card of thoroughbred horse racing at Caledonia Downs was won by Mrs. Helen McDonagh's Bing Crosby, an eight-year-old bay gelding by Distinctive Pro out of the Fire Dancer mare Torch Singer. When Debi Young and Mrs. McDonagh reached the winner's circle for the photograph, Debi scanned the stands for her father and Trick. She was hoping they would come down and be part of the photo. After all, this was her first win as a trainer. Maybe they were shy because they didn't know Mrs. McDonagh very well — at all, for that matter — but Mrs. McDonagh had said, "Of course, the more the merrier," when Debi had asked if her father and his friend could join them in the winner's circle. At least they would wave, she thought, still searching the stands.

But they weren't there. They were on their way to Emergency at Etobicoke General Hospital. Young wasn't badly hurt, but Trick's assessment — completed as he wound several yards of linen hand towel he'd Swiss Army–knifed from the dispenser in the men's room around Young's head — was bruised balls and three or four stitches.

Trick used his manual wheelchair whenever he went to the racetrack because he had Young to propel him through the crowds, and Young, despite his injuries, was able to lift Trick into the front seat of his minivan and stow the wheelchair, unfolded, where the missing middle seat belonged. As Young drove, only slightly woozy, only slightly inconvenienced by the slipping of his turban, Trick couldn't stop talking. "It was beautiful, man. We routed the bastard!"

"Who was he?" Young asked. "That's what I want to know. And what did he want?"

"What did he want? He wanted your wallet. Blew his hard-earned welfare check on the last race. Needed some get-even money. Some start-up money."

"Muggers pick their spots. They don't go after somebody my size."

"Hey, you were alone in the men's room. It was his main chance."

"I never got to hear his advice."

"Probably, 'If you know what's good for you, you'll hand over your wallet,' that kind of thing."

"I don't know. He had a crowbar. He just happen to bring it in from the parking lot?"

"Whatever, but that's the good news because we got his prints all over it. We'll make this guy, Camp."

"At first I thought it was the bare-assed guy."

"What bare-assed guy?"

"There was this bare-assed guy taking a leak when I walked into the john. Pants down around his ankles. Said the last race was fixed. I get sick of that. People can't accept that they just picked the wrong horse, it was their own fucking fault they blew the grocery money. I told him as much. I thought maybe it was him behind me."

"It wasn't him, unless he was a bare-assed black guy."

"No, it wasn't him." They were silent for a moment as Young concentrated on his driving, and then he said, "You were good in there. You were very fucking good in there."

"Just like old times, brother. The adrenalin. Fuck!"

"Very fucking good you were."

At the same time that Young was being attacked in the men's room of the clubhouse at Caledonia Downs, Doug Buckley was only a short distance away, sitting at the bar in the owners' lounge in his salmon leisure suit, and that's where Mahmoud Khan found him.

"When I first met you," Khan said, seating himself on the stool to Doug's left, "at the meeting at Morley Rogers' house, I sensed what kind of man you were. I knew you wanted to become a player."

Doug, halfway through a rye and ginger, nodded. "When you spoke to me as we were leaving Mr. Rogers' house, you said we might see more of each other."

Khan smiled. "That's right, my friend. You have a good memory. You know, I must say that you strike me as an enterprising fellow, a fellow with a future in the more elevated business and cultural circles. And, if you're interested, I would be pleased to sponsor your application to the King County Golf and Country Club."

Doug was taken aback. "Thank you, Mr. Khan. I don't know what to say."

"It would be an important addition to your profile. It would mean that you are well-connected, that you associate with the inner circle."

"Yes, I understand, thank you."

"But there is one small favour I was hoping you might do for me," Khan said, smiling.

"Name it," said Doug.

It was a busy night in the Emergency Ward, and Young had to wait almost two hours before a doctor could look at him. When the doctor asked Young what had happened, Young looked at Trick, and Trick said, "He's so tall, Doc, he's always bumping into things. We were at the hardware store to get some briquettes for the barbecue, and he bumped into one of those big round shoplifter mirrors."

It was almost seven and raining heavily when Young and Trick returned to the minivan. Young had six stitches and several Steri-Strips across his left cheekbone. After stopping at Trick's building, unloading him, and getting him as far as the lobby, Young was driving home when he decided on a nightcap at McCully's. His head didn't hurt that badly.

Standing inside the doorway, shaking the rain off the shoulders of his windbreaker, the first thing Young registered was the dirty white linen of Priam Harvey's plantation suit.

As Young approached the bar, Dexter saw him. It was clear from the expression on his face that Dexter hadn't forgotten Saturday night's incident. Young held up his hands in a gesture of peace. "Two Blue, please, Dexter."

Harvey turned and stared at him unsteadily. His head bobbed this way and that as if it rested on a spring. He made an effort to focus. "What happened to your face?"

"Bumped into a mirror. What have you got on Percy Ball?"

"That's a nasty gash. You should get it looked at."

"It's been looked at. It's got stitches in it, for fuck-sake. Tell me about Percy Ball."

Harvey gave him a crafty look. "Tell you what. Instead of you asking the questions, *I'll* ask the questions. What do you think of that?"

"Are we supposed to be working a case together, or aren't we?"

Harvey raised a forefinger and held it unsteadily in front of Young's nose. "One question."

"Fine. Go ahead."

Harvey cleared his throat, his fist at his mouth, then smiled. "Why did you knock me down the other night?"

Young looked at him. "In the first place, I didn't knock you down. I picked you up and dropped you. Anyway, you know why. You were making fun of Jessy, you insulted her, then you asked me if I was fucking her."

Harvey's jaw fell. "I did?"

"Yes, you did." Young chugged his first beer and started on the second. "But I'm sorry if I hurt you. I shouldn't have done it. I'm a lot bigger than you are."

"No, no, you were perfectly within your rights. I have no recollection of saying those things, but if you say I did, then I must have. I'm sorry and ashamed. Jessy is a most esti ... a most estimal —"

"What about Percy Ball?"

Harvey paused for a moment. He began to fumble through his pockets for cigarettes. "I have not yet had an opportunity to pay Mr. Ball a visit," he said slowly, deliberately, "but you shall be the first to know when I do."

"You working on something for the magazine?"

"That's right, old boy. Profile of a rich bitch. Wants to see her name in print."

"Funny thing, Mr. Harvey, but I got a suspicion you're not working on anything right now."

Harvey continued to fumble for his cigarettes, his eyes lowered. "That's ridiculous. Where the *hell* are my cigarettes?"

"My guess is you got canned. Month or two ago? Come clean, Mr. Harvey."

Harvey sighed and lifted his head. "It's true I'm not working for *Sport of Kings* at the moment. It's all free-lance I'm doing right now."

"Bullshit, you're not doing anything right now."

"I beg your pardon."

"Oh, for fucksake."

Young's stomach ache had been in remission for most of the day, but now it was starting up again. *I've got to get something to eat*, he thought. He stopped at a Chinese takeout place on his way home.

Standing on her tiptoes at the jukebox, a little girl with a ruined face was making her selections. She was dressed in pink overalls, a yellow T-shirt, and yellow sneakers. She had platinum hair that bounced off her shoulders as she danced back to the table where a woman and a man were sitting. Young guessed that the woman was her mother and the man was the mother's boyfriend. He wondered what had happened to the little girl's face. Was it a car accident? Did she hit the dashboard? Was that why the left side of her face was off-kilter, indented, the cheekbone gone, the eye sunken and dead? Was that why her nose looked reconstructed and the left corner of her mouth was twisted into a permanent smile? Young touched a fingertip to the Steri-Strips on his cheekbone. The mother kept repeating, "Missy, come on, I've got to get to work," and the man would say, "Missy, get your raincoat," but neither of them made any move to leave, even though the server had already placed their bag of takeout in front of them. The man was smoking a cigarette.

Young wanted to comfort the girl. He wanted to tell her we all have scars, even though you can't see most of them. What doesn't kill us makes us stronger, he wanted to tell her.

Young ordered soo guy, orange beef, shrimp with garlic and green pepper, and steamed rice. "Give me a Blue while I'm waiting," he said to the waiter.

At a table behind Young sat a fat man wearing a filthy Blue Jays cap. The man announced, to no one in particular, "I'm five foot seven, three hundred thirty-eight pounds."

Young turned and looked at him. From the lilt in his voice Young judged the man to be Irish.

The man said, "My doctor says for my weight I should be eleven feet tall."

"Where you from?" Young said.

"Belfast," the man said. "I've been married thirty-three years. In prison, I should say. I've been in prison thirty-three years."

The waiter brought Young his bottle of beer and, fifteen minutes later, his bag of takeout. As Young pulled on his windbreaker, he heard the mother say, "I've got to get to work," and the girl with the ruined face in a little, pleading half-voice say, "Just one more song, please, Mommy. Back Street Boys?"

Young plodded along the sidewalk. The rain was falling heavily. He turned up the collar of his coat. The liquor store was still open, so he went in. His stomach was hurting seriously now, and he was either out of Jack or close to it, he couldn't remember which.

"We deal in lead, friend," Young said into his portable phone.

"Sarge, is that you? Where are you?"

"We deal in lead, friend."

Then she caught on. "Oh," she said. "That's an easy one. *The Magnificent Seven.* Steve McQueen to Eli Wallach when the bad guys ride into the village. Give me a hard one."

"Okay, smartass," Young said. "How many of them die?" Young had finished his Chinese food, his stomach ache had taken a breather, and he was sitting on a hardback dining room chair turned backwards in front of the open closet door in his bedroom. Except for his underpants, he was naked. He had a harness arrangement attached to his head, with a cord leading up to and over the top of the door and down the other side to a plastic bag containing fifteen pounds of water. A quarter of a century earlier, Young had pinched a nerve in his neck playing football, and once in a while it still gave him trouble; lunging at the man with the crowbar had aggravated it. The idea of this apparatus — recommended by his chiropractor — was that the weight of the water would pull his head upward and, by creating more space between his vertebrae, relieve the pressure.

Wheeler said, "Four died. Robert Vaughn, who played the southern dandy, he died. James Coburn, Charles Bronson, and ... don't tell me."

"Can't remember?"

"Give me a minute."

"Want a clue?"

"Quiet." Wheeler was curled up on the sofa in the living room of her apartment. There was a cat in her lap. "It's the one no one can ever remember, right?"

"That's right." Young had decided not to tell Wheeler about the attack at the racetrack. It was Sunday night. She sounded relaxed, and he didn't want to upset her. Monday would come soon enough. With his free hand, Young took a hairbrush from the bedside table. He reached over his shoulder and scratched his back with it. Its bristles were very stiff, which was why he had stolen it from Debi when she was living with him. It was the best back-scratcher he had ever owned.

"Let me go over them," Wheeler said. "Yul Brynner, Steve McQueen, the horrible Horst Buchholz as the kid —"

"I thought he was good in *Tiger Bay*, with Hayley Mills."

"— Robert Vaughn, James Coburn, Charles Bronson as Bernardo Reilly —"

"And one more." Young owned a copy of the movie; he watched it three or four times a year. He had two VCRs, one on top of the other in his living room. The bottom VCR played his videotapes, but wouldn't rewind them. The one on top wouldn't play them, but rewound beautifully. On his days off, Young liked to watch movies in segments — half an hour at breakfast, an hour at lunch, the rest at suppertime. "Give up?"

"No, I don't give up." Wheeler pushed the cat from her lap, stood up from the sofa, and, carrying her portable phone with her, padded across the broadloom to her bookshelves. She took down the *Film Guide* and flipped through it silently.

"For fucksake, Wheeler, I haven't got all day."

"It's on the tip of my tongue."

"Or all night."

"You haven't got all night? You called me, remember. What's the matter, you got a date? You all dressed up? What are you wearing, Sarge? You want to know what I'm wearing?"

"I couldn't care less what you're wearing."

"Pajamas with feet."

Young put down the hairbrush and worked a finger under his head harness. Gingerly, he patted his Steri-Strips. "Really? Pajamas with feet?"

"Yes, that's right."

"Well, you wouldn't believe what I'm wearing, but I'm not going to get into one of those kinky conversations where you tell me what you're wearing and then I tell you what I'm wearing and pretty soon we're both slapping the monkey."

"But I'm a dyke, Sarge."

"So you say. What of it?"

"Well, I'm sure you don't want your buds to know you get aroused by a dyke."

"You see, Wheeler, what I think is you're one of these elective dykes." Young could lean over just far enough to pick up the bottle of Jack Daniel's by its neck.

"Elective dykes? Oh, you mean a girl who's straight,

but can't attract men so she does the next best thing."

"That's right." He took a swig of the sour mash, sloshed it around a bit, and swallowed. "One of these days you'll see the light and realize I'm the man for you. You attract me, Wheeler, and if you could see me now, you wouldn't be able to resist me."

"You look that good?"

"Mmm hmm."

"Brad Dexter."

"What?"

She closed the book and put it back on the shelf. "Brad Dexter. The one no one can ever remember. He got killed, too."

Young grunted.

"It's late, Sarge. Good night. I'll see you tomorrow."

Sometime later he phoned Debi. He was sitting at the table in his breakfast nook with all the lights on. He had detached himself from the water bag and had removed the head harness and was now wearing a dirty pair of work socks, old gray sweatpants, an oversized navy blue T-shirt, and the green and black, triple-X lumberjack shirt he'd found at a Big 'n' Tall in the shopping mall across from the racetrack. He had a drinking glass with one ice cube in it and the bottle of Jack Daniel's in front of him. Reg was on the floor at his feet. Young's stomach was killing him.

"Hello?"

"Hello, sweetie."

"Daddy, is that you?" Her voice was groggy. "Daddy, it's midnight. What is it?"

"I'm sorry, sweetie, I didn't mean to wake you. I didn't realize how late it was. I just wanted to find out how your horse did."

"We won. Bing came from way out of it and won by two. Where did you and Uncle Artie get to? Me and Mrs. McDonagh, we were waiting for you in the winner's circle. I was worried. I called earlier. Didn't you check your messages?"

"It was police business, sweetie. We had to hurry out. I'm sorry."

"Daddy, you all right? Have you been drinking?"

"I've had a couple, but I'm fine. Is Jamal there?"

"Of course he's here, where else would he be?"

"Can I talk to him?"

"Daddy, it's midnight. You *are* drunk. I'm not going to wake him up in the middle of the night —"

"It's okay, sweetie, it's okay, I just wanted to make sure he was safe."

"Why wouldn't he be safe? Did something happen to you today? Are you all right?"

"I love that little boy."

"I know you do, Daddy." Young could hear Eldridge say something in the background, then Debi said, "Daddy, you're scaring me, are you okay?"

Young didn't know what to say.

"Are you still there?"

"Yeah, I'm here, I'm just being stupid. I'm sorry I woke you up. Just go back to sleep. Tell Eldridge I'm sorry."

Monday, June 12

When the alarm woke him, Young was in rough shape. His cheek was throbbing where the crowbar had struck him, he was badly hung over, and his stomach felt as if talons were dug into it. He phoned HQ.

"Sick?" Gallagher said. "You're never sick."

"I'll be in tomorrow. I'm going to let the dog out and then I'm going back to bed."

He took three ibuprofens and slept until noon. When he got up the headache was gone and the pain in his face had subsided, but his gut hurt so much he could barely stand up.

At 2:00 p.m., he parked his minivan outside McCully's. Inside, as he approached the bar, he could see that Jessy was talking to a man sitting on one of the stools. The man was wearing a floral shirt, white jeans, and a New York Yankees ballcap turned backwards. A magazine was open in front of him, and Jessy was pointing something out.

When Young was close she looked up and said, "Jesus and Mary, what happened to you?"

"Nothing. Cut myself shaving." He nodded at the magazine. "What's so interesting?"

"I was just showing this gentleman my tattoo catalogue. Another rye and ginger, sir?"

"No, thanks," the man said.

Something about his voice. And his clothes. Young looked at the back of the man's head. Black frizzy hair poking out from under the ballcap. Then the man turned and smiled up at him. "Detective Sergeant," he said, "how are you?"

Doug Buckley.

Without taking his eyes off of him, Young said to Jessy, "Since when are you getting a tattoo?"

Jessy said, "I've been thinking about it for a while now."

"What kind you going to get?" Young was still staring at Doug, whose smile was slowly fading.

"A mermaid, I think. Or maybe a tarantula."

Out of the corner of his eye Young could see her touch her hair. "Where you going to get it?"

"There's this place on Queen Street. One of my girlfriends, her brother — "

"No. Where on you are you going to get it?" Young still hadn't taken his eyes off Doug.

"Oh. Well, I was thinking maybe the middle of my back."

"Who's going to see it there? You won't even see it."

"Or maybe on the back of my leg," she said quietly.

"The back of your leg?"

She pointed to the magazine. "There's one in there of Willie Nelson I would just love to have on my calf. It's so good you'd swear it was a photograph."

"Maybe you should get your name tattooed on your arm," Young said, "like the basketball players do. You know why they do that, don't you?"

Jessy shook her head. "Why do they do that?"

"In case they forget their name they can look at their arm and, as long as they can read upside down, they can say, 'Oh, that's right, I'm Tyrone.'"

Jessy said, "Why are you acting like this?"

It was a fair question. Young thought about it for a moment. "I guess it's because you're chumming up to this piece of shit." Doug started to climb down off his stool, but Young laid a hand on his shoulder. "Has he asked you to go out with him yet? 'Cause if he hasn't, he will. And before you decide yes or no, you might want to know a few things about him. Like how he abandoned his family. Like how he lies to officers of the law. Isn't that right, you piece of shit?"

Doug trembled under Young's hand, but said nothing. Just then, Vinny appeared in the doorway of the kitchen and called Jessy's name, and she moved off down the bar.

"So, shitbird," Young said, "why did you move out of the Hilton?"

Doug lowered his head. "I had a little problem there. It had nothing to do with the murder investigation."

"What kind of little problem?"

Doug swallowed. "A masseuse. Things got a wee bit out of hand with one of the masseuses. It was best I leave. No-trace camping, if you know what I mean." He smiled up at Young.

"Where you living now?"

"The King Eddy."

Young raised his eyebrows. "I've never been there myself, but I'm told it's pretty snazzy."

Doug shrugged. "You have to pay for quality."

"So what's someone who can afford the King Eddy doing in a joint like McCully's?"

"The last time I saw you, you asked me if I would be around. I'm just checking in with you. Like with a parole officer."

"How'd you know where to find me?"

"I asked your daughter when I was out at the track the other day. I told her I had something for you, that it was important I see you. She refused to tell me your phone number or where you lived. All she would give me was the name of this bar."

"So what've you got that's so important?"

Doug looked around. Down the bar, Vinny was talking to two drinkers, and Jessy was at the beer taps, filling a pitcher. Doug took a quick, shaky sip of his rye and ginger, looked up at Young, and said, "I know who killed Shorty Rogers."

Young narrowed his eyes. "You do."

Doug nodded. "Yes, indeedy." He slurped at his drink.

"I'm all ears."

Doug was sucking on an ice cube. "It was the bird guy. The birdman of King County. The saviour of birds. I can't remember his name."

"I can. Stirling Smith-Gower."

Doug said "Bull's eye!" and the ice cube he was sucking jumped out of his mouth and slid across the bar.

Tuesday, June 13

Young woke up in so much discomfort he was doubled over all the way to the toilet. If he breathed deeply, a searing pain burned across his abdomen. During the drive to work, he gripped the steering wheel tightly and groaned. As soon as he arrived at HQ, he was summoned into Staff Inspector Bateman's office. Bateman, seated at his desk, eyed the stitches on Young's cheekbone. "Trick's back," he said.

"Good."

"Starts his computer lessons this morning. First time he's been in since he got hit. Nearly three years."

Young nodded.

Bateman fiddled with a letter opener. "He told me what happened out at the racetrack. Why didn't you let me know? He says it was just an 'attempt mug,' but it could have been something else."

"Yeah, well, we got the crowbar. It's in a plastic bag in my van. Wicary can dust it for prints."

"You don't look so good. Maybe you should take a couple more days. Wheeler says you've been having gut aches, too, is that right?"

"Just heartburn, boss. No problem."

"Could be diverticulitis. My wife had that. Watermelon seed. It was supposed to be a seedless." He sighed and ran the fingers of one hand through his silver hair. "Very well, carry on."

Trick was sitting in his wheelchair in the hall. "How you feeling, brother?"

"Shitty. Good to have you back. How'd you get here?"

"Boum-Boum. He dropped me around back, and I came up the freight elevator."

Young gathered Trick, Wheeler, Barkas, and Big Urmson in the conference room.

As people were seating themselves, Wheeler raised a tentative finger to the Steri-Strips on Young's cheekbone. "That looks painful," she said. "My sources tell me it happened Sunday afternoon. Why didn't you say something?"

Young shrugged. "What doesn't kill us, Wheeler, makes us stronger."

When everyone was seated, he said, "Greetings everybody, and a special welcome back for Mr. Trick. As all of you probably realize by now, we're basically working two situations at once, both at the racetrack, but there's a good chance they're more closely related than just that. The first one, the death of the horse that was in Shorty Rogers' barn, my gut instinct tells me was not a natural death. My gut instinct tells me it was killed intentionally. It may or may not be related to the second situation, Shorty's murder, but I'll bet there's a tie-in somewhere. Now, with respect to Shorty's case, I know we've already interviewed all the likely suspects, but I want each of them interviewed again. Only this time by someone different. Barkas interviewed Summer Caldwell the first time; this time, Wheeler, you're going to do it. I want these people to get the impression that everybody in Homicide is familiar with them, not just one person. However, since our friend Mr. Harvey has let us down with regard to Percy Ball, I'll talk to Percy again myself. I think he knows a lot more than he's letting on. Then I'm going to find out about Mahmoud Khan's financial situation. I don't think he's as rich as he looks. I think he's got some serious money problems, which may explain the dead horse. Wheeler, like I said, you've got Summer Caldwell. We need to find out more about her. Is she squeaky clean like she looks, what with the good works and the Feed the Children, or is there more to her than we know about? She was at the meeting at Uncle Morley's house, and it seems she's jealous of his success in the whatchamacallit."

"The Beautiful Garden Competition."

"Right, but did she have any reason to want his nephew murdered? My guess is she'll end up pretty low on the list, but check her out just the same."

Wheeler said, "While I'm at it, I want to see what she knows about Miss Sweet —"

"Good, because I want you to stick with Miss Sweet, at least for the time being. I couldn't get anywhere with her, and she opened up for you like a steamed clam."

He turned to Barkas. "Richard Ludlow, Barkas. Wheeler already did him, so now it's your turn. President of the King County Golf and Country Club. Sniff around. I know he would just love to lay his hands on Uncle Morley's land, but, again, did he have any reason to want Shorty dead?"

His eyes moved from Barkas to Big Urmson. "And speaking of Shorty, I want you out at the track, Urmson. I'll set it up with Debi. She'll meet you at the gates. Talk to people about Shorty. What are they saying? What's the latest theory floating around Shedrow. Hang out in the kitchen for a while, see what you come up with. I know you did Stirling Smith-Gower the first time, and you did a bang-up job. I want you to do the same thing with Shorty."

He swivelled in his chair. "Your turn," he said to Trick.

Trick smiled noncommittally.

"I dropped by McCully's yesterday afternoon, and Doug Buckley, the guy that won the lottery, was in there chatting up Jessy."

"That wasn't wise of him."

"Turns out he was there to see me. Seems he knows who killed Shorty."

"Really?"

"Yup. He claims it's Smith-Gower."

"The bird guy?"

"That's right. Find out if he's back from South America yet."

Trick looked uncomfortable. "How?"

Young shrugged. "Call him up, for starters."

Trick was unconvinced.

Young said, "Look, it's simple, really. Pick up the phone and dial his number. If he's there, ask him about the ring-necked booby, then ask him where he was at eleven p.m. on May 31."

That afternoon, Wheeler drove out to the Caledon Hills, northwest of Toronto, and spent an hour drinking iced tea and eating crustless cucumber sandwiches on a flagstone patio behind a renovated century farmhouse. Despite the cool, overcast weather, Summer Caldwell was wearing a light summer dress and a floppy sun hat. She was an artificial brunette, a fading beauty.

She showed Wheeler photographs of her "children."

"This is Tien," she said, in sing-song baby talk, "he's eight and he lives in Cambodia, and this is Irma, she's six and she lives in Colombia."

Wheeler said, "May I?"

Summer Caldwell passed her the photographs. "Thirty years ago," she said, her voice deeper and raspier now, a smoker's voice, "Thomas made it clear as a condition of our marriage that there would be no children, but he does allow me to sponsor."

"They're beautiful."

"Thank you." Wheeler passed the photos back, and Summer Caldwell replaced them in her purse. "It was a terrible shock when we heard about Delbert."

"You knew him as Delbert?"

"Well, yes. Of course, I knew that everyone else called him Shorty, but it just seemed so common." Summer Caldwell touched her hair. Her fingernails were long and lacquered. "We both grew up out here. We attended the same elementary school. Then when my parents sent me off to private school in Toronto, I lost track of him until I heard he was training racehorses."

"Do you and your husband own racehorses, Mrs. Caldwell?"

She laughed. "No, my dear. Thomas wouldn't dream of doing anything so … I don't know, so … frivolous. He's a financial advisor, don't forget. And an accountant!"

"So far as you know, did Delbert have any enemies?"

Summer Caldwell paused. She studied the platter of little sandwiches. "I know he drank," she said, "and I suspect he gambled. If the two took place simultaneously, it's possible that he ended up owing someone a lot of money."

"Are you just speculating, or do you know something definite?"

"Pure speculation, my dear." She selected a sandwich and held it with her fingertips, as a child might hold an insect.

Wheeler consulted her notes. "Mrs. Caldwell, what can you tell me about Myrtle Sweet?"

For a moment, Summer Caldwell continued to study the sandwich. Then she turned to Wheeler and, with appetite, said, "Oh, she's quite the scandal!"

"What do you mean?"

"Poor old Morley. He advertised for a housekeeper, and when she showed up for an interview, I'm sure the both of them began to drool. She's very voluptuous, you know, in an Ava Gardner sort of way. And despite his religious, God-fearing exterior, Morley's a horny old goat. And I should know, for hasn't he pinched my bottom on more than one occasion! And when that Sweet woman saw how old and feeble he was, she must have thought she'd died and gone to heaven. As well, he was living alone. It didn't take her long, I'm sure, to claw her way into his affections, and now I'm just concerned that she's sinking her teeth into his fortune. I'll bet my Mercedes his will has suffered a codicil or two since her arrival! They're common people, the Rogerses, common as mud, and they're not the brightest people in the world, either, but Morley has been squirreling away money for years, and when he sells his acreage, he'll be very well off indeed."

"Does she —"

"And those two young men she has working for her, well, I'm sure I just don't know what to think of them."

"You mean Eric and Kevin Favors?"

Summer Caldwell put down her sandwich. "My word, you've done your homework, haven't you? I didn't know their last name."

"Technically speaking, don't they work for Morley Rogers?"

"Well, yes, I suppose they do, but my guess is she runs the show. Do you mind if I smoke?"

"Not at all. What do you mean you don't know what to think of them?"

"Well, to begin with, they're black, which is almost unheard of in this community."

Wheeler nodded, waiting.

"And they're twins. Identical. Until that meeting at Morley's house, I thought there was only one — I used to see her with one of them at the Caledon Hills Mall — then lo and behold, there were *two* of them at the meeting. I thought I was seeing double. I thought I'd had one too many martinis!" She leaned conspiratorially towards Wheeler. "And I'm positive there's something going on."

"What sort of thing?"

"You know." She nodded meaningfully.

"Something … sexual?"

Summer Caldwell held the flame of her gold lighter to the end of a cigarette as long as a drinking straw. "Exactly."

"How do you know?"

"That evening at Morley's. The air was positively *charged* with sexual energy. I could feel it. I'm very good at sensing these things, and I kept searching the room to find out who was involved. And then I discovered eye contact between Myrtle Sweet and one of the twins."

"Which one?"

"I'm afraid I don't know, my dear, I can't tell them apart!"

Wednesday, June 14

By the time he went to bed Tuesday night, Young's stomach ache had an evil grip on his guts. It was different this time. This time it wasn't going away.

Earlier in the evening, as he'd watched television, he had deliberately laid off the cheesies and Jack Daniel's. He had drunk milk instead. Still, as he lowered himself into his bed, he knew the demon in his belly was making itself comfortable.

Despite the pain, he was so tired he slept heavily, but as soon as he woke up in the morning he was in agony. He let Reg out, fed her, showered, shaved, dressed himself, skipped his Grape-Nuts, downed six ounces of Pepto-Bismol, and left for work. By the time he reached the end of his street, he was folded over the steering wheel. He could turn right and go to work or turn left and drive himself to East General Hospital. He sat there at the stop sign for so long that the driver of a car behind him honked his horn.

He turned left.

In the emergency ward at East General Hospital, he explained his problem to a receptionist; she asked for his health card and told him to take a seat. Eventually, a doctor whose name sounded to Young like Wallawallabingbang led him into a curtained cubicle, and Young repeated what he had told the nurse: that he had been suffering from a series of stomach aches — one a week for the last three weeks — but he couldn't seem to shake this one. When the doctor, a small man with thick glasses, asked Young to lie down on his back, Young had to bite his lip against the pain. And when the doctor probed the lower right section of Young's abdomen with the four fingers of his right hand rigid as a board, Young screamed and almost came off the table.

An hour later, after x-rays had been taken, Young was told he would be number five on the emergency operation list and that he should phone his place of employment and tell them he was going to be off work for at least a week, probably two.

"But I can't miss work," Young explained.

"Why not?" asked the doctor.

"I'm a detective. I'm working a murder case. I'm —"

"Does your appendix know you are a detective? I don't think so. Your appendix does not care two hoots if you are a detective."

Early that afternoon, Staff Inspector Bateman assembled Young's team in the conference room and told them the news. For a moment there was quiet, then he said, "I talked to the hospital a few minutes ago, and the prognosis is Camp will be gone at least a week, maybe two. I'll let you know when he's ready for visitors." He turned to Wheeler. "Meanwhile, Lynn, you're acting leader of the team."

Wheeler looked around the table and said, "Okay, everyone, you all know your assignments. Tony, have you made any progress with Richard Ludlow?"

"Tomorrow. I'm up to my armpits."

"Don't wait too long. Arthur, you've got Stirling Smith-Gower, right?"

"I'm on it today."

Big Urmson said, "He might still be in South America."

"Good point, Big. What about you?" Wheeler checked her notes. "You're supposed to snoop around the racetrack and find out what people are saying about Shorty."

"I'm heading up there this afternoon. It's already set up with Debi."

"Fine. As for me, I've already talked to Summer Caldwell, but I've still got Myrtle Sweet to do. Have your reports on my desk in two days. That means Friday, before you go home. Any questions?"

Big Urmson said, "What about Mahmoud Khan and Percy Ball? Sarge was going to do them."

"And what about Doug Buckley?" Barkas asked. "Who's got him?"

Wheeler said, "Just do the ones you've got for now. If anyone finds himself with time on his hands, let me know and you can have your pick. Anything else?"

Trick said, "Who's going to look after his dog?"

"Good question. I'd do it, but I don't think Misty would like having a bulldog in the apartment."

"Misty a cat?"

"Yes, a lilac point Siamese. What about you? I could pick Reg up and bring him to your place. There's a nice little parkette right across from your building, isn't there?"

* * *

Young was alone on a bed in a dark room. The pain was very bad. He was so frightened he couldn't stop shaking. He tried to think about the things he loved. It was difficult to concentrate, but he came up with a list of fourteen items and put them in alphabetical order: baseball, beer, Bob Seger, bourbon, Debi, dogs (in general, Reg in particular), Hawkins Cheezies, hockey, horse racing, Jamal, Jessy, movies, Trick, Wheeler.

Then he made a list of his favourite movies: *All Quiet on the Western Front*, *Apocalypse Now*, *City Slickers*, *The Deer Hunter*, *Dog Day Afternoon*, *The Great Escape*, *The Magnificent Seven*, *The Maltese Falcon*, a Paul Newman movie he'd just seen a year ago called *Nobody's Fool*, *One Flew Over the Cuckoo's Nest*, *Serpico*, and another one whose title he couldn't remember about a group of college friends who reunite at the funeral of a classmate; the theme song was "You Can't Always Get What You Want," and William Hurt was in it, and Glenn Close, and Kevin Kline.

Later, he dreamed he was in a forest cutting wood with a chainsaw, and the saw bucked off a knot and cut through the sleeve of his lumberjack shirt and through his forearm, dropping it like a length of stovewood into the dead leaves at his feet. He fell onto his back, the lifeblood spilling, and told Mahmoud Khan — who appeared out of nowhere and knelt over him like a priest — to tell Wheeler he would always love her and to tell Myrtle Sweet that he wanted to fuck her, and could she hurry over before he died.

Debi met Big Urmson at the backstretch gate. Only minutes before his arrival, she had been informed of her father's hospitalization in a phone call from Staff Inspector Bateman. He'd assured her there was nothing to be done until after the operation, and he'd asked if she would still be willing to meet Big Urmson and get him into Shedrow.

"You're lucky you didn't come yesterday," she said when Big Urmson arrived. "Tuesdays are dark, and there's no one around."

"Dark?" Big Urmson asked.

"There's no racing on dark days."

Big Urmson visited the cafeteria. He talked to two trainers, several grooms, and some of the kitchen staff. The woman who dolloped out the mashed potatoes was convinced Shorty had been murdered by the Russian Mafia. The cashier claimed his death was divine retribution for past sins.

Big Urmson left the kitchen and wandered around outside. One of the grooms, an old man with shifty eyes, argued that Shorty's murder had never happened, it was all a hoax, the body found in the stall was someone else's, and Shorty himself would reappear next February during the winter meet at Gulfstream Park in Hallandale, Florida.

Another groom, a young black man with cornrows in his hair who was sweeping inside Barn 1, said maybe it had something to do with The Butcher.

Big Urmson said, "What butcher?"

The young man shrugged and said, "The guy that kills horses."

Big Urmson pressed the young man for more information, but he claimed he didn't know anything else, that he'd only heard of him, and Big Urmson was unable to find anyone else who would admit to any knowledge of The Butcher.

The most popular and most credible theory concerning Shorty's death was that he owed somebody money, but here again Big Urmson was stonewalled because no one promoting this theory was willing or able to identify anyone to whom Shorty might have been in debt.

Trick was sitting in his wheelchair at the desk that had been set up for him opposite Wheeler's. He took a deep breath and picked up the phone. He dialed the number scribbled on the piece of paper in front of him.

A female voice answered. "Ontario Avian Protection Association. Consuela speaking."

Trick cleared his throat. "Consuela, good morning. Is Mr. Smith-Gower available?"

"No, I'm sorry, he's out of town. Would you care to leave a message?"

For a moment the wind left Trick's sails. "Is there any way to reach him?"

She laughed. "No, I'm afraid not. He's birding in Brazil. He's after a particularly elusive life-bird, the Hyacinth macaw. When he goes on trips like this he doesn't even leave a number where we can reach him. The last thing he wants is contact with the outside world."

"When do you expect him back?"

"Next Wednesday. A week today. But you never know with him."

"I see. Well, thank you."

"Would you care to leave a message?"

Trick thought for a moment. "Yes, would you have him phone Arthur Trick at Homicide. I just need to ask him —"

"Homicide?"

"Yes, I just need to ask him a few questions."

"But —"

"Mr. Smith-Gower is not in any trouble, I assure you, Consuela, but he might have information which could be of use to us."

After he'd given Consuela his phone number and hung up, Trick sat immobile. *Camp gives me a job*, he thought, *and I can't even get started*. He shook his head. *Maybe I should phone Boum-Boum and get him to take me home.*

"Lynn," he said.

Across from him, Wheeler looked up from her paperwork. "Yes?"

"You still need someone to look into Percy Ball and Mahmoud Khan?"

"Yes, I do."

"Camp thinks Khan's in financial trouble and Percy's hiding something, is that right?"

"That's right."

"Let me take a shot at them."

The orderly parked the stretcher, with Young on it, in a corridor outside the door to Operating Theatre 2. Then, without saying a word, he turned and walked away.

Young was shivering. His whole body was shaking, and his teeth were chattering. He lay like this for several minutes until a passing nurse noticed him. "My goodness, look at you," she said. She walked over to a compartment in the wall and opened the door to it. It looked like a body drawer in a morgue. Young half-expected her to pull out a frozen corpse. But when she returned she had a white blanket in her arms. As she spread it over Young, she looked like an angel. The blanket was warm, almost hot. Young felt delicious, like a child being tucked in. "It's just nerves," the nurse said. "You'll be fine." Then she disappeared.

A few minutes later he was wheeled into the operating theatre. "We'll need help," someone said. It took four people to transfer Young from the stretcher to the table. There were bright lights above him and all sorts of equipment around him. A different doctor leaned over him. He was wearing a green shower cap. "Mr. Young, my name is Dr. Habib. I'm going to perform your surgery. Do you have any questions?"

"Where's the other doctor?"

"What other doctor?"

"Wallawallabingbang."

Dr. Habib looked puzzled, then laughed. "Oh, Dr. Wadiwalla? He's not a surgeon, Mr. Young. No, no, no, he's a GP. He works exclusively in ER. What did you think his name was? Wallawallabingbang? That's very amusing."

Young's teeth were starting to chatter again.

Dr. Habib said, "Mr. Young? Mr. Young, this is Dr. Chen." Another face appeared. They were both wearing shower caps. "Dr. Chen is the anaesthesiologist. I don't think you can do much with his name!"

The other face leaned over Young. It was smiling. A smiling Asian face with a green shower cap. Young began to feel giddy.

"I going to prace this mask over your face," Dr. Chen said, and he held up a black respirator. "When I ask you, you count down from fi' to one."

Young studied the respirator. "How far will I get?"

Dr. Chen was still smiling. "You will get as fah as fo' but not as fah as three."

The respirator hovered over his face. Young stared at it. It looked like a spaceship preparing to land. Fleetingly, he thought of Richard Dreyfuss in *Close Encounters of the Third Kind*. The swirling lights. The weird music.

He could hear Dr. Chen's voice say, "Begin to count, prease."

As the respirator settled over his nose and mouth, Young closed his eyes and took a last breath. "Five," he said. "Four."

Thursday, June 15

Debi was standing at the backstretch gate as Boum-Boum opened the sliding side door of his Econoline van. He manipulated the lever that lowered the hydraulic lift bearing Trick and his wheelchair to the ground.

Trick and Debi talked for a few minutes about Young's condition, and when Debi mentioned Reg, Trick assured her the bulldog was fine. "I'd better get to work," he said. "Where am I likely to find Percy?"

"Barn 4," Debi said, "so long as you get there before eleven. After that, it's JJ Muggs."

Trick consulted his watch. "It's ten-thirty," he said. "I'd better get a move on." He told Boum-Boum to get himself a coffee at the track kitchen and to be back at the van in fifteen minutes.

Trick was relieved to find the surfaces he had to traverse hard and dry, and he steered his wheelchair quickly and carefully past horse vans, pickup trucks, fat men in fedoras, and small men in flak jackets.

Inside Barn 4, Trick negotiated his way along the shedrow past buckets and brooms and leaning rakes and bales of hay and straw, past dozens of stalls, most of whose inhabitants swung their heads out as he rolled by. A man sweeping asked Trick what he wanted, and Trick said, "Percy Ball." The man pointed further along and said, "Far end."

Trick wheeled himself towards the open door of a dimly lit tack room. Inside, Percy was sitting on a dingy cot cleaning his fingernails with a jackknife. He looked up, studied Trick for a moment, and said, "Who the fuck are you?"

Trick said, "Special Agent Arthur Trick, Metropolitan Toronto Homicide Department." With his left hand he opened a small plastic identification folder and held it in front of Percy for several seconds, then closed it and returned it to his shirt pocket. "I need to ask you a few questions about the Shorty Rogers case."

Percy wiped the blade of the jackknife against the thigh of his pant leg, folded it shut, slid it into his hip pocket, and flipped the blond hair out of his eyes. "I told that big cop everything I know. Which was nothin'. I don't know nothin'."

"Well, I'm confused," Trick said, "because Detective Sergeant Young — the big cop — told me you said Shorty may have owed somebody money. And sometime later, you phoned him and told him Shorty was involved in a disagreement with a man named Buckley over a horse they owned together."

Percy was silent. He pulled a cigarette out of his black jacket.

Trick looked around the tack room. "You allowed to smoke in here? I thought there were rules against smoking in barns."

"Fuck the rules."

Trick narrowed his eyes. "Maybe you don't understand. People in wheelchairs, such as myself, or people who are otherwise disabled, get a little uncomfortable when able-bodied people, such as yourself, break safety rules. If something goes wrong, we can't get out as fast as you can."

"Fuck you, too."

Trick looked closely at Percy but said nothing. He knew dead eyes when he saw them.

"Ask your questions," Percy said. "I don't have all day."

Trick surveyed the room. Junk food trash in a corner. A pair of muddy boots. A pile of soiled clothing. Cigarette butts on the floor by Percy's feet. A filthy sleeping bag balled up on the cot. "You exercised horses for Shorty, right?"

"Yeah, so what?"

"Including the horse that died a while ago?"

"Yeah, so what?"

"We're checking out the owner's telephone records. A Mr. Mahmoud Khan. Has he ever phoned you?"

"Yeah ... no, I spoke to him a couple times when he was out here, that's all. He'd ask me how his horse worked, and I'd tell him. Whichever horse worked that day."

"Any reason to believe Mr. Khan might be strapped for cash?"

Percy laughed. "Are you crazy?"

"So why did he have Download murdered?"

It was a stab in the dark, and Percy looked away. "You don't know what you're talkin' about." He shook his head. "It was colic killed that colt."

"And who killed Shorty Rogers?"

Percy stood up. His hands were shaking. He glared at Trick. "I don't know. I've no fuckin' clue who killed

Shorty." He dropped the cigarette and ground it under the heel of his cowboy boot.

"If there's any information at all —"

"I told ya, I've no fuckin' clue! Now leave me alone!"

Trick studied Percy for a moment, then, with his left hand on the console of his wheelchair, he began to reverse out of the tack room. *The little shit's righteous as hell when he's telling the truth*, he thought to himself, *but it's obvious when he's lying.*

Dr. Habib said, "We have to run a tube down your throat."

Young, who was in a fetal position on the bed, made no response.

Dr. Habib said, "Your abdominal area was traumatized by the operation. We had to handle you rather roughly. As a result, your bowel system has shut down."

Young turned his head slightly.

"So much tissue had formed around your appendix," Dr. Habib continued, "that we couldn't locate it on the x-ray. We performed a laparoscopy — that is to say, we entered through your navel — but discovered that the mass was too large. So we created a traditional incision over the affected area."

"Why did you have to handle me roughly?" Young's voice was weak, barely a croak.

"We had to move things around a bit. To find it. As a result, your bowel system went into shock. In protest, you might say. So now we have to feed this plastic tube down through your nostril and into your abdomen to assist with evacuation."

"You mean I'm going to shit through my nose?"

"Um, yes, basically. For a few days, until your bowel system starts up again."

"And the reason I hurt so much down there is because you had to handle me roughly?"

"Yes. You see, when we finally found it, your appendix was the size of a ... oh, a small grapefruit. It had begun to perforate, and tissue had formed around the appendix to contain the poison."

"It was the size of a grapefruit?"

"A small one, yes."

"And you had a hard time finding it."

"Yes, and we had an even harder time getting it out. It didn't want to come. We had to treat your body rather rudely."

Young frowned. "What do you mean rudely?"

"We had to move quickly."

"I was in danger?"

"Oh yes. If this had happened in some remote area, if you had been on a fishing trip, for example, you might very well have died."

Young swallowed. "No shit."

"That's why we operated on you so soon after you came in."

Young glanced down towards his stomach. "So you had to go in fast, grab what you were after, and get out fast."

"That's right."

"I feel like some animal's been at me."

"Well," Dr. Habib sighed, "like I say, we had to be fairly rough. If you can, just picture a dog digging for a bone."

Richard Ludlow was out of town on business, but his receptionist seemed to take a shine to Tony Barkas, who looked a lot like Tony Danza, the TV star. She offered him a cup of coffee and invited him to sit down. He sat in a deep leather chair beside a glass table with magazines and a bowl of peppermints on it. As she stood up from behind her desk to fetch his coffee, he saw that her black leather skirt was short and tight, and her legs looked eight feet long. She wore a yellow blouse, and her black hair hung down over her breasts. Her complexion was as pale as a geisha's. After she handed him a mug of coffee and once again seated herself at her desk, Barkas explained that he was assisting in a murder investigation and asked if the receptionist, who said her name was Sandi — "with an 'i'" — knew whether or not Mr. Ludlow was acquainted with a man named Shorty Rogers.

Sandi said she'd never heard of anybody by that name, but would Detective Barkas care for a cookie to go with his coffee.

"Sure," Barkas said. He didn't really want one, but he wanted to see her legs again.

Sandi walked to a small pantry in the corner of the office and took a package of Oreos out of the cupboard. "They're double-stuffed," she said. "I hope that's all right."

"That's fine."

When she was seated at her desk again, Barkas asked her how long she had been working for Mr. Ludlow.

"Almost three years now."

"Three years? That's a long time. You two work pretty closely, I guess."

"Oh, yes. He depends on me." She smiled. "He calls me his right hand."

Barkas nodded. "I guess you have to work late some nights?"

The smile disappeared. "Some nights, yes. Why do you ask?"

Barkas scratched his head. "Please don't take this personally, but I was just wondering if you and Mr. Ludlow … well, you know."

"No, I don't know."

"It's just that you're such an attractive young woman. I'm sure Mr. Ludlow —"

"Our relationship," Sandi interrupted, her face suddenly pink, "is strictly professional."

Barkas said, "I'm sure it is, but word on the street is Mr. Ludlow likes the ladies."

"That's not true."

"It's not?"

"No, it's not." Sandi was twisting a pen in her fingers. "Mr. Ludlow is a respected member of the community."

Barkas said, "He's married, isn't he?"

She dropped her head. "I know he's married."

"His wife know what's going on?"

"There's nothing going on! You have no right to talk to me like this. I'm going to have to ask —"

"What I hear on the street is Mrs. Ludlow found out about the others, and now their relationship —"

"What others?"

"— and now their relationship is one of those ones where the husband and wife sleep under the same roof, but not in the same bed, if you catch my meaning."

Sandi snapped the pen in two. Royal blue ink spattered her yellow blouse.

"I'm sorry," Barkas said, standing, "I didn't mean to upset you, but I have to dig as deep as I can. A man's been murdered, and we have to catch the killer before he does it again."

Sandi was sobbing. "I know what you're doing. You're trying to make me say things, but I won't! You don't know him. He's gentle and kind." She dabbed at the ink stains with a Kleenex, smearing them. "He couldn't kill anybody. He couldn't even take a dead mouse out of a mousetrap under my sink, and I had to do it."

"Just because he can't take a mouse out of a mouse-trap doesn't mean he can't kill somebody, or have somebody killed."

Sandi looked across her desk at Barkas. Her eyes were like ice. "You walk in here out of nowhere, you say you're investigating a murder, you start implying things about me and Mr. Ludlow, but you know what? Your little game won't work. I won't say a word against him. Whatever you think he may have done, you're wrong. And you know why? Because he's way too smart to put himself in a situation where he might lose his money or go to jail. He's way too smart for that."

A black nurse and a white nurse helped Young stand up. The black nurse greased one end of a transparent plastic tube. When she looked up at Young, who was looming over her like Frankenstein's monster, she said, "He's too tall." She found a chair, stood it in front of Young, and stepped up onto its seat. Then she slipped one end of the tube into his left nostril. Two or three inches in it stopped. She pushed harder, and Young cried out. She tried again, harder, but Young cried out again, so she stopped.

Down below, the white nurse said, "Try the other side."

The black nurse withdrew the tube, stepped down off the chair, greased the end of the tube again, and climbed back up on the chair. This time she inserted the tube into the right nostril and it slid in smoothly, but when it reached the back of his throat, Young gagged and vomited a small amount of liquid into a kidney-shaped basin the white nurse held in front of him.

Eventually the tube was all the way in, about three feet of it. Young wasn't sure he would be able to stand it. It felt like a spoon down his throat.

Friday, June 16

Trick, reasoning that Mahmoud Khan was the kind of man who didn't like to spend more money than he had to — how many millionaires entrust their precious thoroughbreds to the cheapest trainer on the grounds? — looked up websites for all of the storefront investment advisors he could find. The websites offered a lot of general information about the companies — locations, fees, guarantees — but no access to databases.

Now what? thought Trick. He looked across his desk at Wheeler. "Lynn," he said, "I've got a hunch about Mahmoud Khan, but I don't know how to prove it."

"What do you need?"

"I need Evan."

Evan was the technician who had taught Trick how to use a computer. Within the hour they were seated side by side as Trick watched Evan work. The young man was tall and skinny with greasy brown hair and a bad case of acne. In minutes, his grubby fingers flying over the keyboard, Evan had determined that Mahmoud Khan was a client of The Clifton Group, whose offices could be found in strip malls all across North America, and that he was hundreds of thousands of dollars in the red. He had invested heavily in a condominium complex in British Columbia that had been condemned because of soil contamination, as well as in a number of new Canadian stocks that had stumbled out of the starting gate and never recovered. Among his assets, Khan listed his farm, Dot Com Acres, its buildings, machinery, and livestock, and his Internet business, whose fortunes, according to the graph Evan accessed, were on the wrong side of the mountain.

Trick was propelling himself past Wheeler's desk towards the elevator when she said, "I just phoned Fingerprinting to find out when we'll get the lab report on the crowbar, and Wicary said, 'What crowbar?'"

Trick's heart almost stopped. He thought for a moment. "It must still be in his van."

A phone call was made to the hospital. A nurse was sent to Young's room to ask him where he had parked his minivan when he drove himself to Emergency. When she came back to the phone, she said that Young couldn't remember.

After several more phone calls and a short search, the minivan was discovered on a side street adjacent to East General Hospital. Two parking tickets were tucked under the passenger-side windshield. The crowbar in its plastic bag was found on the floor under the driver's seat.

Young still looked like a truck had hit him: his incision was covered by a large white bandage freckled with bloodstains; his navel was stapled shut and protected by a dark red crust of scab; an intravenous needle lay against his arm like a poison dart; the plastic tube ran from his nose to a small wheeled machine called a GOMCO — about the size and shape of a pull-around vacuum — on the floor beside his bed; and his eyes were vacant, the bags beneath them dark and heavy.

"Hi, Daddy," Debi said.

Young's eyes flickered and focused, and he became aware that his daughter was standing at the foot of the bed. His eyes moved to another shape beside her, and there was his grandson, his jaw hanging, his eyes wide with horror.

"How are you feeling?" Debi asked, her voice shaking.

Young understood that he had been asked a question and was expected to answer it. He tried to think of what to say. He licked his dry lips with his tongue, but all that came out when he tried to speak was a sound like the one the old Vauxhall he had owned as a teenager used to make when he turned the key but the battery was dead.

He opened his eyes again and slowly focused. Jamal had vanished behind his mother; his arms were wrapped around her legs.

Wheeler had all the reports assembled on the desk in front of her. She began to read through them.

Trick thought Stirling Smith-Gower an unlikely suspect. "Some of these do-gooders," he wrote, "can be real screwy, even dangerous, but not this one. Even though I haven't met him yet, the impression I get is he's not one of these militant types who kill doctors to save babies. His secretary, Consuela Martin, seemed helpful, and she's going to ask Mr. Smith-Gower to phone me as soon as he returns from South America. Although the timing of his trip — so soon after Shorty's murder — looks suspicious, my guess is he's clean." On the other hand, he felt that the money-strapped Mahmoud Khan should be high on their list: "How the death of Shorty Rogers could benefit him I still don't know, but he bears watching. I haven't met him yet, either, but I know he's dug himself in pretty deep financially, and my guess is he's looking for some way to climb back out." Of Percy Ball he wrote: "This guy is a piece of work, and my money says he has his hand in somewhere. I don't expect he was the brains behind the operation, but he might have done the dirty work. He may be small of stature, but that doesn't mean he's not dangerous."

She looked at Big Urmson's report next. He described his visit to the racetrack and briefly outlined the theories people had offered to explain Shorty's murder: money owed, the Russian Mafia, divine retribution. He also made mention of someone called The Butcher.

"The Butcher?" Wheeler said aloud.

Big Urmson had written, "A young black groom with irrigated hair told me The Butcher whacks horses for a living."

The research Tony Barkas had done on Richard Ludlow was more conclusive: "Smart businessman," Barkas wrote, "not so smart about sex life. But is he killer? No way, unless better motive than plain greed shows up. True, with Shorty out of inheritance picture, Ludlow might have easier time getting hands on Morley's land, but Ludlow already stinking rich. Not smart enough to keep pants on, but way too smart, as his secretary said, to lose money or go to jail. Not enough motive to kill Shorty. What about Khan? What about Buckley (who might have killed him in order to sell Someday Prince)? What about old man himself? What about housekeeper?"

Wheeler pursed her lips in thought. She didn't regard Mr. Rogers as a legitimate suspect. Despite his dismissive attitude towards Shorty on the videotape, he hardly fit the profile of a killer. As far as Khan was concerned, Wheeler took him very seriously, although Trick's research suggested that Khan did not have the funds to get himself out of debt, let alone buy Mr. Rogers' property. Doug Buckley certainly had motive, as Barkas mentioned, but he also had $8 million. Unlikely. Miss Sweet, on the other hand, was another story.

On Thursday, Wheeler had put out a nation-wide inquiry on Myrtle Sweet, and when she returned from lunch twenty-four hours later there was a response from the Quebec Provincial Police on her desk. Sweet was Myrtle's maiden name; she was thirty-five years old and had grown up in the fashionable Westmount section of Montreal, the daughter of an investment banker and his socialite wife; she had quit McGill University in 1981 to live with a student radical, a French Canadian; she was legally disowned by her parents a year later; after two years of living on a commune in Rivière du Loup, she gave up a baby girl for adoption and acquired a restraining order, citing physical and psychological abuse, against her boyfriend; she was married briefly to a chartered accountant named Raymond Leclerc of Valleyfield, Quebec; since the dissolution of her marriage, she had been arrested twice for fraud and once for tax evasion, using the aliases Marcelle Sauvage, Marguerite Savory, and Monique St. Louis; she had served a total of four years and three months in federal penitentiaries, satisfied the conditions of her parole in November of 1993, and disappeared not only from the province of Quebec but also, so far as anyone knew, from the face of the earth.

In her summary of the reports, Wheeler wrote, "Best bets: Myrtle Sweet, Percy Ball, Mahmoud Khan.

Continue to check out Doug Buckley, Richard Ludlow, Stirling Smith-Gower, Summer Caldwell; follow up on Ronald Outhouse, Trinidad Grant. Find out more about Favors Bros. & The Butcher. Need to see Mr. Rogers' will. Need results of lab test on crowbar."

Saturday, June 17

Young was becoming familiar with the various nurses who tended to him — not by name, but by action. The day nurses were talkative and laughed a lot and moved through his room like whirlwinds. The night nurses were silent and humourless and slow to respond when he rang for them. In the daytime the ward was a noisy, busy place, but at night it was like a museum after dark, with just the thin sound of the radio at the nurses' station to suggest that anyone except Young was there. Young felt like a mummy, unable to move or speak. He couldn't concentrate on anything for more than a few seconds and rarely turned on the television Debi had rented for him. Mostly, he just lay on his side in bed with his eyes closed, conscious of the tube through his nose and the irritation it was causing at the back of his throat. He hardly thought about anything at all, and he wasn't aware of the passage of time. One night he was startled when he heard a nurse shriek and then in an angry voice say, "I don't care what you do in the privacy of your own home, Mr. Christiani, but that sort of behaviour will not be tolerated here!"

One of the night nurses was especially nasty. She was a blonde woman whose face Young never clearly saw, but one night when he was suffering more than he thought he could bear and rang for more Demerol, she entered his room without a sound and, without warning and without even swabbing him down, stabbed him in the hip with a needle. Young howled in shock and pain, but when he turned to confront her, she was gone. When he began actively thinking again, he developed a theory that night nurses didn't really like people; they were happiest when the halls of their wards were dark and gleaming and all their patients out cold.

"Where's Jamal?"

"He's at his friend Ryan's house."

"Oh."

"I brought you tomorrow's *Form*. I know how you like to keep up." Debi put the *Racing Form* on the bed near Young's hand.

"Is he really at Ryan's?"

She looked at him. "Yes, he's really at Ryan's."

"Did he know you were coming to visit me?"

She hesitated. "Yes."

He nodded. "He didn't want to come."

"Daddy, you have to understand. When he saw you the other day, it was very frightening for him. It was frightening for me."

"Do I look any better now?"

She looked at him critically. "A little, I guess."

"Do you think he's … I don't know … traumatized? Maybe he'll never want to see me again, if I scared him that much."

She put her hand on his arm. "It wasn't just the way you looked, it was that you didn't seem to know him. You didn't respond. That really affected him."

"I tried to, but I couldn't talk."

"Anyway, I've told him you're going to get better, and he's praying for you."

"He's what?"

"He's praying for you. As you may or may not be aware, Eldridge is very religious, and he's got all three of us down on our knees in Jamal's room at bedtime, and we pray. Eldridge has us pray for all sorts of things: that he won't fall off a horse or be involved in a bad spill; that Jamaica will have a soccer team for the next World Cup; that Bob Marley will show up someday, not really dead after all. Right now, we're praying for you. You should hear Jamal, Daddy, he's so sweet. 'Dear God, please make my Poppy better.' It makes me cry."

"It's the tube up my nose that freaks him, right?"

"No, Daddy, it's — "

"One of the nurses taught me how to disconnect it so I can go for a walk. Maybe if I'm out of bed the next time he comes, he won't be so scared. We could go for a walk around the ward. Of course, I'll still have the IV in my arm and the little trolley I have to drag around behind me. But the tube shouldn't bother him. There'll just be about six inches of it coming out of my nose, tied in a knot so nothing leaks out."

Sunday, June 18

When Wheeler and Trick entered room 614 at East General Hospital, Young was sitting up in bed reading the *Racing Form*.

Trick said, "What's that tube up your nose for?"

"I shit through it," Young said.

"Nice," Trick said, "and it's transparent, too."

"They think of everything around here. Stick around long enough and you can watch me go. It's kind of like TV, only different. How's Reg?"

"Good. We seem to get along."

"Is she getting enough exercise?"

"Well, she runs around my apartment almost constantly, and I take her to the park."

"How often?"

"Once or twice a day, depending. She's fine, Camp, but I wish she wouldn't drag her ass across my carpet."

"You giving her milk and cereal in the morning? A small amount?"

"No, I'm giving her Louisiana Hot Sauce on a bed of peppers."

"You're a laugh riot."

Wheeler said, "How are you feeling?"

Young turned to her. "Not bad. Well enough to do a little reading." He rattled the *Racing Form*. "Speaking of which," he said, turning to Trick, "you going to the track today? It's Sunday."

"No, it wouldn't be any fun without your sorry ass there for amusement. Besides, who'd cart me around?"

Young nodded. "I'm the only one stupid enough." He reached for a tattered *Sports Illustrated* on his bedside table. "You two might be interested in this. There's an article in here about The Sandman."

Trick said, "The who?"

"The Sandman. He's this guy in the States that killed horses for a living. We were talking about him a while ago, before you came aboard, but I forgot all about it."

Wheeler said, "But The Sandman's in jail, right?"

"Right, somewhere in Illinois, I think." Then he turned to Trick. "Do you remember Alydar?"

"Of course. Only horse to finish second in all three Triple-Crown races."

"Beaten by Affirmed in all three."

"That's right." said Trick. "By a length and a half in the Derby, a neck in the Preakness, and a head in the Belmont. One more race and he would have got to him."

"Well, Alydar died in 1990, and now they're saying he was murdered."

"Get out of here. He was an amazing racehorse. Why would anybody murder him?"

"For the insurance?" Wheeler said. "Maybe he was worth more dead."

Young nodded. "That's right. Thirty-six million dollars, to be exact. Plus, he'd turned out to be no great shakes at stud. People weren't sending their mares to him."

"Was The Sandman involved in that?"

"They don't know. That was five years ago. But if Mr. Harvey's right, he's in jail now, so for sure he didn't kill that horse in Shorty's barn. But if I'm right, somebody did."

"Well," said Wheeler, "if you remember, Sarge, just before you had your operation, you sent Big Urmson up to the track to see what he could find out."

"Yeah, so?"

"People gave him all sorts of explanations for Shorty's death — creatures from outer space, wrath of God, et cetera — but this black kid he talked to mentioned somebody called The Butcher."

"Who's he?"

"According to the source, he's like The Sandman. He kills horses for money."

Monday, June 19

After five days with three feet of tube through his nostril and down his throat, Young thought he was going to snap. When Dr. Habib stopped in to check on him, Young said, "Doc, you have to take it out. If you don't, I'll go crazy."

Dr. Habib said, "What about your bowels, Mr. Young? Am I right in thinking there's still no movement?"

"It's coming, it's coming. I can almost fart."

Dr. Habib shook his head. "I don't know, Mr. Young, we really need — "

"Please, Doc, please. I'm begging you. I'm not kidding, I can't stand it."

Dr. Habib put down his clipboard. "All right," he said. "If you insist."

For the first time in a long time, Young felt a flutter of excitement in his chest. He prepared himself for what he thought would be a gradual, inch-by-inch process, as Dr. Habib slowly drew the length of tube out of his body.

But Dr. Habib, after disconnecting the tube from the GOMCO machine and placing his left hand firmly on Young's forehead, took hold of the tube close to Young's nose with his right hand, and — like a man pulling the cord on a lawn mower — drew out the tube in one swift motion. There was a sharp wet sound and a fine spray.

Young breathed in. He breathed deeply and enormously.

He felt freed, as if buried alive for days under a fallen building, he'd been discovered, dug out, and pulled up to fresh air and sunlight.

Wheeler phoned Fingerprinting. She asked Wicary how he was coming with his report on the crowbar.

"Tomorrow," he said. "First thing."

"I need it today," she said. "Please."

"Sadly, you're not the only one who requires my services, and my assistant had to go to a funeral in Brampton ... or Brantford — some fucking place. In any case, he's gone for the day. Tomorrow for sure."

She phoned Elliot Cronish and asked if his friend in Guelph had completed the tests on the horsehairs Young had clipped from the stallion Sam McGee.

"I thought the results would have been sent directly to you," he said. "You haven't received them?"

"No. It's been ten days."

"Well, that's very strange. I shall ring her post-haste and inquire."

"Thank you."

"How's our favourite philistine?"

"Who?"

"Your superior officer, my angel."

"Oh, he's doing well. I talked to him an hour ago.

He'll be going home in about a week. He's all excited because they took the tube out of his nose."

"He had a tube up his nose, and I missed it?"

"If you'd gone to see him you would have seen it."

"No, sorry, I have to work in hospitals, I never visit them. Too much death."

"I thought you liked death. You're a pathologist, after all."

Cronish laughed. "I used to, when I started out. Fascinating in its various forms. But no, not anymore. I'm like the porn fan who gets a job at the adult video store. After a while, it loses its appeal."

Tuesday, June 20

Late in the afternoon, Young was told he was getting a roommate and did he want to move from the door side to the window side. Up to that point he had been alone in his semi-private. Yes, he said, and two orderlies came in and moved him and his bed and slippers and suitcase and get-well cards and magazines and half-empty cans of Mountain Dew to the window side of the room.

An hour later the roommate arrived. His name was Bill Compton. Like Young, he was a big man in his late forties, and after he had settled in, they began a conversation in which they discovered that not only had they both played football, but they had played in the same league at the same time, and may even have faced each other in the same game at Etobicoke Municipal Stadium in 1970, when Young was playing defensive tackle for the police college and Bill was playing offensive guard for an independent team called the Oakville Black Knights. The thought that they may have hunkered down in their three-point stances opposite each other and growled and insulted the other guy's sister made them laugh.

Young and Bill talked about their respective illnesses — Bill had suffered a heart attack on the golf course — and about a whole slate of other things: family and work and dogs and baseball and hockey and how precious life was.

They talked until they were exhausted. When they couldn't talk anymore and were both quiet, Young felt like he'd met a long-lost brother. He promised himself he would look Bill up after they were released from the hospital. Then a nurse came in, gave Young a shot of Demerol in the buttock, and drew the curtain between the beds.

Wheeler waited all day for the report on the crowbar to arrive, and just before she went off shift, she asked Gallagher to phone Fingerprinting and find out what was going on. She was putting on her windbreaker when he appeared at her cubicle. "Wicary says it's been sent," he said.

"I haven't seen it, have you?"

Gallagher shrugged and walked back down the hall.

Wheeler took off her windbreaker and sat back down at her desk. She phoned Fingerprinting to ask Wicary if he could tell her the results, but a taped message stated that the department's hours were eight to four. Wheeler looked at her watch. It was 4:02.

She put her windbreaker back on and went home. She changed into her pajamas, heated up a frozen lasagna, and fed her cat. She tried to watch TV, but couldn't concentrate. Halfway through *Jeopardy*, she sat up straight on her sofa and said, "Wicary says it's been sent." She got dressed and drove back to HQ. She began a methodical search of the offices and cubicles on her floor, but it was 11:30 before she found two sealed envelopes under a pizza box on top of the mini-fridge beside her desk.

The first envelope contained the results of the analysis conducted on the hairs Young had snipped from the fetlock of Mahmoud Khan's stallion, Sam McGee. The report began by stating that most equine DNA profiling was carried out at the request of horse owners who were interested in confirming a horse's pedigree — sometimes mixed-up foal papers or clerical errors concerning horses' lip tattoos caused confusion. And although this type of profiling was usually based on blood work or follicle samples taken from the roots of mane hair, sufficient information was extracted from the hair clippings taken from Sam McGee to establish a DNA match with the hairs removed from the wound on Shorty Rogers' temple.

Alone at her desk, Wheeler nodded. Sarge had been right: Bing Crosby didn't kill Shorty. But who did? Mahmoud Khan? Why would he have ordered a hit on a man who had no immediate influence on what might happen to Mr. Rogers' land? And Trick's determination — courtesy of Evan's hacking — that Khan was hardly the multi-millionaire he claimed to be argued against his being interested in or capable of buying the land even if it did come on the market. Unless Shorty knew that Download's death was a murder and threatened to blow the whistle, or maybe blackmail Khan. Or maybe someone else clipped those hairs from the stallion and planted them on Shorty in order to frame Khan. Still, it was a bit of a stretch to think that someone would conceive such an unlikely plan and go to such lengths. *Well*, she thought, *if Sarge was right about the hairs, maybe he's right about Percy Ball knowing more than he's saying. Every time he's squeezed, Percy comes up with a little more juice. But is there some other reason Khan would want Shorty dead? Am I missing something?* Wheeler shrugged her shoulders and peeled open the second envelope.

Wicary had positively ID'd the man who had attacked Young with the crowbar. A known felon, he had served five years of a seven-year sentence in Collins Bay Penitentiary for assaulting a store clerk with a deadly weapon. As well, there were two convictions for common assault and an acquittal on a charge of forcible confinement after he kept a woman in his apartment for three days before letting her go. An illegal immigrant from Jamaica, he was deported after his last release from prison — a year, time served, for selling crack cocaine to an undercover cop — but his prints on the crowbar confirmed he was back in Canada. Present whereabouts unknown: no address or phone number, no record of recent employment. Thirty-four years old. Five foot eleven, two hundred ten pounds. Brown skin, brown eyes. No distinguishing features. Eric Alonzo Favors.

Dressed as an orderly in a green smock and green shower cap, Eric Favors entered East General Hospital and took the elevator to the sixth floor. He found a cart of rumpled bed linen to push in front of him and kept his head down as he made his way along the empty hall to room 614.

It was almost midnight.

Favors abandoned the cart in the hall. As he entered the unlit room, he accidentally knocked the silencer attached to the muzzle of his .357 Magnum against the door jamb.

From the bed near the door a man's voice said, "Nurse?"

Favors saw the silhouette of a large man sitting up in bed. He raised the gun, aimed, and fired. The shot made a *phump* sound. The silhouette reclined. Favors stepped closer and fired a second bullet into the man's chest, and, feeling for the man's face in the darkness with his left hand, fired another through the right eye. Favors heard footsteps in the hall, tucked the gun under his smock and into the waistband of his jogging pants, stepped out of the room, and almost collided with a nurse walking towards him, who said, "Old man in 620's buzzing me right in the middle of Leno!"

Favors kept his head down.

The nurse looked at him. "Do I know you?"

Favors slid his right hand under his smock.

"Where's your ID?" said the nurse.

Favors hesitated, then turned and sprinted towards an exit sign. He leaped down the six flights of stairs, ran through the lobby and out into the cool night air. He jumped into a tan, ten-year-old Chrysler Cordoba, screeched out of the parking lot, and sped for the free-way. It was only when he was eight or ten miles from the hospital, well on his way back to the Caledon Hills, that he was calm enough to dial his cell phone.

Myrtle Sweet answered. "Well?"

"I done it," Favors said.

"You're sure?"

"Three bullets sure."

"Good."

"614, right?"

"That's right, 614."

"I done good, Miss. I done like you wanted."

"That's good. Straight home now."

After Favors ran off down the hall, the nurse turned the lights on in room 614. In the bed beyond the drawn curtain, Young was awakened by her screams.

Wednesday, June 21

Just before 3:00 a.m., a coroner pronounced Bill Compton dead. The pathologist — Cronish's night shift equivalent — discovered two bullet wounds to the chest and another to Compton's right eye. An evidence man found gunpowder residue on Compton's cheek. Staff Inspector Bateman sent a car to pick Wheeler up at her apartment and gave her the task of preliminary investigation; while Wicary dusted for fingerprints, she interviewed the nursing staff. Photographs were taken. The body bag boys came and went.

Wheeler stayed behind after everyone else was gone. From his bed, Young said, "The nurse who saw him in the hall said he was a black man, five ten, five eleven, stocky build. That description matches the man who came after me at the track."

Wheeler said, "It's the same man, Sarge. I showed the nurse some mug shots, and she picked him out no problem. It's one of the twins who work for Morley Rogers. One of the bodyguards."

"What's his name?"

"Eric Alonzo Favors."

"How'd you ID him?"

"The prints Wicary got off the crowbar. He's got several priors."

"Took that long to make him?"

Wheeler sighed. "You may not remember, Sarge, but the crowbar got forgotten in your van for a while when you got sick, then it took us a while to find your van. Then, unfortunately, the lab report got delayed."

"What do you mean delayed?"

"It got buried under a pizza box."

Young stared at her. "You know what the bottom line is here, don't you?"

"Yes. Mr. Compton's dead because we didn't ID Eric Favors fast enough."

"That's right."

"It was my responsibility. I'm sorry."

"No, no, you got it wrong. How long was the crowbar in my car?"

"I'm not sure, Sarge."

"Fucking well tell me."

"Five days."

"Five fucking days it was in my car. How could I fuck up like that?"

"We all knew about it, we just forgot."

Young rubbed his face with his hands. "All right, listen, we have to move on. Tell Urmson to get back out to the track and find the groom who talked about The Butcher. See what else he knows." He looked up at Wheeler. "What else have we got?"

"The lab report on the horsehairs."

"And?"

"And the hairs you cut off Mr. Khan's stallion match the hairs found in Shorty Rogers' wound."

Young nodded. "So the killer brought them to the track from Khan's farm."

"Do you want me to bring Mr. Khan in?"

"Yesterday I would have said yes, but things have changed. It was Eric Favors who attacked me at the track and it was Eric Favors who killed Bill Compton. Interesting, isn't it, that he lives right next door to Khan's farm. I think he brought the horsehairs into Shorty's barn. I think he killed Shorty."

"But why?"

Young looked up from his bed at Wheeler. "'Cause he was told to."

Wheeler nodded slowly. "Mrs. Caldwell did say that Miss Sweet and one of the twins were, well ... involved."

"So what's your next move?"

"If Miss Sweet is the brains behind Eric Favors, and if I were her, I'd get out of town. There was a bunch of reporters downstairs about an hour ago, so the story will probably make the morning edition. Miss Sweet's going to find out very soon that Eric killed the wrong man. If I were her I'd either be hightailing it, or ... I think I'm going back out to Caledon, see if Mr. Rogers is all right."

"Okay, but get an APB out on Myrtle Sweet and Eric Favors, and listen, if you get the old guy talking, find out about his will."

"Right, but Sarge, if I think the old man's in danger, I'll need to move him."

"You're the boss. And get Mr. Harvey to go after Percy Ball. I mean really go after him. That little prick knows more than he's saying." Young paused. "On second thought, get Urmson to do that while he's out at the track. We can't count on Mr. Harvey. What about Barkas and Trick?"

"Tony's still working on Richard Ludlow. Trick's talking to Stirling Smith-Gower this afternoon."

"Good," Young said. "You got it all under control. Does Debi know about this?" He gestured at the other bed.

"I don't think so."

"Good. Keep it that way."

"She'll find out soon enough."

The two of them sat in silence for a minute, then Wheeler said, "You look a whole lot better than you did a few days ago. Maybe they'll let you out early."

"Not till my bowels kick back in."

"But they took the tube out. Doesn't that mean you're ready?"

"Not yet. Habib says most likely Sunday."

"Well, that's not so bad."

"I farted yesterday and again this morning. I'm close, partner, I'm close."

In her short tenure as trainer Debi had learned that most owners rarely visit their horses; most owners are wealthy and conduct their business by cell phone while, Debi imagined, relaxing poolside or driving out to the golf course. Whether their wealth was earned or inherited, they were almost never seen backstretch unless it was race day for one of their horses or they had a guest, often a business associate, whom they wanted to impress. In fact, Mrs. McDonagh, Bing Crosby's owner, who stopped by every Saturday morning, was Debi's only regular visitor. So what surprised Debi this Wednesday morning as she stepped out of Software's stall with a pitchfork full of manure was not only the coincidental appearance of two of her owners, Mahmoud Khan and Doug Buckley, but the sight of Khan, whom Debi regarded as a cold fish, leaning conspiratorially close to Doug.

The two men stood at the end of her shedrow, out of earshot. Debi watched them for a moment, waiting for them to notice her, but they were absorbed in their conversation. She smiled at their secrecy, unloaded her pitchfork into a wheelbarrow, and returned to Software's stall.

"One hundred thousand dollars," Khan was whispering to Doug, "is of no consequence to a man of means, and my best advice is to hang on to the colt. He has a chance to be a good one, and good ones don't grow on trees. Besides, it is my opinion that the developing nations — and here I'm talking about 'developing' in terms of the thoroughbred horse racing industry — should develop their own breeding stock. The Japanese should be no exception. We must learn to keep what is ours to ourselves, and that goes for Someday Prince, who could very well become not only an important racehorse but also an important sire. In fact, my friend, you might give some thought to syndication."

"You mean sell shares in him?"

"Precisely."

Doug, flushed with a confusion of feelings — social acceptance, well-being, greed — said, "You're a treat, Mr. Khan, but I think I'll keep him to myself." Then, affecting a seriousness incongruous with his salmon leisure suit, white belt, and white shoes, he said, "Any news on my application to the golf club?"

"Patience, my friend," Khan said. Then, lowering his voice, he added, "You did sow the Smith-Gower seed I asked you to, I hope?"

"Oh yes," Doug replied, "but I don't know whether it did any good."

Khan said, "The man's a nuisance. If he gets the animal rights activists agitated, they'll picket and demonstrate and go on hunger strikes and chain themselves to trees until some sort of wetland protection is conferred on the old man's land."

"He didn't actually kill Shorty, did he?"

Khan laughed. "I imagine he could kill a human being a lot easier than he could kill a sparrow, but, no, I doubt very much that he killed Shorty."

"You don't know for sure?"

"The point is, if I have any chance of getting my hands on the old man's land, I have to eliminate that meddling fool from the competition." Khan placed a hand on Doug's shoulder and looked him in the eye. "Listen, my friend, I may have one more favour to ask of you. In fact, I would appreciate it if you would be my guest tomorrow afternoon at Dot Com Acres for a swim and a barbeque, and I'll explain then."

"I'd love to. What kind of favour?"

Khan wagged a finger. "I said we'll discuss it tomorrow afternoon. How's two o'clock sound? Now let's find Debi." He took Doug by the elbow and turned him into the shedrow. "Ah, there she is!" he exclaimed, as she emerged from the stall with another laden pitchfork. "How are you this morning, Miss Young?" he called.

Debi looked around. "Not bad, Mr. Khan." She emptied her pitchfork into the wheelbarrow, dug its tines into the dirt floor, and leaned on it. "What brings you out here?"

"Just passing through. Wanted to see the steeds. Mr. Buckley and I crossed paths in the parking lot."

As they came closer, Doug said, "Any plans for Someday Prince, Debi? I'd like to bring a few friends out to see him run."

"He's entered in the Afleet Stakes a week from Sunday."

"What's the purse?"

"Hundred and twenty-five."

Khan laughed and said, "That's just pocket change to you, my friend. Small potatoes, am I right?"

Doug said, "Every penny counts." Then he said to Debi, in as sincere a manner as he could muster, "Thanks for entering him. I really should do a better job of staying in touch —"

"I didn't enter him," Debi said. "Shorty did, back in May when he claimed him."

"Oh. Well, anyway, maybe you and I could sit down someday and talk about his training schedule and his upcoming races. I have a few ideas —"

"Just for your information, Mr. Buckley, if Prince does win, you don't get the whole hundred and twenty-five. You get sixty percent of the winner's share, less the jock's ten percent, less my ten percent. Sixty thousand dollars. Now, if you'll excuse me, I have to finish my chores." She tugged the pitchfork free of the floor and returned to her mucking out.

Twenty minutes later, when she was leading Gigabyte outside for his bath, she caught sight of Khan and Doug in earnest conversation with Tom Wright over by the walking machine. She puzzled over this as she hosed and sponged the colt.

At 10:00 a.m., when she walked to the track kitchen for something to eat, she saw Wright in line at the cashier, his food tray on the slide in front of him.

"Tom," she said, approaching him, "I see you've found some new friends."

He looked down at his egg sandwich and his quivering cube of Jell-O. "I don't know what you're talkin' about."

"Khan and Buckley."

He looked up at her. "They came to me, not the other way around."

"What did they want?" Debi asked.

"They wanted to know what my rates were, and if I might be interested in trainin' for them." He looked her straight in the eye. "I think they're lookin' for someone with a little more experience."

"What was your answer?"

"I told them I run a small operation, no more'n four horses at a time, but I provide quality care and attention."

"Did you ask them what my rates were?"

"Didn't have to. They told me."

"And then, let me guess, you undercut me."

"My rates are reasonable —"

"You snake. You goddamn snake."

"Young woman, you got a lot to learn. You don't think before you speak. Mr. Khan and Mr. Buckley, they said so themselves. You gotta be polite with owners. They're the ones payin' the bills."

"Just because some jerk wins the lottery doesn't give him the right to tell me how to train horses."

"You gotta give them what they want."

"Brown-nose them, you mean? Like you do?"

"When you're older —"

"What was it? What made you stab me in the back? Was it because Shorty's owners kept me on? You think you've got better claim to his horses than I do? You're just afraid I might be successful someday, and you've been training for what, fifty years, and all you've got is a broken-down old mare."

Tom turned on her, his face red. "Now you listen to me, you upstart. Horse racin's man's work, but you women've wormed your way into everything. Women grooms, exercise girls, even jockeys. But trainin's the last straw. Women can't train."

"Why not?"

"I told you, it's man's work. Always has been. Women are too soft. They don't get enough out of their horses. They —"

"Wait a minute. You treat that mare of yours like a family pet. She's —"

"That's different. She's over the hill. If I had some fresh stock, some young horses with real potential —"

"What? You'd train the hell out of them?"

"No, I'd get the *most* out of them, that's all. You just don't understand that horse racin's a business, and you have to treat it as such."

"And there's no place for women in it."

"You got that right."

"Next thing I know, you'll be telling me we shouldn't have the vote. Barefoot and pregnant, is that what you want? What is it, don't you think we're smart enough?"

"You're not. You're not smart enough and you're not tough enough."

Debi tilted her head. "Goddamn it, Tom, I liked you, I respected you, but you're no different than anybody else." She jammed her thumb into Tom's Jell-O and mashed it around. "Enjoy your lunch."

An hour later, Debi was sitting on a hay bale outside Bing Crosby's stall studying Thursday's *Racing Form* when her cell phone rang. It was Mahmoud Khan.

"I am phoning really just to give you a pat on the back," he said. "You are doing a terrific job under difficult circumstances — taking over the stable so soon after Shorty's death."

"I saw you and Mr. Buckley talking to Tom Wright," Debi said. "Aren't you happy with my work?"

Khan laughed and said, "You are an observant young lady, aren't you? No, no, we were simply having a casual conversation … about breeding."

"Really. Well, if you're ever unhappy with my work, I hope you'll speak to me first."

"No, please, my dear, I am entirely satisfied with your work. You seem to have learned your profession thoroughly."

"Shorty was a good teacher, and I was a good student."

"I wonder," Khan said, "could you please give me a progress report on Gigabyte? What are his prospects?"

Debi hesitated, then said, "I'm sorry to tell you this, Mr. Khan, but he's a dud. He's got bad action and no heart. He's got about as much chance of winning a horse race as I do."

There was a moment of silence on the line before Mahmoud Khan said, "I regret that Shorty was not as forthcoming as you about the horse's limitations."

Wheeler had just returned to HQ from the murder scene at East General Hospital when Priam Harvey showed up.

"Lynn," he said, leaning on her desk, "got a minute?"

"What is it, Mr. Harvey?"

"Give me something to do. Please."

Wheeler looked up at him. His eyes were bleary, his hair was dirty, his clothes looked like he had slept in them, and his hands were shaking. "I can't, Mr. Harvey. Sarge was going to send you out to the track to follow a lead, but he changed his mind."

"What lead?"

"Remember a while ago you were talking about a horse killer in the States called The Sandman?"

"What about him?"

"It seems there's a copycat out at Caledonia Downs. Apparently a groom mentioned it to Big Urmson when he was out there. He referred to him as The Butcher. Sarge wants us to find the groom and see what else he knows."

"I'll do it."

Wheeler shook her head. "I told you, Sarge changed his mind. He told me to send Urmson instead. He's on his way out there now."

"That boy's thick as a brick."

Wheeler favoured Harvey with her brown eye. "He may not be the sharpest, but he comes to work every day and does his job, which is more than I can say for some people."

Harvey stood in front of her, trembling.

"How many drinks have you had today, Mr. Harvey?"

He shrugged. "A couple."

She opened her desk drawer and took a five-dollar bill out of it. "You'd better get yourself another. Take this. Have one on Homicide."

As Priam Harvey walked unsteadily towards the exit, he passed Barkas, who had just reached Richard Ludlow by telephone. Ludlow was loud with anger, and Barkas held the phone several inches from his ear.

"In the first place," Ludlow shouted, "I would remind you that I am president of the King County Golf and Country Club, I am president of Ludlow Real Estate, the premier realtor in the Caledon Hills, and I am a millionaire several times over! While it would be nice to add the old fogey's twelve acres to the golf course, and while

I could easily acquire the permits necessary to build a condominium complex right next to the fourteenth tee, I can certainly live without it, and I certainly wouldn't kill anyone in order to make it happen. But rather than suggest that the Homicide Department is full of cretins, I will instead offer a helpful hint: if you're looking for suspects, you should talk to that controlling bitch the old fogey has living with him. There's a gold digger if there ever was one! And in the second place, my receptionist tells me you and she had quite an interesting little chat the other day. Is this true?"

Barkas said, "We did have a conversation."

"Well, my young friend, Sandi has got it into her pretty little head that I'm a bad boy, and there's tension in this office I could cut with a knife. You wouldn't by any chance have said anything that might have upset her?"

"What could I have said, sir, that might have upset her?"

"Don't be coy with me, son. All I have to do is make a phone call and you'll be out in the rain walking the beat. Or wearing shorts and riding a mountain bike with a whistle in your mouth and one of those idiotic helmets on your head!"

"Sir," Barkas said slowly, clearly, "I am part of a murder investigation. You're not a suspect, necessarily, but you are involved. You knew who Shorty Rogers was, you went to the same meeting he did at his uncle's house, and it's just possible that you might be interested in his uncle's property and that you could, therefore, have had a motive for killing his uncle's sole living heir. Now you tell me you're going to make a phone call and have me put out on the street. Well, be my guest. My badge number is five-seven-four-four, my staff inspector's name is Bateman, and his phone number —"

Ludlow hung up.

* * *

Priam Harvey walked across the street and entered an establishment called Hughie's. As he approached the bar, he took the five-dollar bill Wheeler had given him from the pocket of his trench coat. The bartender said, "What'll it be?"

Harvey's hand was shaking so much the money broke free and fluttered to the floor. Harvey looked at the bartender, and the bartender looked back at him. Harvey swallowed, clenched his teeth, turned, walked out of the bar, recrossed the street, trudged up the long staircase to the Homicide offices, passed through the big double doors, and walked down the corridor to the end near the water cooler, where he found Trick sitting at his computer.

"Arthur."

"Mr. Harvey," Trick said, "what a surprise. I haven't seen you since Camp dropped you on your head."

Harvey lifted his chin. "Where's Lynn?"

"You just missed her. She was getting on the elevator as I was getting off. She's on her way to Morley Rogers' place."

Harvey frowned. "Listen, Arthur, I'm going out to the track this afternoon to see if I can find Percy Ball."

"I already talked to him. A week ago."

"I know, but I want to talk to him myself. He may know something about The Butcher. That little guttersnipe has his nose into everything."

"You short of funds, Mr. Harvey, or did Camp tell you you don't get paid unless you do some actual work?"

"You might think it's something like that. I wouldn't blame you."

"But it's not?"

"No, it's not. Can you get a car for me? And a driver?"

Trick hesitated. "I don't know how much authority I have around here. I'll try."

"Anything I should know before I go out there?"

Trick thought for a moment and nodded. "I talked to Percy about both cases, Shorty's murder and the death of the racehorse. Maybe I was imagining things, but it seemed to me he was telling the truth about Shorty — that he had nothing to do with his death — but he was hiding something about the horse. See what you think. And ask him about The Butcher."

After Harvey left, Trick phoned the offices of the Ontario Avian Protection Association and spoke to Consuela Martin, who informed him that Stirling Smith-Gower's plane had returned from Santiago, via Chicago, and that he had phoned from the airport to say he would stop in at the office on his way home. "I'll be sure to tell him you called," she said.

Shortly before 2:00 p.m., Smith-Gower phoned.

"Thank you for returning my call," Trick said. "Good trip?"

Smith-Gower made a *puh-puh-puh* sound as he lit his pipe. "Wonderful, thank you. Consuela tells me you've been trying to get hold of me. What can I do for you?"

"Well sir, as part of the ongoing investigation into the murder of Delbert Rogers —"

"Murder? I thought it was an accident. I thought a horse kicked him. You're talking about Morley Rogers' nephew, right?"

"Yes sir, Delbert Rogers, or Shorty, as most people knew him. I'm sorry you weren't aware, but Mr. Rogers was murdered."

"My God, I had no idea."

"Well, you've been away. Two weeks, was it?"

"Um, yes, I was away two weeks."

Trick checked his notes. "Actually, sir, the cause of death was upgraded to murder on June 2, five days before you left on your trip."

Smith-Gower emitted a high-pitched sound, which, to Trick's ears, was either a profound sigh or a tremor of hysteria. "My God," he said, "my God! Have you caught the murderer yet?"

"No sir, that's why I would like, if possible, to ask you a few questions."

"You want to ask *me* a few questions? What kind of questions? I didn't even know the man."

"It's true, is it not, sir, that you attended the same meeting at Morley Rogers' house that Delbert — or Shorty — did, on May 17?"

"Yes, I was there, but I never even spoke to him. That was the first and only time I ever laid eyes on him."

"I see. Can you account for your whereabouts late in the evening of May 31, around eleven o'clock?"

"My God, do you think I ... surely you don't think I had anything to do with his murder? My God —"

From his end of the phone, Trick could hear rapid breathing, then a clatter as the phone made contact with a hard surface, and then a heavy thump. He heard a scream, footsteps, Consuela's voice saying, "Mr. Smith-Gower, are you all right?" and then her voice on the telephone, "He's unconscious! What happened? What did you say to him?"

Big Urmson found his way back to Barn 1, where he had spoken to the groom with the cornrows. But he hadn't written the groom's name in his notebook, an oversight that disappointed but didn't surprise him. Had he even asked the groom what his name was? He couldn't remember. *Procedure*, he kept repeating to himself, thumping himself on the side of the head with the heel of his hand. *Procedure.*

He walked up and down both sides of the barn three times, but he couldn't find the kid. Eventually, he wandered outside, where he found a woman walking a lathered, panting horse.

Big Urmson approached the woman and said, "How'd he do?"

The woman stopped. "Who are you?"

Big Urmson said, "Police," and showed his badge.

The woman, who was skinny, wore her bright yellow hair spiked, and had a tattoo of a teddy bear on one sunburned shoulder, said, "So?"

"I just want to ask you a question."

"I'm clean and sober, baby. You got nothing on me."

"I'm not after you," Big Urmson said. "I just want to ask you a question."

"Yeah, I heard your question: 'How'd he do?' In the first place, he's a she, and since you're so curious, I'll tell you. She did shitty. Hasn't earned a penny since we been here."

Big Urmson lifted his hand to pat the horse's forehead. The horse jerked back.

"You want to lose your fingers?" the woman said. "This little thing would just as soon bite you as look at you, wouldn't you, bonehead?"

Red-faced, Big Urmson said, "I talked to a black kid the other day. A groom. He works in Barn 1. I'm looking for him."

"What's his name?"

"That's just it, I don't know his name."

The woman folded her arms across her flat chest. "You don't know his name. Some cop you are. What did he look like? Don't tell me he was black, 'cause you already said so."

"He wasn't very tall. He was thin. His hair was all irrigated."

"All irrigated?" she laughed. "I expect you mean Marvis."

"You know him?" Big Urmson fumbled in his pocket for his notebook.

"Sure, I know him. Marvis Clutterbuck. We both work for the same stable, or I should say worked for the same stable. He's gone."

She started walking the filly again, and Big Urmson hurried after her. "What do you mean gone?"

"He got caught with substance. He's banned from the grounds."

"Where'd he go?"

"Beats me. In this business, people come and go. You don't ask questions. He was a nice enough kid, but I didn't know him real good. Why do you want to talk to him?"

"You heard about Shorty Rogers?"

The woman stopped and looked off into the distance. "I heard about it."

"Well, this kid told me about someone who might be involved … someone called The Butcher. People hire him to kill their horses. For the insurance."

The woman laughed again and rippled the shank she was leading the filly with so that it rattled up against the halter. "I oughta hire this butcher fella to kill this here hayburner."

"You never heard of The Butcher?"

The woman turned and faced Big Urmson. "No, and I'll tell you something else: I wouldn't believe anything Marvis told you, neither. He's nice enough, like I said, but he's pretty much permanently high on crack all the time, or hash." She nodded emphatically. "And that's telling you way more than I should."

Big Urmson said, "Just one more question. Do you know Percy Ball?"

The woman's face darkened. "Yeah, I know him."

"Do you know where I could find him?"

The woman considered the question for a moment. Then she said, "Under a rock someplace."

Priam Harvey stuck his head inside the door at JJ Muggs, discovered that Percy was not there, resisted the urge to have a pint, returned to the car, and told the driver to take him to Caledonia Downs. He was entering the track kitchen when he bumped into Big Urmson coming out of the men's room.

"Mr. Harvey," Big Urmson said, "what are you doing here?"

"I'm looking for Percy Ball," Harvey said. "You seen him?"

"That's why I'm here. Lynn said I was supposed to talk to him."

"She changed her mind. You can head back to HQ."

"But —"

"But nothing, sailor. I've got it covered."

Harvey found Percy Ball nursing a coffee in a far corner of the cafeteria. "The sun's way past the yardarm, Percy," Harvey said, "why aren't you at JJ Muggs?"

"Hey, Mr. Harvey," Percy said, sitting up straight.

"Back from the dead, I see."

"What do you mean? I ain't dead."

"Well," said Harvey, pulling a chair out opposite Percy, "there was a rumour circulating that you were, indeed, dead. Funny thing about that rumour: it started up not too long after I floated you a loan."

"What loan?"

"What loan, you ask? About a year ago I loaned you ninety dollars —"

"No, you never."

"How much was it?"

"Sev ... oh, fuck."

Harvey laughed. "Good gravy, that was easy. I thought you'd give me more of a battle than that."

Percy lowered his head. His blond bangs fell over his red eyes. "It don't matter. I ain't got seven dollars, never mind seventy."

"That is a shame. Have you got anything else to offer — in place of money?"

"Like what? I told you, I ain't got nothin'."

Harvey smiled. "How about some information?"

Percy looked back up. "Information? What kind of information?"

"You give me straight answers to a few questions, and out of the goodness of my heart I will forgive you those seventy simoleons."

"Go ahead and ask."

"Do you know a groom who works for the Four Aces Stable in Barn 1? Kid with cornrows?"

Percy narrowed his eyes. "Sure, I know him. Marvin, or something, but he got ruled off."

"He did, did he? Drugs, I suppose."

Percy shrugged.

"Well," said Harvey, "the important thing is that before he went, he gave a cop some information about someone who kills horses for a living. Someone called The Butcher. Ever hear of such a person?"

Percy looked back down at his shoes. "People keep askin' me questions. That big cop asked me about Shorty's murder, then some nigger in a wheelchair asked me some more, and now you're askin' about somebody who kills horses? You're the third person askin' me questions. I'm gettin' tired of it. Don't tell me you're a cop, too. I thought you were some kind of a writer."

"Seventy macaroons, Percy. You'll be off the hook."

Percy was quiet for a moment, then said, "I've heard people talk."

"What do they say?"

"They mention that skinny bitch works for Four Aces. Tough girl type. Tattoos. Don't know her name. Spiky yellow hair. Come to think of it, her and Marvin worked together."

"Why do people mention her, do you think?"

Percy shrugged. "I don't know. Just what people say, that's all."

"Anything else?"

"No."

"That's not very much for seventy dollars."

"It's all I got."

Harvey sighed. "Very well, I'll reduce your debt by half, but you still owe me thirty-five."

As he walked back out to the parking lot where his driver was waiting, Harvey paused to light a cigarette. His hands had stopped shaking.

Thursday, June 22

"How were I supposed to know there were another mon in the room? You didn't say nutting about no other mon."

"Twice you've failed me. And you've been seen both times. You were seen at the racetrack, and tonight a nurse saw you. You have to disappear."

"What you mean?"

"You have to go away."

"But, Miss, you say we always be together. I don't want to go away. I want to stay here and look after you."

"Look after me? You can't look after yourself. You can't carry out a simple plan that a moron could carry out."

"It were dark, Miss. I couldn't see nutting. Then this big mon sit up in he bed and I figure it him and I shoots him. I were in the right room! How were I supposed to know —"

"Now listen carefully. I'm going to give you some money, and then I'm going to put you on a plane to Montreal —"

"Montreal? But don't they all speaks French down there? How I'm gonna get along where they all speaks French?"

"Well, I guess you'll have to learn to speak French, too, then won't you. Or maybe you won't. It's up to you. Now come on, you have to hurry up and pack. You have to leave today. This afternoon. I'll drive you to the airport."

"Ask Kevin come with me. I might can get lost udderwise."

"No, he stays here. Remember, Eric," and she leaned close to his ear, "you're twins, identical twins. If they see him by himself, they'll think he's you. They'll catch him instead of you. That's why we mustn't tell Kevin what happened. And when you get to Montreal, you mustn't phone me. I'll phone you."

Eric's black skin looked gray in the bright light of Morley Rogers' kitchen. "But he my brother."

"He's your insurance policy is what he is. He stays. Someday you'll thank me. Someday when you and I are sitting under a palm tree with our feet up and those fancy rum drinks in our hands, you'll thank me."

But Eric's mouth was set. "I won't go 'less Kevin go."

"You'll do exactly what I tell you."

Eric shook his head slowly. "I won't go 'less Kevin go."

Myrtle was silent. "Well," she said finally, "if you won't go without your brother, then maybe the best thing is we all go. We'll all go to Montreal and learn to speak French."

* * *

Doug Buckley was early for the barbeque at Mahmoud Khan's, so he parked in the little strip mall across from Dot Com Acres and, when no one was looking, slipped into the adult video store. He read the titles on the boxes and studied the copy and still photos on the back. When he left the store at ten past two, he was carrying a brown paper bag containing a videotape entitled *Pregnant Party Girls*.

Doug rang Khan's doorbell five minutes later, fashionably late by his calculations. Khan greeted him warmly and gave him a whirlwind tour of the stables and the main house. When he proposed a swim, Doug ran out to his SUV and fetched a gym bag containing his bathing suit and a towel from the King Edward Hotel.

After their swim, sitting on the deck in their sunglasses, Khan and Doug sighed with contentment. Khan summoned his daughter Cheyenne and asked her to bring Doug a rye and ginger. The rich brown of Cheyenne's skin, Doug couldn't help but notice, was accentuated by her lime green bikini. Cheyenne slipped into the pool and swam to the far end. Beyond the diving board, beneath a Marlboro umbrella, stood a bar cart.

Khan said, "Let's get down to business, my friend. Yesterday, I told you I had another favour to ask."

Doug watched Cheyenne climb out of the pool. Her brown legs glistened.

"It concerns a rather delicate situation," Khan continued, "one that has the potential to cause me considerable embarrassment."

Doug looked down at his own legs. He wished he weren't so pale.

Khan said, "I have a suspicion the police think I killed Shorty. I wish I *did* know who killed him, then maybe I could protect myself. I've already been questioned by a homicide detective."

Doug looked up at Khan. "I've been questioned, too," he said. "No biggie." He wouldn't want to be as brown as Khan, of course, he wouldn't want to be mistaken for an East Indian.

"Yesterday a young man phoned me at my downtown offices and said he had some information I might be interested in. I asked who he was, but he wouldn't tell me. In any case, I agreed to meet him in a coffee shop on Yonge Street. I gave him a hundred dollars. He wanted more, but I told him that's all I had with me, so he took it. He wouldn't tell me his name, but he did tell me he worked for the police department as a computer technician and that he had been instructed to hack into my financial records."

"What for?"

"I asked him the same question, but he didn't know. The police hadn't told him anything. But that's all right; once I thought about it, the answer was obvious. They wanted to know if I had anything to gain financially by killing Shorty Rogers. What they found out was — and this, my friend, is the source of my embarrassment — I'm close to bankruptcy."

Doug's eyes widened. "But that's impossible. You're a member of the golf club!"

"I'm afraid it's true, due to certain unanticipated downward trends and some poorly considered investments. Ironic, isn't it, that a business mogul such as myself should be toppled by a computer nerd with tape on his glasses."

"What are you going to do?"

"That's where you come in, my friend."

"I'm listening."

"First off, I know it's silly of me to even mention it, but my humiliation will be even greater if news of my financial difficulties should —"

"No fears there, Mr. Khan," Doug said, "I won't tell a soul."

"Well," Khan said, "to be direct about it, I was hoping you might lend me some money."

Doug was taken aback. "Why me? Why not go to a bank?"

Khan smiled. "Unfortunately, my credit at the moment reflects discredit on me. In fact, the bank that holds the mortgage on this farm is preparing to foreclose."

"I don't know what to say. I —"

"It was eight million you won, wasn't it, Doug? If I could have half, say, I would return it all within the year at seven percent interest."

"It's already invested, Mr. Khan, all but five hundred thousand, which I'm going through like a hot knife through butter. My financial advisor said I shouldn't put all my eggs in one basket, so I acquired a diversified portfolio — mutual funds, guaranteed investment certificates, a shitload of Nortel stocks." Doug paused. "And I have to tell you, Mr. Khan, I'm looking at a nine percent return on most of it."

Khan glowered. "Can't you *un*invest some of it?"

Doug hesitated, then said, "I'm not sure it would be a good idea."

"Even a few hundred thousand."

"I don't think it would be wise."

"My friend, can't you see I need your help?"

"I can see that, yes, but if you don't mind my saying so, you seem to be a bit of a risk at the moment."

"Now listen, Doug, once I've purchased the old man's land, I'll be able to develop Dot Com Acres into a world-class breeding operation on a par with anything in Kentucky."

"I'm sorry, Mr. Khan, I'm very sorry, but the answer is no." Doug paused. "On the other hand, once I'm a member of the golf club, I might be in a better position to help you out."

Khan's face was black. "But new memberships take months to process! They have to do a background check, and you need character references. There's an interview."

"For all I know, you haven't even actually put my name before the committee."

"Of course, I have. I —"

"All I know," said Doug, watching Cheyenne walking towards him with his drink on a little round tray, "is that I really want to be a member of the golf club."

"But there's no time, the bank's going to foreclose the end of July!"

"That's all I really want," Doug said, his eyes locked on Cheyenne's thighs.

Wheeler drove up the weedy driveway that led to Morley Rogers' sagging verandah. She was unaware of the conversation taking place next door, on the cedar deck beside Mahmoud Khan's swimming pool, and she was also unaware that five minutes earlier a tan Chrysler Cordoba containing Myrtle Sweet and Eric and Kevin Favors had sped away from Morley's farmhouse.

She parked, climbed the steps of the porch, opened the screen door, and knocked loudly. She heard a car on the highway behind her, turned anxiously, and watched until it passed. She knocked again and heard a shuffling sound. A moment later, the front door opened, and there stood the humped old man she remembered from the videotape. He could barely lift his head high enough to look her in the eye. He wore a soiled white shirt, brown trousers, red suspenders, and plaid bedroom slippers. A cowlick of white hair stood up like static on the back of his small head. The farmer's tan on his face and neck had faded to a sickly pallor.

"Mr. Rogers?" Wheeler said.

"Who are you?" the old man said.

"Detective Lynn Wheeler, sir, Homicide Division, Metropolitan Toronto Police Department. I need to speak to you."

As best he could, Morley looked her up and down. "Come in," he said, and slowly turned and manoeuvred his walker into the living room.

"My grandmother has a walker," Wheeler said brightly, as she scanned the photographs on the walls and the knick-knacks on the mantle, "but hers has wheels. Wouldn't you rather have one with wheels?"

"Of course I would," Morley said, backing up slowly towards an overstuffed wingchair, "but I don't expect she'd allow it. She doesn't want me too mobile."

"You mean Miss Sweet?"

Morley let himself fall into the chair. He fell slightly to one side but didn't attempt to straighten himself. He sighed, his head jammed sideways between his right shoulder and the chair's wing, and breathed rapidly, like a fish in the bottom of a boat.

Wheeler said, "Are you comfortable like that? Do you want me —"

"Don't touch me!" he snapped. Then he narrowed his gaze at her. "What do you want?"

Wheeler stood directly in front of him. "You held a meeting here several weeks ago at which you discussed the possible sale of your property with a number of interested parties. Is that right?"

The old man coughed. "It was a ploy, really. I wanted to see how much interest there was in my land and who the interested parties were, and I wanted them to see each other, to promote competition and raise the value of my land."

"But in the end you didn't sell it."

"I never intended to. Bright's Kill is my home."

"What was Miss Sweet's role at the meeting?"

"She helped me organize it. She knew who all the interested parties were."

"You trust Miss Sweet to handle your affairs?"

Morley considered. "She's good to me, God bless. She's the only person in the world who cares whether I live or die." He blinked and grunted. "So I do, yes, I trust her."

Wheeler said, "We have reason to believe, Mr. Rogers, that Miss Sweet may have been involved in the murder of your nephew."

His eyes swivelled towards her. His breathing was quick and shallow. "What are you saying? Myrtle couldn't possibly —"

"And furthermore that she was involved in the attempted murder on Sunday, June 11, of Detective Sergeant Campbell Young —"

"Nonsense!"

"— and the subsequent attempt on his life on Tuesday, June 20, which resulted in the fatal shooting of an innocent man."

"Get out of my house!"

"Mr. Rogers, you should also know that Detective Sergeant Young's attacker has been positively identified. It was the same man in both incidents. A man currently in your employ by the name of Eric Favors."

"Eric? That's ridiculous."

"His fingerprints were found on a crowbar used in the first attack, and a witness to the second attack, a nurse in the hospital where it took place, identified him from a group of photographs. There's a strong possibility Eric killed your nephew. Are Miss Sweet and Mr. Favors currently on the premises, sir?"

Morley's breathing was laboured, his face still trapped sideways against the wing of the chair. "Myrtle left a little while ago to run some errands. I don't know where Eric is. I haven't seen him all day."

"I'm going to call for backup and a search warrant, Mr. Rogers, and we're going to see if he's here."

The old man was silent for a moment. Then, with considerable effort, he turned his head and let his chin fall to his chest. He said, "The Lord is my shepherd; I shall not want."

"Sir, your life may be in danger. You may be the next victim. If we can't locate Eric, I'm going to have to ask you to leave the house."

"He maketh me to lie down in green pastures —"

"Even if we do find him, you should leave. We don't know who else might be involved. The other twin, maybe."

"— he leadeth me beside the still waters."

After Doug had devoured a thick strip loin and drunk an entire bottle of Wolf Blass Yellow Label, and after he had spoken inappropriately to Cheyenne and ignored the other daughter and giggled at Khan's wife Chandra's turquoise sari, and after he had staggered out to his Ford Expedition and his taillights had disappeared into the darkness, Khan contacted The Butcher by telephone.

The Butcher said, "Are you sure? It's only been a couple of months since the first one."

"I can't wait," Khan told him.

"The insurance company's gonna be suspicious."

"I need the money now."

"What do you need money for? You're a rich man."

"I was a rich man, and I will be again. This is a bad situation, and sometimes the options available to correct a bad situation are limited. Besides, if you do your job properly it will look like the horse died of natural causes, and no one will be the wiser. So just do it."

"How much is the colt insured for?"

"That's none of your business."

"I just wanna know so I can figure my cut. By rights, I should get fifteen percent."

"I'll double what I gave you last time. Ten thousand."

"It's too risky. I'm gonna need more."

"How much?"

"Twenty."

Khan was quiet for a moment. "All right," he said, "but I want it done tonight."

"Tonight? It's already eight o'clock."

"Tonight."

"When will I get my money? Last time, I got half up front."

"What's tomorrow, Friday? I'll have it for you Monday. I'll contact you and tell you where to pick it up."

"I want half up front."

"I paid you last time, didn't I? I'll pay you this time. Just do it!"

By 9:00 p.m., the search squad had covered every inch of Morley Rogers' property. At Wheeler's request, the old man fetched his will and pointed out with a shaking finger the changes he had initialled a month earlier, changes that Myrtle Sweet had composed, rendering her his sole beneficiary.

No sign of Myrtle Sweet or the Favors brothers was discovered. There were no suitcases in the twins' bedroom closets, no wallets or personal identification cards on their bureaus. An open valise was found on the floor of Miss Sweet's bedroom, and several articles of clothing lay across her bed.

The search concluded, Wheeler left with Morley Rogers' will under her arm, but without Morley himself. "I won't leave Bright's Kill!" he declared. "Bright's Kill is my home, and I won't be driven from it. I was born in this house and I'll die in this house, in my bed or sitting on the shitter, God bless, or lying on the same kitchen table I was born on — or under it on the floor, for all I care, among the dust and ashes, in sure and certain hope of the resurrection unto eternal life!"

Before she left, Wheeler posted a uniformed officer outside Morley's front door.

One of the first things The Butcher did when he decided to become a horse killer was purchase a ninety-eight-foot-long Woods outdoor-use extension cord. He cut off the female end with a box-cutter, split the casing of the cord open for about ten feet, and fastened alligator clips to the ends of the exposed positive and negative wires. All he had to do then was attach one clip to the ear of the target horse and the other to its anus. Then, before the horse could shake the clips free, the Butcher would signal his accomplice to plug the male end of the extension cord into the nearest outlet.

Because of his professional approach to his business, The Butcher had no trouble preparing the murder of Gigabyte, the three-year-old colt Mahmoud Khan had paid $375,000 for as a yearling, but who had yet to break his maiden. In thirteen career starts — six at age two and seven at age three — Gigabyte's best finish was a distant third.

It was almost midnight as The Butcher and a young man named Tyler — who was not only The Butcher's accomplice but also his nephew, a skinhead with a brass nose ring and a Manson-style swastika amateurishly tattooed on his forehead — drove through the backstretch of Caledonia Downs Racetrack in The Butcher's rusting half-ton.

"How much are we gettin' this time?" Tyler asked at one point.

"Three hundred," The Butcher said. "Same as last time. And same as last time, I'm lettin' you have one hundred out of that."

Tyler said, "Why are we even killin' the horse?"

"Same as last time. The Paki wants it dead."

Tyler nodded. "Remember last spring when me and you hauled that load of firewood over to his place?"

"What of it?"

"You know the bitch next door that looks after Shorty's old uncle?"

"Black-haired bitch?" The Butcher said.

"Yeah, her. I talked to her, eh, that time. I talked to her over the fence. She said, 'You're a fine-lookin' young man.' She invited me over for lemonade."

"Bullshit," The Butcher said, switching off the headlights of the truck and turning into the lane that led to the barns. "Next thing you're gonna tell me is you fucked her."

"No, no, I didn't, but I'd like to. She's got a nice rack on her. And she was plenty willin', too."

"Bullshit she was willin'."

"No, it's true, Uncle. I went right in the old guy's kitchen with her. I was just gettin' ready to put my hands on her when this nigger walks by the window, and she told me to take off, so I run out the front door, and when I got outside I could hear you yellin' for me, so I run back over to the Paki's place and jump the fence, and you never knowed any different!"

The Butcher studied his nephew in the darkness of the truck. "You seen her since?"

"No I never, but I hope to one day."

The truck came to a stop in the shadows behind Barn 4. The Butcher said, "You stay away from her. She's off limits."

"Why's that, Uncle? You got your brand on her?"

"Just stay the fuck away from her."

The two men unloaded their equipment from the bed of the truck and walked quickly and silently through the moonlight past Barns 5 and 6. Inside Barn 7, they made their way along the shedrow by flashlight until they located Gigabyte's stall. Inside the stall, The Butcher had to hold the flashlight in his teeth as he secured one end of a shank to a vertical bar in the front wall of the stall and fastened the other end to the horse's halter. He attached one alligator clip to the horse's ear and then, moving along the length of the horse, lifted the tail and attached the other alligator clip to the hide close to the anus. Skittish, Gigabyte tried to pull away, but The Butcher patted his neck and spoke soothingly until he settled down. With his free hand he waved the flashlight above his head, and Tyler, standing outside the stall with the male end of the extension cord in one hand, licked his lips nervously.

The Butcher whispered loudly, "On three, boy. One. Two. Three!"

Tyler leaned down and jammed the plug into a wall socket. The Butcher let go of the halter. The horse's eyes bulged, its tongue shot out of its mouth, its legs shook uncontrollably, and it collapsed straight down — like a dynamited building. The Butcher had retreated to the far wall to avoid injury, but the horse went down without incident. Sometimes a horse will hurl itself across the stall, or even once it's down its hooves might thrash wildly, and a man can get killed. One time, down at Richmond Park in Massachusetts, a horse The Butcher was murdering had whipped its head against his shoulder, dislocating it.

The Butcher left the wires clipped for another two minutes before he signalled Tyler to unplug the cord. Then he panned the beam of the flashlight across the horse's still form. Thin plumes of smoke rose from its ears and nostrils, from its open mouth, and, further back, from its anus. The air in the stall stank of burnt hair.

The Butcher removed the alligator clips, wound the extension cord into a tight coil as Tyler did the same from his end, stepped out of the stall, and slid the door closed. The two men walked through the nighttime shadows of Barn 7 until they were outside. As much as possible they avoided the moonlight and made it back to The Butcher's half-ton without seeing a soul.

Friday, June 23

A t 5:45 a.m. Debi discovered Gigabyte dead in his stall. She informed racetrack security, then phoned East General Hospital. By rights, she thought later, she should have phoned Mahmoud Khan first — it was his horse — but even as she was staring at the carcass lying in the straw, its blue tongue protruding, its copper eyes popping, she recalled the telephone conversation she'd had with Khan several hours after he and Doug Buckley had shown up at the barn on Wednesday morning. She remembered his tone as he'd said, "I regret that Shorty was not as forthcoming as you about the horse's limitations"; he had sounded resigned, and he had sounded cold in the way that a man who has decided to take bloody action sounds cold.

Young was sitting in a chair in his hospital room when Debi called. Even though it was only six in the morning, he was up and dressed. In place of the backless blue gowns he'd had to wear for the past ten days, he was sporting a green cotton button-down shirt and an old pair of jeans Debi had brought in for him. With only two days to go until he went home, he was preparing for re-entry into the world. The last of the IVs had been removed the day before — the nurses had used up so many sites on his arms that the last one had been inserted into the back of his forearm, close to the elbow. He had stopped the Demerol shots, too, but his hips were so sore he felt like a pincushion.

The ringing of the phone startled him, and he fumbled the receiver. "What?" he said, when he'd picked it up.

"Daddy," Debi said, "it's me."

"Hi, sweetie —"

"Gigabyte's dead."

"What?"

"Mr. Khan's colt. He's dead."

"What happened?"

"I found him in his stall fifteen minutes ago. His tongue's sticking out, his eyes are bugged out. I saw what Download looked like when he died, Daddy. Gigabyte looks exactly the same. He's been murdered."

Young scratched his head. "I'll see what I can find out. Are you okay?"

"Yes, but I'm mad as hell."

Young searched the corridors of the ward until he found Dr. Habib, who was with an elderly woman in her room. Young waited impatiently outside the door where Dr. Habib could see him. Eventually, Dr. Habib stepped into the hall. "What is it, Mr. Young?" he said. "Can't you see I'm with a patient?"

"You have to get me out of here."

"You want to be discharged?"

"There's an emergency."

"What kind of emergency, if I may ask?"

"It's police business."

Dr. Habib waved his arms and said, "This police business, does it have eyes, does it have ears, can it see that you are still a sick man? You are still under observation, and you cannot go home until I say so, and if all goes well, I will say so on Sunday, no sooner, now please excuse me, I have patients who are very very sick, much more sick than you are."

Young hobbled back to his room. He phoned HQ and asked Desk Sergeant Gallagher to put Wheeler on.

An hour later Wheeler was sitting beside Young at a large table in the patients' lounge. Trick appeared at the door, pushed by Big Urmson and followed by Barkas, who said, "How's she hanging, Chief?" A few minutes later, Priam Harvey arrived, as gray and dishevelled as ever. Young whispered to Wheeler, "What's he doing here?"

"You'll see," she replied.

After briefing the team on the death of Gigabyte, Young asked each member to update him.

Barkas began by describing his last telephone conversation with Richard Ludlow, who had seemed more concerned about his secretary going cold on him than anything else. "He's an asshole, no question," Barkas told the table, "but he didn't kill Shorty, I'd bet my life on it. He's too smart for that. He may not be smart enough to keep his zipper up, like I wrote in my report, but there's lots of rich, brilliant businessmen like that, right? Politicians, too. And anyway, it's not his style. He may be a killer businessman, but he ain't a killer."

Next, Trick described his preliminary conversation with Stirling Smith-Gower's secretary at the Ontario Avian Protection Association, and then his brief but light-shedding chat with Stirling Smith-Gower himself. "Buddy keeled over while I was talking to him on the phone," Trick said, shaking his head. "Just because I wanted to ask him some questions. He's not our guy."

"Wait a minute," Wheeler said. "Doesn't the fact that he fainted make him more suspicious? Like maybe he had something to hide?"

"I don't think so," Trick replied. "I get the impression he's kind of fragile. Delicate, like. He could no more kill a man — or a horse, for that matter — than he could kill a fly. He'd collapse just thinking about it."

Young said, "If that's the case, I'd like to know why Doug Buckley pointed the finger at him."

Wheeler said, "Red herring."

"But why?"

She shrugged. "I guess we'll have to ask Mr. Buckley that question."

When it was Big Urmson's turn, he talked about the information the Four Aces groom had given him concerning Marvis Clutterbuck's disappearance. "Which makes me think, timing-wise, that he might have had something to do with the death of Gigabyte. Marvis disappears; Gigabyte dies. Maybe he had something to do with the death of Shorty Rogers, too."

Young said, "Marvis is the black kid who told you about The Butcher?"

Big Urmson nodded.

Priam Harvey said, "That's interesting. Percy Ball told me we should check out the Four Aces groom. He claims she might be The Butcher."

Young said, "Percy thinks The Butcher's a woman?"

"He thinks maybe."

"You finally talked to Percy?"

"I did indeed."

"Well, what do you think? Is he involved?"

Harvey shook his head. "Percy's far too stupid to mastermind something like this, what with horsehairs cut from the other horse and a horseshoe nailed to a baseball bat. Which reminds me: do we know for certain the murder weapon was a baseball bat? Has it turned up yet?"

"No to both questions," Wheeler said, "but it's our best bet at the moment."

Young was still looking at Harvey. "Anything else on Percy?"

"No, that's it."

Young turned to Wheeler. "What about Uncle Morley?"

Wheeler nodded. "All right, well, we did a sweep of his farm looking for Eric and Kevin Favors and Myrtle Sweet and came up empty, so we put out an APB on them. We just have to hope that wherever they are, they think they're safe, and that they don't know we've ID'd Eric. And then, if everything goes smoothly, when they make their next move we'll be ready."

Young said, "How'd the old man take the news that his faithful employees aren't so faithful?"

"At first, he refused to believe Miss Sweet or Eric could be plotting against him, but I convinced him his life was in danger. He even gave me his will for safekeeping."

Young's eyebrows rose. "What's in it?"

"Everything goes to Miss Sweet."

"What a surprise. Is it a new will?"

"No, it's the old will, but sentences have been crossed out and new ones added. Originally, Shorty was going to inherit ten percent and the rest of it was going to go to various charities, including the institution where his brother Harold was living."

"Harold died last year, right, so the changes must be recent?"

"Harold died six months ago, and the changes to the will were made two months ago. But Mr. Rogers authorized all the changes. He initialled each one of them."

Young compressed his lips. After a moment he said, "If Myrtle knew that Shorty was no longer going to benefit from the old man's will, why would she have him killed? Maybe we're barking up the wrong tree."

Harvey said, "Perhaps she was afraid Shorty'd contest the will. After all, she'd only been with the old man a year or so, and a court might have decided Shorty had better claim. Perhaps she was afraid the initialled changes wouldn't stand up in court."

Wheeler said, "And even though Mr. Rogers initialled the changes, Miss Sweet was the only witness."

Young nodded. "Okay, listen. I'm going to mix up your assignments again, just like I did last time. To confuse the enemy. Barkas, you first: I want you to check out the Four Aces groom, the one Urmson was talking to. See what else she knows. See if she might be The Butcher."

"What's her name?"

Young looked at Big Urmson. "What's her name?"

Big Urmson began to open his mouth, then closed it again.

Young said, "You didn't get her name?"

Big Urmson's eyes gave him away.

Barkas said, "That's okay, she works for the Four Aces Stable, right? I'll find her."

Big Urmson said, "She's got yellow hair, if that's any help, Tony. And a teddy bear tattoo on her shoulder."

Young said, "That's not all, Barkas. I want you to go to the institution in Barrie where Harold Rogers lived. I want to know cause of death."

"I could maybe get that with just a phone call."

"No, I want you to make a personal visit, let them know you're investigating a murder. Just in case we have to deal with them in the future, I want them to know this is serious business. Show a little muscle."

"No problem."

"Wheeler, your job is to find Eric Favors and Myrtle Sweet."

"Right, Sarge."

Turning to Big Urmson, he said, "I want you to go up to the track with Barkas, help him find the Four Aces groom, but then your job ain't human, it's equine. The dead horse, Urmson. I want you to get Forensics involved, I want Cronish to scope the horse. I know he's not a vet, and more than likely he'll put up a fight, but tell him it's important. Tell him to look for burn marks on the horse's ears and asshole. And singe marks. Can you remember all that?"

"Ears and asshole, Sarge. I got it."

Harvey said, "Anything for me?"

Young regarded him. "You really back on board?"

"Yes," Harvey said, "I'm back on board."

Young looked at Wheeler and raised his eyebrows. She said, "He came to me yesterday wanting to help. I told him no, like you said, then all on his own he went out to the track and, like you just heard, he got Percy Ball to give us the Four Aces groom."

"Wait a minute," Young said. "Let me get this straight. Urmson went to the track looking for the black kid who told him about The Butcher, couldn't find him, and ended up, quite by accident, talking to the Four Aces groom, the woman with the yellow hair and a teddy bear on her shoulder, who Percy ends up ID'ing as The Butcher. Is it just me, or would you say it's from the it's-a-small-world department that Percy should give us somebody we didn't even know existed till Urmson stumbled on her a few minutes earlier?"

No one said anything.

"What I'm getting at," Young continued, "is maybe there's a connection between this woman and Percy. Check it out, Barkas."

"Right, Chief."

"Now, what about Mahmoud Khan? We haven't talked about him yet. If I'm right that he was behind the death of the first horse, is he crazy enough to do it again? Is he that desperate for money, or is someone trying to frame him?" Young looked at Harvey. "Okay, you've got Khan. I want you back out at the track snooping around. See what you come up with. But remember, you're not a cop, so stay in the shadows." Young paused to take a breath. "Now, last but not least, Doug Buckley."

There was silence around the room.

Finally Wheeler cleared her throat and said, "I don't believe you assigned him to anyone, Sarge, and neither did I. Sorry. An oversight on my part."

Young looked at her for several seconds, then turned to Trick. "See if you can find him. If you're right that Smith-Gower didn't kill Shorty, then why did Buckley make a special trip to McCully's just to put me on his trail."

Trick nodded. "I'm on it."

"Okay, that's it."

As people were filing out, Young held Wheeler back. "I know Bateman made you team leader while I was under the weather. I shouldn't horn in like this —"

"Sarge," she said, holding up a hand like a stop sign, "I'm glad you're back. I'm delighted you're back."

After she hurried off down the hall to catch up with the others, Young began his slow, shambling journey back to his room. He had to lie down; his heart was jumping like a jackhammer.

Saturday, June 24

Doug liked to be touched. He liked to be handled. For the last few years that he'd lived with his family, he had seen a massage therapist every three or four months for treatment of lower back stiffness. The therapist, a sixty-year-old Latvian woman with hands like meat hooks, received her clients in the basement of the bungalow she and her retired husband owned only a few blocks from Doug's house. While she was pouring baby oil over his back and kneading his muscles, she would talk aimlessly about her grandchildren, or the night school reiki class she taught, or the role God played in her life. Doug only half-listened; he concentrated on the enjoyment he received from being manipulated. He felt like a baby, safe in the capable hands of this much older, very maternal woman.

After he won the lottery and during the time he lived at the Airport Hilton, however, his interest in being touched changed. He wanted something sexual. He could afford it, after all, so why not? One night — a night he'd already mentioned to Young — when he suggested to the masseuse he'd ordered from room service, a masseuse he'd used twice before and now asked for by name — Sigrun — that she might be more comfortable if she removed her blouse, she smiled and said, "I've forgotten my lotion, I'll be right back," and left the room. Ten minutes later Doug was visited by the house detective, who told him he had fifteen minutes to vacate the premises.

Doug was angry and humiliated. He believed that a man of his wealth shouldn't be treated like a common pervert, and he felt an almost overpowering compulsion to wreak havoc. He didn't know how or when he would do it, but the desire to do evil was taking definite shape in his mind. For almost two weeks after moving to the King Edward Hotel, he agonized. He regarded himself as a pillar of society — he was a Cub Scout leader, after all — but finally he couldn't contain himself any longer, and he did something he'd never done before in his life: he hired a prostitute.

After supper in the hotel dining room, he went for a walk. It was drizzling, but he didn't care, and after a few blocks he saw a woman standing under a pink parasol at the corner of King and Jarvis. He approached and said hello. She smiled and asked if he was looking for company.

He escorted her back to the hotel and up to his room, offered her a drink, and proposed they relax on the sofa before "getting down to business," as he put it, smiling in what he hoped was a worldly way. She responded by telling him that she charged one hundred dollars an hour, so he — "Ryan," as Doug had decided to call himself — should plan his entertainment accordingly. "My name, in case you're interested," she said — she was half-white, half-Filipino, maybe twenty years old — "is Shar-Day."

"Welcome, Shar-Day," he said. "Mi casa es su casa." As he sat down beside her on the sofa, he spread his arms to include the entire suite. "And, Shar-Day, I want you to understand something right from the git-go. Money is no object."

For the first time since entering the suite, she took a real look around. The walls were marble, the decor oriental, the layout split-level. "Wow," she said.

"Three thousand dollars a night," he said.

"You can't be serious!"

His room — or, more correctly, rooms, or, more correctly still, the Royal Suite — boasted a sunken living room featuring the twelve-section, three-sided sofa complete with seventeen pillows — Doug had counted them — upon which they were making themselves comfortable, a spacious dining room with a glass table and seating for twelve, a complete kitchen that dwarfed Doug's kitchen at home, two bathrooms, and a master bedroom with a four-poster bed and a computer keyboard whose functions Doug was unable to fathom.

"Catherine Zeta-Jones and Michael Douglas stayed in here not long ago."

"In here?"

"Yes indeed. The bellboy told me. Catherine probably sat right where you're sitting. Do you want some nuts or something?"

"Who else stayed here?"

"Who else? Well — again, this is all according to the bellboy — Céline Dion and her husband used it last year. Farther back, Marlon Brando, Elizabeth Taylor, the Beatles."

"The Beatles? Wow."

"Shar-Day," Doug said earnestly, patting her hand, "I feel like we're really getting to know each other, and I'd like you to stay the night." He stood up and walked up out of the sunken living room, across the dining room, to the mini-bar. He brought back two glasses, the ice bucket, airplane bottles of scotch, gin, and vodka, a can of tonic water, and two Heinekens, and placed them on the coffee table beside a dragon's head fruit bowl.

As he sat back down beside her, she said, "You must be rich."

He couldn't resist telling her that he had won the lottery, that he was a millionaire many times over.

Her attitude changed. If she had been formal and businesslike on the street, she was all his now. She snuggled close to him. She nuzzled into his armpit. "Anything," she whispered.

"What?" Doug said as put his feet up on the coffee table.

"Anything you want me to do, I'll do it."

Doug didn't know what to say. He had waited all his adult life for a woman to say those words to him.

"Tell me what you want me to do."

Several images flashed across his mind's eye.

She stood up. "Do you want me to dance for you? Do you want me to be your private dancer?" She started to move rhythmically, sensually, to a music only she could hear. As Doug watched, she began to strip. She was wearing open-toed high heels. She kicked them off. She wriggled out of her jade miniskirt. She turned around so that Doug could see her black thong panties disappear between her buttocks. She slipped a finger under the waistband and peeled them down. He watched as the panties clung between her legs before they let go. She sat down bare-assed on the coffee table, pulled her panties free of one foot, hooked them on the big toe of the other foot, then sling-shot them eight or ten feet across the room where they coiled like a traumatized snake on the broadloom. She unbuttoned her blouse, slipped it off, and tossed it to him on the sofa. She wasn't wearing a bra. Her breasts were small with almost no areolae, but her nipples stood out like cocktail wieners. She got down on all fours and backed towards him, waving her fanny as she came. "Maybe you want it like this?" she said, looking back over her shoulder. "Your wildest fantasy, Ryan, is my command."

She let him have a good long look at what he'd always wanted to see, to study, to examine at his leisure. Here it was spread out before him like a feast, ready and waiting, and he was as soft as a baby. Panic prickled across his shoulders and down his spine.

"I'm sorry," he said, "I don't feel well. I think you'd better go." He dropped four fifty-dollar bills on the coffee table. He walked up out of the sunken living room, across the foyer, through the master bedroom, and entered the bathroom, locking the door behind him. He sat on the toilet and covered his face with his hands. *What a fool*, he thought. *She must think I'm a fool.*

When he came out twenty minutes later, she was gone. So were the four fifties, and so were the two cans of Heineken and the three tiny liquor bottles. So was the dragon's head fruit bowl.

Mahmoud Khan took a call on his cell phone out by the swimming pool. "Khan here," he said.

"Mission accomplished."

"Well done, my friend."

"I want my money."

"You'll have it."

"I want double what we said."

"Don't be ridiculous. We agreed —"

"And a month from now I want another five."

"Are you out of your mind? I don't —"

"What I'd really like is a reg'lar allowance. Five thousand a month. That's sixty thousand a year. Sixty thousand a year I could live fairly comfortable."

"Listen to me and listen very carefully: I don't have that kind of money. Why do you think I hired you? And even if I did have that kind of money, what makes you think I'd let a petty criminal like you blackmail me?"

There was a moment of silence at the other end of the line. Then, "That's an easy one, Mr. Khan. 'Cause if you don't pay me, I'll leak it to the Jockey Club that you hired me to kill your horses."

"We're on the phone, damn you! Do you want —"

"And while I'm at it, I'll leak it to that fancy country club of yours, and your insurance company, too, and whoever else I can think of. Your Paki wife and your Paki daughters."

When he spoke again, Khan's voice was murderous. "And who, my pathetic friend, do you think they're going to believe — scum like you, or a man of means?"

"Well, my guess is once they hear the tape I'm makin' of this call, they'll go with scum like me."

Sunday, June 25

Young hadn't been outside in eleven days. As he stood in front of the hospital waiting for Debi, he breathed in deeply, and even though the air he was inhaling was normal city air, redolent of car exhaust and industrial pollution, it was elixir to him.

Debi picked him up in his minivan, and when they arrived at his apartment, he headed straight for the La-Z-Boy and collapsed into it.

From her mat on the floor Reg opened one eye. Then she struggled to her feet, waddled over, and lay down beside him. "Long time no see," Young said, looking down at her. "You smell like old socks."

From the kitchen Debi said, "I picked her up from Uncle Artie's this morning and brought her back so she'd be here when you got home. I don't think he bathed her."

"He can barely bathe himself, how's he going to bathe her? Besides, I never bathe her either."

"I picked up some lunch things, some treats."

"Oh, yeah? Like what?"

"Like tomato rice soup. Like fresh Italian bread and salted Lactantia. Like some Schneider's summer sausage, sliced thin like you like it. Some hot mortadella. Some creamy havarti."

"Not light, I hope."

"Of course not light. This lunch is supposed to be bad for you, right?"

"Right. Where's Jamal?"

"I also stopped at Baskin-Robbins and picked up some of that cherry ice cream you like so much."

"Where's Jamal?"

"Today's *Racing Form*'s on the little table beside your La-Z-Boy."

"Where's Jamal, for fucksake?"

The rattle of cutlery. "What?" Debi stepped out of the kitchen where she could see him. "What did you say?"

"You heard me. Why won't you answer my question? Where's my grandson? Is he still scared of me? How come you don't swear anymore?"

She put two plates down on the kitchen table. "I decided to quit swearing. I have to set an example for Jamal. I made up my mind while you were in hospital. It's no different than quitting anything else. Smoking, for example. Or drinking. I've been clean for almost four days."

"Don't you think you're overdoing this motherhood thing?"

"No, it's for the best."

Young shrugged. "Suit yourself. So where is he?"

"He's at home with Eldridge."

"Why didn't he come with you?"

"He's still a little antsy about seeing you. He still prays for you."

"Well, that's good. I need all the prayers I can get."

"He's afraid you won't know him."

Young scratched his ear. "Of course I'll know him. Why wouldn't I know him?"

"I'll see if he'll come tonight."

"You'll see? Just bring him. Who's the boss in your house, a six-year-old?"

After Debi left, Young phoned Trick. "I'm back."

"Welcome home, brother."

"You watch the hockey game last night?"

"No, I lost interest months ago."

"Can you believe we're still playing hockey on June 24?"

"I know, it's crazy."

"And was Canada represented in the Stanley Cup? No, we weren't. And Detroit — an 'original six' team — manages one shot, one shot, in the third period, and ends up not only losing but being swept by New Jersey. The New Jersey Devils win the Stanley Cup. New Jersey, for fucksake. What do they know about hockey in New Jersey? All they know about is gangsters and pollution."

Trick said, "Don't they call it the garden state?"

"Garden state, my ass. You ever been there?"

"No," said Trick, "have you?"

Doug Buckley had a drink with Mahmoud Khan in the clubhouse bar at Caledonia Downs. He was feeling very dapper in his powder blue leisure suit, white belt, and white shoes. After some small talk, Khan said that he had another proposal for Doug.

"I'm sorry, Mr. Khan," Doug said, "but I thought I made myself clear: I can't lend you any money."

"No, nothing like that," Khan said quietly. "This is something different." He steepled his fingers in front of him. "It involves the commission of a crime."

Doug stared at Khan for a moment, then closed his eyes. *You want to be a player*, he said to himself, *you've always wanted to be a player, this is your chance. You want to play with the big boys, don't quit on yourself.*

He opened his eyes. "I might be interested," he said. "What's my motivation?"

"My word, sir, on the heads of my daughters, that you will be a chartered, tenured, lifetime member of the King County Golf and Country Club by first of September."

Doug looked at him carefully. "What do I have to do?"

Khan leaned towards Doug and whispered, "I am being bothered by a small-time hoodlum. He's threatening to blackmail me. I want you to threaten him back."

"Threaten him back?"

"If necessary, rough him up."

Doug began to laugh. "You mean like break his legs?"

"You're a strong man, I can tell," Khan said. "A gym teacher, weren't you?"

Doug's hands began to tremble. He trapped them between his knees below the table's edge. He remembered the whore, how badly he'd wanted to fuck her, how he'd gone soft.

"He's not a big man," Khan said. "You're much stronger than he is."

Doug chewed at his lip. "There's something else I want. I want the golf club membership, but I want something else, too."

"Name it, my friend."

"I want Cheyenne."

Khan blanched.

"I'll marry her, of course."

"She's seventeen years old." Khan's voice was tight.

Doug laughed nervously. "I'm sure girls become brides much younger than that where you come from, but I'll wait till she's eighteen. I'll have my divorce by then. I'll be your business partner *and* your son-in-law! What do you say?"

Several seconds passed before Khan replied. "Tonight," he said. "It has to happen tonight."

At seven that evening, there was a knock at Young's door, and he and Reg both struggled to their feet and made their slow, plodding way across the living room.

It was Debi, Eldridge, and Jamal. Debi was carrying Jamal, whose face was buried in her neck.

"Hey, Captain," said Eldridge. "How you feelin'?"

"Not so bad. Any winners lately?"

"Had one yesterday for Peter Mayfield. You know the horse. Baby Brother. Peter claimed it off Shorty last year."

Debi said, "Baby was my favourite horse in the whole world."

Young was watching Jamal. "Well, I'm glad you had a winner. You still riding in the mornings?"

"Yes, I exercise all of Peter's horses, and I pick up a few others. I think I'm catchin' on with Jim Sylvester's stable."

"That's a good outfit," Young said. "That's a good barn. Well, come in, come in. Me and Reg were just watching *Sesame Street*."

The boy's face came out of its hiding place.

"Big Bird got his beak stuck in a jar of peanut butter," Young went on, "and Bert and Ernie had to help him get it unstuck."

The boy's eyelids flickered.

"Then they went to Mr. Hooper's store and ate some ice cream."

Jamal looked at him.

"The show's over now, so I was just going to have a bowl of ice cream myself. Your mom put some Cherry Jubilee in my freezer when she came by this afternoon. You like Cherry Jubilee, don't you?"

The boy nodded, unsmiling.

"Would you like some?"

The boy put his arms out, and Young took him and carried him into the kitchen.

Doug Buckley was standing in front of a restaurant near the St. Lawrence Market. He wasn't dressed in one of his pastel leisure suits for this occasion; he was wearing blue jeans, a windbreaker, and a ballcap.

Doug didn't know the name of the man he was waiting for, but Mahmoud Khan had told him what he looked like. Doug had called the man at 8:00 p.m., using the number Khan had given him, and told him he had been instructed by Mr. Khan to deliver an envelope. When the man, who sounded as if he had been asleep, asked what was in the envelope, Doug said it was payment for a job well done. The man's spirits were raised momentarily, but when Doug told him where and when to meet him, he went sour.

"Tonight at ten? Maybe I got somethin' planned, ever think o' that? You can't just expect a person to drop ever'thin' —"

"Do you want the money or not?"

"But I'm way up at the north end of the city. The market's way downtown. Why do I have to come all the way downtown?"

"Do you want the money?"

"How am I gonna get there? A cab's gonna cost me a fortune."

"Don't you have a car?"

"Maybe I do, maybe I don't. Maybe I don't like drivin' on the freeway, ever think o' that? Maybe I've had a few drinks."

"That's your problem," Doug said. "Do you want the money or not?"

"Okay, okay. Where do I go? How will I know who you are?"

"Brown jacket, Yankees cap. In front of The Golden Griddle at the corner of Front and Jarvis. Ten sharp. Don't be late." He hung up.

Doug had been waiting half an hour. It was almost ten-thirty. He and Shar-Day, who was standing kitty-corner across the intersection in the light of a streetlamp, had been eyeing each other for some time when a taxi pulled up to the curb a short distance away.

A man climbed out of the taxi and stood for a few seconds looking up at the lights and tall buildings. Doug recognized him immediately from Khan's description. The man looked like a little boy lost in the big city. His eyes met Doug's, he did a double take, and he strode towards him saying, "Thirty-six dollars for a fuckin' cab ride. What the fuck's goin' on with this city?"

Doug said, "Come with me," and led the man away from the restaurant, across the street, and towards the market.

"Where we goin'?" the man said, hurrying to keep up.

"Don't worry," Doug said. "It's not far."

"You're Mr. Buckley, right?" the man said. "I seen you at the track."

Doug tugged the brim of his Yankees cap low over his eyes. "You must be confusing me with someone else."

"No, I never forget a face, you're Mr. Buckley."

"Come on, it's not far."

"But why do we gotta go anywhere? All you gotta do is gimme my money."

"There's something extra that comes with it."

"Whattaya mean, somethin' extra?"

They crossed in front of the market, which was housed in a vast old warehouse.

A few security lights inside showed the empty booths, the barren tables. On Saturday mornings, the place was abuzz with activity — the fishmongers, cheesemongers, and vegetable vendors, the hawkers who set up their wagons outside the building and sold hats, hubcaps, homemade greeting cards, quilts, candles, rag dolls — but tonight no one was there, and the eerie silence of the place made the man edgy.

"Whattaya mean, somethin' extra?" he repeated, beginning to puff behind Doug's fast pace.

"Just a little farther," Doug said, and turned down an alleyway that ran the length of the market. It was so dark it was difficult to see, but he sprinted ahead. Behind him he could hear the man bang into a trash can and curse. When he came to the far end of the building, Doug turned left, and a few feet later turned left again into a truck bay. A bare bulb on the ceiling provided faint illumination. There was an empty oil drum and a small mountain of garbage off to the side of the bay. Inside the oil drum was a metal baseball bat.

As the man came chugging around the corner, he called, "Where are you?"

Doug said, "I'm right here," and turned to face him, the bat in his hands.

The man stopped. He breathed in sharply.

"If you know what's good for you," Doug said, sliding one hand up and down the barrel of the bat as he approached the man, "you'll stay away from Mr. Khan. If you go anywhere near him or try to blackmail him —"

"Gimme my money," the man wheezed. "I know who you are."

Doug raised the bat. "I don't want any trouble with you. My job's just to tell you —"

"Gimme my fuckin' money," the man snarled, "or I'll tear your fuckin' throat out."

"There isn't any money. I'm just —"

"What!" The man leapt at Doug, who stepped to the side, swung the bat, and caught him sharply on the back of the head. The man fell to the ground, lay there for several seconds, then rose to his hands and knees. Khan had told Doug just to scare the man, at most to break a few bones, but the man had identified Doug, so Doug lifted the bat high above his shoulder and brought it down solidly on the man's skull. The sound would have sickened most people, but it had the opposite effect on Doug. It exhilarated him. It was a bell tolling a new chapter in the story of his life, a new beginning, and to keep the bell ringing he raised the bat over his shoulder again — like a man chopping wood — and swung it down, raised it again and swung it down, raised it again and again — viciously, ecstatically — until the man's head collapsed like a pumpkin.

Panting, Doug leaned on his knees to catch his breath.

He dragged the man's body deeper into the truck bay.

He overturned the oil drum, stuffed the man's body into it, feet and hands foremost, stood it upright, and wheeled it on a tilt back into the corner.

He picked up the blood-stained baseball bat, wiped it on some crumpled sheets of newspaper, exited the truck bay, rounded the corner into the darkness of the alleyway, and began a concentrated stroll towards the lights of Front Street. *Breathe*, he said to himself, swinging the bat like a man in the on-deck circle, *breathe*.

* * *

Crawling out of his den of leaking, fuming garbage bags, a grimy young man struggled to his feet, shuffled over to the oil drum, and felt around for the wallet he hoped he would find on the protruding ass-end of the body. He found it, extracted the twenty dollars that were in it, picked up a Yankees cap he spied on the floor, placed it on his head, tugged it low over his eyes, said, "Who's a happy camper?", then began a sequence of ballet movements that carried him across the blood-stained floor of the truck bay and into the street.

Monday, June 26

Young was sitting in his La-Z-Boy waiting for *Geraldo* to start. According to the listings in the *Toronto Star*, the theme for the day was "breasts." Other topics for the week included "mothers and daughters in love with the same man," "satanic cults," and "fat-free living." Scheduled for Jenny Jones were shows on former child TV stars and interracial sex. Maury Povich was featuring unhappy reunions and bickering twins.

The phone rang.

"What?"

"It's me. How's the patient?"

"Not bad. Say, you notice anything wrong with Reg when she was with you? She seems kind of sickly."

"Nothing except her dragging her ass across my carpet."

"No, not that. She hasn't been eating. She just lies on her side, and it looks like she's putting on weight."

"Don't look at me. All I fed her was what I was told to feed her. Listen, I got some news."

"Where are you?"

"Homicide."

"So what's so important you'd tear me away from *Geraldo*? They're talking about breasts today. Maybe they'll show some."

"Percy Ball's been murdered."

"What?"

"A junky found him behind the market."

"No shit."

"No shit, brother."

Young sat forward and hit "mute" on the remote. "What happened?"

"Details are sketchy at this point, but it looks like he was beaten to death. The killer folded him up like a suitcase and stuffed him in an oil drum."

"Junky see it happen?"

"He says he did. He says he was having a little siesta near the loading docks when these two men arguing woke him up. Then a minute later one of them was beating the crap out of the other with a baseball bat. After the victim — well, Percy — was dead and the killer took off, the junky went up to 51 and reported it."

"Very civic-minded of him." Young pondered. "You say Percy was killed with a baseball bat. Maybe Eric Favors did it. We know Eric killed Bill Compton, and it's still a possibility that Shorty was killed with a baseball bat. Junky get a good look at the killer?"

"No, he says it was too dark."

"Could he tell if the killer was black?"

"I don't know if he was asked that."

"Well, tell 51 to ask him."

"Okay, but there's something else, too."

"What?"

"Well, the junky arrived at 51 wearing a Yankees cap, but our colleagues in blue realized it was too clean to be his. They know him well. His street name's Filth."

"A Yankees cap."

"Yeah, at first he claimed it was his, but eventually he gave up that he'd found it at the scene."

"Did he take anything else? Percy have any money on him?"

"No, his wallet was on the ground, but there was nothing in it besides his driver's licence."

"How about Filth? They search him?"

"Yeah, they did. He had some change in his front pocket and two fives and a ten in his hip pocket."

"Tell them to dust the money."

"I expect they've already thought of that."

"It'll at least tell us if it was Percy's. And if it was, then maybe Filth's the killer. What did *he* say about the money?"

"He said it was his."

"No surprise there."

"But the boys at 51 don't think he's the killer, Camp. Apparently, this guy's scared of his own shadow."

"Well, if they're right, and they probably are, then Percy got hit for some other reason, and I'll bet dollars to donuts it has something to do with Shorty's death."

"Or the horse murders."

"Right. But wait a minute. You said this Filth guy found him behind the market? You mean St. Lawrence Market, right, where I buy my farmer's sausage?"

"The ones you hang in your kitchen and gross everyone out with?" Trick said. "Yeah, that market."

From his chair, Young cast his eyes towards the kitchen. He could see the sausages hanging from their knobs. They'd been there since before he went into hospital. They'd be good and hard by now. His mouth watered. He said, "But that's way downtown. What was Percy doing downtown? He never wandered any further from the track than the nearest bar."

"Beats me."

Young thought for a moment. "I'm coming in. I'll be there in twenty minutes."

"No, wait. You're supposed to be resting. You're not supposed to do anything for a week."

"Tough shit. And listen, when you phone 51, tell them to look for hair in the ballcap. If it wasn't Filth's ballcap, maybe it was Percy's, and if it wasn't Percy's, it was probably the killer's. Maybe it was Eric Favors'."

"I'm sure they're checking it out, Camp, they're not idiots down there."

"Just tell them."

"Now I'm sorry I phoned. I just wanted to bring you up to speed."

"That's okay, you did the right thing." Young made an effort to get up out of the La-Z-Boy.

"Camp," Trick said, "don't come in yet. It's too early."

As he stood up Young felt something pull in his stomach. A staple, maybe. He fell back into the chair. He sat there for a few seconds: there wasn't much pain, but his heart was throbbing, and he could feel how weak he was. He probably couldn't make it to the corner store, never mind HQ. "Okay," he said, "you're right. But what's today, Monday? I'm coming in on Wednesday. Warn the troops."

Doug Buckley was in his suite at the King Edward Hotel. He was on the phone to Mahmoud Khan. "Yes, it's done, but there was a slight complication." Doug, who had never smoked in his life, was puffing on a cigar.

He had acquired the habit the night before while sitting in The Consort Bar after returning to the hotel following the murder of Percy Ball. He had felt a need to calm down and an urge to celebrate, so he had ordered a Montecristo No. 4, because the menu notes described it as "very discrete in the floral range" and "enjoyable at any hour of the day." The cigar had cost him twenty dollars, and the Scotch he had with it — a twenty-five-year-old Macallan — had cost thirty-five dollars. He had stood alone in the bar admiring the Mappemonde wallpaper and a display of antique radios and birdcages and typewriters, and he had felt a surge of well-being. He'd enjoyed himself so much that he'd bought a second cigar to take to his room, which he was smoking now, as he spoke to Khan.

"What kind of complication?" Khan asked. "Remember, we're on the telephone, so we must be careful what we say to each other. No names. We don't want any of our competitors to gather any information that might prove useful to them."

"Quite right, Mr. ... umm ... Mr. K."

Khan laughed. "I repeat, what kind of complication?"

"There was a problem last night. The man you sent me to meet took a lot of convincing."

There was a pause. Khan said, "Can you be more specific?"

"Well, let's just say he won't bother you anymore."

There was another, longer pause. Khan said, "I'm not sure exactly what you mean, but it sounds as though you got the job done."

"Oh, I got the job done."

"Well, good work, my friend. Tomorrow morning I'll see how things are going with the membership committee."

"Thank you, Mr. K."

"I'm sure you'll be up at the club swinging your Big Bertha in no time."

"I appreciate that."

"Oh, I should tell you I had another chat with our prospective trainer this morning."

"Who? Oh, you mean Tom Wri — "

"No names, my friend, can't you remember that?"

Doug tapped the ash off the end of his cigar onto the carpet. "Sorry, Mr. K."

"Anyway, I'm satisfied he'll be a worthy replacement for our current trainer, who is too independent by half, too stubborn and willful, and as well she's the daughter of a man I would rather avoid. So I think the new candidate may be the answer. He's malleable. He'll follow instructions without questioning them, which is what I like in an employee. It's what I like in you, as a matter of fact."

"No offense, Mr. K., but I'm not your employee. We're more like partners." Doug sucked mightily at his Montecristo.

"Equal partners?" Khan said.

Before Doug could answer, he began to choke on the cigar smoke. He coughed for a solid thirty seconds, and when he was finished, his eyes red and his nose running, he said in a voice that squeaked and broke, "Well, maybe not equal partners — not yet — but partners just the same. Not to mention that in a year or so I'll be your son-in-law." He tried to clear his throat, but his voice remained falsetto. "It's sort of like the old barter system: I give you something, and you give me something in return."

"And speaking of that something I wanted from you: you're sure there's no possibility the third party might file a report that could make trouble for us?"

"I'm sure, Mr. K. In fact, I'm positive."

"You're making me nervous, my friend. Is he ..."

"Yes, Mr. K.," Doug giggled, "he's no longer with us."

Khan was silent.

"Mr. K.?" Doug said.

"I think it best if we conclude this conversation. I'll call you in a day or two."

"Righty-o. But before you go, could I ask a small favour?"

"What is it?"

"Say hi to that beautiful Indian princess of yours."

Khan swallowed. "I have to hang up now."

"Notice that I didn't use her name. I'm trying to be careful here, like you said."

Khan said, "One final question, just to put my mind at ease. I can assume, can't I, that no evidence of any kind was left at the place where you and our friend met?"

"No problem, Mr. K., it's all looked after."

But after Mahmoud Khan hung up, Doug Buckley began to chew at a thumbnail. He had disposed of the baseball bat — he'd windmilled it deep into a vacant lot off Eastern Avenue — but when he'd awakened this morning and dressed to go down to the lobby to buy a newspaper, his Yankees cap was nowhere to be found.

Tuesday, June 27

Trick phoned Young to see if he was well enough to go out for a few beers.

"I don't know," Young said, "I'm still feeling kind of iffy."

Trick said, "I figured if you're okay to go to work tomorrow, you'd be okay to go to McCully's tonight."

"To be honest with you, I don't want to leave Reg alone."

"She still won't eat?"

"No, all she does is lie on her side. And worse, if I try to pet her, she snarls at me. She's never snarled at me in her life. I better stay here."

Trick decided he could tolerate the mess and dog smell at Young's apartment for one evening. On rare occasions, Trick would invite Young to his apartment, but Young would usually decline. He felt uncomfortable in rooms whose armchairs bore antimacassars, whose carpets showed the streaks of recent vacuuming, whose

appliances gleamed, and whose tenant was given to saying, "Camp, would you please get your huge, stinking
feet off the coffee table," or "For Christ's sake, Camp,
you've got cheesie debris all down your front. I'm going
to have to cover the chesterfield with plastic!"

Trick called Metro Cabs and asked the dispatcher if
Boum-Boum was on shift. Twenty minutes later, Boum-
Boum arrived at Trick's building, and half an hour after
that Trick was drinking a beer in Young's living room
while Young drank milk. There was a ballgame on TV —
the Blue Jays were in Boston — but Young was fretting
about Reg, whose belly, Trick had to admit, was alarm-
ingly swollen. "It's probably just gas," he told Young.

"She can't have put on weight," Young said, staring
down at the bulldog on the floor. "She hasn't eaten anything in two days."

"That's when you first noticed something wrong —
two days ago?"

"Well, yesterday really. But her gut's even bigger now."

"Have you called the vet?"

"I called this morning, but he's on vacation."

"Don't they usually give you an emergency number
if they're going on vacation?"

"Yeah, there was a number on the message, but I
don't want a stranger, especially in some walk-in clinic,
doing whatever to her. Some of those wackos practically flunked out of vet school."

"Well, it's probably just gas."

They sat in silence for a while watching the baseball
game, but Young couldn't focus. Trick tried to distract
him. "Which ballcap do you like best?"

Young looked up. "What, between the Jays and the
Red Sox?"

"No, in the whole major leagues."

Young shrugged. "I don't know."

"Come on."

"Cubs, I guess."

"That's a nice cap. A classic. Myself, I like the Yankees."

Young nodded. "Yeah, now that I think about it, I suppose that's my favourite, too. I like the way the N and Y are sort of, like, intermingled." He was trying to arrange his thick fingers in a configuration similar to the Yankees insignia, and at the same time a separate and yet somehow related thought concerning the significance of Yankees caps was glimmering in his mind, when, from the floor, Reg squealed in pain.

"Good Christ!" Young said, and struggled out of the La-Z-Boy. He fell to his knees beside the dog and watched helplessly as she convulsed. "Holy shit," he said, putting his hands to the sides of his head. "Holy shit, holy shit!"

Trick propelled himself to the phone on the TV table beside the La-Z-Boy.

Ten minutes later, they were on their way to the emergency vet clinic in Boum-Boum's cab, Young in front with the dog across his knees and Trick parked behind him by the sliding side door. Reg kept baring her teeth and trying to snap at Young.

While Young lurched into the clinic with Reg in his arms, Boum-Boum unloaded Trick. By the time they caught up, the vet, a gray-faced man in a soiled lab coat, had Reg on a stainless steel table and was probing her abdomen.

After a minute he looked up at Young and said, "She's flipped her intestine. Her stomach's distended like this because it got tied off at each end like a sausage and filled up with gas. It's called gastric torsion, which is a form of colic."

Young said, "So what do we do?"

"I'll try to force a tube down her throat. While I'm doing that, you have to decide if you want her operated on. How old is she?"

Young had to think. "Eleven, almost twelve."

The vet shook his head. "She might not even survive the anaesthetic."

Young held Reg's head in his hands as the vet fed the tube into her mouth. Reg was calmer now, and she stared up at Young. She laid a forepaw across his wrist.

"It won't go," the vet said, and pulled the tube back out. "What's it going to be?"

Young said, "You'd have to open her up?"

"Stem to stern. It's a very serious operation. We have to correct the position of her whole insides. The anaesthetic itself is a real danger for a dog this old. As well, there's a high risk of infection after we staple her up. And there's no guarantee the whole thing won't happen again."

"Why did it happen this time?"

"She probably swallowed something she was chewing on, and it made her gag so violently she tore her stomach loose."

Young looked over to where Trick was sitting in his wheelchair with Boum-Boum standing behind him. "While you were looking after her, could she have gotten hold of any kind of ... I don't know, like a foreign object?"

Trick said, "I took her outside twice a day, morning and night, but I never let her off the leash. We just went around to the little park behind the building where the kids play. They got a swing set there, a teeter-totter. She did her business and we went back up."

"She never chewed on anything?"

Trick looked uncomfortable. "I wasn't watching every minute. I was busy looking at the moms." He laughed feebly. "But, yeah, the other day she was down on her belly chewing at something. A stick, I think. She had it in her mouth all the way back to the apartment. I tried to take it away from her, but she wouldn't let me. I don't know what happened to it. I never saw it again."

"That would do it," the vet said. "She probably swallowed a piece of wood, and that's what she was trying to throw up when she flipped her stomach. Listen, I'm sorry, but you have to make up your mind. Do you want me to operate?"

Young looked back down at Reg, who was still watching him — quietly, patiently. "How come she's so peaceful now? She was trying to bite me earlier."

"She's gone into shock."

"She's never tried to bite me in her whole life."

"Sir, we don't have much time."

Young swallowed. "You don't recommend the operation, do you?"

"It's your decision. It's expensive, and it may not save her."

Young looked over at Trick again. "What do you think?"

Trick shook his head. "How should I know? What do I know about dogs? I caused the whole fucking thing, why are you asking me?"

Young looked back down at Reg. Her eyes had gone opaque. They were like two buttons.

He said, "We're losing her, aren't we?"

The vet took a hollow-point puncture tool the size of a corkscrew from his tray of instruments, raised it above his head, and stabbed it into Reg's flank.

Gas hissed out.

Young gasped.

The vet raised the tool a second time.

"No, don't!" Young said. He grabbed the vet's wrist. "Don't hit her again." Tears were streaming down his cheeks. "Let her go."

* * *

An hour later Young, Trick, and Boum-Boum were sitting in McCully's. When Jessy came to take their order, Trick told her that Young's dog had died. She leaned over and kissed Young's cheek and patted him on the back. "I'm sorry, big guy."

Young nodded.

"What was it?"

"The vet had some fancy name for it, but it was basically colic. Her intestines got all twisted up. I need a drink."

Jessy turned towards the bar and yelled, "Dex, a double Jack over here." Then she said, "This your first time in here since you got out of hospital?"

"Yeah. I was just starting to feel better, then my dog dies."

"His name was Reg, right?"

"Her name, yeah."

"Reg was a she?"

Young nodded.

"How come you named her Reg? Is it short for Regina or something?"

"It's short for Reginald."

"Why would you name a female dog Reginald?"

"When I was a kid I had a favourite uncle named Reg. She's named after him."

"But why would you name a female dog after your uncle?"

Young looked at her. "For fucksake. I wanted a dog, right, and I wanted to name it Reg after my uncle, and when I went down to the pound to look for a dog the only one they had that I liked was a female."

"You don't have to snap at me."

"Why didn't you visit me in the hospital?"

"What?"

"Why didn't you visit me in the hospital?"

Jessy gulped. "I'm sorry, big guy, I've been so busy —"

"Not even a card."

She stalked off. Dexter brought the Jack Daniel's over to the table. Young knocked it back and waited for the burn.

Trick said, "Wasn't it colic that killed that first colt in Shorty's barn?"

Young said, "According to the vet."

"What about the second horse?"

"Results aren't in yet. But if the black groom was telling the truth, The Butcher — whoever he is — killed them both."

"Or," said Trick, "if you believe Percy, whoever *she* is."

Young stood up and walked to the bar. He said, "Dexter, four Blue for me and Trick, and the cabby's drinking Diet Pepsi." A fat man in a Yankees cap climbed down off his stool and squeezed past Young. Young shook his head as if he were clearing cobwebs. He returned to his table with the drinks and sat down.

Jessy was at the next table, taking an order.

"Jessy," Young said.

She glanced at him over her shoulder. "Hold your horses," she said. A moment later, she was standing in front of him. "What?"

Young said, "Do you remember that time I came in and you were talking about getting a tattoo?"

"I don't understand you. Five minutes ago you bite my head off because I ask about your dog, and now you want to know —"

"Just answer the question, Jessy. You remember

that time I came in and you were talking about getting a tattoo?"

She looked at him. "Sure I do. Willie Nelson on the back of my leg. I never did get it, though."

"Do you remember there was a guy sitting at the bar, and you were showing him the catalogue?"

She nodded and smiled. "You didn't seem to like him."

"How was he dressed?"

"How was he dressed? How am I supposed to know how he was dressed? A hundred guys come in here every day, and I don't look at how they're dressed. Besides, that was, what, two weeks ago?"

"Jessy, this is police business, so don't bullshit me. You were flirting with him. I know you know how he was dressed."

Jessy put her hands on her hips. "He was wearing one of those tropical shirts, pink and green. And he had a baseball cap on his head, turned backwards."

"What colour was the baseball cap?"

"It was a dark colour, black or navy blue."

"That's right." Young turned to Trick. "It was a Yankees cap. When Doug Buckley came in here looking for me, he was wearing a Yankees cap."

Wedneday, June 28

"The first thing we're going to do," Young told the assembled, "is take down Doug Buckley. He's a worm who'll turn."

Young had waved off all the greetings and the welcome-backs. A cake in the shape of an immense raised vanilla donut with his name on it in red icing was waiting on the lunch table, but he wouldn't let Wheeler cut it up and serve it during the meeting; he said they would eat it later. "I appreciate the gesture and all that," he said, "but we've got work to do."

The first item of business was Doug Buckley's Yankees cap.

Young surveyed the faces arranged around the conference table — Trick, Wheeler, Barkas, Big Urmson, Priam Harvey, Elliot Cronish — and said, "The junky who watched Percy Ball get killed found a Yankees cap on the ground. Two weeks ago, before I went in the hospital, when I saw Doug Buckley at McCully's, guess what he was wearing?"

Harvey said, "Lots of people wear Yankees caps. How does that make him the killer?"

"Because the scene of the murder is exactly two blocks from the King Eddy, which is where the little shit is currently residing, that's how. It was close to home."

"That's hardly the sort of evidence that will hold up in court."

"I realize that. It's time we moved on him."

"We better move quickly," Wheeler said, "before he disappears."

Young said, "Soon, Wheeler. This morning, in fact. But first, I want all of you to fill me in as quick as you can on your research. Trick, you first. What did you find out about Buckley?"

Trick cleared his throat. "As you just said, Buckley's still in residence at the King Eddy, and according to the front desk concierge I spoke to half an hour ago he's made no mention of checking out. As to why he visited you at McCully's and fingered Stirling Smith-Gower, my guess is he was doing someone's bidding, maybe Mahmoud Khan, whom he's frequently been seen with lately — your Debi said as much herself, Camp, that the two of them were thick as thieves out at her barn a week ago — but why Khan or Buckley or whoever wanted the rumour spread I don't know. I tried several times to reach Buckley at the King Eddy, but either he wasn't there or he wasn't answering the phone."

Young said, "Okay." He turned to Elliot Cronish. "I asked Urmson here to contact you with regard to the second dead horse. What can you tell us?"

Cronish smiled his inscrutable smile. "Horses are hardly my area of expertise, as you know. However, it proved a most enlightening experience. Fruitful, too." He opened a folder in front of him and began to read. "The carcass of the dead thoroughbred racing colt Gigabyte showed definite signs of scorching on the edge of the left ear and on the hair immediately adjacent to the anus. These burns and their accompanying attachment marks are consistent with a case of electrocution, which could have been performed with equipment such as alligator clips connected to a car battery or even an ordinary extension cord plugged into a wall." He looked up from his notes. "Secondly, I prevailed upon my associate from Guelph to conduct the necropsy, which she did at short notice and considerable inconvenience to herself."

"What did she find?"

"It's what she didn't find that's interesting. The track vet's report said the horse died of colic, but my associate found no evidence to support that conclusion. There were signs of distress — the horse's eyes and tongue were extruded — but its intestines were normal."

"The report on the first horse said colic, too. Did the same vet do both autopsies?"

"Yes, he did. One moment, please." Cronish referred to his notes. "Here it is. Bay colt: Download. Cause of death: colic. Yes, same conclusion and same sawbones. Charles Noble, DVM."

"Did you talk to this Noble?"

Cronish looked over his half-glasses at Young. "I spoke to him by telephone. He was rather evasive, but I don't think he's complicit, if that's what you're getting at. I don't think he's incompetent, either. He's just lazy. If he had any suspicions about the horse's death, it probably seemed a lot easier to him simply to let the matter slide. From the outside, the horse looked like it might have died of colic. He didn't bother to look inside. I just think he's not the type of man who welcomes complications into his life."

"Maybe he's in Khan's pocket."

Cronish shrugged. "I'm not a detective, Detective, but my guess is he's just slothful. Wouldn't it be to Khan's advantage to have as few people as possible on the payroll? It's cheaper, for one thing, and it means fewer traitors lined up to knife you in the back when the opportunity arises."

"But how did Khan know he'd get a favourable result from the vet?"

"I don't know. Maybe he knew the man's reputation as a human slug."

"Maybe he slipped him a G-note."

"Maybe he did."

Young paused for a moment, then said, "You're prepared to testify about all of this?"

"About the factual information, certainly. My speculation into the moral fibre of the track vet is merely that — speculation."

"So your answer is yes?"

"My loins are girded."

Young turned to Priam Harvey. "I asked you to check out Khan. Any results?"

Harvey shook his head. "Not really. He's an elusive character, a bit of a mystery man, never in his office, and nobody at the track seems to know anything about him. The only person I talked to who proved useful was the golf pro up at King County. He told me the word around the clubhouse is that Khan's a delegator — his word — that he gets people to do his bidding, which supports what Trick said earlier."

Young nodded and turned to Barkas. "What about the Four Aces groom?"

Barkas leaned forward in his chair. "I did a check on her, both through our files and Jockey Club security. Turns out she's thirty-eight years old. Grew up in Moncton, New

Brunswick. Various minors for drugs and prostitution. Her name — get this — is Florabelle Salmon."

"According to what Percy Ball said, she's The Butcher. What do you think?"

"No way. I went out to the track and met her. Talked to her face to face. It's the other way around. She said now that Percy's dead, there's no point in keeping it a secret any longer. According to her, Percy Ball was The Butcher."

Harvey laughed. "Why should we believe her? I've told you, Percy was too stupid for anything like that. She's probably just trying to take us off the scent."

Barkas regarded him. "Too stupid to attach a clip to a horse's ear and another to his asshole and plug a cord in a wall? How smart do you have to be to do that?"

Young said, "What about Harold Rogers? Did you go to the institution in Barrie?"

Barkas turned back to Young. "Yeah, the Elmdale Nursing Home. Pretty depressing place. All these zombies wandering around in pajamas. I walked into the chronic ward by mistake. That wasn't a pretty sight, let me tell you. This one old guy was standing barefoot in a pile of his own shit, banging his head against the wall. And about as far away as I am from you, Chief, a nurse was sitting at a desk rolling these foot-long cigarettes in a machine and cutting them up with scissors. Like she didn't even know the old guy existed."

"What did you find out about Harold Rogers' death?"

"The whole place smelled like the runs."

"For fucksake, Barkas."

Barkas blinked at Young. "Sorry, Chief. Yeah, they let me see his records. His death was natural. Died of pneumonia."

"Well, so much for that theory."

"What theory?" said Trick.

"I thought maybe Myrtle and her pals were knocking off Uncle Morley's relatives one by one. First Harold, then Shorty. Still, Harold's death might have made Morley's money seem that much closer. It might have spurred them on." Young turned to Wheeler. "What have you got on Myrtle and Eric?"

Wheeler nodded. "Quebec police found Mr. Rogers' Chrysler Cordoba in the parking lot at Mirabel Airport outside Montreal. They found it last night, but we don't know how long it's been there. They haven't been seen or heard from since last Thursday. They're number eight and nine on the most wanted list, and there's an all-points out for them, but they could be in Costa Rica by now."

"Or back here," Young said.

Trick said, "Why would they come back here? They're hot."

"Maybe they won't come back, but maybe she will. She didn't do the killing, so she still thinks she can walk the streets with — what do you call it, Wheeler?"

"Impunity."

"Thank you, and she's still the big winner in Morley's will."

"But Morley's not dead yet," Harvey said, "and shows no signs, so far as we know, of imminent demise."

"All the more reason for her to come back. Maybe she'd like to speed up his imminent demise."

Wheeler said, "What about Mahmoud Khan, Sarge? Should we move on him, too?"

"Not yet. He's still the key to the whole thing, but he's not dangerous on his own. He gets other people to do his dirty work. We'll leave him alone for the time being and see where he leads us." Young checked his watch. "It's oh-nine-forty. Wheeler, Barkas, Urmson, go get ready. It's time to pay Doug Buckley a visit."

* * *

After abandoning the Cordoba at Mirabel Airport, Myrtle Sweet, Eric Favors, and Kevin Favors had remained in Montreal, holed up for five days at The Clarion Hotel on rue de Maisonneuve. The Clarion catered to business travellers and European tourists who preferred rooms with housekeeping facilities, and Myrtle and Kevin took turns cooking. Eric watched television.

Wednesday morning she proposed a tour of the Laurentian Mountains, an area north of Montreal renowned for its ski slopes and pricey resorts. "You boys have been cooped up for too long," she said. "Poor dears, you need an outing." Kevin drove their rented Ford Taurus and Myrtle sat cross-legged beside him with a map in her lap. Eric dozed in the back. At first they followed the main highway, then Myrtle directed Kevin to turn onto a secondary highway, then a paved road full of potholes that twisted and turned like something out of a nightmare. A few miles outside a remote hamlet called Perdu River where Myrtle's parents had once owned a summer cottage, Myrtle instructed Kevin to turn onto a dirt road that ran past rocky fields and gutted trucks and falling-down barns. Lastly, they came to a grassy road, little more than a farmer's lane, which led them into a tiny uninhabited valley bordered by pinewoods — a miniature Shangri-La — where Myrtle, at age fifteen, had lost her virginity on the hood of a Camaro to a business associate of her father's. "Here," she told Kevin. "We'll stop for lunch here."

Before checking out of the hotel, she had prepared egg salad sandwiches and carrot sticks. There were oranges and store-bought brownies for dessert. There was a bottle of Chardonnay nestled against a freezer pack in the wicker hamper she had borrowed from the kitchen of the hotel. As she laid out the picnic under a spreading oak tree, the two men stood by awkwardly. They had not enjoyed their week in Quebec. They could not speak French and were reluctant to speak at all or even to go outside their room for fear of drawing attention to themselves. They feared that identical black twins — strangers to the city — walking the streets of Westmount or Notre Dame de Grace would be not only an uncommon sight but an unwelcome one. Now, here, in this rural setting, surrounded by wildflowers and insects, they felt just as much like fish out of water.

As well, there was sexual tension. Sexual tension of a new kind. For several months, Myrtle had been sharing her bed with Eric, but their second night in Montreal, she'd told Kevin she wanted him to sleep with her. Embarrassed, Kevin declined. Myrtle insisted. Kevin refused.

Although identical to his brother physically, in every other way he was different. He attended church on Sundays. He read his Bible at night. He turned a blind eye to his brother's relationship with this woman who wasn't officially their boss but from whom they took their orders. Kevin had been kept in the dark about the errands of a criminal nature his brother had performed. When he asked why they'd left the Cordoba at the airport, Myrtle made up a story about leaving it there for Morley's French Canadian grandson to pick up. "It's a birthday present," she said. The car was old, and the young man enjoyed mechanics. She even told Kevin the purpose of their trip to Montreal was to check out a nursing home Morley was considering moving into.

"Why Quebec?" he had asked. "Why so far from his home?"

"Oh, Montreal is his home," Myrtle lied. "He was born in Montreal. He wants to go home to die." She even had to leave their hotel for an hour Tuesday morning under the pretext of inspecting a nearby seniors' residence. She used the time to buy herself a new outfit — a dove gray pantsuit.

When Kevin refused her advances in Montreal, Myrtle made a decision. She had already made a decision regarding Eric, who had outlived his usefulness and who, in any case, was not very bright. And now that he was wanted for the murders of Bill Compton and Shorty Rogers and the attempted murder of Campbell Young, he was a liability as well. Kevin, on the other hand, was intelligent and more refined than his brother, and Myrtle had thought it would be an easy transfer, one man to the other, once Kevin overcame his scruples. She had shivered with anticipation wondering whether two men who looked the same would fuck the same. Too bad, she thought, that it had taken her so long to distinguish between them. For the first few weeks after Morley had hired them — through an agency, the first week of April — she had barely noticed them, let alone realized how different they were. But now that it was too late, she regretted taking Eric as her lover instead of Kevin. And now that Kevin had refused her, she had steeled her heart against him, too. Because she was a woman who was used to getting what she wanted, she did not accept rejection any more than she accepted threats or disappointment or failure.

As she drew the .38-calibre revolver from inside a package of paper napkins in the hamper, Eric, sitting facing her, looked at her with curiosity, like a little boy being shown a new toy, but then, as she raised the gun and pointed it at him, his expression changed to disbelief, and his eggy mouth fell open.

The first shot took off part of his ear. His eyes went wide, but he didn't move. Using both hands, Myrtle gripped the gun more tightly. The second shot hit him in the Adam's apple, and as he rolled onto his back, gurgling and clawing at his throat, she turned towards Kevin, but Kevin had bolted and was halfway to the pinewoods. Her shots resounded emptily around the little valley.

She rose from her sitting position, stood over Eric, and pointed the gun at his forehead. Blood foamed from his nose and mouth. She listened to the ingress and egress of air through the hole in his windpipe. When she squeezed the trigger for the *coup de grâce*, nothing happened. She tried again. Nothing.

She quickly gathered the picnic supplies and threw them and the gun into the trunk of the Taurus. As she surveyed the area to make sure she hadn't left anything behind — just as she had done before leaving the hotel room, checking under the bed for a dropped earring or a forgotten bra — she observed that Eric had stopped moving. Good, she thought, wiping her hands on the thighs of her slacks. She wasn't going to leave him there alive, she'd known that. She would have had to stab him with the paring knife she'd brought to peel the oranges, or beat him with as large and heavy a rock as she could lift. She made a mental note to reload the gun from the box of extra bullets she was carrying in her vanity case.

As she drove alone towards the Ontario border at Hawkesbury, she cursed herself for her one mistake: she should have shot Kevin first. The clever one. Eric would simply have sat there in confusion until she turned the gun on him. Instead she shot the slow one first, and the quick one got away.

* * *

Doug Buckley's hands were shaking even before Young sat down opposite him in the Café Victoria of the King Edward Hotel. And even though Doug must have noticed Young's arrival, he kept his eyes focused on the industry of his knife and fork.

"Nice joint," Young said, when he was settled. "Lots of marble. Big painting of Edward the Seventh in the lobby. Took a peek in the bar before I came in here. Thought I might find you there. Anyway, very nice bar. Very elegant, very spacious."

The progress of knife and fork had stopped, but Doug said nothing.

"Then I had to use the men's room. Also very nice. Little towels folded individually for your convenience. They were paper towels, right, but they weren't made of any paper I ever seen before. It was like real cloth." Young sighed and looked around. "There was a painting on the wall in the men's room, too. Painting of a ... well, you're a schoolteacher, what do you call one of those half-man, half-horse creatures?"

Doug said nothing. He still had his eyes down.

"A satyr?" Young said. "No, that's a half-goat, I think. A centaur? Yeah, that's it, a centaur. So, this centaur had a jockey on its back, only it's a woman. She's wearing racing silks up top, like you would expect a jockey to wear, but she's bare-assed, eh, her ass up high in the air, and she's waving a whip in the centaur's face, and he don't look too happy." Young laughed. "No, he don't look too happy at all. I think it's one of those modern paintings you're supposed to interpret. I think maybe it's got something to do with being pussy-whipped. What do you think?"

Doug said nothing.

"Is that the special?" Young said, looking at Doug's plate. "I saw the menu by the entrance. Twenty-one fifty buys you a sautéed calf's liver. Where I come from, that's a lot of money for lunch. It also says you can have a half-roasted Bartlett pear for ten and a quarter. For that kind of money I'd want it fully roasted. What's that you're eating?"

Doug kept his eyes down. He still hadn't moved.

"Crab cakes, right? Yeah, I saw those: 'Our Award-Winning Crab Cakes.' Eighteen fifty, right? They better win a fucking award." He looked appraisingly at Doug, who was wearing an avocado leisure suit. He had his orange aviator glasses on. "Too bright for you?" Young said, jerking his chin at the chandeliers.

Doug's right hand travelled slowly, erratically, towards a glass of white wine.

"You know why I'm here, right?" Young said.

In a small, tight voice, as if he couldn't trust it off the leash, Doug said, "I have no idea why you're here."

Young eyed Doug's water glass. "You don't mind, do you?" he said. He reached forward, picked up the water glass, and drank noisily until it was empty. Then he said, "I'm here to arrest you."

Doug raised his head and met Young's gaze. Carefully, he removed the aviator glasses. His baby face had lost its innocence. Something had died in his eyes: they were bloodshot, dark bags beneath them. He hadn't shaved in three days. "What for?" he said.

Young looked around the dining room. Wheeler was speaking quietly to the maitre d', who was flapping his hands. Big Urmson was at the other end of the room, his back to them, examining the emerald drapes that hung like giant bloomers from the ceiling. Barkas was just now seating himself at a table two back of Doug Buckley in the shadow of a vase the size of a Volkswagen.

Young leaned forward. "We know about Percy Ball."

Doug's eyes showed nothing. "I don't know anybody by that name."

"It was an accident, wasn't it? I mean, you didn't mean to kill him, did you?" Young laughed in a friendly way. "You're not the killer type, are you?"

Doug shook his head. "I'm not the killer type, no."

"Of course not. You didn't mean to kill him."

"I don't know who you're —"

"Doug," Young said quietly, "look at me. I'm talking about the man you killed down at the market. In the truck bay."

Doug closed his eyes.

"It's over, Doug. We know you did it. Things will go a lot easier if you cooperate." Young paused. "Are you with me?"

Doug sat motionless.

Young said, "You didn't mean to kill him, did you?"

Doug opened his eyes and looked at Young. "All I meant to do was … was threaten him, but …"

"But what? Things got out of hand? Did you have to defend yourself, is that it?"

"Yes, he … he attacked me."

"Percy did?"

"I don't know his name."

"Okay, let me get this straight: a man attacked you, and then you — in defending yourself — you killed him."

"Yes."

"His head was completely caved in, Doug. What did you hit him with?"

"An Easton Triple 7."

"A baseball bat?"

"That's right."

Young nodded slowly. "Good, good. That feels better, doesn't it? Getting all that off your chest." Young gestured at Doug's face. "I can see how you've been troubled by what happened."

"It's been awful," Doug said, staring at the wreck-age of his crab cakes. "It's been just awful."

Young leaned back in his chair. "But you have to help me with something here, Doug. Why were you and this man, whose name happens to have been Percy Ball, down-town near the market? That's what puzzles me. Were you doing someone a favour, or delivering something?"

Doug's eyes became slits.

Young said, "Don't clam up on me, Doug." He reached forward and put a hand on Doug's wrist. "Even though we know it was an accident, you're still in a bit of a jam. It'll go a whole lot easier for you if you tell me why you were there."

Doug swallowed and said, "Mr. Khan."

"Mr. Khan?" Young said, his hand still touching the dull green of Doug's sleeve. "Mahmoud Khan told you to kill Percy Ball?"

"No. He told me to scare him. To rough him up."

"How much did he pay you?"

Doug shook his head. "It wasn't about money."

"Really? What was it about?"

Doug hesitated, then said, "He told me he'd get me a membership in the golf club."

Young stared at him. "You killed a man to get into a golf club?"

"I didn't mean to kill him."

"But you did kill him."

"And you know what?" Doug began to laugh. "I don't think he meant it. I don't think he's even men-tioned my name to the committee. I think he's been stringing me along."

"He promised to get you into the golf club if you roughed up Percy Ball?"

"Yes. And he promised me his daughter."

"What?"

"He promised me his daughter. Cheyenne. I was going to be his son-in-law. But I don't think he was serious about that, either." Doug's face was ashen. "And his business partner. He told me I was going to be his business partner." He lifted his glass of wine and gulped down what was left. "I want to go home now. Take me home, please. Kathy and the kids need me."

Young stood up. He nodded to his colleagues, and they began to move through the tables towards them. "You can bet I'm taking you somewhere, but it ain't home. Well, let me correct myself: it's your new home. Barkas, step over here, please. I know it's a little late, but read Mr. Buckley his rights."

Mahmoud Khan was standing at a payphone in the Yorkdale Shopping Mall. He was speaking to a man named Tallon, an adjustor with Reliant Insurance. Tallon said, "No, I'm sorry, Mr. Khan, but according to my information your claim regarding the death of the racehorse Gigabyte is still under review, and compensation has not yet been approved. I'm glad you called, though, because my superior, Mrs. Shantz, mentioned to me just a few moments ago that she would like to make an appointment to see you at your earliest convenience, this afternoon if possible. Hang on for just one moment, please, and I'll put her on the line."

"Thank you," said Mahmoud Khan. As soon as he was put on hold and Muzak replaced Tallon's voice, he hung up.

Kevin Favors hid in the bush for an hour, crying and shaking. He hardly noticed the mosquitoes on his neck and arms. Eventually, he began to make his way back towards the clearing. Peering through the lower branches of a tamarack, he could see the motionless body of his brother lying on the ground. There was no sign of Myrtle or the car.

He crept forward, his eyes darting left and right. He was afraid Myrtle would reappear any second, but he had to see Eric. He was ashamed that he had run away and left him to die. He knelt beside the body and pressed his forefinger into his brother's throat for a pulse, but he couldn't find one. He closed his eyes, his thumb on Eric's wrist, but felt nothing. He leaned his cheek, his ear, against his brother's open mouth, but there wasn't even the whisper of a breath. The blood around his brother's lips and nostrils was congealing. There was blood in the corners of his eyes, which were wide open, rolled back, and yellow as yolk. Convulsing, Kevin turned away and vomited.

Minutes later, still on his hands and knees, his chest still heaving, Kevin heard the distant crunch of tires on gravel. He abandoned Eric's body and ran back into the woods.

At HQ, Doug Buckley was booked, fingerprinted, and put in a cell. His avocado leisure suit, his orange aviator glasses, his white belt, and his Elton John platform shoes were taken away, and he was given gray prison garb. He placed a phone call to his wife. He asked her to find him a lawyer, a good one, money was no object. She told him to find his own lawyer.

The bank manager spread his hands, palms upward, in a gesture of helplessness. "I'm sorry, Mr. Khan, but we've already extended your line of credit well beyond the normal limits." He tapped a fingernail against the folder lying on his desk. "And currently you're repaying us at the minimum allowable rate, seven and a half percent. In order for us to lend you any more money, especially anything in excess of a hundred thousand dollars, we would need collateral additional to what you've already offered. If you —"

"Mr. Stokes," Khan laughed, "this is ridiculous. You act as though I were some sort of risk. Have you forgotten who I am?"

"No, Mr. Khan, I certainly haven't forgotten who you are."

"I'm president of Dot Com Enterprises, I'm a member of Rotary and the Better Business Bureau, not to mention the King County Golf and Country Club. May I remind you that I started my business from scratch, from the bottom up."

"Please, Mr. Khan —"

"Hell, man, I've been your client for almost seven years, you're familiar with my dossier, my holdings —"

"Mr. Khan, please. We've been over this. My hands are tied. I simply cannot —"

"What about my boat? I have a thirty-six-foot yawl in dry dock at the yacht club. The *Chat Room*. It's worth ... oh gosh, I've no idea what it's worth!"

The bank manager looked down at the folder, then up again. "It's already on the list, Mr. Khan. You've already used it as collateral."

There was a mint on the pillow, and two pears, a plum, and a peach in a bowl on the dresser. Myrtle Sweet smiled.

She had arrived at The Daffodils, a women's spa on Lake Simcoe an hour's drive north of the Caledon Hills, at 8:00 p.m. After exchanging the Taurus for a Ford Fiesta at a car rental in Hawkesbury, she had driven the rest of the way in seven hours. Over three hundred miles. She was exhausted, and when she checked in she was gratified by the warm reception she had received. "Welcome to The Daffodils, Ms. Wilson," a young woman at the front desk had said. "You're in the Hollyhock Suite. Down the hall, past the atrium, first door on your left. Luis will help you with your bags."

Myrtle congratulated herself for having planned so thoroughly, for having selected the spa in the first place, and for having made the reservation.

She chose the plum.

Thursday, June 29

At 9:00 a.m., Doug Buckley was standing shoulder to shoulder with five other men in the lineup room at HQ. On the other side of the one-way glass, an anxious, malodorous drug addict named Justin Greenspan identified Doug as the man he'd watched murder Percy Ball in the truck bay behind the St. Lawrence Market.

At 9:30 a.m., Young was informed that Forensics had removed two human hairs from the New York Yankees cap, but that follicle samples from Doug Buckley, Justin Greenspan, and the corpse of Percy Ball were needed for comparison purposes, and that it would be at least a day before a DNA match with any of them could be determined. Justin agreed to provide a sample; Doug declined, pending instruction from his court-appointed lawyer. A search warrant was quickly obtained, and at 11:15 a.m. a number of Doug's personal belongings, including his hairbrush, were retrieved by Big Urmson and Tony Barkas from the Royal Suite of the King Edward Hotel.

At 2:00 p.m., Doug hobbled into Courtroom 7A of the University Avenue Courthouse. He was wearing an orange jumpsuit, and a short length of chain connected his wrist cuffs to his leg shackles. The arraignment was heard by Judge Nolan Bigsnake. Doug's lawyer said, "Your honour, my client is not only innocent, but the eyewitness who identified him this morning is a well-known heroin user and documented schizophrenic, and, furthermore, my client's confession was coerced and will most certainly be deemed inadmissible during pre-trial, should this classic case of police bungling and mistaken identity ever reach pre-trial. On behalf of my client, I therefore request bail." Judge Bigsnake denied bail, and Doug was led out of the courtroom.

At 3:30 p.m., in a telephone conversation with Dr. Charles Noble, the track veterinarian, Young asked whether there was any possibility that Dr. Noble might have been wrong about the conclusion he had come to regarding the death of Mahmoud Khan's colt, Gigabyte. Dr. Noble said that he had gone over his notes following the visit he received from Dr. Elliot Cronish, and he would be prepared to testify that he hadn't specifically examined the ears or anus of the dead horse, nor had he performed a necropsy and, therefore, it was entirely possible that he had missed some crucial pieces of evidence that Dr. Cronish and his associate from the Guelph School of Veterinary Medicine had found. Gigabyte's carcass had been preserved by police order, but the carcass of the other colt, Download, had long since been turned into dog food, so there was no recourse there. Dr. Noble confirmed that he had conducted the examination of Download — again without a necropsy — and his conclusion had been the same: colic. And, yes, he allowed that he may have misinterpreted the trauma in both horses — the bulging eyes and exposed tongue.

All in all, Young was satisfied. Dr. Noble's willingness to amend his report suggested that he had not been bought off by Mahmoud Khan and that he was, if anything, merely lazy — as Cronish had suggested.

Phone calls to Mahmoud Khan's Toronto office and his Caledon Hills farm came up empty. Staff Inspector Bateman wanted to issue an APB, but Young argued that it might be a better idea not to alarm Khan, that they would have a better chance of apprehending him if he were allowed to go about his business unsuspecting. "I'd like to know what he's up to before we move on him," Young said. "Let's find him first and put him under surveillance."

At 4:45 p.m., just as Young was finishing the paperwork on Doug Buckley, Trick phoned to say that he and Priam Harvey were at McCully's, and would he join them.

Young packed up his notes and headed out of the office. As he passed Wheeler at the pop machine, she said, "What's up?"

"Beer," he said. "Beer's up. Want some?"

"Not today," she said, "but thanks."

"It's Thursday, for fucksake, Wheeler. It's almost Friday. Come on, have a beer."

She shook her head. "Another time."

"Listen, I'm going to need you early tomorrow."

"How early?"

"Six. We have to take a little drive out to the Caledon Hills."

As he continued towards the double doors and the stairs leading down to the parking lot, Young heard Desk Sergeant Gallagher call his name.

* * *

"Rasheed," Mahmoud Khan said into the telephone, "as my younger brother there are certain obligations you are expected to fulfill. I know you have your hands full with a young family, as well as caring for our parents and grandmother, and I'm sure living in San Diego must be expensive, but my advisors tell me plastic surgery is very lucrative these days, especially out where you are with all those aging movie stars, and I am sure you will agree that one hundred thousand is not an unreasonable request. One hundred thousand is small potatoes these days to a man of means. Pocket change. And may I remind you that it is only a loan, little brother, a loan that I will repay within six months at a rate of interest I think will surprise and please you. And you know —"

Khan hung up the phone, waited several seconds, picked it up again, dialed his brother's number, listened, waited, and said, "Rasheed, it's me again, your tape ran out. You should allow more space for messages. It could be Bette Midler calling for a facelift! Anyway, I just wanted to say that if you are ever in any kind of difficulty, you know I will be the first to offer you my home, my counsel, my personal funds. Please call back soon. You have my number. I am depending on you."

Kevin had walked for miles through pine forest and barren fields. He avoided roads and laneways. He worried that he would wind up in the hands of rednecks who would tie him to a cedar rail and torture him or hang him from a tree in the village square, that his supplications and his explanation of his brother's murder would fall on deaf or uncomprehending ears. Babble as he might, his pleas would mean nothing to backwoodsmen whose only language was French and whose only interest would be the colour of Kevin's skin and the licence it gave them.

After a sleepless night and a day of eating berries, drinking out of streams, and wandering without direction, Kevin stumbled onto a highway. Filthy, hungry, and covered in scratches and insect bites, he stepped to the shoulder and extended his thumb. It was almost dusk; perhaps his black skin would not be so noticeable. He had to hope that once he was picked up, the driver would not kick him out or, worse, feign friendship and drive him to some remote cabin or secret order lodge where his lifeblood would be ceremoniously spilled. He stood there for an hour before an eighteen-wheeler hissed to a stop fifty yards past him. He ran, his heart pounding. He was so full of hope on the one hand and fear on the other that as he climbed the steps into the enormous cab of the truck he thought he might pass out.

The driver, a thin man with dark, lanky hair down to the shoulders of his red and black lumberjack shirt, took one look at him and said, "*Maudit!* What happen to you, man?"

Out of breath, Kevin collapsed into the passenger's seat. "I got to get to Toronto," he gasped.

The driver reached into the cooler beside him and pulled out a can of iced tea. He opened it with one hand and offered it to Kevin. "You been lost in the woods, I think."

Kevin nodded and accepted the drink.

The driver was putting the truck into gear and checking for traffic in his mirror. "Where you from, man?"

"I ... uh, north of Toronto."

"No, I mean like where you from?"

They were on the highway and slowly gaining speed. "Jamaica."

"I thought so!" the driver said, shaking his head. "I been there, eh, it's ver' beautiful, but my wife, she prefer Miami. So that's where we go. But I don't drive," he laughed. "When it's my 'oliday, I don't drive, no sir. I fly ... like the birds, eh." He let go of the steering wheel momentarily and spread his arms like wings. Then, one hand back on the wheel, he reached into the cooler again. "Here," he said, and handed Kevin a sandwich. "Hope you like turkey, eh. My wife make it."

Kevin unwrapped the sandwich. A minute later, his mouth full, he said, "Where are we?"

"Highway three-twenty-seven south. It's your lucky day, eh. I'm going to Toronto myself. St. Jovite to Toronto. My truck, she's full of bathtubs. A funny load. We be there by midnight. You just relax and let Sylvain do the driving."

Kevin finished the sandwich and the iced tea. Sylvain told him to crawl into the sleeping compartment and rest for a while. As he lay on Sylvain's blankets listening to country music waft in from the cab, he felt safe for the first time in what seemed an eternity. He thought about what had happened and realized that, since she'd killed once, there was no reason to believe Myrtle wouldn't kill again. And her next victim, Kevin realized, would be either him — sole witness to Eric's murder — or the old man whose money she was after.

Once he was settled and Jessy had brought him two bottles of Blue, and after he had filled Trick and Harvey in on the arrest of Doug Buckley, Young said, "But what I don't get is what this means in terms of the two murders. We know Doug Buckley killed Percy, and we're pretty sure Eric Favors killed Shorty, but who's the brains behind it all? According to Doug, it's Khan. But where does that leave Myrtle Sweet?"

Harvey lit a cigarette. "Khan's the brains behind it all. He's the key. Two of his horses are dead under suspicious circumstances. His trainer's dead. And his dead trainer's exercise rider is dead. According to the Four Aces groom, Percy Ball and The Butcher were one and the same. I didn't believe it at first, but if it's true, then maybe Khan-brought Buckley in to shut Percy up. Maybe Percy was blackmailing Khan over the horse murders."

Trick said, "Maybe Shorty knew about the horse murders, too. Maybe *he* was blackmailing Khan."

"And Khan hired Eric to take out Shorty?" Young asked. "It's possible — Eric lived right next door to Khan. But I still don't know where Myrtle fits into all this."

Harvey said, "Myrtle wanted Shorty eliminated as beneficiary to Uncle Morley's will. Her interest is in Uncle Morley's money, nothing else. She and Eric may not even have known about the horse murders. They still may not know. And anybody can nail a horseshoe to a baseball bat, although if I were going to clobber someone with a horseshoe, I wouldn't attach it to a bat. Too round."

"Funny you should mention that," Young said. "Just as I was leaving to come over here, Gallagher got a phone call from King County Homicide. Some guy was out walking his dog a few miles from the racetrack, and the dog chased a rabbit into the woods, and when he came back out, he was dragging a three-foot length of pressure-treated four-by-four."

Trick and Harvey looked at him expectantly.

"With a horseshoe nailed to it."

Harvey said, "Aha! Didn't I tell you? Too damn round! And, now that I think of it, the whole horsehair business was a bit of a stretch, right? The experts all said it was unlikely that any horsehairs would have gotten stuck to the wound on Shorty's head."

"Unlikely," Trick said, "but not impossible."

"The whole thing shouts out to me that whoever masterminded Shorty's murder didn't know diddly about horses."

"Well," said Young, "that describes Myrtle, which leads me to another question. Why did Eric try to kill me?"

Trick shrugged his left shoulder. "Myrtle didn't like you sniffing around. She was scared you'd sabotage her plans for Uncle Morley."

Harvey said, "Exactly. Don't mix Myrtle and Eric up with the dead horses. Their only interest, as I said before, is Uncle Morley's property." He paused and scratched his head. "That two crimes involving Shorty Rogers were happening simultaneously and in the same place was pure coincidence. The real question is whether Shorty was killed because of his involvement with Mahmoud Khan's horses or because he was Uncle Morley's nephew."

Jessy arrived with a basket of wings. "Mediums, right?" she said. She put the basket on the table.

Young looked from Harvey to Trick. "Somebody order wings?"

"They're on the house," Jessy said. "Courtesy of Vinny."

"Vinny?" Trick said. "That cheap bastard never gives anything away."

Young looked over towards the swinging doors to the kitchen. Vinny was standing there watching. He nodded to Young.

"Take them back," Young said to Jessy.

"Are you serious?"

"Yeah, I'm serious, take them back. I know what he's up to. This is about the bookies. A few weeks ago I yanked his chain about the bookies. He's trying to buy me off. Take them back and tell him I don't take bribes."

"Wait a minute," Harvey said. "I'll eat them."

Young shoved the basket towards Jessy. "Take them back!"

"Okay, big guy. No need to get rough."

When she was gone, Young drank his second beer in one motion. His right knee was pumping like a piston. He checked his watch. "I gotta go."

Trick said, "Don't let that fat little prick spoil your evening. He's just nervous, that's all. You make him nervous. You make a lot of people nervous."

"It's true," Harvey said. "You make *me* nervous."

"I'm going," Young said.

"Why?" said Trick.

"I've got … well, I've got sort of an appointment."

Harvey said, "With whom do you have sort of an appointment?"

Young said, "Can you get home okay?"

"Yeah," Trick said, "I'll call Boum-Boum. But I don't get it, what's the rush? Have another beer. One more beer never hurt anybody. I'm buying."

"No, I can't. There's something I have to do."

"What's so important," Harvey said, "that you can't have one more beer?"

Young was standing now. "I told you. There's something I have to do."

Pat the stud groom was leading Sam McGee in from the paddock. The horse snorted and pranced, its fine head and arched neck gleaming in the slanting sunlight of early evening.

Mahmoud Khan was standing near the doorway to the stable. "What a glorious day it's been, Mr. Khan," Pat said, but Khan didn't respond. He was staring at the stallion. "*Here*," Khan said to himself, "*is my cre-ma-tor-eum.*"

"Goddamn it."

"I thought you gave up swearing."

"I tried, but it didn't take."

"Pass me the spade."

"She didn't suffer, did she?"

"No. Well, not for long. She went into shock, and after that she was pretty confused. Shock's a great thing. I imagine that's what happens to people when they're being tortured: they go into shock. After the first few teeth or fingernails are pulled out —"

"Daddy, please!"

"— they don't feel much of anything. Too bad you can't bottle it and sell it. Have you told Jamal yet?"

"I was hoping you would. It would be better coming from you."

"Why would it be better coming from me?"

"I don't know. You're his grandfather. That's what grandfathers are for."

"What, to tell their grandsons about death?"

"Yeah, to teach them, I guess. Besides, you know how to talk to kids."

"I do?"

"Yes, you do. You sure it's legal to bury her in the backyard like this?"

"Sure it is. She's just ashes now."

"How are you going to mark her grave?"

"I figured I'd make a cross, or maybe an *R* out of some of those bricks I've got on the balcony."

"The *R* sounds nice. When are you going to get another dog?"

"Not for a while. Maybe never. I don't need the aggravation."

"Oh, Daddy, you loved her."

"Yeah, but she's dead now, and I'm looking forward to not having to look after a dog. To not having to walk her every night, or find her turds all over the top of the sofa —"

"She just got excited whenever you pulled in the driveway."

"Yeah, well, I can do without that kind of excitement. I can do without having to scoop about nine thousand of her little excitements out of the yard every spring when the snow melts."

"Isn't that deep enough? You're halfway to China."

"I suppose. Let me catch my breath."

"You know what?"

"What?"

"You're going to need another dog."

"No, I'm not. I just told you —"

"Yes, you will. You need something to take care of. You don't think so, but you do. "

"No, I don't. What I need is nothing to take care of. Nothing and nobody. Pass me the urn."

"Who's going to sleep with you?"

"What?"

"Now that Reg is gone, who's going to sleep with you?"

"Who's going to sleep with me? Who's going to sleep with me? I was hoping maybe a woman might sleep with me."

* * *

Myrtle relaxed all day. She availed herself of everything The Daffodils had to offer — pilates, a mud bath, massage therapy, twenty minutes in the tanning bed, seminars entitled "The Woman in the Three-Piece Suit" and "Don't Start Over — Make Over!", happy hour, an amazing Prince Edward Island lobster supper, a late-night swim, and a poolside chat with several women she found almost as interesting as herself. But all the while she was planning her next move. In her mind, she was inviolate; so far as the police knew, she had done nothing wrong and was perfectly within her rights to stake her claim to Morley's fortune. Hadn't she cared for him for more than a year, hadn't she cooked for him and fed him, hadn't she changed his diapers and washed his clothes and run his household? Hadn't she let him paw and nuzzle her? Hadn't she done him certain favours that revolted her? She deserved every cent he had, and she was running out of patience.

But first I have to find Kevin, she thought as she prepared for bed. *And figure out how to pin Eric's murder on him. And the old man's. Keep cooking*, she said to herself. It was what Eric used to say as she ravished him: "Oh, Miss, you cooking now." She smiled at herself in the mirror above the washbasin. The bathroom was panelled in cedar. She loved the smell of cedar.

Friday, June 30

Young and Wheeler rolled slowly up the red brick driveway of Dot Com Acres until Young stopped their unmarked Crown Victoria beside the Dodge Ram pickup truck he'd seen when he first visited. While Wheeler climbed the steps of the verandah and walked to the front door, Young headed for the barn. It was 8:00 a.m., the resident red-winged blackbirds were calling *kong-ka-ree* to each other, and beyond the farm buildings the sun was boring holes through the mist that lay heavily over the fairways of the golf course next door. As he entered the stable, Young heard someone singing, and as he walked along the centre aisle towards a wheelbarrow half-filled with manure and soiled straw, he recognized Pat the stud groom through the bars of one of the stalls.

"Morning," Young said.

The old man jerked around, leaving off "Danny Boy" in mid-phrase and dropping his pitchfork. "Mother of

God!" he said. "You'd scare the pigs off Ireland! You mustn't sneak up on an old man like that."

"Mr. Khan around?"

Pat bent over and picked up his pitchfork, then peered through the bars at Young. "You're the detective, aren't you? I remember when you was here before. You watched us breedin' the stud." He spat into the straw at his feet. "He's out that way. Looks like he's goin' on a trip." He raised his chin towards the far end of the stable then clicked his dentures twice, three times, and returned to his work.

Emerging into the weak sunlight, Young saw Khan lifting a white suitcase into the open trunk of his Porsche Carrera, which was parked in the mouth of the lane that led down from the main house past Sam McGee's pasture to the barn. The stallion was grazing peacefully in the middle of the field while Khan struggled with the suitcase, which was one piece of luggage too many for the small car.

"Good morning, Mr. Khan," Young said as he drew near. "Off somewhere?"

Khan turned and, in the second before he smiled broadly and said, "Ah, Detective Sergeant, how nice to see you," a shadow of anger darkened his face. "To what do I owe the pleasure?" Despite the coolness of the morning, Khan's pink golf shirt was already sweat-stained.

"Off somewhere?" Young repeated.

"Yes, business," Khan said.

"Where to?"

"Chicago."

"Overnight?"

"Yes, just overnight. I'm leaving for the airport in a few minutes."

Young jerked his chin at the Porsche's trunk. "That's a shitload of baggage for just one night."

Khan licked his lips but said nothing.

Young studied Khan for a moment, then cleared his throat. "Mahmoud Khan," he stated formally, "you are under arrest for the murder of Percy Ball."

Khan took a step into the lane that led back to the house, but Wheeler was striding towards him. Young had the handcuffs ready, and Khan turned and faced him and thrust his wrists, belly-up, towards him. "I'm not saying anything until I speak to my lawyer."

In the car a few minutes later, Wheeler, driving, looked at Khan in the rear-view mirror. "Should we tell him who gave him up?" she asked Young.

"Go ahead," he said.

"Doug Buckley gave you up."

Khan looked impassively out the side window as Wheeler turned the car around in front of his monster home. His daughters — the beautiful one dressed in jeans and a halter top, her navel ring glittering; the plain one still in her Mickey Mouse pajamas and bearpaw slippers — stood motionless on the front steps. Khan waved to them, and the plain one waved back.

"I have a couple of questions," Young said, half-turning to look at Khan. "Of course, you don't have to answer them — not yet, anyway — unless you want to. But I'm curious: we know Doug killed Percy — to shut him up about the deaths of your racehorses, right? — but why did he kill Shorty?"

Khan met Young's eyes. "To the best of my knowledge, Detective Sergeant," he said, "that fool had nothing to do with Shorty's death, and neither did I." He chuckled joylessly. "And if anyone had reason to kill him, I did."

"Why's that?"

"He was blackmailing me."

"Shorty was? Because of the horses?"

Khan turned his attention back to the view outside his window. "I've said too much already."

Young nodded. Trick had been dead on.

"But I repeat," Khan said quietly, as if he were speaking to himself, "I had nothing to do with his death. I swear it on the heads of my daughters."

"Well, if Doug didn't kill Shorty, then Percy must have. Then you had Doug kill Percy to shut him up about the horses and about Shorty. It's all starting to make sense."

Khan looked back at Young and shook his head. "Are you deaf? I told you — I swore to you — I had nothing to do with it. Percy tried to blackmail me, too, but the only thing he was good for was killing horses."

Young smiled. If Khan was telling the truth, then Priam Harvey had been right, too. That put Eric Favors number one on the who-killed-Shorty chart. But where the hell was he? And where the hell was Myrtle?

Myrtle Sweet was having tea in the lounge of The Daffodils when she came upon an article in the *Toronto Star* concerning the investigation into the discovery of a body found near the St. Lawrence Market late Sunday night: "The body has been identified as that of Percival James Ball, 41, an exercise rider at Caledonia Downs Race Track." *Percy*, she thought. *Somebody's killed Percy.* She laughed out loud, and a woman sitting in a nearby armchair looked over and smiled. Myrtle smiled back. She had first spoken to Percy one afternoon in late April over the fence that separated Morley's twelve acres from Mahmoud Khan's farm. Although Myrtle hadn't known it at the time, Percy had been there to collect his pay for electrocuting the first horse, Download. As he bragged to her that he was a jockey, that he had won two Queen's Plates, Myrtle sensed he was lying, trying to impress her, and she knew she could use him. A month later, when she saw him whitewashing Mahmoud Khan's paddock fences and waved him over to ask if he would clip a dozen hairs from the leg of Khan's stallion, he had wanted to know why she needed them. "I want them for a pillow I'm making, a horsehair pillow," she had said, "and I need a few white hairs to finish it off. That stallion has a white stocking on one of his back legs, but I'm afraid to go near him. You're not afraid, are you?"

"Are you kiddin', lady?" Percy had said. "I'm a natural 'round horses." Then he'd leaned towards her and whispered, "In fact, if there's ever a horse you need put down — if it's sick or whatever — I can look after it for you."

"Put down?" she had replied. "Why would I want a horse put down? I don't even own a horse."

Percy had looked uneasy then, as if he had said too much, and hurried away.

An hour later, he had brought her the hairs. And now, six weeks later, he was dead.

Like Kevin and Eric, Percy had been on her list. Like them, he had known too much. But someone had done her work for her. She wondered who and she wondered why. *Oh well*, she mused, *sometimes things have a way of working out on their own*.

She read the rest of the article. It concluded by saying that the police "were continuing to search for clues in the brutal murder."

She finished her tea and touched a napkin to her lips. Time to move on. Time to pay Morley a visit.

Kevin Favors knew what Detective Sergeant Campbell Young looked like long before he saw him step outside the back entrance of HQ. When Eric had returned agitated from a Sunday at the racetrack several weeks earlier, Kevin at first chalked it up to gambling losses, but when he noticed dirt smears on his brother's pants and the torn col-

lar of his shirt, he had pressed him for an explanation. Eric
had finally told him he had been attacked by a gigantic
red-headed policeman in the men's room of the clubhouse
restaurant. He even knew the policeman's name. Kevin
thought it peculiar that a policeman would start a fight
and then provide his name. When he asked what pro-
voked the attack, Eric wouldn't reply. When he asked if it
was racially motivated, Eric shook his head. Then Eric
said something that baffled Kevin. He told him if anything
ever happened to him — anything bad — Kevin should
contact this same Detective Sergeant Young. Despite
Kevin's pleas, Eric refused to say anything further. He
could be stubborn when he wanted. Even as children in
the slums of Kingston, Eric had always been the moody,
intractable one, and Kevin had been the obedient one, the
pleaser. As teenagers, Eric had become a ganja-smoker and
had affairs with older women, some of them married. He
was simple but dangerous, and they couldn't resist him. At
any moment, it seemed, he might explode into violence or
retreat into gloom. Kevin, meanwhile, had kept up his
studies and attended church every Sunday.

It had not been difficult to determine where Detective
Sergeant Young worked. One phone call to TIPS with the
promise of information on a murder was all it took, and
now, as Kevin stepped towards Young from between two
parked cars, his clothes still mud-stained from his trek
through the bush and rumpled from the night he'd spent
at the hostel on Queen Street where Sylvain had dropped
him after their arrival in Toronto, he was unaware of the
impact his appearance would have on Young.

It was mid-afternoon. Young had returned from
Caledon with Wheeler and Mahmoud Khan and had just
finished booking Khan. He had stepped outside to smoke
a cigarette when he saw a black man approaching him. A
familiar-looking black man. Young looked around quick-

ly to see what advantage his surroundings might provide, then, as Kevin Favors drew near — dirty, dishevelled, a stony expression on his face — he charged.

As he threw himself at the other man, Young was surprised that he met no resistance. Kevin turned his head to the side, his hands raised defensively, and went down without a sound under Young's bulk. Young rose up astride Kevin, squeezed his neck with his left hand, and cocked his right fist. "Eric Favors?" he said.

Kevin, his eyes shut tightly, said nothing. One ear was scraped and bleeding, and there was a wad of gum with a cigarette butt stuck to it in his hair. Young eased his grip on Kevin's throat.

"You're Eric Favors, right?" Young said.

Kevin opened his eyes. "He my brother."

Young stared at him intently. "You ... he tried to kill me. How do I know you're not him?"

"We twins."

"How do I know you're not him?"

"You fight with him, right? At the racetrack?"

Young removed his hand from Kevin's neck and lowered his fist. "Your brother fights like an animal," he said. "You fight like a girl." Slowly, he got to his feet and brushed himself off. "What are you doing here?"

Kevin continued to lie on his back on the pavement. "I come to tell you something."

Young leaned over and extended his right hand. Kevin took it, and Young raised the smaller man to his feet like a father one-handing his little boy out of a swimming pool. "What?"

"It about Eric."

"Where is he? I want to talk to him."

"He dead."

Young looked at Kevin and whistled, a slow one-noter, like a kettle.

Kevin said, "Myrtle Sweet kill him. She shoot him. She try to shoot me, too, but I run away."

"When did all this take place?"

"Not yesterday. Day before. Wednesday."

"Where?"

"I don't know. Near Montreal."

"Where's Myrtle now?"

"That why I come. She back here by now, I expect. Eric tell me if anything happen to him, I should find you." Kevin wiped his forehead with the back of his hand. "Myrtle kill my brother, sir. She shoot him in cold blood. Now she want to kill me. But first she going to kill the old man."

Morley Rogers wasn't happy about being spirited out of his house. It was done late in the afternoon with only two unmarked police cars in evidence. Young and his team did not want to spook Myrtle, who, for all they knew, was spying on them from the bushes, but they had no choice: they had to move the old man before she showed up.

"I'll go," Morley said, slapping at Wheeler's hands as she funneled him into his cardigan, "but under duress. Bright's Kill is my home, God bless, my home! I want my objection noted — duly noted, I say! 'My house shall be called the house of prayer; but ye have made of it a den of thieves.' Matthew, twenty-one, thirteen. Liars and fornicators. Whores of Babylon. 'Father, forgive them; for they know not what they do.' Luke, twenty-three, thirty-four. Where's my teeth, woman, where's my jeezly teeth?"

Barkas wasn't too happy about being spirited into the house, nor about donning the old man's urinous clothing, affecting his stoop, hobbling around behind a derelict, food-encrusted walker someone had rescued from Properties, or lying between the sour sheets of the old man's bed.

Just before 5:00 p.m., Young was summoned out to one of the unmarked cruisers to take a call. "Homicide," Big Urmson said, and passed him the handset.

It was Desk Sergeant Gallagher. "Forensics just checked in," he said. "They got the results on the four-by-four and the Yankees cap."

"I'm listening," Young said.

"The blood and hair on the four-by-four, they're Shorty Rogers'."

"Right, good, and …?"

"And the hair that came out of the cap is the same as the hair that came out of Doug Buckley's hairbrush."

"*Very* good. Have we found the bat yet? He used a bat, one of those aluminum jobs — an Easton."

"No sign of it yet."

"Any fingerprints on the four-by-four or the horseshoe?"

"Nope, sorry."

"Fuck," Young said and went back inside the farmhouse.

When everything was in place and Morley was on his way downtown to a Best Western and Barkas was nodding off in Morley's recliner and Wheeler and Big Urmson and the unmarked police cars were gone, the only thing left to do was wait. And wait Young did, huddled in his raincoat in the root cellar beneath Bright's Kill, his only companions onions, apples, yams, potatoes with long, sickly tentacles, his flashlight, his police-issue Glock automatic, half a dozen granola bars, a two-litre bottle of Mountain Dew, and a spider the size of a baseball.

Saturday, July 1

Young woke to a thumping sound. When he opened his eyes he couldn't see anything. For a moment he didn't know where he was. He had been dreaming about riding on a sailboat with a group of tanned, wealthy-looking men and women, but none of them would speak to him. He said, "Hello, hello," but they didn't respond. They weren't rude to him; they seemed not to see him. Maybe he wasn't there. In the dream he held his hands up in front of his face, but he couldn't see them. Maybe he was dead; maybe he was a ghost. When the thump woke him and his eyes snapped open, he went from a sunny day on a lake — creak of rigging, flap of sails, slap of waves against the hull — to pitch darkness. Then he remembered where he was: he was in the root cellar under Morley Rogers' house. He fumbled in the darkness for his flashlight, turned it on, and shone it at the face of his wristwatch. 4:28 a.m. He heard another thump and stood up. As he made his way quickly, stiffly, towards the stairs, he remembered to bend his head so as not to bang it against the floor joists.

The door at the top of the stairs was shut, but Young could see a crack of light below it. He listened for more thumps and heard what he thought were footsteps on the flight of stairs that led to the top floor of the house. Carefully, he eased the cellar door open. The light in the kitchen was on. Where was Barkas? he wondered. Maybe they were Barkas's footsteps he heard. Of course they were. What had he been thinking? Young shook his head at his own stupidity. Then he heard a voice above him say, "Who the fuck are you? Where's the old man?" followed by the sound of scuffling. Young moved from the kitchen into the hallway. As he chugged up the stairs, gun in hand, it occurred to him that the voice had been a man's, not a woman's, let alone Myrtle's. Then he heard a thud and a groan. The light was on in the upstairs hall, and as Young swung round the newel post at the top of the stairs, there — in a pair of pale blue pajamas and with blood on the back of his head — lay Barkas. Keeping an eye on the doorways along the passage, Young knelt beside Barkas, whose eyes were open and blinking.

"You okay?" Young whispered.

"I'm okay, Chief. Radio for backup."

"Who hit you?"

"Don't know." Barkas groaned. "Never seen him before. Tattoo on his forehead. Radio for backup."

Young stood up, took four steps, and, with his Glock held at chest level, swung into the doorway of the first room. A bedroom, the bed unmade. A table lamp turned on. The old man's room — the room Barkas had been in.

Young returned to the hall. He heard a crash — outside. He took several steps further along the creaking floorboards and swung into the next doorway. Another bedroom. A woman's things scattered across the bed. A suitcase open on the floor.

Along the hall to the next doorway. A bathroom. Young waited a moment, stepped in, and, with his gun in his right hand, hit the light switch and yanked back the shower curtain with his left. Nothing. Young turned to the window. It was open. Low in the night sky, streaks of gray were beginning to appear. Young stuck his head out the window and, in the light from the kitchen, saw the solarium below. One of the panes of glass in its ceiling was gone, and Young could see shards and slivers glinting on the ground. He scanned the gloom around the solarium. A movement some distance away caught his eye. It was the silhouette of a man vaulting the fence that separated Morley Rogers' property from Mahmoud Khan's. The man disappeared into the darkness.

Young stabbed at his radio with a forefinger. "Where's the backup!" he shouted

Once he was on the other side of the fence, the man sprinted through the low mist towards a distant pool of light. In the next paddock, a horse snorted in the darkness, and the man ran even faster until he came to another fence, climbed it, and arrived at the door of Mahmoud Khan's breeding shed.

"Well?" Myrtle Sweet demanded as he brushed past her into the building. She was still dressed in the dove gray pantsuit she had worn that afternoon when she left The Daffodils.

"He wasn't there," the man said, breathless. He was bleeding from a gash on his forehead. "There was someone else ... dressed up like an old man. A cop, I think. You said there'd be no problem!"

"What did you do?"

"I whacked him!" He brandished a steel spanner. "I'm gettin' outta here. Someone was comin' up the stairs."

Myrtle said, "You've cut yourself. What happened?"

The young man just had time to say, "I had to jump out the bathroom window" when Myrtle raised the .38 revolver from behind her hip and shot him in the face. The spanner fell from the young man's hand, his eyes rolled up in his head, and he fell backwards into the dirt.

Myrtle was replacing the gun in her purse when Pat the stud groom, in pajamas and slippers and carrying a flashlight in one hand and a shank in the other, appeared in the doorway. "Who're you?" he said. His eyes dropped to the body of the young man. "What —" he said, but Myrtle raised the gun again and fired. She meant to shoot Pat in the face, too, but she was rattled, her hands shaking crazily, and the bullet struck him in the left shoulder, spinning him backwards through the doorway.

Myrtle stepped out of the breeding shed, kicked off her high heels, picked them up in one hand and, carrying the .38 in the other, ran up the dark lane in her stockinged feet towards the lights of the strip mall. Across the highway, an OPP cruiser, its blue lights rotating, squealed out of the parking lot, crossed the road, and disappeared down Morley Rogers' driveway. Myrtle broke out of the shadows beneath the "Khan's Dot Com Acres" archway and hurried towards the Ford Fiesta, which was parked in front of the adult video store.

* * *

Young did a football roll across the top rail of the
fence and began to lope across a small field in the
direction he thought the man had headed. Away from
the light of Morley's kitchen window, the darkness
was complete, and because he didn't want to use his
flashlight and draw attention to himself, Young had
to go by instinct. After a few seconds, he saw a yellow light in the distance. He swerved towards it.
Through the darkness he heard what sounded like a
four-stroke drumbeat that repeated itself, faster and
faster, louder and louder. He stopped. He stood per-
plexed. At the last second, he pulled the flashlight
from the pocket of his raincoat, flicked it on, and
shone it towards the sound. "Aarrrrhhhhhhhh!" he
bellowed, and the huge bay stallion Sam McGee drew
up just short of trampling him, reared in the flashlight beam, snorted, and pawed the air. Young
retreated, shouting, "Down boy, down boy!" until he
backed into the fence he'd just rolled over. His eyes
fixed on the stallion, Young rolled back over the top
rail and hit the ground. He was breathing so hard he
was afraid for his heart. The stallion whinnied and
threw its head savagely, then swung away into the
darkness. Young turned off the flashlight. When he'd
caught his breath, he felt his away along the fence
until he came to a corner. He crossed a grass lane,
climbed a fence into what he hoped was an empty
paddock, stumbled across it towards the light he'd
seen earlier, came to a gate, climbed it, and found
himself at the breeding shed.

In the yellow light spilling out of the doorway,
Pat the stud groom lay curled on his side, the shoulder of his plaid pajama top black with blood. Young
knelt beside him, and Pat said, "There's someone
in there."

Young looked through the doorway and saw a body on its back, eyes open, a spreading puddle under the head. "What happened?"

"I been shot," Pat said. "That woman next door, the one looks after the old man, she shot me, then run up the lane." He closed his eyes and said, "I was sleepin'. Then I heard the stallion all akimbo, kickin' his stall and cryin' out. My room's right above him, eh, so I gets out of bed and comes downstairs to soothe him. But no matter what I says to him or how I pets him, he won't be soothed, so finally I turns him out. I does that sometimes when he's unruly, eh, I puts him in his paddock. Then when I'm about to go back inside, I hears a bang, and I thinks it's Cheyenne lightin' firecrackers for Canada Day, so I come over for a look-see."

"How bad are you hurt?"

"T'other one wouldn't do such a thing, but Cheyenne gets herself in mischief."

"How bad are you hurt?"

"What does she want? Is she after the horses?"

"I'll get help for you."

"I'm all right."

"Can I leave you?"

"Go on, lad, I'm all right."

Two uniformed officers appeared, guns drawn, in the light at the corner of the building.

Young said, "Where were you?"

"Across the road, sir," one of them said, red-faced. "We didn't see anybody come in."

"That's because they came in this driveway," Young said, and he pointed. Through the trees they could see the night security lights of the little mall, and the head-lights of a car just leaving it, pulling onto the highway. "You," Young said to the red-faced policeman, "stay with this man." He turned to the other policeman. "There's an undercover officer down on the second floor of the farmhouse next door. He's yours. Get going." Young stood up, punched his radio again, and said, "Suspect just pulled out of mall across from Khan's farm. Late-model compact. Dark red. Headed right for you. Take all precautions, armed and dangerous. Get two ambulances out here on the double, one to Khan's, one to Morley Rogers'." Young clicked off and stepped into the breeding shed for a closer look at the body. Lying on his back with a stunned expression on his face was a teenaged boy Young had never seen before, a skinhead with a bullet hole in his forehead — square in the centre of a swastika tattoo. The crimson pool under the boy's head was as big as a beer tray. Young studied the boy's face. *You're younger and you're bigger and you don't have the blond mop*, he thought to himself, *but you're the spitting image of Percy Ball.*

By the time Young returned to the Crown Victoria he'd parked behind a shed on Morley's property, opened the door, climbed in, started the ignition, turned on the headlights, gunned the car down the driveway, and sped east a half-mile along the highway to the roadblock, three police officers were positioned around Myrtle's Fiesta with their guns drawn. A fourth officer was shining a floodlight into the interior of the vehicle, which had come to rest at an odd angle on the shoulder of the road, its tires shredded by the spike belt the police had laid across the pavement. As Young climbed out of his car and lumbered towards the scene, he could see Myrtle still seated behind the wheel. Her right hand was out of sight on the far side of her head, up by her ear.

"Secure?" Young called out as he approached.

One of the officers said, "Yes sir, we got her, but she's —"

"Who's she talking to?"

"She's —"

"Keep me covered," Young said. He stepped closer to the car and said loudly, "It's over, Myrtle, put down the phone." He looked in through the windshield and saw her floodlit face, white as death, her thick black hair, and the .38 she was holding to her temple.

"Good Christ," Young said.

She raised her eyes to his, and her lips moved, but he couldn't hear her.

He made a winding motion with his hand. "Roll down your window."

Stepping closer to her door, he slid his hand inside the lapel of his raincoat and eased the Glock out of his shoulder holster.

He watched the window lower. When it was all the way down, he said, "Lay the gun on the seat beside you and put your hands on the steering wheel."

She was still looking up at him, and she still held the gun to her temple.

"Put the gun down."

"I didn't return the hamper."

"What?"

She made eyes at him. "I borrowed a picnic hamper from the hotel the boys and I were staying at — The Clarion, I highly recommend it — and I forgot to return it. I imagine it's still in the trunk of the other car, wherever *it* might be!" She giggled, turned away from Young, raised her left hand from the steering wheel and — as Young brought the Glock into firing position — lowered the sun visor. She studied her reflection in the mirror on the back of the visor and patted her hair. "Truth be told,

I didn't actually forget to return it. I deliberately didn't return it. Very naughty of me. One should always return the things one borrows." She smiled at herself in the mirror and batted her eyelashes. "I should really be ashamed of myself," she said to her reflection, "I know I should" — she turned her gaze back up at Young, and her eyes were as cold and dead as cinders — "but I'm not." She took the gun from her temple and pointed it through the window at Young. "Please tell someone to turn off that horrible light."

"Put the gun down," Young said, aiming the Glock.

Myrtle nodded, took a deep and dramatic breath — like a little girl about to begin a recital — and closed her eyes. Young ducked to the right as she squeezed the trigger. He heard the explosion, and he heard the *pop-pop-pop* the police guns made. The windshield crystalized and dropped like a waterfall across the dashboard into Myrtle's lap. Her head rolled back against the headrest. Her eyes fell open. Empty. Black. Beautiful.

Several seconds passed, but it wasn't until the blood sluiced out of her nostrils in two scarlet streams that Young holstered his gun and turned away.

Sunday, July 2

Debi was scheduled to saddle Bing Crosby for the third race at Caledonia Downs, a mile-and-a-sixteenth claiming event for older horses, and Someday Prince for the eighth race, the seven-furlong Afleet Stakes for three-year-olds. Back in May, Shorty Rogers had thought the Afleet might be a good fit for Someday Prince, and before his death he had completed the nomination payments. When Doug Buckley and Mahmoud Khan had visited Debi's shedrow, and Debi had told Doug that Someday Prince would run in the Afleet, he had been delighted at the prospect of inviting some of the country club people to come out and watch the colt, but Doug never was admitted to the country club; instead, he was awaiting trial for the murder of Percy Ball. Mahmoud Khan, who on that same occasion at Debi's barn had referred to the purse money as "small potatoes," was also in jail — for conspiracy to commit murder. Debi had expected some lawyer to tell her she couldn't run Someday Prince in the stake, that Doug Buckley's assets were frozen until further notice, but no one had said a word, so she intended to run him. After all, if he won she earned ten percent of the sixty percent winner's share. That worked out to $7,500. To Debi, $7,500 was big potatoes.

Tom Wright's Doll House was entered in the same race as Bing Crosby. As the horses were being loaded into the gate, Young, sitting in the clubhouse dining room with Trick, lifted his binoculars to his eyes.

Bing Crosby was 3-1, and Young had bet $200 across the board on him. Doll House, at 12-1, took the lead from the gate and, because no one pressed her, was able to set a slow pace. At the head of the stretch, she was in front by six lengths when Bing Crosby began to close on her. Twenty yards from the wire, she took a bad step, and Bing Crosby galloped past her and won easily.

Young kept his binoculars focused on Doll House. The jockey pulled her up just past the wire and dismounted. She was standing on three legs; the fourth — her right fore — was shattered at the fetlock, just above the hoof. Young located Tom Wright over by the rail and watched him hurry across the track and kneel in the dirt by the old mare's broken leg.

The horse ambulance was brought out from the backstretch, and six men surrounded Doll House and practically carried her up the ramp and into the trailer. Then someone closed the tailgate and the ambulance was driven away.

Young and Trick made their slow, laborious way down to the winner's circle, where they joined Debi and Mrs. McDonagh for the photograph. Mrs. McDonagh stood at Bing Crosby's head, holding his bridle. Debi stood beside her, ready to intervene should the horse become fractious. Young stood behind Trick, his hands resting on Trick's shoulders. Mrs. McDonagh patted Bing Crosby's nose, and the photographer took the picture. Trick looked up at Debi and said, "Too bad about that other horse," and Debi said, "It's awful about the mare, Uncle Artie, but Tom Wright deserves what he gets."

Two hours later, eleven three-year-old colts went post-ward for the stakes race. Young was up over $1,000 on the afternoon and bet all of it on Someday Prince. And Debi had a chance not only to earn $7,500 but also to win her first stakes race. When the starting gate opened, Someday Prince dwelt, and by the time Trinidad Grant got him going, he was twenty lengths behind the rest of the field. He made his customary late kick, picking up two horses on the backstretch and two more at the head of the stretch, but he was too far behind and finished fifth.

That evening, Young was sitting in his La-Z-Boy, with Jamal on his lap. The Blue Jays had played an afternoon game, and the TV was off. Jamal was facing his grandfather, just as he had done when he was a baby and he would tug at Young's ears and mash his lips together, and Young, like a patient old dog, would endure his attentions. But Jamal had outgrown tugging and mashing. Now he made other demands on his grandfather. "Poppy," he said, "can we put Bob Seger on?" Young looked down at the boy. What song do you want?"

Jamal scampered off his grandfather's lap. "'Betty Lou'!"

"Oh," Young said as he pried himself out of the La-Z-Boy, "you want to dance."

When the music started Young lifted Jamal into the air. At first he held him in waltz position, the boy's feet dangling, exactly as he had done with Debi twenty years earlier. Same song, same dance. Young took the boy in his right hand and extended his arm, so that Jamal seemed to fly out into the middle of the living room. Then Young brought him back to his chest again, passed him to his other hand, and the boy rolled out in the other direction. When he brought him back again he raised him over his head, careful of the ceiling, and Jamal touched the stippling with his fingers, then down he came, and Young leaned forward, passed him over one shoulder and down his back, then reached around with his other hand, grabbed him, and brought him up under his armpit and back into waltz position. This routine was repeated, Jamal squealing with excitement, until the music ended.

Debi had asked Young if Jamal could spend the night at his house; she and Eldridge were driving to Fort Erie Monday morning to look at a horse, and they had to get an early start. "Tonight's the Twist Contest, don't forget," Young had told his daughter.

"Are you going?"

"I always go."

"What about Jamal?"

"Don't worry, I'll get the girl across the street to come over."

"Okay, well, maybe me and Eldridge will come for a little while, too."

When the babysitter arrived ten minutes after Bob Seger had finished singing "Betty Lou's Gettin' Out Tonight," Jamal was still bouncing around the room like a rubber ball. "Goodnight, honey," Young called from the door, and Jamal waved from mid-bounce. "Good luck, Angela," he said to the babysitter, a tongue-studded fifteen-year-old whose hair was midnight blue, then he closed the door behind him and walked down the front steps to the street where his minivan was parked.

"Ladies and gentlemen!" DJ Dan shouted, waving his hands, the sweat running down his face. "Let's do The

Twist! That's right, it's time for your regular monthly McCully's Tavern Twist Contest!" He stood on the little karaoke stage and waited until the cheering and hooting and whistling died down. "Choose your partner and get out on the floor. We'll begin with the song that started it all, 'The Twist' by Chubby Checker, then we'll hear the same artist doing 'Let's Twist Again,' then we'll seg-way into Parts One and Two of 'Peppermint Twist' by Joey Dee and the Starliters, then we'll hear The Beatles' 'Twist and Shout,' then we'll hear 'Pimp Twist,' by the Kottonmouth Kings, and we'll finish up with Sam Cooke's rendition of 'Twisting the Night Away.' Six songs in all. Six dances. Tonight's judges will be Vinny Dinunzio, owner of this fine establishment, and Dexter Bynoe, master of the mixed drink. Take your places, everybody!"

At the table where Young was sitting with his daughter and Eldridge and Trick, he waited for Eldridge to ask Debi to dance, but Eldridge didn't like to dance — he felt it was heathen. Eldridge knew better, however, than to force his views on Debi, and she looked over at her father. Young raised his eyebrows and inclined his head towards the dance floor. She smiled and nodded.

Ten minutes later, halfway through "Twist and Shout," someone screamed over by the far wall. Young hurried off the dance floor, Debi right behind him, and forced his way through the crowd until he found the new barmaid, Freedom, standing beside the shuffleboard table and staring down at a spreading lake of beer, an upended pitcher, and an upside down basket of chicken wings.

"What's going on?" Young roared over the noise.

Freedom was red in the face. "He decided to take a little nap under there, but his arm flopped out, and I tripped over it."

Young leaned forward and peered into the shadows beneath the shuffleboard table, and there was Priam Harvey passed out on his back.

"Vinny's gonna make me pay for all this!" Freedom wailed.

Young extricated his wallet from his hip pocket and handed Freedom a twenty-dollar bill. Before she could respond, he started back towards the dance floor.

Debi followed him. "That was nice of you," she said, "to help that girl out."

"Your Uncle Artie's got the hots for her."

"You're kidding."

"Nope."

"But he's … he can't …" Her voice trailed off.

Her father, twisting again, said, "Oh, yes, he can. There's things he can do. If he wants something bad enough, your Uncle Artie can do just about anything."

After Sam Cooke finished singing "Twisting the Night Away," there was a short pause while the judges conferred. Then DJ Dan announced that Young and Debi had been named Twist King and Twist Queen. They had to kneel so that squat little Vinny could place paper crowns on their heads. As he got to his feet, Young whispered to Vinny, "If you think being voted Twist King is gonna influence me where the bookies are concerned, you're barking up the wrong fucking tree."

When they returned to their table, Eldridge put his arm around Debi's neck and kissed her cheek. Freedom was bending over Trick and had her ear close to his mouth. Before Young could sit down, Jessy suddenly appeared at his shoulder, her face flushed with heat and activity. She tugged at his sleeve, and he lowered his head. Leaning up against him she said, "Come over later, big guy."

His immediate inclination was to nod, and he almost did. Instead, he looked down at her and shook his head. Her expression stiffened, but she remained where she was, planted in front of him. He turned away and made his farewells to the others at the table, waved away their protestations, waded through the gyrating crowd on the dance floor, pushed open the door to the street, breathed deeply, and crossed O'Connor Avenue to the beer store parking lot where he'd left the minivan. He unlocked the driver's door and lowered himself onto the seat. He was exhausted. For a minute before putting the key in the ignition, he sat quietly, his forehead against the steering wheel.

Angela lived only a few houses away, so Young watched her from his front door until she was safely home. He checked on Jamal, who was deeply asleep in the middle of Young's king-size mattress. Young placed pillows all around him, as he had done since Jamal was a baby. He patted the boy's damp forehead.

As he lay down on the sofa in the living room, he felt a chill and, despite the humidity in the apartment, pulled a blanket and an old sleeping bag over his legs and chest.

Monday, July 3

Young woke up, his bladder pressing. He had been dreaming about horses in a meadow. His ex-wife was there, wearing shorts and a T-shirt and carrying a picnic basket. She was smiling, and the sun was in her hair. Debi wasn't there. Maybe she wasn't born yet. There was a red and white checked tablecloth on the green grass. The horses came right up to Tanya and nuzzled at her clothes and hands, looking for carrots and sugar cubes. One of the horses turned to Young and said, "Lucky Doctor in the sixth."

Young lay still, thinking about the dream. Then he wondered whether or not his bladder discomfort was serious enough to make a trip to the bathroom absolutely necessary. He faced this dilemma in the middle of most nights, especially if he'd been drinking beer the evening before. Even one beer after 10:00 p.m. and he pretty much knew he'd be up at 2:00 or 3:00 a.m., stumbling down the hall to the bathroom.

Finally he gave in. If he didn't get up now, he'd just have to get up later. Ten minutes or twenty minutes or an hour. He flipped the sleeping bag and the blanket back and swung his legs out, careful not to disturb Reg, who was asleep at his feet. Then he remembered that Reg wasn't asleep at his feet, that she was dead, her ashes buried in the yard. He sat on the edge of the sofa, his head in his hands. He remembered how sometimes when he woke up in the middle of the night Reg wouldn't move; she would remain curled at the foot of the bed, maybe one eye open. If she did stir, he knew he would have to let her out, and that meant he would have to stand yawning on his little balcony for ten minutes while she fussed and sniffed in the yard below, and that he would have to plead with her, "Reg, hurry up, will you, I'm freezing my ass off up here," or threaten her, "I'm going in now, I'm going in. Here I go."

He padded down the hall, huge and naked except for the stained bandage that covered his appendectomy incision. He flashed back to the dream he'd had a month ago, the morning Debi had awakened him with the news of Shorty's murder, the dream in which he'd chased a young girl wearing a private school uniform — Black Watch skirt, green knee socks — through a maze of alleyways. Why had he been chasing her? he wondered. Was she running away from him, or was there some unseen danger from which he was trying to protect her? What were his intentions? It troubled him to think that his intentions might not have been honourable. He remembered she was flipping her blonde hair out of her eyes as she ran, and she was laughing, but that proved nothing, except maybe that she wasn't afraid of him, that what was really happening, possibly, was that she was leading him on. Was there anything sadder than a big ugly man chasing after a vision of beauty?

He leaned his forehead against the jamb of the bathroom door. Tanya had left six years ago, Debi had her own life, Reg was dead. No wife, no child, no dog: he was alone in the world. Even the grandchild sleeping in his bed was, for the moment, no comfort.

He tried to remember the other dream he'd had that night, something about the racetrack and an old man whose head swivelled 180 degrees. He wished he could make sense of his dreams; he wished they would come clear for him.

He did not turn the light on in the bathroom. He knew where the toilet was. He leaned one hand against the wall above it, aimed, and let go, his eyes closed the entire time. Sometimes when he was alone in the apartment he would pretend he was blind and move around with his hands in front of him like antennae. He figured he'd manage all right if he were blind. *I mean, look at Trick*, he thought. *He doesn't let anything stop him. He does what he wants. He goes where he wants. He goes after what he wants — Freedom, for example. And even Priam Harvey — smart as he is, alcoholic as he is — he gets by, too, just like me, living alone. Hell, we all live alone. All my friends live alone. Even Wheeler — who shouldn't live alone — lives alone. All she's got is her cat. I've never seen it, of course, never having been invited over. I've never seen her pajamas with feet, either. I don't particularly want to see her cat — being as I hate cats — but I wouldn't mind seeing her in those pajamas with feet. Maybe I should give her a call.* Young opened one eye and peered at the clock radio on the shelf beside the medicine cabinet: 5:26. He was surprised how quickly the night had passed, but it was still too early to phone. Then he realized it was Monday morning. *I have to go to work today*, he thought. *I have to get dressed and wake Jamal and get him ready*

*and take him to Mrs. Ferri's. And then go to work. But
not yet. Another hour of shut-eye.*

Young shook himself and flushed the toilet. He
dabbed the tip of his penis against a towel hanging on
the back of the bathroom door. As he started back
down the hall, he remembered hearing someone at
McCully's say it wouldn't be long before there was a
horse racing channel on TV. Maybe when he retired
he'd sign up for it. Then he could bet by phone. That
would be all right. And the idea of retirement was
attractive, too. He could go any time he wanted — he
already had his twenty years — but he was afraid he
wouldn't have enough to do to keep himself busy. He
was afraid he'd start drinking first thing in the morning. That wouldn't be very good. *Maybe*, he thought,
*I'll go into private practice. Campbell Young: Private
Eye. Or I'll call myself an investigative consultant.* That
was the new label being bandied about.

He opened the door of his bedroom a few inches.
Inside his fortification of pillows, Jamal slept soundly.

Young wandered into the kitchen and poured himself a glass of water. He opened the door onto the balcony and stepped out. It was warm, but clear, and the
stars were putting on a show. He squinted down into the
darkness of the yard. *When I get home from work*, he
thought, *I'll make the* R.

He stepped back into the apartment and shut the
door. He walked through the kitchen and down the
hall to the living room. It was light enough that he
didn't smack his shin against the coffee table or trip
over Jamal's Hot Wheels. He hoped his blanket and
sleeping bag would still be warm when he crawled
back into them, and he hoped he'd be able to retrieve
the dream about Tanya and the horses in the meadow,
so he could crawl back into it, too.

Acknowledgements

For their help and encouragement, I would like to thank the following people: Harry Baillie, Barry Bellchamber, Michael Blair, Andy Brakas, Joe Broughton, Helen Brown, Dale Campbell, Hadley Carpenter, Peter Carpenter, Reeves Carpenter, Tommy Cosgrove, Frank Courtney, Terry DeRoche, Pat Dubyk, Brian L. Flack, Paul Game, Terence M. Green, M. T. Kelly, Larry Krotz, Athena Maikantis, Victor Matanovic, Stephen Murphy, Karen Ralley, John Ross, Lawrence Scanlan, Rick Short, Terry Sprague, Jim Swan, Kandy Welsh-Hotston, Brian Wilson.